Horse
of a Different
KILLER

"A sleuth who communicates with animals...You'll love taking a walk on this 'Wilde' side!" —HEATHER BLAKE, national bestselling author

Maura Morrigan

National Bestselling Author of *A Tiger's Tale*

BERKLEY
PRIME
CRIME

$7.99 U.S.
$9.99 CAN

S > EAN

ISBN 978-0-425-25721-0

9 780425 257210

5 0 7 9 9

Berkley Prime Crime titles by Laura Morrigan

WOOF AT THE DOOR
A TIGER'S TALE
HORSE OF A DIFFERENT KILLER

Horse of a Different KILLER

Laura Morrigan

BERKLEY PRIME CRIME, NEW YORK

THE BERKLEY PUBLISHING GROUP
Published by the Penguin Group
Penguin Group (USA) LLC
375 Hudson Street, New York, New York 10014

USA • Canada • UK • Ireland • Australia • New Zealand • India • South Africa • China

penguin.com

A Penguin Random House Company

HORSE OF A DIFFERENT KILLER

A Berkley Prime Crime Book / published by arrangement with the author

Berkley Prime Crime Books are published by The Berkley Publishing Group.
BERKLEY® PRIME CRIME and the PRIME CRIME logo are trademarks of
Penguin Group (USA) LLC.

For information, address: The Berkley Publishing Group,
a division of Penguin Group (USA) LLC,
375 Hudson Street, New York, New York 10014.

ISBN: 978-0-425-25721-0

PUBLISHING HISTORY
Berkley Prime Crime mass-market edition / March 2015

PRINTED IN THE UNITED STATES OF AMERICA

10 9 8 7 6 5 4 3 2 1

Cover illustration by Mary Ann Lasher.
Cover design by Diana Kolsky.
Interior text design by Kristin del Rosario.

For Mom. I love you.

ACKNOWLEDGMENTS

There are many people without whom this book could not have been written. Heartfelt thanks to:

The wonderful team at Berkley Prime Crime, especially my editor, Faith Black. Faith, you're one in a million.

My friend Lois Ann Gavin and fellow writer Terry Conway. True "horse people" who proved to be a wealth of knowledge and ideas.

The Honorable Pat Kinsey, for answering random questions about the justice system, providing kitten inspiration and letting me "borrow" Pretty Girl.

The members of my writers group: Amelia Grey, Frances Hanson-Grow (AKA Mom), Geri Buckley Borcz, Hortense Thurman, and Sandra Shanklin. Your support means more than I can say.

My aunt, Oma Laura, for Jacksonville history and insights.

I claim responsibility for all mistakes, embellishments, and other tweaks to reality.

And finally to my loving and supportive family and friends who may not always understand the writer-crazies but are willing to put up with it. Thank you!

CHAPTER 1

Some days you're the windshield, some days you're the bug.

Other days, you're the girl wading thigh-deep in frigid swamp water trying to talk a koala out of a cypress tree.

Well, if you're me, anyway.

My name is Grace Wilde, and I am the dog, cat, elephant, and at the moment, koala whisperer.

I waded closer to the base of the tree and squinted up.

Percy, the koala, sat in the crook of one of the bare branches. He was still soaked from his frantic swim to reach the tallest tree in the area. Wet is not a good look for a koala. The tufts of fur on his ears drooped and the rest of his gray and white coat was clumped and matted. In addition to looking pitiful, the poor little guy was confused, agitated, and in a pretty foul mood.

I couldn't blame him.

He'd been on his way to his new home in Orlando when disaster struck. The transport vehicle was involved in an accident on I-95 that left the driver with a concussion and an injured leg. During the crash, the van's rear doors and the koala's cage had popped open. Thankfully, Percy had chosen to run away from the six lanes of speeding traffic and flee into the adjacent swamp.

Someone called 911. Kai Duncan, whom I've been dating and who happens to be a sergeant with the Jacksonville Sheriff's Office, called me. I, in turn, had called reinforcements. And here we were . . .

"What do you think, Grace?"

The question came from my friend and colleague, Sonja Brown.

Sonja was an animal behaviorist with a big heart and had great instincts. Like the rest of the would-be rescuers gathered around us, she was willing to drop everything to go on a mission to find a rogue koala. Unlike the other volunteers, Sonja knew my secret.

I can communicate with animals.

Some would say I'm psychic, some would use the term *telepath*. A few too many would call me crazy, a freak, or both, which means I tend to be a selective sharer.

I looked at Sonja. She stood in the murky water a few feet to my right and wore an expression of calm concern on her lovely, dark face.

So far, I'd coaxed, cajoled, and visualized a eucalyptus utopia.

Percy wasn't interested.

He wanted someone he called Teddy, and that was that.

I motioned Sonja closer. She slogged slowly to where I stood.

"What was the driver's name?"

"Mark somebody. Why?"

I lowered my voice so the other rescuers wouldn't hear. "He keeps asking for Teddy."

"Teddy, huh?" She looked up at the koala. "Even if we figure out who Teddy is, it would take a while for them to get here, right?"

I nodded, understanding what she meant. Though I hadn't sensed any physical trauma from the koala, I couldn't be sure and we couldn't take any chances.

Drawing in a lungful of marshy air, I focused my thoughts and tried again to persuade Percy to come down the tree.

Hungry? I pulled the image of eucalyptus leaves to the front of my mind and offered it to the koala.

Teddy! Was the response.

I don't know who Teddy is! The frustrated thought came out a little more forceful than I'd intended.

To my surprise, instead of being startled, the koala answered with a series of sensations and images. The feel of soft fur. Bright, black eyes, a velvet nose.

"I've got it," I said.

I splashed over to where we'd set Percy's transport cage, got on my hands and knees and started digging through the contents. Eucalyptus, eucalyptus, a little more eucalyptus . . . I found a baby blanket and, buried in a corner, a stuffed bear.

"Hello, Teddy."

• • •

"Even though I've seen you do your stuff before, I'm always impressed," Sonja said twenty minutes later as we walked to the construction site where we, and the other volunteers, had parked.

I shrugged and shifted my gaze to the people around us. I had always been uncomfortable with compliments and especially so when it came to my ability.

Having only recently told a handful of people, I was still getting used to talking about it openly. Doing so within earshot of those who didn't know made me feel exposed.

I cast a meaningful look in the direction of the other volunteers.

"What?" She followed my glance, stopped, planted her hands on her hips, and stared at me in silent challenge.

"I'm not ready to tell everyone I meet what I can do, okay?" I whispered.

"Did I say anything about your ability? No, I did not. I didn't use the word *telepathy* or *psychic* or anything like that, did I?" She didn't wait for my answer. "No, what I did was pay you a compliment. The proper response to which should be: 'Thank you, Sonja.'"

She waited expectantly.

I huffed out a breath. "Thank you, Sonja."

"See? Was that so hard? Grace, honey, listen. I understand your reluctance to open up to people. Even though I don't agree with it, I understand."

"You sound like Emma."

My sister had been encouraging me to let the cat out of the bag, so to speak, for years. I'd resisted. Mostly out of fear.

"I know what happened with that idiot old boyfriend of yours, but by now you must've learned that there are plenty of people who will accept what you can do. Not without question, maybe. But they'll at least give you a chance. Speaking of chances . . ." She looked over my shoulder and smiled.

I glanced back to see who she was talking about and felt a smile tug at the corners of my mouth as well.

"I've been trying to call you," Kai said.

"I left my phone in Bluebell." I motioned to where my vintage, light blue Suburban was parked.

Kai nodded a quick greeting to Sonja and said to me, "I need to talk to you. Privately."

Sonja gave me a wink, we said our good-byes, and I turned back to Kai. "What's up?"

He waited for my friend to be out of earshot before he started to answer. "Did you talk to—" He broke off at the sound of tires crunching over the oyster-shell parking lot. Kai went still, then shifted his weight, turning his body slightly to cast a clandestine glance over his shoulder.

"Shit," he muttered.

"What is it?" I asked, leaning to peer around him and see who had driven into the parking area. Kai moved to block my line of sight.

I gazed a question into his troubled face.

"Listen, I don't have time to explain." His words were punctuated by the slam of a door and footsteps on the loose shells. "The woman walking toward us is a cop. She's going to want to ask you questions. Don't panic, no matter what she says."

Here's the thing—when someone tells you not to panic, what's the first thing you do? Yep. I swallowed hard against the sudden tendrils of fear tightening around my throat.

The footsteps crunched closer.

"Kai, what—"

"You're going to have to stall," he said, lowering his voice. "Redirect. But whatever you do, don't tell her anything about Emma."

"Emma?" The tendrils grew into thorny vines at the mention of my sister's name. My heart rate surged, pounding in my chest almost painfully.

"You don't know anything. I don't know anything. I'm just here to take you to a late lunch. Okay?"

I nodded.

"Now, smile and ask me where we're going to eat," he murmured.

I bared my teeth—it was the best I could do in that moment—and said, "So, what are you hungry for?" just as the woman reached us.

The first thing I noticed when I shifted my attention to her was the flame-red color of her hair. Natural, if the freckles dusting her nose and cheeks were any indication. Her hair was cut short and, along with her heart-shaped face and petite frame, made me think of Neverland and pixies.

She didn't look at all scary, which was more unnerving than if I'd turned to see the Blair Witch.

Kai shrugged at me, still pretending not to have noticed her.

"It's up to you. I was—" He stopped and turned, a look of surprise on his face. "Detective Boyle, what are you doing here?"

She gave him an unfriendly look. I admit my understanding of people is limited, but I know the stink eye when I see it. Whoever this woman was, she didn't like Kai.

"Oh, I'm sure you know, Sergeant Duncan."

"I don't, actually," Kai said, his tone so honest and forthcoming, I almost believed him.

She turned to me and her features softened. "Grace Wilde?"

"Yes."

Her tone was much warmer, almost apologetic, when she said, "I have a few questions for you if you have a moment."

I felt Kai reach over to clasp my hand in his. Though we'd been dating, in the few times we'd gone out he'd never held my hand.

The sensation of his warm, rough palm pressed to mine should have sent a happy flutter through me. All I felt was dread.

I could sense Kai trying to tell me something through his steady grip.

What?

Get ready to run?

Stay calm?

"Sure," I said.

"Great. Would you mind coming with me?"

"Like this?" I motioned to my stained clothes. "I should probably head home and change before—"

She waved my comment away and said, "You were going to lunch, right?"

Damn. Busted.

"Drive-through," I said with a shrug. "Bluebell is used to the dirt."

"Who?"

"Bluebell." I pointed.

"Well," Detective Boyle said after eyeing my old, enormous SUV, "I'm sure we can manage."

"What's all this about, Detective?" I asked.

"We'll explain once we get to the sheriff's office."

"Why don't you explain now?" I felt Kai's hand tighten in mine so I tacked on a "please."

"I have questions about your sister, Emma."

"Emma? Is she okay?"

"She's not hurt."

That wasn't the same thing as being okay, but relief poured over me anyway. I blew out a sigh and said, "I'm not sure I understand why you want to talk to me about Emma."

"She's just been arrested."

"Arrested? For what?"

"Murder."

CHAPTER 2

My ride to the Police Memorial Building had given me the one thing I'd needed. Time.

I'd learned at a young age to keep a firm grasp on my emotions.

The more control I had, the better equipped I was to handle the raw flood of feelings from an injured or frightened animal.

Sometimes, there's an overlap between the animal's emotions and my own. That's when things get tricky. But usually, given enough time, I can project an aura of calm even in the middle of the storm.

More recently, I'd been learning meditation techniques, which I put into practice to center my thoughts during the thirty-minute drive and brief waiting period in the interview room. Ironically, I seemed to be better at focusing my mind when under acute stress than under normal circumstances.

Consequently, when Detective Boyle entered the small room and sat across from me, I was able to remain composed when I asked, "Where's my sister?"

"She's speaking to another detective right now."

"When can I see her?"

"Soon. But we need some information first."

"You said my sister's been arrested for murder. Of who? When?"

"Before we can get to all that, there are a few things we need cleared up. Grace, I know you want to help us and we want to help your sister. Being honest is the best course."

"Okay." I nodded as if that was my intention. "But you should know this, Detective. Whatever you think Emma's done, you're wrong. My sister could never kill anyone."

Even as I said it, I knew it wasn't true. Technically, Emma was more than capable of killing someone. She had a black belt in aikido and had trained in other martial arts, even practiced some MMA and street-style fighting.

My sister was, quite frankly, a badass. But murder? No.

"If that's the case," Detective Boyle said with reassuring friendliness, "we'll figure it out. First, we have some questions, okay?"

I nodded. I knew this was all an act. She was playing the good cop, but her warm tone and pixie looks didn't fool me. I'd seen the look she'd given Kai. There was a bad cop, hard and cold as frozen granite behind the disarming smile. I was going to be ready for her.

"You live with your sister, correct?"

I thought about Kai's warning and decided telling her my living arrangements couldn't be that incriminating. I might even be able to stall.

"My old landlady booted us after she bought a new pair of glasses and got a good look at Moss."

"Who?"

"My dog, Moss. He's big and scary-looking, so we ended up at my sister's place on the beach."

"We?"

"Moss and I. It's only temporary, though. I've actually been house hunting. Have you ever done that? It's kind of stressful."

Detective Boyle made a noncommittal sound, then

moved on to her next question. "Did you see your sister this morning?"

I shrugged. "I see Emma just about every morning. She makes me coffee, which is really nice because she doesn't even drink coffee. Emma likes green tea. Do you?"

"Not really."

"Me either. Tastes like dirt, if you ask me."

She nodded amiably, though I could see she was not pleased by my rambling answers.

"Speaking of which, I'm a little thirsty," I said. "Could I trouble you for some water?"

"Sure."

She rose, stepped to the door, poked her head out, and then returned. I'd hoped for a longer reprieve from the questioning but the water request had taken all of five seconds and she plowed on as soon as her rump hit the chair.

"So, you saw your sister this morning. What time was that?"

"Gosh, I don't really remember." I looked up at the ceiling, pretending to think about it, and noticed an inverted dome, which I knew shielded a camera. I wondered who was on the other end watching. Kai? Probably not. My only other real contact in the JSO was Detective Jake Nocera. A gruff, tough, homicide detective, Jake was a Yankee transplant and one of my few friends. Would that exclude him from the case as well?

I got my answer a moment later when the door opened and Jake ambled in holding a paper cup in one beefy hand. Not looking at me, he set the cup on the table, turned, and walked out the door. Something about that made my heart sink.

I picked up the cup and took a sip.

"Thanks," I said to Detective Boyle.

"Sure. Can you remember what time you saw your sister this morning?"

I shook my head. "Like I said, I love my coffee. I can't really think straight until I have at least one cup."

"Do you remember when you left or if she left before you?"

"I got an emergency call to go deal with a situation off 95. But you know that—you guys came and picked me up there."

"You know Detective Nocera, don't you?"

"Yes."

Kai had told me not to answer questions about Emma; he hadn't said anything about Jake—or himself, for that matter. So I figured I was in the clear.

"He's told me he doesn't know your sister very well."

"He doesn't."

"Which is why he's still on this case." She waited a beat, then added, "He vouched for you. I think you should know that." She let the silence stretch out between us as she studied me.

I didn't know what to say, so I kept my mouth shut.

"So." She leaned in, eyes locking on mine. "Why are you playing with me?"

"Playing with you?"

"You're not answering my questions."

I started to weave an elaborate line of BS but thought better of it, deciding a partial truth was the best bet.

"Look, Detective, this situation is . . ." I paused, searching for the right word. "It's surreal. Quite honestly, it's freaking me out. When I get upset or nervous I either babble like an idiot or clam up completely. As I believe the second option is not what you're hoping for, I've been doing my best to answer your questions."

I was lying, but only about the last part.

"You're doing your best?"

I nodded. I *was* doing my best—to misdirect, deflect, and stall. Though I still wasn't sure why. Kai's warning had fallen pretty short in the clarity department.

"But it's hard," I said. "I'm worried about my sister and I'm afraid I'll say something that will give you the wrong idea."

"Like what?"

"Nothing. There's nothing I can tell you that will help because, I promise you," I said, looking her dead in the eye, "my sister would never kill anyone."

"Even her ex-husband?"

"Her—" I stopped as the words sank in. Drawing in a slow breath, I tried to will the color to remain in my face. "Tony Ortega is dead?"

"He is. And your sister was caught standing over his body—minutes after his death."

She waited for a response. I exercised my right to remain silent. I was pretty sure anything I had to say about Ortega could be used against me. Especially since the first thing that popped into my head was, *He probably deserved it.*

Boyle amped up her stare, honing it to a hard point. I could almost feel it pressing into me. I'd been right about the cold, granite cop under the pixie dust.

Luckily, as a woman who faced apex predators on a regular basis, I was not easily intimidated. People can try to posture and pretend, but very few can beat me in a stare-down.

The look in her eyes made one thing clear: She would no longer be playing nice.

Worked for me. I had always been more of a runs-with-scissors than a plays-well-with-others kind of a girl.

"You knew Anthony Ortega."

I nodded.

She glared at me for a long moment, waiting for me to elaborate.

"He was married to my sister, of course I knew him."

"When was the last time you saw him?"

I shook my head with a shrug. "I'm not sure."

"Guess."

I thought about it. I knew I'd seen him a few weeks before he and Emma divorced, right before he'd put her in the hospital. "I haven't seen him in years."

"Not at all?"

"No. Not at all."

"But he has contacted you."

I shook my head, though I knew where she was going with her question. "He won the bid for my services at a silent auction last weekend, but I've had no contact with him."

She angled her head to study me.

"You say your services. You mean as an"—she opened the file in front of her for the first time—"animal behaviorist?"

"It's the only thing I do."

"Aren't you also a veterinarian?"

"I keep my license current, but I don't have a practice."

"Why's that?"

"Sometimes it helps to be able to treat or quarantine an animal in the field."

"Right. You helped with the Richardson murder a few months ago."

"I did."

"The dog—a Doberman, wasn't it? Had to be put down after you'd given the okay for it to be adopted."

"Yes." Actually, the Doberman in question was alive and well and living with a certain surly detective I knew. I'd fudged on the papers, and Jake had gotten a great dog who was only vicious when murderers were attacking people he cared about.

Detective Boyle was trying to goad me by questioning my skills, but she was barking up the wrong tree, so to speak. People had been questioning my skills for years, and I was not easily goaded.

"Quite a mistake," she added.

"Everyone makes them."

"Detective Nocera tells me you're very good at your job, despite your *mistakes*. But I'm having a hard time understanding why Anthony Ortega would need to hire an animal behaviorist."

"Hmm . . ." I tried to sound thoughtful but was pretty sure my restraint was starting to slip and let some sarcasm through. Kai had advised me to stall and redirect, but I was reaching my limit. "Typically, people need me to help with animal behavior."

"Even people who don't own an animal?"

I should have been surprised but I wasn't. Tony Ortega had never been what I'd call pet-friendly.

"No. That would be unusual."

"I agree."

I flashed her a smile. "Just when I thought we weren't going to see eye to eye." Yep, definitely letting loose with the sarcasm.

She ignored my comment. "You must have some idea what he wanted."

I shook my head. Actually, I'd suspected Ortega had wanted to weasel back into Emma's life and was using me to do it. Learning he didn't own a pet seemed to confirm that theory.

"Sorry, Detective. I have no clue."

"Because you and your sister have no contact with him, correct?"

"Yes."

"Why not?"

Part of me wanted to tell her what a raging asshole Ortega was. A total narcissist and someone I wouldn't want to hang around with even if he hadn't beaten my sister so badly she'd been almost unrecognizable when I'd seen her lying in the hospital bed.

The image of that moment filled my mind. Emma's beautiful face so swollen and bruised it looked like a horrible, bloated mask.

The truth was, I was glad Ortega was dead. But I kept that to myself and said, "We didn't have anything to talk about."

"So, all the times he called you in the last few days . . ." She paused to consult her notes. "Thirteen times according to your phone records—you never spoke to him?"

"No, I didn't."

"You were avoiding him?"

"We didn't get along."

"Why's that?"

I had a feeling she knew the answer. But I wasn't about to take the bait. Telling her Ortega was abusive to my sister until she escaped their marriage sounded too much like a motive for murder.

I shrugged, looked her in the eyes, and said, "Ever just meet somebody who rubs you the wrong way? You just can't help it. You don't like them, right off the bat?"

She kept her gaze steady on mine and smiled ever so slightly. "You know, every once in a while, I sure do."

"Well then, we seem to have reached an understanding."

I stood, gave her a departing nod, and walked out into the corridor.

Marching over to the double doors leading into the homicide unit, I pulled one open and spotted Jake already striding toward me. He'd probably been watching my interview with Boyle on one of the wall-mounted monitors.

Though I thought he knew me well enough to predict what I wanted, I stopped and, with a very calm voice, said, "I'd like to see my sister. Please."

Jake's jowly face was made more dour by the stern, downward tilt of his mouth. He glowered at me, then glowered a little harder, finally ticking his chin up in a quick nod.

"Come on," he growled, leading me through the room to a solid wood door exactly like the one I'd left. "I'll tell Boyle we'll learn more if we let you two talk."

"Because you'll be listening?"

He gave me a what-do-you-think? look before unlocking the door and swinging it open.

Emma sat at the table on the far side of the tiny, gray room. Not a hair out of place, not a smudge in her lightly applied makeup, she looked like she always did—polished and elegant. At least she would have if she hadn't been sporting an ill-fitting muddy green shirt with the word *INMATE* printed over the left pocket. The corner of her lips quirked up into a wry half smile when she saw my face.

"I know." She cast a disparaging glance at the shirt. "This is not my color."

Her flippant comment made me want to sigh with a mixture of relief and exasperation. I wasn't sure what I would've done if I'd walked in to find her crying and terrified.

Blithe, irreverent Emma I can handle. Scared, helpless Emma is not something I processed well.

A flash of memory hit me again: my sister's bruised and battered face, tears leaking from the corners of her swollen eyes as she recounted what Ortega had done to her.

And, again, I was glad the man was dead.

"You're worried about your clothes?" I asked, lowering into the plastic chair across from her.

"Not really. Though they did take my favorite pair of Gucci boots . . . which I sincerely hope to get back unscathed." She directed the last comment to the camera bubble over our heads.

"Emma—"

"I'm kidding. They're my second-favorite pair of Gucci boots." She grinned.

Only Emma.

"Where's Wes?" I asked, referring to our friend and attorney Wes Roberts.

"On his way and ready to spit nails."

"Good." Wes lived in Savannah now but still practiced in Florida. He was a great lawyer. I felt a wave of optimism wash over my worry. The sensation lasted about half a second.

"Listen," she said, her face growing serious, "there's something I need you to do for me."

I had a feeling I knew what she was going to ask.

"Don't worry. I'll call Mom and Dad," I told her with as much stoic nonchalance as I could muster.

She shook her head. "It's not that. You wouldn't get through to them, remember?"

Relief hit me hard enough to force a grateful breath from my lungs. I slumped back in the chair. "Right. They're in Big Bend."

Our parents had called when they'd reached the national park the day before to say they'd be out of cell range for a few days. They'd been traveling the country in their RV, having a ball. I didn't want to be the one to ruin it. Nor did I want to unleash our mother on the Jacksonville Sheriff's Office.

Mom's an ex-teacher. She has that "teacher's voice" thing, and she wouldn't hesitate to use it.

"By the time they're back to civilization this will all be handled," Emma said. "But that's not what I need to talk to you about."

"Okay."

"You have to promise that you'll do it."

"Of course."

"Even though Wes is on his way, I'm going to be stuck her a while, so I need you to take care of a party tonight."

"Beg pardon?"

"It won't be a big deal."

"But—" Nothing about handling social situations was easy for me. My sister, on the other hand, was an events coordinator and a very good one.

That didn't change the obvious, which I felt obligated to point out.

Straightening, I leaned forward and said, "Em, don't you think you should be more worried about being arrested for murder than a party?"

"Murder? Is that what they told you?"

"Yes. They said a witness saw you at the crime scene lurking over Tony's dead body."

"Lurking, was I?" She shook her head slowly, eyes bright with amusement. Before I could ask her to let me in on the joke, she said, "You know the cops are under no obligation to tell you the truth, right?"

I blinked at her while that sank in. "Wait. So all this stuff about Tony being dead and you being there—"

"All true," she said. "I *did* go to speak to Tony. When I went in, I found him in the office very much dead."

"Em, why would you go to his house?" I had a sinking feeling I knew. "This is about the auction, isn't it?"

"I went to return his money and explain that he was not to contact you again. Which, in hindsight, was stupid."

"Yes it was. You should have let Wes deal with Tony." Wes had handled my sister's divorce and made it clear Ortega was never to have contact with our family again.

"Like I said, hindsight." She lifted a shoulder.

I leaned forward. "You went inside?"

"The door was open, and by open I mean *standing* open." She spread her arms in a combo, this-wide and what-was-I-supposed-to-do? gesture.

My lips parted as I gaped at my sister.

"What? It was my house, once."

I shut my mouth, then opened it again but Emma cut me off before I could speak.

"Don't," she said.

"What?"

"Say whatever it is you're thinking about saying."

She hit me with a pointed look and I wasn't sure if my sister was warning me to keep my trap shut because she didn't want to hear any flak or as a reminder that we were being observed.

Probably both. She would get an earful from Wes when he got here and the bigger deal I made about her interacting with Ortega, the more weight the police would give it.

I could think of a dozen questions to ask her, but ended up going with one the cops knew the answer to.

"So, what are you in here for if not murder?"

"They charged me with trespassing."

"Trespassing?"

"Yep. Even though the door was open and I knew the owner, going inside was trespassing. At least that's what they tell me."

"Bogus."

"Probably. Wes will sort it out, but not in time for the party tonight."

"Em—"

"Listen. Everything you need is on my laptop in my brief-case at home."

"But I—"

"It's important, Grace. I have a friend, well, you know Kevin."

"Aikido Kevin?" I asked, thinking of the tall guy who sometimes joined us in my sister's private dojo for class.

Emma nodded. "His brother, Tyler, was just diagnosed with a rare form of cancer. He's an artist, and though the cancer is treatable, his insurance doesn't cover it."

"And the party is to raise money for his medical bills?"

"Sort of. Tyler will be teaching guests how to paint one of his original designs."

"Like an art class?"

Emma shook her head. "It's a painting party. We serve champagne then heavy hors d'oeuvres, everyone paints, there are breaks so there's time to chat and have a glass of wine. Tyler's work will be on display and many of the guests own galleries or are influential in the art scene. We're hoping to get him a gallery show from this event."

I blinked at her.

"It's easy. All you have to do is welcome the guests, introduce Tyler, then make sure everyone is having a good time."

I could feel my eyes bulging out as she spoke.

"Grace? Are you breathing?"

"No."

My sister canted her head and studied me. "Okay. On second thought, I have a better idea. I know the events coordinator for the Ritz. Call the hotel and ask for Kendall. She owes me a favor."

"What do I say?"

"Tell her you're my sister and you need help with an event. She'll likely be busy but that's the nature of the party business. Kendall's good. She'll be able to get the ball rolling once you get her the file."

"File?"

"On my laptop. It's labeled 'Painting Party' with the date. You'll see it. Transfer it to the yellow flash drive—it's in the zipper pocket of my briefcase. Okay?"

"The flash what?"

"You know, a portable USB stick."

"Right—the little rectangle thingy."

"Make sure you use the yellow one."

"Yellow USB stick. Got it."

"Get the file to Kendall and she'll handle it."

"So, I won't have to go to the party?"

"That will be up to Kendall. Just follow her lead, do what she says, and you'll be fine. Trust me."

CHAPTER 3

I hit the first snag before I made it out of the sheriff's office. Jake informed me that he and Detective Boyle would be coming to the condo to take possession of Emma's computers. I tried to explain to Jake that I needed one of her work files but he just shook his head.

I thought I could get around it by beating them home, until I realized they were my ride back to Bluebell. I assumed they would drop me off in the lot and follow me home.

Sometimes I hated being right.

After depositing me next to my SUV, they waited, then escorted me all the way back to my sister's beachfront condo. I muttered a quick plea to the heavens that I'd be able to copy the file before they took Emma's stuff. Or, even better, that Wes would somehow get Emma out of the pokey in time for the party.

I looked at the dashboard clock as I pulled into the condo's parking lot. It was after four, which didn't give me much hope. I was going to need that file.

Maybe they would let me print a copy of it?

With a bit of renewed hope, I climbed out of Bluebell and turned to the detectives.

"Emma asked me to fill in for her tonight at an event she's supposed to be handling. I need the file from her computer."

"We can't let you have access to the computer," Detective Boyle said. "It's being taken into evidence."

"I understand. But I really need the information on that file. Maybe I can print it? Or, hell, you can read it to me and I'll take notes."

"I can't allow that, Miss Wilde. I'm sorry," she said, not sounding at all sorry.

"Look, she ain't askin' for much." Jake tried to intercede but Boyle was having none of it.

"She's asking to violate chain of custody."

He made a derisive noise. "Come on, Boyle . . ."

She ignored his intended meaning and motioned toward the condo building. "After you, Detective Nocera."

In that moment, I kind of wanted to strangle Detective Boyle. Actually, I knew a tiger who owed me a favor . . . Maybe a good maiming would teach her to be a little less obdurate.

The look on my face must have been broadcasting my feelings loud and clear because Jake stepped toward me and said, "Let's go, Grace."

I followed him to the building and up the stairs. Detective Boyle stayed close on my heels until we reached the top.

"Where's Yamada?" she asked, looking around.

I assumed she was talking about Charlie Yamada, an investigator with the Jacksonville CSU. He was one of Kai's friends and, apparently, his replacement on this case.

"He's supposed to be here," Jake said.

With a scowl, Boyle pulled her phone out of her pocket and paced away from us.

As soon as she was out of earshot Jake asked, "What about your dog?"

"Moss? What about him?"

"Don't you need to put 'im up?"

"You afraid of the Big Bad Wolf?"

"Nope." He cast a meaningful glance toward Detective Boyle, who had ended her phone call and was on her way to join us.

Being slow on the uptake, it took me a second to realize Jake was trying to give me the time I needed to snag the file off Emma's computer before it was confiscated.

"Um . . ." I turned my attention to Detective Boyle and said, "I need a minute to get my dog."

"Why?" she asked.

I could feel Moss's presence on the other side of the door. Roused from a nap by the sound of my key in the lock, he was ready for dinner and a potty break.

"He's cranky," I said, at the same time urging Moss to bark. He growled in protest, not in the mood for games.

Hungry, he told me, then added a howl for emphasis.

Not what I was aiming for but, whatever works.

Boyle took a step away from the door. "That sounded like a wolf."

"Yes it did. No wonder you're a detective."

"You can't keep wolves in Florida," she said.

"Actually, you can. Florida Fish and Wildlife categorizes wolves as a Class II animal and thus legal to own. Though, to be honest, most people probably shouldn't."

"And you're the exception?"

Jake snorted at that, earning a quick glare from Boyle.

Unlike Jake, Boyle had no idea how much of an exception I was, and I had no desire to enlighten her.

"Yep. Even so, Moss can get ornery. So I'd like to go in and put him in another room so you can get what you need and leave in one piece. He's only part wolf, but he doesn't like strangers."

It was all a load of hooey.

Moss can be a willful and stubborn beast, even a bit territorial around some people, namely Kai, but he was never vicious. The exception being when in the presence of sociopaths and people who mean me harm.

In truth, Moss would wag his tail in greeting, give the two visitors a quick once-over before demanding to go out and be given food. But I needed to buy time and I was will-ing to resort to slander to get it.

Boyle's eyes narrowed. "You have two minutes."

It took me three. First, I had to contend with Voodoo, our new kitten and resident nutcase who'd begun to climb my bare leg as soon as I stood still long enough.

Up!

"Okay, crazy." I scooped her up and held her in the crook of my arm, letting her bat and play with a strand of ponytail that had fallen over my shoulder.

Most of my time, however, was spent blocking Moss's insistent nudges as I placed Emma's briefcase on the kitchen counter, pulled out her laptop, and began searching for the yellow flash drive.

Hungry.

I know, buddy. I urged him to be patient.

Hungry.

Nudge.

"Hang on," I muttered.

Out.

Nudge-nudge.

"Stop that," I whispered as I fished around the pockets of the briefcase for the USB stick.

"Got it." I smiled when I spotted the bright yellow rectangle.

Out! Moss insisted.

Just a second. "Hey!" My dog shoved his head under my forearm, causing the flash drive I'd been trying to plug into the laptop to go flying from my hand. I heard it bounce off something in the kitchen behind me as it skittered off to who knew where.

When I turned and scanned the room, the thing was out of sight.

"Crap!"

I started to look for it when a trio of knocks sounded on the front door. Loud and authoritative.

No time. I decided to send myself an e-mail with the file as an attachment. Charlie or whoever checked over Emma's mail would see what I'd done but I couldn't worry about that now.

A few keystrokes and mental reprimands to my canine later, I was turning off the laptop and had just shut the lid when the front door opened and Detective Boyle came striding into view.

"What are you doing?" she demanded.

I tried to took innocent when I turned to her. Holding Voodoo up in one hand, I said, "Had to grab this little girl. Moss is very protective."

To emphasize my point, I kept a firm grip on Moss's collar. Not that I could have kept him from doing something if he'd wanted to—my dog outweighs me by at least twenty pounds—but I was still trying to make him seem dangerous.

"I was just trying to find his leash," I added.

"Really? Does it look like this?" She held up Moss's leash, which she must have spotted on the foyer table as she walked in.

"That's it! Thanks. He really has to pee."

I took the leash from her as Moss and I passed, then paused when Charlie Yamada stepped through the front door.

He didn't seem to notice Detective Boyle's disapproving look when he greeted me with a smile and said, turning his full attention to Moss, "Hey. So this is the famous wolf-dog?"

"Yep. Moss this is Charlie. Charlie, Moss." I patted my dog and clipped on his leash.

"Wow," Charlie said, his face alight with admiration. "He's beautiful."

Moss, beautiful. Moss agreed with a slow swish of his tail.

"Thanks," I said, ignoring my dog's self-affirmation.

A lot of people would be apprehensive around a dog like Moss. Not Charlie. When we'd met, I'd learned Charlie was a big dog person. Meaning he liked dogs a lot and big ones even more.

"Can I pet him?" he asked, finally tearing his eyes off Moss to look at me hopefully.

"Sure."

"Yamada," Boyle snapped. "You're not here to play with the dog."

"Right. Sorry, Detective."

"Here," I said, handing him Voodoo, who had started squirming against my grip. "Can you hold her a minute so she doesn't try to escape when we go out?"

I didn't wait for Boyle's veto, just turned and slipped out the door.

Moss watered his favorite bush with relief and we were back inside in less than a minute. We came back in to find Charlie standing right where he'd been, still holding Voodoo, who was trying to wriggle up the short sleeve of his polo shirt.

"Thanks," I said, taking back the kitten, who promptly hung a claw in Charlie's shirt and squeaked out a plaintive meow at being removed from her new "toy."

Mine!

No, I tried to scold her mentally while I untangled her kitty claw from Charlie's sleeve.

Voodoo voiced her complaint again. Ignoring me entirely.

Mine!

I distracted her by pulling out the Saint Francis medal I always wore from where it hung under my shirt and dangled it in the kitten's line of sight. She lunged for the pendant and I captured her against my chest.

"Sorry," I said to the room at large.

Charlie was grinning at the kitten, who really is a rather adorable black fluff-ball.

Boyle, on the other hand, was looking at Voodoo like she was something that belonged in a toilet bowl.

Jake had ignored us and, holding up my sister's laptop, stepped from the kitchen.

"I've got this. Yamada, you need help with the other computer?"

"I'm on it. Just might need you to get the door." He looked at me. "Grace?"

It took me a second to realize he was asking where he could find Emma's office.

"It's this way." I led them down the hall, pausing to deposit Voodoo and Moss in my bedroom as we passed.

I opened the door to my sister's office and clicked on the light.

Like evil laser scanners in a sci-fi flick, Detective Boyle's gaze tracked over every inch of the room when we entered. She shot a glance at Charlie, then nodded at my sister's sleek, new iMac.

Taking his cue, Charlie unhooked the computer and carried it out of the room. Jake followed to manage the door and I was left alone with Boyle, who continued her perusal until her focus homed in on the large antique wardrobe Emma used to stash her gift-wrapping supplies and other random clutter best kept out of sight.

She squinted at it as if wishing she had X-ray vision.

"It leads to Narnia," I told her, deadpan.

Boyle didn't react for a moment, and when she finally turned to me, her eyes were hard, her mouth pressed into a thin, closed-lipped smile. "Cute."

"Thanks. I'll be here all week."

"You and your sister seem to find this amusing. I don't."

"You're wrong, Boyle."

Jake's large form filled the doorway.

"We're done here," he said, though I couldn't be sure whom he was addressing. I hadn't taken my eyes off Boyle long enough to notice anything more than Jake's dark shape materialize in my periphery.

We filed out of the room and I led the way to the front door, holding it open as the detectives passed.

Jake paused and turned to me before following Boyle down the stairs. "You okay?"

"Yeah."

"Look," he said, keeping his voice low. "I know Boyle seems—"

"Like a constipated Chihuahua with hemorrhoids?" I supplied.

His lips twitched with humor at the description. "Call her what you want. She's a hard-ass, true enough, but she's a good cop. Let us run this down. If Emma's got nothin' to hide, you got nothin' to worry about."

CHAPTER 4

My sister had recently upgraded to the newest iPhone, insisting I take her old one. It was a huge improvement over the prehistoric Nokia I'd been using, but after a month, I still had almost no clue how to use it apart from a couple of apps, making phone calls, and snapping the occasional photo.

Emma had always enjoyed taking advantage of my *tech-neptitude*, as she called it, by programming "fitting" ring tones for different people.

Sometimes, I longed for my phone to emit a simple ring, but that didn't stop me from lunging for it when it began playing the familiar salsa tune she'd programmed for Wes.

"Wes?"

"You want the good news or bad news?"

"There's bad news?"

"I'm pulling off of I-95 onto Union Street now. That's the good news. Unfortunately, the only bail bondsman I've been able to get in contact with is asking for cash and it's Sunday."

"So, Emma's stuck in jail."

"Just for the night."

"Crap. That means I'll have to do this party gig."

"That's one of the things I love about you, Grace, always thinking of others," he teased.

"At least I got the file before they took Emma's stuff."

"Before who took Emma's stuff?"

"The cops—" I had a sudden sinking feeling.

"Grace, tell me they had a warrant."

"I don't—I just assumed . . . Did I screw up?"

There was a brief pause. "No. But the cops have if they think they're going to get away with conducting an illegal search before I get to town."

"Jake told me if Emma had nothing to hide I shouldn't worry."

"He's right. You shouldn't. Warrant or no warrant, I'll handle it," he promised before hanging up.

I knew he would, but it didn't stop me from wanting to throttle Jake.

A glance at the clock told me throttling would have to wait. I needed to get in touch with this Kendall chick if I didn't want to be hosting a painting party by myself. The thought brought on a wave of queasiness.

Social occasions made me uncomfortable. Being the person *responsible* for a social occasion was going to require a bottle of Pepto-Bismol and, quite possibly, a few cc's of bear tranquilizer.

I took a fortifying breath, looked up the Ritz-Carlton, and dialed the number listed for special events.

"I'm sorry, it's Kendall's day off," the woman told me, making my stomach clinch.

"Is there any way you can get a message to her? It's kind of urgent. My sister, Emma, has an event scheduled for tonight and she can't"—my insides burbled—"make it."

"Emma? You mean Emma from *E Squared*?" The woman's words got noticeably higher when she said the name of my sister's company.

"The one and only."

"Oh!" The woman let out an excited gasp. "We just love Emma. She's such a doll. Everything's okay?"

We? Who was we?

"Just a scheduling conflict," I said.

"Well, let me see if I can get ahold of Kendall for you. What's your number?"

I gave it to her and made a beeline for my bathroom to find the Pink Stuff. I took a giant, chalky swig and was thinking about locating the bear tranquilizer—I had a vial of it, by the way—when my phone rang.

"Hi, I'm trying to reach Grace Wilde."

"Kendall?"

"That's me. You're Emma's sister?"

I confirmed and explained that Emma needed someone to oversee a painting party that night.

"I know it's incredibly short notice," I said, setting down the Pepto long enough to look up the file on my computer's e-mail. "But if there's any way you can help, I'm not"—my insides squirmed and let, out a long, gurgling groan—"good at this sort of thing. I have the file you need."

"Well, then we should be able to come up with something. Where and when?"

"Hang on." I started scanning the file and winced. Many of the details were followed with notations done in Emma's personal shorthand. I was one of the few people who, given enough time, could decipher it. Which was probably one of the reasons she'd asked for my help. At least the host's contact information was easy to identify, displayed at the top of the page. "At someone's house in the Omni plantation." I gave her the address. "Seven thirty."

"Why don't we meet there at six?"

I looked at the clock. I'd make it, if I hauled my cookies out of the house within the next fifteen minutes.

"Sounds like a plan."

Not wanting to lug my laptop with me, I opted to print the file, hitting the icon and waiting to hear the printer start up before I jumped in the shower. No time to do more than strip and rinse, I clipped my hair on the top of my head, jumped in and out of the shower, and froze when I realized I had no idea what to wear.

My sister often dressed the part when doing themed

events. She had a closet filled with costumes and accessories ranging from punk to Southern belle. I knew a hoop skirt would not do for a painting party but beyond that, I was lost.

I tried to call Wes for advice, but got his voice mail.

"Crap, crap, crap."

I ran to my sister's bedroom, flipped on the light as I stepped into her closet, and pivoted in a semicircle, hoping inspiration would strike.

Instead, I wondered, *Why me? Out of all the people Emma could have asked—*

"She didn't ask them," I said, cutting off the internal whining. "And you are not going to mess up because you don't know what to wear. So think."

Focusing on the clothes, I let out a long breath and thought.

"Paint, painting . . ."

People wore smocks when they painted, right? What the heck was a smock, anyway?

"I've got it."

With an about-face, I hit the lights and rushed back to my room. My dad had given me one of his old, long-sleeved button-down work shirts to wear when I'd volunteered to help him paint the shed before my parents sold the house.

"It's here, somewhere," I muttered as I rifled through the bottom drawer of my dresser.

"Ha!"

I held the shirt up like a prize. Moss, who was lounging on the floor nearby, lifted his head and blinked, unimpressed with the wrinkled, yellow-and-white-spattered garment.

"Do you have a better idea?" I asked, but my dog had already returned to his nap.

"Didn't think so." I shrugged off the canine critique and buttoned the voluminous shirt over a pair of dark jeans, stepped into my favorite duck boots, and was ready.

Shoving the bottle of Pepto into my purse, I hurried to the office and snatched up the pages I'd printed.

I did a double take. The ink had come out a lovely shade of fuchsia. Grinding my teeth, I folded the pages in half and stuck them in my purse next to the matching bottle of Pepto-Bismol.

Rolling up the shirt's giant sleeves, I rushed out the door and galloped down the stairs. I had cranked Bluebell and was pulling out of the condo's lot almost on time.

At the first stoplight, I plugged the party's address into my phone's GPS app and it plotted the fastest route—approximately forty-one minutes. It was just shy of five thirty. I stepped on the gas and was shooting up Interstate 295 when my phone began playing "Hot Blooded," Emma's idea of an appropriate ring tone for Kai.

"Hey. I heard you walked out on your interview with Boyle."

"You heard right. And you can tell Jake I'm not impressed with his little 'don't worry' speech. Trying to give me a pep talk doesn't make up for the fact that he took my sister's things without a warrant."

"He didn't need a warrant."

"I thought that was part of the whole due-process thing."

"Normally. But Emma gave her permission."

"Who told you that? Boyle?"

"No, Jake did."

I snorted. "Please. Emma's not that stupid."

"Actually, it's not at all stupid. If we'd gotten a warrant, it would have been for every type of computer and data storage device in the house, including your stuff. Anything Emma had access to."

"Oh."

"I also heard you were tampering with evidence."

"Do you know where I am?" I asked.

"No."

"I'm going to a *party*. Where I'm supposed to make sure people are having *fun* and drinking *wine*."

"That sounds"—he paused—"terrible?"

I ground my teeth.

"It is! I have no idea what I'm doing, Kai. Don't you get it? I needed to get the info on this party so I could get help. Boyle can think what she wants. I did what I had to do."

Wow. *Melodramatize much, Grace?*

"Sorry," I said. "I just don't want to let Emma down."

"Do you trust your sister?"

"Of course."

"Then you should be fine."

I guess he had a point.

"I've got to head to a scene," he said. "Have fun."

I didn't make any promises.

Following along with the dot on the GPS, I zipped through a couple of roundabouts and found the Omni without any problem.

The house was harder, but, again, the app pulled through and I navigated the winding roads without a problem, turning into the cobblestone driveway at only a couple minutes past six.

I parked next to the caterer's van and followed one of the workers inside.

A lean, energetic woman dressed in a T-shirt and yoga pants was standing just inside the entrance to the kitchen, speaking to an older, black woman wearing dark slacks, a fashionable leopard-print blouse, and a look of uncertainty.

I approached and overheard the last snippet of their conversation

"Emma put you in charge?" the woman asked, taking in the girl's appearance, from her damp hair down to her flip-flops.

"She did. And don't worry, this is going to be great." The young woman's enthusiasm, genuine as it sounded, didn't seem to put the older woman at ease.

"You are . . . ?"

"Kendall. I've just got to hop into the powder room to change." She smiled and lifted a garment bag into view. "I'll be out in two seconds."

Kendall stepped back into the hall and swept through a door, closing it with a soft *thump*.

The woman, who I assumed was Mrs. Smith, stared after her for several seconds then glanced at me, the worry lines in her brow deepening when she saw my paint-splattered smock.

I canted my head toward the door. "I'm with her."

With a look of dismay, Mrs. Smith turned and walked back into the kitchen.

"So far, so good, Grace," I muttered.

True to her word, Kendall emerged from the bathroom a couple of minutes later. Dressed in a black skirt suit with a deep purple satin blouse and her hair slicked back into a stylish bun, she looked older and utterly professional. The warmth and exuberance were still there but she no longer looked like a yoga instructor.

"Kendall?"

She turned, her smile broadening when she saw me.

"You must be Grace. You look just like your sister."

"Um . . ." I'd never thought we looked much alike, being that my sister is tall and lithe and I'm short and curvy. But it certainly wasn't an insult. "Thanks."

Kendall's smile remained bright as she took in my outfit.

"Looks like you're ready to paint."

"Yeah, I wasn't . . ."

Looping her arm through mine, she pulled me into the hustle and bustle of the kitchen. "Don't worry about it, I'll take care of everything. You have the file?"

"Yep." I handed her the pages.

She frowned at them and glanced up at me.

"Sorry, I had an issue with my printer. I know it's hard to read but I promise that's everything."

She blinked at me for a second, probably wondering how Emma and I could possibly be related, then shrugged.

"Okay, let's get this situated."

Kendall took charge—pointing, directing, and answering questions with ease.

I helped whenever an extra hand was needed but mostly tried to stay out of the way.

"Looks like we're good to go," she told me a half hour later.

"I'm amazed and eternally grateful."

"No problem. The only reason I got a job with the Ritz in the first place was because of Emma. I owe her."

"I'll make sure to tell her thank you."

"You look a bit worn out," she said with an appraising once-over that reminded me so much of my sister it took me a moment to respond.

"Yeah," I said finally. "Parties aren't my thing."

"Well, you're off the hook now. I can take it from here."

"Really?"

"Yep."

I thanked her again and headed to Bluebell. My shoulders didn't begin to relax until I made it out of the neighborhood.

With a heavy breath, I slumped back in the seat and headed home. How was it possible for me to be so exhausted at barely seven o'clock at night?

On a whim, I decided to take the ferry rather than loop all the way around the Saint Johns River. The thirty-minute ride would save gas, if not time, and help me relax.

Ten minutes later, I eased Bluebell over the bump leading onto the ferry's deck and parked behind a compact car. Once we were under way and I knew the diesel fumes from the boat's chugging engine would be carried off, I cranked the window down and let the evening breeze flow over my face.

The air was cool, hinting at a fall that would never really come.

November in North Florida could be cold one day and hot the next but it never managed to morph into true autumn.

Oh well. There were worse things.

Like snow.

Wes called about half a second after I'd closed my eyes and leaned my head back to rest it against the seat.

After learning Emma was fine, I asked about the warrant. Wes confirmed what Kai had told me. Emma had given the police permission to take her computer and her laptop.

"Basically, when Jake asked her if they'd find any connection to Ortega on her computers she invited them to check for themselves." Wes didn't sound happy about it.

"Kai said it was probably a good thing. Otherwise, they would've taken my stuff, too."

"That's assuming they would have been granted a warrant in the first place. Anyway, what's done is done. Emma assures me there is nothing incriminating on either computer, so it doesn't matter."

"And the trespassing charge?" I asked.

"An intimidation tactic, I suspect. They don't want to arrest her for Ortega's murder until they have substantial evidence."

"Which they won't get."

"Correct."

I wasn't naïve enough to believe people weren't arrested and even convicted for crimes they didn't commit.

"Boyle seems to really have it out for Emma, Wes." And for me, for that matter. Not that I cared what the woman thought of me.

"Emma mentioned something about that."

"It doesn't worry you?"

"Worry? No. Irritate? Yes. I plan to see her tomorrow morning to express my . . . ire."

"Good." It really ticked me off that she'd lied to me about Emma being arrested for murder. It would serve her right to have a taste of irate Wes for breakfast. "Boyle said there was a witness."

"Jasmine El-Amin, Ortega's fiancée."

"Fiancée?" I winced at the idea of him getting married again. "What's her story?"

"It's interesting, actually. Jasmine is a well-known fashion model from Europe. I'm not sure how long she and Ortega had been together, but it seems she's very recently moved in with him. She and her driver came home and found Emma standing next to the body."

"Her driver?" I scoffed.

"Now, now, don't judge." I knew Wes was referring to the fact that he often employed a driver himself.

"That's different, Wes. You work in your car. It's an extension of your office."

"That's what I keep telling my accountant. In any case, the driver was the one who made the 911 call."

The ferry's horn blared and Wes said, "Sounds like some party."

"I'm on the ferry on my way home."

"Already?"

"Thanks to Emma's friend Kendall."

"Who?"

"It's a long story. Call me tomorrow and let me know about Em?"

"You know I will."

CHAPTER 5

It was a dun-gray morning and, though I knew the sun was up, not a ray penetrated the thick fog. It clung to the dunes and shrouded the horizon, enveloping everything in its moist ephemeral embrace. The tide had come and gone, leaving deposits of coquina shells that crunched underfoot.

Moss was itching to go for a long run. I was not so enthusiastic. I started down the beach anyway at more of a feeble jog than a run, which caused my dog to tug on the leash and cast impatient glances over his shoulder at me.

Run?

"Working at it, big guy," I puffed.

Moss slowed to a measured trot, a pace he could easily keep up for several miles without a whisper of fatigue.

I tried not to hold it against him.

It took a while, but I finally increased my speed—though not enough that Moss had to shift into the loping run he loved so much.

People talk about the joy of running—of the endorphins and reaching a Zen-like clarity of mind. This had never happened to me. Mostly, all I thought about when I ran was how much farther I had to go before I could stop.

That morning, however, my mind was clouded with questions and worry.

Emma was in jail. She'd been arrested on a trumped-up charge, but it seemed the police—read: Detective Boyle—were looking pretty hard at Emma. I didn't like it.

And why had Ortega really contacted me?

I'd wanted to know as soon as he'd won the bid at the auction granting him my help—presumably with an animal. But Emma had told me it would be better to ignore him and let Wes handle it.

That had worked until I'd gotten the first phone call. The message had been short and, if not sweet, at least succinct.

"Grace, this is Tony Ortega. I need to speak to you. You're the only person who can help."

When I'd played the message for Emma, she'd rolled her eyes and said, "Please. Who does he think you are, Obi-Wan Kenobi?"

"Is there a chance he has a real problem with a pet?"

"Tony, with a pet? You know what he said when I told him you were studying to be a veterinarian?"

I hadn't.

"Who would bother to care for a sick animal?" she'd said, perfectly mimicking his light Spanish accent.

After that, I'd erased all the other messages without listening to them, except . . .

I stopped so abruptly Moss jerked the leash out of my hand. *Run!*

Suddenly freed from the dead weight holding him back, Moss turned on the afterburner and sprinted down the beach. Within seconds he was thirty yards away.

"Moss!" I called between panting breaths.

I squinted into the hazy distance, scanning for anyone who might be alarmed to find a large, white wolf running toward them, and blew out a relieved sigh when I saw the coast was clear.

No pun intended.

Nevertheless, the damp, dim morning wouldn't keep everyone away. Soon, someone was bound to come along. I looked back toward the condo, praying my dog-hating neighbor, Mr. Cavanaugh, would not be that someone. He'd call the authorities and file a complaint with the condo association before I could blink.

I looked back to where Moss had been but he was nowhere in sight.

Moss! I reached out mentally, easily zeroing in on the familiar hum of his canine brain.

This, oddly enough, helped me see him and I got a fleeting glimpse of his white form as it disappeared into the fog.

Too far.

"Moss!"

Get back here. Now.

I put more than a little force of pure will into the last word. The weight of She Who Must Be Obeyed.

It would have been overkill for almost any other dog, causing a panic response.

Moss is not any other dog.

In a pack he would be alpha—a fact he reminded me of repeatedly.

Run!

He materialized out of the fog. Speeding toward me at a full run. Wolves can sprint at thirty miles per hour—I was guessing Moss was close.

He was making a happy-wolf face. Golden eyes bright. Mouth open in a toothy, tongue-lolling smile.

The exuberance hit me as soon as he did. Warmth radiating through him into me. Though the contact was only a glancing bump, it was enough to nearly knock me off my feet. Penance for calling him back.

I whooped out a laugh and snagged his furry neck when he came in for a second pass.

For a minute I was lost in wolf wonderland, but finally remembered to snap Moss's leash on and try to recall what I was thinking about before his grand escape.

Ortega. Had there been another message from him? One I'd missed?

I pulled my phone out of my pocket to check and it started ringing. Nearly dropping it in surprise, I blinked at the caller ID.

Anthony Ortega.

What the hell?

"Hello?"

"May I speak with Grace Wilde, please." The voice was British and belonged to a woman.

"Speaking."

"Miss Wilde, this is Jasmine El-Amin. I'm sorry to ring so early." The words were rushed and filled with nearly palpable anxiety. "Do you have a moment?"

How to answer? Now that I knew I was talking to Ortega's fiancée—the witness Wes had mentioned—I wasn't sure.

Normally, I'd be handing the person accusing my sister of murder a list of short piers on which to take a long walk but curiosity triumphed pettiness.

I wanted to hear for myself what she and her driver thought they'd seen.

Keeping my tone polite and professional, I asked, "What can I do for you Miss El-Amin?"

"I very much need your help. If you could meet me at my house as soon as possible—it's a matter of life and death."

• • •

I told Jasmine I would be there in forty-five minutes. It took closer to an hour because in addition to having to take a shower, I'd decided to do a quick Google search for her to get a little background info. Skimming over the Wikipedia entry as fast as possible, I learned she'd been born in London to a British mother and a father who was of mixed English, Mediterranean, and Middle Eastern heritage. Which was pretty vague but might not matter anyway.

"'Began her modeling career at age ten,' blah, blah," I read aloud. There was no mention of Ortega or their engagement, making me wonder how long they'd been together. It listed her hair color as dark brown and her eye color as hazel. Her height was five feet ten inches, only a few inches taller than my sister.

The only image included was a photograph of her stalking down a runway. I supposed the clothes would be called avant-garde, her makeup and hairstyle just as cutting-edge. She wore the slightly sullen, yet somehow severe expression you often see on runway models.

Paging back to the other search results, I quickly found a host of photos. I started to scan over a few to get a more realistic idea of what she looked like—then chided myself for wasting time. I'd see what she looked like soon enough, or would if I got a move on.

A few minutes after eight, I pulled through the open gate leading to the Ortega house. The place looked almost exactly as it had the last time I'd seen it over six years ago. An interesting mix of Southwestern and Art Deco with a dash of Aegean, the front of the house had no porch and few windows. The stucco walls were stark white, making the focal point the enormous double doors set into the cylindrical, two-story entry.

The strangest detail was the railless steps that wrapped the side of the entry, curving up to nowhere.

They reminded me of photos I'd seen of Greece, where stairs leading to rooftop terraces were decorated with pots of bright flowers and the occasional lounging cat. Here, it seemed a pointless architectural adornment.

To the left of the stairway to nowhere, carved wood doors were embedded in the semicircle of the house's façade. I climbed out of Bluebell and had started toward the doors when one opened and a young woman carrying an assortment of cleaning supplies in a plastic caddy stepped onto the landing and began scrubbing the wood. It took me a moment to realize she was wiping away the smudges and dust left over from fingerprint powder.

A moment later, the door opened again and a second woman appeared. She was older and dressed in a navy skirt suit and low heels. Her dark hair was pulled up into a tight

French twist. She spoke quietly to the woman cleaning, then looked up when she noticed my approach.

The flash of recognition caught me off guard and it took me several seconds to remember her name.

"Mary," I said with a forced smile. "I didn't know you still worked for Tony."

Emma had described Mary as more of a house manager and personal assistant than a housekeeper. Whatever her title, something about her had always rubbed me the wrong way. I wasn't sure what I had against the woman. Other than thinking anyone who could stomach working for Ortega had to have a screw loose.

"Grace. It's been too long. Come in." She opened the door and ushered me inside, through the foyer. Here, there were more windows than walls, making the view of the Atlantic spectacular.

Emma had loved this house. It had been in midconstruction when she'd met Ortega, and though it had been years, I vividly remembered how excited she'd been when he'd suggested she design the pool area, which was visible through the wall of glass opposite the entry.

Ortega trusted Emma and valued her opinion. *Yeah, right.*

It was all a ruse, like the steps leading to nowhere.

Mary led me down the corridor, past the kitchen into the living room.

"Jasmine had to take a phone call. I'm sure she'll only be a moment. Make yourself comfortable."

Again, the views of the Atlantic were sweeping. But it wasn't the vista that drew my eye.

On the far wall was an enormous black-and-white photograph of Jasmine, her eyes deeply kohled and her semi-profile striking and exotic. She held her hair away from her face, her gaze focused in the distance.

As beautiful as Jasmine was it was the other figure in the photograph that held my attention. The rest of the frame was filled with the neck and head of a gorgeous black horse.

Her horse. I realized with certainty.

"Hello, handsome," I murmured to the photo. Could this be the reason Jasmine had called me?

For that matter, could it be the reason Ortega had been trying to reach me? A knot of worry began to twist in my gut at the thought.

I'd despised Ortega for what he'd done to my sister, but that didn't mean I'd let an animal suffer for it. Another disturbing thought entered my mind. If Ortega had genuinely needed help with an animal, why ask me? Why risk the wrath of Wes to reach me?

The sound of a woman's voice speaking a foreign language called my attention from the photograph. I crept over to the closed door and pressed my ear against the wood.

I wasn't sure what I hoped to glean, given that the only foreign language I'd ever studied was as dead as Anthony Ortega.

The conversation must have ended because the only sound I heard was that of muffled footsteps. I had just taken a step away from the door when it opened.

The startled woman standing in the doorway was tall, lovely, and visibly upset.

"Sorry," I said. "I was just about to knock. I'm Grace Wilde."

Jasmine blinked at me for a moment before gathering herself.

"Of course," she said, motioning toward the sitting area. "My apologies—family drama. Please, have a seat."

We settled across from each other on two identical linen sofas and a moment later, Mary appeared and asked if we needed anything.

"I'd love a cup of tea, Mary," Jasmine said, then looked at me. "Grace?"

"Tea sounds good. But only if it's iced and sweet." Mary nodded then moved into the kitchen to fulfill our requests.

"Thank you for coming so quickly."

"You sounded upset when we spoke."

Nodding, she opened the fashion magazine she'd been holding to a dog-eared page and handed it to me. The photo in the full-page spread was similar to the one adorning the wall, though the magazine version had been tweaked so that the focus was on the jewelry being advertised. Highlights had been added to the pieces sparkling on Jasmine's finely boned hand, wrist, and neck.

Her hair was wavy and wind tossed, matching the horse's thick mane.

"A Friesian?" I asked, referring to the breed.

She smiled with a nod. "Beautiful, isn't he?"

"Very. He's your horse?"

"What makes you say that?"

I tilted my head toward the enormous photo. "You can tell by the way he's looking at you."

Worry lines pinched her brow as she gazed at the image. "Heart. That's his name, and what he is to me. Especially now." She paused then looked at me, eyes bright with tears. "He's missing."

"Missing? You mean Heart's been stolen?"

"Not quite."

"I'm not following."

"Right, sorry." She rubbed her forehead with shaking fingers. "I don't know where to begin. You see, Heart isn't mine. Though I think he was going to be."

I waited, hoping she would say something that made sense.

"Tony was going to buy him for me. In fact, I think he already had."

Mary approached and handed us our drinks. Jasmine looked up at the older woman, her face strained and hopeful. "You think so as well, don't you, Mary?"

"Yes," she said gently. Turning to me, Mary added, "I heard Mr. Ortega talking about arranging for shipment of something from Morocco and speaking to someone about a horse trailer."

"Morocco?" I looked from Jasmine to Mary. If they were trying to clarify, it wasn't working.

"Perhaps you should start at the beginning, dear." Mary patted Jasmine on the shoulder. "Should I get the note?"

"Yes, thank you," Jasmine said and watched the older woman walk away. "I don't know what I would do without her. So odd. When I first arrived, I found Mary to be quite cold toward me. Things can change so quickly."

I didn't think Jasmine expected a comment, so I waited, figuring the note, Morocco, and everything else would factor into the story once it began. Jasmine let out a measured breath and took a sip of her tea. After what seemed like an hour, she finally spoke. Her British accent made her sound more pulled together than she probably was.

"I expect you already know I'm a model. A month or so ago I was hired to do a photo shoot on location at the estate of Nicolas LaPointe outside Casablanca."

"LaPointe as in LaPointe and Company that makes watches and jewelry." I glanced at the ad, noticing for the first time the company's logo, a set of crossed spears, at the bottom of the page.

Even I had heard of Nicolas LaPointe. Eccentric in the way that only the obscenely wealthy can afford to be. Last I'd heard, he'd bought an island and was populating it with rare and endangered species of birds.

"Mr. LaPointe collects cars, art, horses—things he finds beautiful. He wanted to include both his cars and his horses in the shoot to celebrate the company's hundred and twenty-fifth anniversary."

"Okay," I said, following so far. "So you went to Morocco for a photo shoot."

"We shot the commercial first. It took weeks. Heart and I bonded immediately. I've ridden horses most of my life, which was one reason I got the job."

"They let you wear that jewelry while riding on a horse?" I'd have been afraid I'd lose an earring to the Sahara desert.

"No. Those are copies. We took photos of the real pieces in the studio with perfect lighting and a number of armed guards. They merge the two images together in postproduction." A smile ghosted her lips, giving me a glimpse of the radiant woman under the mask of grief. "You'd be amazed at what they can do with Photoshop."

I bet.

She took a sip of her tea. "The day after Tony arrived, it happened."

"Tony? He was with you?"

She nodded. "He always popped in to see me if I was going to be on location for a while. We would never have seen each other otherwise."

Tears pooled in her eyes and I tried to steer her away from a breakdown by asking a question I already knew the answer to. "Is that where the picture of you and Heart was taken—Morocco?"

She looked at the photo again, though her eyes seemed to lose focus as she immersed herself in the memory.

"It was the first day of the still shoot. We'd set up at the far side of the estate, near some hillside ruins. That shot was taken not long before it hit."

"Before what hit?"

"A storm, unlike anything I'd ever seen. It came out of nowhere. The wind and dust. The lightning and sand . . . a *haboob* it's called."

"A sandstorm?"

"A very sudden and violent sandstorm," she amended and turned back to me. "There were two other models working, but I was the only one who knew how to ride. The concept of the ad was to focus on the jewelry, no other accessories or adornments. So there was no saddle, no bridle, or even reins."

"You're telling me you were left sitting bareback on a horse during a sandstorm? Where was Heart's trainer?"

"There was nothing he could do. Just as the storm hit, one of the large lights was blown over. The bloody thing exploded.

"Heart bolted. I managed to hang on, but within seconds it became almost impossible to see. Heart was panicked—running back and forth, blinded and confused."

"That sounds kind of . . . terrifying."

"It was. Until I began talking to him. I had my arms around his neck, holding on as tightly as I could, and when he heard my voice, he started to calm down. It was as if he'd forgotten I was there then suddenly understood he wasn't alone." She paused. A brittle smile danced over her features. "I managed to lead him to the shelter of a cluster of palms and we weathered the storm together."

"You were able to lead him? With what?" I asked, dubious. Unless Jasmine was the only other person I'd met with the ability to communicate with animals telepathically, I was gonna have a hard time believing her story.

"The dress I was wearing was layer upon layer of black chiffon. I tore one layer off and used it as a blindfold. Once his eyes were covered, he was fine. But ever since then, he's been terrified of storms. If he has a blindfold he'll stay calm. If he doesn't . . ."

"You're afraid he might hurt himself or someone else."

"I'm sure of it. Three days after the first storm it happened again—though we had more warning. By the time we were able to calm him, Heart had injured two people, including Yosef, and had a gash on his side as long as my forearm."

"Yosef?"

"Yosef Kalil. He was Heart's trainer. Very experienced."

Over a thousand pounds of panicking horse was nothing to sneeze at. I'd seen how seriously a horse could injure itself, even in the relative safety of a stall.

"You're worried that whoever has him may not know about his phobia," I surmised.

"Precisely."

"Have you told the police about this?"

"Yes. But I'm afraid they don't seem to care about Heart as much as I do. And, more to the point, I have no proof that he's here in the U.S."

"You don't?"

"No, but"—she raised her shoulders in a helpless shrug—"I believe he's here, Grace. A fortnight ago, not long after I first arrived, I heard Tony on the phone talking to someone about a horse. I asked him about it, but he just teased that I'd have to wait and see. I knew he was planning a big surprise, but decided not to dig and spoil it. Then he—" She broke off, her gaze drifting toward the office.

Thankfully, Mary arrived to distract Jasmine. "I found this in the trash this morning," she said, handing me a piece of paper torn from a notepad.

Scrawled on it were the letters *R n R brd stab.*

I looked a question at Mary, then Jasmine.

"It's Mr. Ortega's writing," Mary said. "I've gotten good at deciphering his notes. I think it's the name of a boarding stable."

"R and R," I said, studying the note. "But that doesn't mean Heart's there. He could still be in Morocco."

"He's not. I wasn't able to reach Mr. LaPointe's assistant, but I spoke to one of Heart's former trainers," Jasmine said. "He confirmed that Heart had been sold and was being sent to America."

"And you think someone stole him after he arrived?"

She shook her head. "I'm not sure. That or, more likely, there's been a mix-up. And now with Tony gone—" She swallowed hard. Mary offered to get her another cup of tea but Jasmine declined. Her fingers clutched the ceramic so hard I wouldn't have been surprised to see it shatter.

With a sad nod and a parting glance to me, Mary went back to doing whatever house managers did.

"Is Heart a valuable horse, monetarily?" I asked.

"To me, he means the world. But no, in terms of money . . ." Jasmine shook her head. "He's a gelding. And though he's gentle with a good temperament, he has no extensive training nor pedigree."

"So you want what, exactly, from me?"

She lifted a shoulder as if to say it was obvious. "I'd like you to help find him. I'll pay you, of course."

Finally, I just couldn't stand it anymore.

"Okay, I have to bring up the elephant in the room," I said.

"Which is?"

"The fact that the person accusing my sister of murder is asking me for help."

She balked at my words. "You're mistaken. I never accused your sister of murder. I simply told the police what I saw."

"Which was what?"

"Mac and I came into the house and Tony was . . ." Her gaze slid toward the office then snapped back to me.

"Mac?" I prompted, hoping to prevent a tearful breakdown. "Is he your driver?"

"Yes. His last name is MacEntire, so he asks to be called Mac. And before you ask why I would need a driver, I grew up in England and I've never been great at driving on the wrong side of the road, so Tony suggested it."

Handy, too, to keep tabs on the little lady and keep her dependent.

"Did you and Mac come in the front door? Or through the garage?"

"The garage."

"What about Mary, where was she?"

"She had that morning off."

"And you didn't hear anything when you got home? A scream? A gunshot? An argument?"

"No. Nothing. He was just—" She wiped away a tear, then lowered her head, pressing her trembling lips together.

I took a moment to regard the lovely young woman quietly crumbling in front of me and wondered if she knew how lucky she was.

Unlike Emma, Jasmine would never have to see the ugly side of Tony Ortega. The true side.

We sat in silence for a few minutes as she gathered herself. I wanted to offer comfort but couldn't. Honestly, Anthony Ortega's death was probably the best thing that could have happened to her.

When she finally lifted her face she said, "Please, Miss Wilde. Help me find Heart. I believe you're the only one who can."

"Why would you think that?"

"Because of Tony. Mary told me he'd been trying to reach you. She said you work with animals. And there's this—" She stood and motioned toward the office. I followed her to the desk and waited as she turned the computer's monitor to face us then hit the space key to turn it on.

The screen blinked to life. On it was a copy of an article from the *Times Union* website. The headline read: *Woman Catches Killer*.

It was about me.

I stared at the accompanying photograph. My arm was

in a sling, and even Emma's expertly applied makeup couldn't hide the bruises on my face. I looked pitiful.

Of course, I remembered when the photo was taken. It's not every day the governor gives you a $100,000 reward for helping solve the murder of his son.

"And, what? You read this article and thought because I'd helped with one crime I would be able to help with another one?"

"I didn't look this up. Tony did. I saw it this morning."

We both stared at the photo.

"I checked the browser's history. This was the last thing he pulled up on the computer before he died," she said.

"And why do you think that would be?" someone asked from the doorway.

I turned to see Detective Boyle strolling into the room. Charlie shuffled in a moment later, his eyes were fixed on a spot on the designer rug a few feet from toes of his shoes.

"Detective." I showed her my teeth in a way that could never be mistaken for a smile. "What a nice surprise."

"Likewise, Miss Wilde."

Mary hurried into the room, her stance stiff and defiant as a posturing rooster. "I am so sorry, ma'am," she said to Jasmine. "Apparently these officers decided to show themselves in."

"The door was open," Boyle said.

Mary slid her an indignant glare. "I very much doubt it."

I remembered something—the woman cleaning the front door.

"You bullied your way in," I said to Boyle.

The detective looked at me, brows raised with feigned concern. "What was that?"

"You saw my truck parked in the drive and wanted to eavesdrop, so you intimidated the poor cleaning girl into letting you in."

Boyle gave Charlie a do-you-believe-this? look, but he didn't commiserate. Instead, he said, "Sorry, ma'am. We have a warrant for Mr. Ortega's computer and other data-storage devices."

"Certainly," Jasmine said. "Whatever you need. Mary?"

Mary gave Charlie a once-over. "Do you have a list?"

Boyle handed her the warrant, then turned back to me. "You didn't answer my question. Why would Mr. Ortega be looking at a photo of you?"

"I have no idea."

"Of course you don't. I'll ask this then: What are you doing here?"

"I asked Grace to come." Jasmine stepped forward; she towered over Boyle, and me, for that matter. "I've retained her services, hopefully."

"As an animal . . . behaviorist?" She screwed up her face in an expression that was both disparaging and dismissive.

"Her horse is missing," I said.

"*Her* horse? I was told it was Mr. Ortega's."

I wasn't going to get into semantics; I wanted to know one thing. "What are the police doing?"

"Looking into it."

"What have you found?" Jasmine asked.

"So far, only that no horse matching the description you gave entered the Port of Miami in the last month."

Jasmine's shoulders slumped. "But—I don't understand. Heart must be here."

"Have you considered that something may have happened to the horse and Mr. Ortega kept it from you to spare your feelings?"

"Something happened? What are you . . . you're saying—"

Boyle either didn't notice or didn't care that her words had pulled the color from Jasmine's face.

"That the horse never made it into the country."

Tears sparked in the model's eyes. "You don't mean . . ." Her voice wavered. "You think Heart could be—"

"No," I said, keeping my eyes on Boyle.

I knew Ortega wouldn't bother to spare anyone's feelings but his own. He'd have told Jasmine, then found a way to use her heartbreak to further manipulate her.

I turned to Jasmine and, when I saw the devastation and

despair on her tear-streaked face, a cold fire began to smolder in my belly.

This young woman, so far from family, already dealing with her fiancé's death and now, thanks to Boyle, fearing she'd lost a friend.

Boyle's callousness was uncalled for, and it pissed me off.

"No?" Boyle asked. "You have a better theory, Miss Wilde?"

I didn't bother to look at the detective. Instead, I spoke to Jasmine in the same gentle, confident voice I would use with a wounded fawn.

"Tony wouldn't have been calling me if Heart had died. He's here and I'm going to find him. I promise."

With a silent sob, Jasmine buried her face in her hands and nodded.

I left the room, edging past Charlie and Detective Boyle without another word. The magazine and note still sat on the coffee table. I picked them up and turned back to the office. Not surprisingly, Boyle had followed me out. I handed her the note. "Tony's handwriting. It's probably the name of a boarding stable."

Boyle handed the piece of paper to Charlie without sparing it a glance.

I headed toward the front door.

"Miss Wilde," Boyle's voice echoed behind me.

The way she said my name set my teeth on edge. I kept walking until I heard her footsteps approaching, then I turned.

"You shouldn't make promises you can't keep," she said.

I locked eyes with her. "Animals are not things, Detective. Heart—yes, the horse has a name—is a *he* not an *it*. I will find him. And I don't make promises I can't keep."

CHAPTER 6

Before I could begin to make good on my word to find Heart, I had an appointment with a man who was being outsmarted by his escape-artist border collie, Pepper. The solution had been simple enough. If he wanted to keep his dog happy and off the streets, she needed a job. Being a people pleaser at heart, and possessing an admirable intellect, Pepper could have been assigned just about any task.

After talking it over with her, I discovered the thing Pepper enjoyed most was catching Frisbees. This idea surprised her owner, who assumed she hated the toys after she'd destroyed the two he'd gotten her.

"Nope," I'd told him. "She just got frustrated when they didn't fly through the air like they used to."

Impressed by my "uncanny insight" (wink, wink) Pepper's owner was happy to dedicate part of his morning and afternoon routine to Frisbee training. I suggested he come up with some complicated tricks to stimulate Pepper's mind and recommended keeping the discs out of reach when not in use.

I also gave him a list of cool doggy puzzles to try, pointing out the most difficult and thus, suitable for a border collie.

The appointment had taken longer than I'd anticipated. It was past noon by the time I made it out of their neighborhood.

My stomach grumbled—protesting how little I'd offered it that day—and I set out to find some fast food.

I pulled into a Wendy's and, while waiting in line for my fries, decided to use my phone to Google R-n-R Boarding Stables. When I looked at the screen, I noticed I'd missed a text from Kai asking if I'd like to meet for lunch. Rather than send a lengthy text message to explain what was going on, I called.

"Hey," I said. "Sorry I missed the invite to lunch, I was with a client."

"Jasmine El-Amin?"

"Word travels fast at the crime lab. What did Charlie tell you?"

"Just that you were going to be looking for a horse that may, or may not be Jasmine's."

"He's Jasmine's," I declared. "Did Charlie also happen to tell you how uninterested Detective Boyle was in looking into it?"

"He mentioned it. Listen, there are some things I want to talk to you about the case, can we get together later?"

"Sure."

As we often seemed to do, we made plans to make plans.

After hanging up with Kai, I Googled R-n-R Stables, finding one listed, not surprisingly, near the Jacksonville Equestrian Center.

Bingo.

I plugged the address into my GPS app and it came up with a route and estimated it would take around forty minutes to get there. I used the time to scarf down my fries and Frosty and think about what I'd learned about Heart.

He was afraid of storms and had to be blindfolded to remain calm. The last bad thunderstorm had been over a week ago. Maybe I should call a couple of equine vets to ask about an injured Friesian. Jasmine was worried no one would know about Heart's fear. I was more concerned that Boyle seemed to be washing her hands of it.

What was the woman's problem?

Wes called, pulling my mind away from uncharitable thoughts about the detective. "Hey," I answered. "Good news?"

There was a pause then a buzzing hiss.

"Wes?"

"Yes. Emma will be on her way home shortly . . . What?" His voice was muted and laced with static.

"I think I'm in a dead zone," I told him.

Pause.

"Hello?"

"Okay," he said. "Just call . . . -en you're in a better—"

His words devolved into fragmented syllables and the call dropped. I checked the GPS app. It was lagging as well.

"Crap," I muttered, pulling into a gas station to check the map the old-fashioned way. After orienting myself and plotting a course, I continued on my way.

Longleaf pines towered above undergrowth so thick it formed a tangled wall of green along both sides of the road.

Rather than rely on the dot on my GPS app to indicate when I was approaching the turn leading to R-n-R, I had to drive at a snail's pace and carefully look for the road.

"Archaic," I said and chuckled.

My fellow drivers were not as amused, and a couple of cars got fed up with my crawling speed and zipped around. One car loitered behind me for so long I finally rolled down my window and waved the driver around. The car dropped back instead. I shrugged. It wasn't my fault. They could blame it on the lack of cell towers.

I finally spotted the turn and soon found myself bumping along the dirt lane that led to R-n-R Boarding Stables.

At least that's what I gathered from the double *R*s dangling from the high, metal archway over the open gate.

I slowed as I passed under the arch, to get a feel for the place.

To my left, a low-slung ranch house sat sprawled under a clump of sweet gum trees, their star-shaped leaves just beginning to change color, green giving way to ruddy purple, orange, and gold.

To the right, a barn and stables jutted out at an angle. The barn was painted a muted yet cheerful yellow. On one side a low-pitched roof, which I assumed housed the horse stalls, extended into a pasture.

There was an old, beat-up Jeep Cherokee parked past the house near the barn. I pulled up to park beside it, hopped out of Bluebell, and looked around.

The areas around the house and barn were tidy. The thick grass was deep green and, judging from the sharp, verdant scent in the air, had recently been cut. In contrast, a large field just beyond the barn looked like it could use a good mowing—the work in a place like this was never done.

Aside from a few huge pines, the pastures were flat and open. I saw two horses standing along the fence at the far end of the property. Too far away to talk to.

I decided to see if I could find a human to ask about Heart and had started toward the barn when I heard a hollow, scraping sound of metal against metal.

Turning to the sound, I followed it past a small shed and around a clump of tall, glossy-leaved camellias, already beginning to bud.

A man was scraping the last bits of manure out of an upturned wheelbarrow, transferring it to a compost pile the size of a Volkswagen Beetle.

"Hey," I said as I approached.

He looked up from his task and swiped the sleeve of his checked shirt over his face to wipe the perspiration from his eyes.

Not a man, I realized. A kid. Maybe sixteen, with the rangy build some teenage boys have that hints at the height and strength of the adult he would soon become.

"Ma'am?" He squinted against the sun and straightened toward me. A quick stab with the manure rake lodged it into the soft earth.

"I was hoping to speak to someone about a horse that may have been boarded here some time in the last couple of weeks."

"Well, Mrs. Parnell isn't here. She had to go out of town. Mr. Parnell will be around tomorrow, though."

"Maybe you can help me . . . Sorry, what's your name?"

"Hunter."

"I'm Grace. The horse would've been solid black. A Friesian," I said, opening the magazine to show him Heart's picture.

Hunter was thoughtful enough to pull off his soiled work gloves before taking the magazine.

He studied the photo for a moment then shook his head.

"Nope. I don't remember seeing any Friesians. But I'm not here every day. I tell you who is, though—Boomer. He's probably somewhere in the barn if he's still around. Usually heads out about now. He'd know better 'n me."

I took the magazine back, thanked Hunter, then hurried off to search for Boomer. A wide gate stretched across the barn's opening, barring my way. Finding the latch to one side wasn't locked, I pulled the gate open and slipped inside.

The stalls were all vacant and I assumed the occupants, like the two horses I'd seen earlier, had been turned out to pasture for the day.

I felt the presence of another animal and paused to cast out my mental net and get a bead on its location. It didn't take long to understand where and what I was sensing.

A cat. Intensely focused on stalking a mouse somewhere over my head in the rafters.

Trying to chat up a cat when it's hunting is a lesson in futility I'd learned years ago.

I left the cat to its sport and continued looking for Boomer. Within minutes, I'd located both the tack room and the feed room—both empty. Then I came to the breezeway at the other side of the barn and felt . . . something.

The animal's thoughts were caught in a single-minded loop.

Eat, eat, eat.

Ooh, different!

Eat, eat, eat.

Had to be a goat.

I canted my head in concentration.

Maybe a pig—but I was leaning toward goat.

I turned in a semicircle, trying to pinpoint the critter's location, and saw Hunter had finished his composting and was walking down the center aisle toward me.

"Y'all have goats?" I asked.

"Yep."

"Man, I'm good," I said to myself.

"Pardon?"

"Nothing." I waved off the comment.

"Came to tell you I saw Boomer headed to his truck." He motioned out the breezeway to my right, and I walked in that direction. Sure enough, as I stepped out into the bright midday sun, I caught sight of a man about thirty yards away, climbing into the cab of an old, maroon pickup truck. I also happened to notice a small brown and white goat munching on a weed several feet in front of me.

I started toward the truck.

Curious, the goat lifted its head to watch my approach.

Boomer, on the other hand, was facing away from me as he slammed the truck's door and, therefore, hadn't noticed me at all. The truck's engine rumbled to life and I started to jog forward yelling, "Hey!" and waving the magazine in the air in an attempt to get his attention.

This startled the goat, who staggered to the side, toppled over, and lay unmoving—all four legs sticking straight in the air.

"Oh my God!" I rushed forward, alarmed. I knelt by the goat, thinking I'd somehow given the poor thing a heart attack.

Oops. The goat's thoughts popped into my mind, telling me he was still very much alive.

Are you okay? I asked, placing my hand on the side of his wide belly.

Okay.

I stared at the animal in confusion. He was trying to move, but couldn't.

"Oh, don't worry about him," Hunter said, coming up behind me. "He's okay."

Okay, the goat confirmed.

"That's Cappy, he's—"

"Myotonic." The word came out on a relieved half laugh as understanding dawned. *You're a fainting goat, aren't you?* I asked.

Yep.

"I've never met a fainting goat." I knew they didn't actually faint but had a disorder that caused their muscles to stiffen when startled.

"We used to have two of 'em, but the storm last week dropped a limb on the fence. Nelly got out and we haven't been able to find her."

Nelly gone. The pang of longing that rippled from the little goat forced a deep sigh from my chest.

I'm sorry, Cappy.

Nelly . . . As he thought of her, an image of a goat entered my mind. Similar in coloring, the only visual difference between them was that Nelly had a white star on her otherwise brown face. Now that I knew what she looked like, I'd make a point to keep my eye out for Nelly while I was running around the area asking about Heart.

Cappy rolled to his feet, gave himself a good shake, and looked up at me.

Okay.

Good. I gave him a pat and glanced to where the truck had been, not surprised to find it, and Boomer, were long gone.

"Crap."

"He'll be back in the morning," Hunter said. "Always is."

I stood and glanced around, noting that the horses I'd seen earlier were still grazing at the far end of the pasture.

"Is anyone else here?"

"Not 'til tomorrow."

"Does that mean you have to bring the horses in all in by yourself?" I asked, thinking I might be able to help and talk to the horses in the process.

He chuckled. "They'll come easy enough when I shake the feed bucket."

"I bet." Darn it.

I would have asked Cappy about Heart. But the little goat

had trotted off to stretch still-stiff legs and find a new batch of something interesting to munch.

That's when I remembered the cat.

What better vantage point from which to see all the comings and goings of the stables than in the barn, perched on a beam? Who needed a fly on the wall when you had a cat on a rafter?

Now, I just had to get rid of the kid long enough to find the cat, get it to talk to me, and ask about Heart.

I must have been gazing up at the roof of the barn as I contemplated my options because Hunter asked, "What?" And squinted up at the glinting sheet metal.

"Just thinking," I said, suddenly inspired. "The architecture of this barn is beautiful. It's a classic, you know, barn shape. Mind if I take a closer look inside?"

"Uh, sure."

"Great!" At least now I had an excuse to go inside and look for the cat who was up in the rafters somewhere.

As I'd hoped, after a minute or two of watching me wander around, gazing up at the barn's cobweb-coated interior, Hunter excused himself to finish other chores.

When in doubt, be boring.

The cat had abandoned its hunt and was somewhere above the tack room, the flat roof of which looked to have been used for storage since the dawn of time. A hodgepodge of items— old dining chairs, fencing materials, buckets, and other barn-type stuff—were visible from where I stood. Well, partly visible. The rest was covered with dust and cobwebs.

Somewhere, tucked into a comfy nook, the cat was napping.

I was torn between hoping the kitty had spent a good amount of time with humans, therefore having a larger vocabulary, and hoping it preferred the company of horses, thus having a better chance of noticing any type of skullduggery that might have gone on in the barn.

Well, you know the old saying about wishing in one hand and spitting in the other . . .

It didn't matter. I was going to get what I was going to get.

"Kitty, kitty," I called softly.

Nothing.

Getting a cat to talk can be tricky—depending on the cat, its mood, and the number of distractions present. Distractions being anything more interesting than me.

"Kitty, kitty!"

Hey!

This time, I added a little cognitive charge to the word. A sort of mental exclamation point.

The cat's interest stirred, quick and focused precisely in my direction. Cats can go from snooze to centered in a millisecond. As someone who needs morning coffee to insure brain cells begin working, I can't help but be impressed.

A moment later, a cat's face emerged from the shadows.

"Hi there, gorgeous," I said with a smile.

I wasn't just playing to the infamous feline ego. The cat was beautiful.

Dark, almost symmetrical calico markings fanned out from her chin past her nose all the way to the points of her tufted ears. The deep browns, orange, and black of her face made her long white whiskers stand out as if lit from within.

I knew instantly the cat was female because as soon as we made eye contact she introduced herself.

Minerva.

I'm Grace.

Animals are usually intrigued the first time I brush brains with them. I'm not like other humans and don't try to be. Reaction to this knowledge varies from species to species and even between individuals, but one thing I can usually count on as a conversation starter is a cat's curiosity and, as it seemed in this case, the famed feline sense of pride.

Minerva regarded me expectantly and I was reminded of the T. S. Eliot poem "The Ad-Dressing of Cats." Not having a dish of cream or Strasbourg pie to offer, I decided to stick with simply inclining my head and saying, "It's a pleasure." Then, looking back up at her added, "You're quite pretty, aren't you?"

Minerva blinked at me, then glanced away, bored.

I was stating the obvious. She knew she was pretty. I'd need to move on to other things if I wanted to keep her interest.

I'm looking for someone . . .

With a combination of imagery and words, I asked if Minerva had seen Heart or at least a Friesian.

Black. She projected a very clear image to me. The point of view, not surprisingly, was from somewhere above, looking down at the hindquarters and long, flowing tail of what looked like a Friesian horse.

I wanted to ask when she'd seen him, but the concept of time does not translate well. To animals, time isn't exactly linear.

The only thing I'd found to work as a semiaccurate gauge of time was that the more clear the memory, the more recent—usually. But as far as asking for specifics? Pointless.

Instead, I requested more details about the black horse. After a pause, Minerva expounded. Using a series of images interwoven with words and more than a few sounds, the cat explained that the black horse had arrived one afternoon. She had visited the newcomer to inspect the horse's tolerance of cats and do an assessment Minerva called a "spot check," whatever that meant.

Finding Heart to be cat-friendly, she went about her day, which mostly consisted of napping. Just when I thought I'd gotten all I was going to from the cat, she told me something unexpected. After a nice nap, Minerva was awoken by voices.

Men angry. The echo of raised voices accompanied her words.

There were men arguing?

Yes. Coming to investigate, she was distracted by the sound of jingling.

Shiny bells, she told me. And I heard the jingling sound from her memory.

Someone had bells?

Shiny bells, she confirmed.

Bewildered, I pushed for more detail but the cat had said all she was going to. A tendril of cobweb had settled onto her back and she twisted around, intent on cleaning the spot.

It always helped if I could touch the animal I was talking

to, something about the physical connection intensifying the mental link.

I called up to her. "Minerva, why don't you come down and chat? I can brush that web off for you."

She ignored me.

Minerva? But it was no good. She had no more to say, at least for the time being.

Before giving up completely, I decided to look for Cappy, but both a visual and mental scan of the area in and around the barn yielded no sign of the little goat.

I headed toward Bluebell and saw Hunter standing at the fence, refilling an aluminum water trough. I walked over to ask him something that had occurred to me while I'd been looking at the stables.

He turned off the hose as I stepped up beside him.

"I was wondering how many horses y'all have."

"Two right now. Scout and Lucy."

"And they're long-term boarders?"

"Yep."

"It's just I noticed there are eight stalls."

"We get a lot of short-term boarders. People going to the equestrian center or driving up from Wellington will stop in for a few nights."

"So it's not unusual for a horse to stay for just one or two nights?"

He shook his head. "I guess you could say we're kind of like a campground. See?" He pointed to an adjacent pasture and I saw a row of square posts about thirty feet apart jutting out of the tall grass.

"Water and electricity?"

Hunter nodded. "People can park their camper-trailers and still be close to their horses."

It was a neat idea. "The horses get to stretch their legs and their owners can relax, because you deal with the logistics."

"Right."

I wondered if any campers had been staying the same time as Heart. A question that would have to wait until morning. I thanked Hunter and headed to Bluebell. As I was driving through the main gate, I noticed a section of new fencing running along the perimeter to my left. I thought of Nelly, Cappy's lost companion, and stopped to study the spot.

The area beyond the fence was densely wooded—a good place for a goat to hide or get lost. I drove on slowly, looking for any sign of Nelly. When a dirt road veered off into the woods in the general direction of the repaired fence, I turned. Bumping along steadily, Bluebell's struts squeaked and bounced as we went.

I squinted into the woods and muttered, "Where are you, Nelly?"

The underbrush along the road was too thick to see much. Often, a burst of goldenrod exploded from the ditch, its bright yellow flower plumes blocking the view completely. The little goat could have been five feet into the woods on either side and I would never see her.

At least she'd have plenty to eat.

Unlike horses and cows who are grazers, goats are more closely related to deer and, therefore, browse for their food. Stripping tender foliage and shoots from shrubs and trees was their specialty.

They did, however, tend to be sensitive when it came to their water supply. I hoped Nelly wasn't drinking out of the murky ditch; she might end up being a very sick goat.

After a few minutes I came to a bigger, paved road and turned onto it. Within twenty minutes, I was as lost as Nelly.

Crap.

I tried my GPS app but had no signal.

Double crap.

Grousing, I continued along, finally coming to a dead end at a trailhead leading into Jennings State Forest. The dirt road itself was closed to motor vehicles—or so claimed the sign dangling from a chain stretched between two sturdy-looking posts.

Having never visited Jennings, I was not familiar with the area. But, as I backed up and started a three-point turn, I noticed two people who probably were.

About thirty feet back and off to one side of the trail was

a small, dusty turnaround. A couple had pulled into it, parked, and were hauling backpacks from the trunk of their car.

They were nice enough to give me a very simple map of the park along with directions to the closest main road. Somehow, I had made it to the other side of Jennings and was facing the wrong way.

When I mentioned my lack of cell reception, the man informed me that one of the cell towers in the park was being used as a nesting site by a pair of bald eagles. A recent storm had damaged the tower, but because of the nest, no repairs could be done.

I thanked them and made a mental note to nix the bad attitude about lack of cell service.

Bald eagle babies trumped modern conveniences any day.

I was surprised to discover the trail was actually very close to a residential neighborhood. It seemed strange, but I supposed state parks acquired land after homes were built, which meant little pockets of suburbia would appear in the middle of parkland.

In fact, I thought, as I slowed at a corner and scanned the area, you'd never know by looking at the houses how close Jennings was. One house in particular stood out, with its trimmed lawn and cheerful little faux wishing well overflowing with flowers.

I wondered if the folks who lived in this area were in tune with nature or at odds with it.

Once I got my bearings, I headed for the interstate. By the time I made it past the 295 exit on I-10, the setting sun was a giant orange ball in my rearview mirror.

It glinted off the windows of the buildings of downtown, heralding the end of a cloudless day.

I thought about Heart, his fear of storms, and hoped the clear weather would hold.

• • •

"Em?" I called out for my sister as I opened the door to the condo but got no response. Tossing my keys and purse on the foyer table as I passed, I did a mental scan for Moss and

Voodoo. They were both content and napping in my bedroom. I paused at the kitchen when I saw a bottle of wine sitting open on the counter.

Walking over to it, I lifted the bottle to read the label. A pinot noir from a vineyard in France I could not begin to pronounce. One of Emma's special-occasion wines. I recognized it only because when I'd first moved in she had pointed out the bottles that shouldn't be opened without good cause.

"I think this qualifies," I said and poured myself a glass.

Armed with my celebratory libation and anxious to tell Emma what I'd learned and get her thoughts on all that had happened, I made my way toward her room, where I could hear a blow-dryer blasting.

I found my sister in her bathroom with her head flipped over and the dryer aimed at her dark hair. She'd obviously showered and was now sporting black, lacy underwear.

"Hey!" I said over the noise.

My sister straightened. "Hey, back!" Grinning, she turned off the dryer and pulled me into a quick hug.

"A toast to freedom?" I asked, raising my glass.

She plucked hers off the bathroom counter and clinked it against mine.

"I'll drink to that," she said and tipped back the wine.

"So," I started, then paused, not sure where to begin. I wanted to tell her I'd met Jasmine and about everything I'd learned at R-n-R stables, but I also wanted to hear the full story on what happened at Ortega's house. Then there was the lovely Detective Boyle, about whom Emma was sure to have an opinion.

I decided to start there, but my sister spoke before I could utter another word.

"Do me a favor, Gracie," she said, turning to the mirror to run her fingers through her hair. "In the laundry room, there's a black dress hanging in the steamer. Can you grab it?"

"You're going out?"

"I have a date with Hugh." She met my eyes in the reflection and did a wicked, one-brow arch à la Vivien Leigh.

That explained the lacy underwear.

It was understandable. My friend Dr. Hugh Murray was melt-your-milk-shake hot. An exotic-animal veterinarian with the zoo, he was the type of man women fawned over.

Most women, anyway. Emma being Emma, I was pretty sure Hugh would be the one doing most of the fawning.

"He's going to be here any second." She flipped her head again, turned the dryer back on, and continued working on her hair.

I retrieved the dress, returning to find she'd finished blow-drying and had moved into her closet to peruse the dozens of pairs of shoes lining one wall.

"It's too bad you murdered my Louboutins." She shot me a weighty glance as she pulled a pair of deep burgundy boots out of a box.

"Um . . ."

It had been an accident. Fancy footwear and I do not mix.

The doorbell rang, Moss let out a deep, bark-howl-bark, heralding the arrival of an unescorted visitor and warning said visitor that the area was under his protection.

It's okay. It's Hugh!

Moss didn't care.

Having met Hugh, and knowing he was my friend, didn't stop my dog from maintaining the Prime Directive. Which was, basically, to jealously guard whatever he believed was his.

Males and their territory—what can I say?

"Tell him I'll be two minutes," Emma said.

I glanced in at Moss and Voodoo as I passed my room.

Be nice, I ordered and continued to the front door.

I pulled open the door and gaped at the man before me.

He wore a deep olive button-down dress shirt tucked into a nicely tailored pair of black slacks. I felt my eyebrows shoot to my hairline when I saw the loafers.

"Clean up good, don't I?" Hugh asked.

"I never would've guessed," I said, opening the door and ushering him in.

"And just think, all of this could have been yours."

He was teasing, of course, so I ignored the comment. It

had taken me a while to get my head around the idea that Hugh's flirtations were his way of showing he cared. I wouldn't call the way he acted harmless, but he wasn't the lecherous jerk I'd once believed him to be.

Moss trotted out of the hall, slowed as he angled toward the entry, then stopped a few feet from us. He stood stock-still—fierce wolf-eyes locked on Hugh.

Hugh, being a man with a good deal of experience with large predators, froze.

Moss let out a low growl.

"Stop it, Moss."

Guard. He insisted.

Guard who? From what?

The answer came a moment later when a blur of black fur the size of a large grapefruit came tumbling into view.

Voodoo slid over the tile, scrambled to gain purchase, then scampered to Moss. The kitten leapt onto my dog's hind leg and began to climb him like a lemur scaling a baobab tree.

Moss's kitty, he declared.

Oh, good grief. No one wants to take your kitty.

"Hey!" Emma emerged from the hallway with a smile bright enough to light the Gator Bowl. It hardly flickered when she noticed Moss, who was stubbornly playing sentinel.

"Move, you beast," she said, and nudged his flank with her thigh. With a low grumble, he allowed her to push past.

"Brave," Hugh said, with open admiration. For all the times he'd made suggestive comments or given me a roguish smile, I'd never seen him look at anyone the way he looked at Emma.

"He can't hurt me," my sister said, brushing white fur off the skirt of her dress. "Grace wouldn't let him."

I made a rude noise, but neither Emma nor Hugh seemed to notice. They were both too involved in checking each other out.

I couldn't blame them. They made a cosmically good-looking couple.

"You got with Kendall, right?" my sister asked as she lifted her purse from its spot next to mine on the entry table.

"Yep."

"See? I knew you could do it." Emma gave me a hug and

murmured against my ear, "Don't wait up." She pulled back with a wink, looped her arm through Hugh's, and sauntered out the door. It closed quietly in my face.

"No, I didn't have anything I wanted to tell you," I said to the closed door, suddenly a little disappointed.

Moss came to stand at my side and nudged my hand with his muzzle.

Okay?

"Yeah, I'm fine. Just kind of wanted to—"

Before I could finish my thought, he caught the scent of lingering barn odors wafting in the air around me and became fixated on sniffing.

"I guess that means I need to shower," I said.

It was probably too late to call Kai and ask him over for dinner. What would I make, anyway?

"Maybe I could order pizza," I said to Moss.

Pizza. He swished his tail in agreement. Moss always appreciated pizza.

If I timed it right, I could call for a pizza, text an invite to Kai, and be in and out of the shower before either arrived. Thanks to the new waterproof supercase Emma had gotten me, I could even text Kai while I was in the shower.

Grabbing my phone from my purse, I ordered a large half veggie and cheese, half supreme. Refilling my wineglass, and ignoring my dog's continued sniffing, I was just turning down the hall when there was a knock at the door.

Moss let out a distracted half bark and zeroed in on something on the toe of my shoe.

As I often did, I paused to consider answering the door. It couldn't be the pizza already and Emma had a key. I shrugged. Whoever it was could come back.

In my room, I took off my shoes and socks, kicking them into the corner to encourage Moss to sniff them somewhere out of the way. I had dropped my T-shirt on the floor when I heard the knock again. Then the doorbell rang. Growling, I snatched the shirt off the floor, yanked it back on, and stomped through the condo to the front door to pull it open with a scowl.

It was Kai.

"Oh—I, um . . ."

"Sorry to just drop by," he said.

"It's okay. I was getting in the shower. But I was going to text you."

"You were going to text me while you were in the shower?"

"Well, yeah. I smell like farm animals and I ordered pizza, so . . . That came out wrong. Come in."

"You sure?" he asked as he stepped into the foyer. "You seem a little annoyed."

"I am. But not with you," I added hastily. "My sister went on a date with Hugh."

"And that bothers you?"

"I wanted to talk to her about some stuff and she goes out to have fun." I stopped. Frowned. "Wow, that sounded really bratty, didn't it?"

"A little," he said with a teasing smile.

I led him into the kitchen and held up the bottle of wine. "Deblubles?" I massacred the name.

"Can't. I'm on call. I'll take a Coke if you've got one."

"Sure." As I was poking my head in the fridge to grab the soda, I noticed my shirt was inside out.

And backward.

"Um . . . here." I handed him the can of Coke and walked out of the kitchen. "I'll be right back."

Zipping back into my room, I yanked off the shirt, turned it right-side out with a snap, and tugged it back on.

I was glad Kai had decided he wanted to date me before he'd realized what a bobblehead I could be.

Spotting my glass of wine where I'd left it on the dresser, I snatched it up and took a deep swig. With a forced sigh, I squared my shoulders and walked back to the kitchen.

Moss had decided to harass Kai and was standing in the entrance to the kitchen, glaring at him.

Cut it out, Moss.

I nudged him on the rump and moved past.

"Why does he do that?" Kai asked. "Does he want something?"

"Yes. To prove he's manlier than you."

"No contest—I've seen his teeth."

"Just ignore him and he'll stop."

"What if I give him a treat or something?"

Treat? Treat!

Moss sidled up to nudge under my hand.

"Because," I said to Kai, "giving positive reinforcement for negative behavior is a no-no." I said the last part looking pointedly at my dog.

Please, treat?

When I ignored his request, he tacked on an image of Kai giving him the treat. *Friends.*

"You are so full of it," I told him.

"What?" Kai asked, looking from me to my dog.

Before I could answer, Moss stepped up to Kai, tail swishing gently, sat at perfect attention, and cocked his head.

Brows arched, Kai looked down at Moss then up at me. A slow grin pulled one corner of his mouth into a lopsided smile.

I shook my head.

Just to drive it home, Moss placed one giant wolf-paw on Kai's knee and made what I like to call the Hopeful, Hero-Worship Face.

"Am I supposed to resist this?" Kai asked, gesturing with his can of Coke.

"No, you're not." I let out a belly breath and leaned against the counter.

Treat! Moss repositioned his paw, gently tapping Kai's leg twice before letting it drop to the ground. He cocked his head to the other side and let out a pitiful whine.

"Come on, Grace."

"Oh, good grief," I said, giving in. "Top shelf of the pantry."

Kai found the treats, opened the box, and handed one to Moss, who took it gently and trotted into the living room to enjoy his victory.

Voodoo, who'd been crouched near the base of the cabinets, leapt out at Moss as he passed.

Ha! Mine! The kitten clasped her claws in the fur of Moss's tail and hung on for the ride.

"I was being manipulated, wasn't I?" Kai asked when I turned back to him.

"Don't feel bad," I told him. "Happens to me all the time."

I took another sip of wine, nearly polishing off the glass. Kai noticed, picked up the bottle, and gave me a refill .

"So," he said. "You were saying something about farm animals."

"To be clear, I tried to ask the humans about Heart—that's Jasmine's horse—first. But the kid I talked to didn't know anything and when I tried to ask another guy, Cappy fainted, which distracted me."

"Who fainted?"

"Sorry, Cappy's a myotonic goat."

"A what?"

"A goat. They're called fainting goats or stiff-leg goats. They don't really faint though, it's a type of muscle malfunction. Their muscles are hyperexcitable. You know how if you're startled, your muscles will tense up right before you react?"

He nodded.

"Well, these guys tense up but they can't relax."

"And they fall over?"

"Sometimes. Depends on the goat." I shrugged. "This one did. I thought I'd given him a heart attack before I realized what was going on. By that time, the other guy who might've had information on Jasmine's horse was gone. But I did have a chance to talk to Minerva, and she told me she definitely remembered a solid black horse being in the stables recently."

"Minerva would be?"

"A calico. She also said some other weird things. I'm not sure what they mean, if anything. But I'm definitely on the right track." I raised my wineglass in a self-salute. "I'm going to prove Heart is in the country and I can't wait to see the look on Detective Boyle's face when I do."

"Actually, that's why I came by," Kai said.

I waited.

"I need to explain a few things about Detective Boyle. She and I have been friends for a long time."

"Friends? She wasn't being very friendly with you yesterday."

"Yeah, well, Tammy's sort of pissed at me right now."

"Tammy? Really? She seems—I don't know—more like a Maleficent or a Bellatrix."

"She's really not like that."

"Like what?" I asked, my temper stirring. "Like a woman who bullies and lies to people? Because in my experience, that's exactly what she's like."

"Okay." He held his hands up in surrender. "Just listen for a minute."

I raised my brows and waited.

"Have you ever heard of Occam's razor?"

"Ocular what?"

"Occam's razor. It's the theory that the simplest solution to a problem is usually the correct one."

"Oh, right." I hadn't been aware it had a name.

"Detective Boyle is a fan."

"You're not?"

"When it comes to certain scientific theories, no. But in regards to investigations and police work, I'd say the rule often applies."

"So because Emma was at the crime scene and because she's Ortega's ex-wife, Boyle is willing to believe she killed him, without looking at anyone else? That's not just simple it's *lazy*."

"Tammy's not lazy. She's a good cop."

The fact that he was defending her rankled.

A little voice in my head reminded me that Kai hadn't been at Ortega's house and hadn't witnessed Boyle's callous and dismissive actions.

He heaved out a sigh.

"I'm not explaining this very well."

I had to agree with him there.

"Occam's razor is just part of it. She's also tends to be a little hyperfocused and suspicious.

"Four years ago when Charles Sartori was put away for

fraud, it came out that he had some connections in the sheriff's office."

"Not surprising."

"Well, Tammy and her partner were both under investigation."

"Like you were?" I asked, feeling a little spear of guilt poke my gut at the thought. Kai had gotten involved with the mob boss because I had asked for help.

He nodded. "When it turned out her partner was in Sartori's pocket, they really put the screws to her."

"Guilt by association."

"Right. The heat on me is nothing like what she went through."

I took a moment to think about his words. "I thought you were done with all that."

He blinked at me, brows drawing together.

"You said, 'is' not 'was,' implying there's still something going on," I explained.

He shrugged off my concern. "It's not," he said. "But Tammy thinks . . ."

"What?" I asked when he didn't continue. "Not that you're involved with Sartori?"

He shook his head slowly. The wine must have been making me slow, because it took me a while to get what he was implying.

"She thinks *I'm* involved with Sartori," I said, slowly. "Doesn't she know I helped catch the bad guys?"

"Not all of them."

"You're talking about Logan." I didn't phrase it as a question because I knew the answer. "Really? A guy nicknamed *the Ghost* eludes capture and she thinks that's somehow my fault?"

"She also knows Logan contacted you after he got away."

I wanted to defend myself. Point out that Logan, AKA the Ghost, was tying up loose ends under Sartori's orders, which involved me only situationally. But something else popped into my head.

"Let me get this straight. Boyle, a woman who was judged harshly because of her *association* with her guilty partner, is ready to vilify me because of my. . . *association*, however remote, with Logan? Am I the only one who gets the irony here?"

"I hear you," Kai said, and I realized my voice had been rising steadily. I forced a slow breath and reminded myself not to kill the messenger.

I frowned at my wineglass and set it on the counter.

"The thing is," Kai said, "Tammy stuck by her partner until the end. She was a hundred percent convinced he couldn't possibly be involved."

"And she thinks you're blinded by my charm?" I'd meant it sarcastically. Just about everyone who meets me finds me lacking in the charm department.

But Kai's gaze held enough heat to burn the house down around us as it locked on to mine. "Something like that."

I cleared my throat. "What about Jake?"

"Jake is playing it close to the vest."

"Meaning?"

"Meaning even though he expressed his belief that you're not the Mafia type, he wasn't as"—Kai paused, giving me a wry half smile—"vehement as I was."

"I get where she's coming from, Kai. But I'm still going to look for Heart."

"I'm not saying you should back off. In fact, I think you should look for him. The truth is, Jake and Tammy are going to be focused on solving Ortega's murder. A missing horse is going to be put on the back burner."

Though I appreciated his honesty, it didn't make me feel much better.

"The owner of R-n-R wasn't around today but I'm going to head back tomorrow and talk to him and see what I can find out from the horses."

His phone buzzed in his pocket. He checked the screen and said, "I've got to go. Let me know what happens after you talk to Mister Ed."

"Their names are Scout and Lucy," I told him as I walked him out.

"Of course they are," he said, turning as we reached the

front door. He leaned down to brush a kiss first on my cheek then on my jawline. He stopped and pulled in a deep breath. The sensation sent a shiver of electricity down my side. "Just so we're clear—I like the way you smell."

And he was gone.

I don't know how long I stood there, weak-kneed and flushed, but a knock at the door had me snatching it open. I half expected to see Kai, but that was just wine and desire fogging my brain. I must have looked a little crazed because the pizza delivery guy took a step back when he saw me.

The pizza smelled good, not that I was terribly hungry, having filled up a little too much on wine and not enough Kai.

I shared a slice with Moss anyway and tried to process what Kai had told me.

Not that he liked the way I smelled, though I replayed his words over and over with a goofy smile on my face as I headed to the bathroom to finally take my shower.

I understood Boyle's suspicions, but still didn't think it gave her the right to dismiss the fact that Heart was missing.

Suddenly, I remembered I hadn't listened to the last message Ortega had left me, the one from the day before—the morning he was killed.

I stared at his number on my voice mail for a few moments, then tapped the screen to play the message.

Ortega's voice filled the room, echoing off the marble and glass.

"Grace, I know what you must think of me, and I deserve it. But, please, call me as soon as you can. This isn't just about me, it's about Emma."

CHAPTER 7

It was a stunning, mild, November morning. Waves glittered as they swept over the beach. The rising sun turned the wet sand along the water's edge into a wide ribbon of glowing, orange light.

I should have taken more than a millisecond to admire the sight, but my head ached from too much wine and my shoes seemed to be lined with lead.

The beautiful weather was not lost on the rest of the population, however, and there was a plethora of people and dogs out and about. I looped Moss's leash around my wrist and gripped it tightly. Distracted or not, today was not the day to have him running loose.

Usually, my sister was up and annoying me as early as possible. But Emma had still been asleep when Moss and I had left for our run. Her delayed start to the day meant two things: no pre-run coffee for me—I couldn't convince Moss to wait while I got a pot going—and I still hadn't had a chance to discuss Ortega's message.

It nagged at me like a sore hangnail.

What could he have meant? He and Emma were no longer

connected—Wes had seen to that. The divorce had severed every tie. They didn't co-own property or a business. How could anything Ortega was involved in pertain to Emma?

I'd wanted to call as soon as I'd heard the message but rather than interrupt her date with Hugh, I'd decided to leave her a note in the kitchen.

E—Need to talk re: Ortega!!!

Adding plenty of exclamation points and underlines for emphasis.

I also needed to talk to her about a dozen other things, not the least of which was what happened at Ortega's murder scene.

Looking forward to coffee, ibuprofen, and an overdue conversation with my sister, I turned Moss toward home.

The pit bull came out of nowhere.

A blur of muscle and smooth, fawn-colored fur, he hit Moss square in the side. The blow caught us both off guard. Moss stumbled but recovered quickly. He spun with a growl.

Reflexively, I opened my mind completely and hurled it into the fray. Stupid.

A wave of pure joy hit me. Energetic enough to make me stagger sideways, the emotion inspired a fit of near-psychotic-sounding giggles to erupt from my throat.

"Zeke!" A young teenager sprinted over the dunes toward us. "He won't hurt—" He stopped, eyes widening.

I wasn't sure whether it was the sight of a wolf tackling his dog or the sound of my deranged laughter, but the kid looked like he was about to faint.

"It's fine," I said with effort, still winded from the run and buzzed from the joy-zap. "Just playing."

And play they did. Though in a limited way, because I, unlike the kid, still held Moss's leash.

"Okay, enough," I told the dogs, feeling like Officer Unfriendly of the Fun Police. They stopped with reluctance. I bent, picked up Zeke's sand-coated leash, and held it out to the kid.

I could hardly give him much grief, having just been given the slip by my own dog the day before. Still . . .

"You need to be careful," I warned the kid.

"Yes, ma'am."

"There are people who would panic if a pit bull tackled their dog, even if Zeke just wants to play. Panicked people can be dangerous."

As soon as the words were out of my mouth, I realized what bothered me most about the message I'd gotten from Ortega: He hadn't just sounded upset, he'd sounded desperate.

What would make a guy like Ortega, who lived to control everything and everyone around him, lose his cool?

Could it have something to do with his murder?

The buzz I'd gotten from the pit bull had worn off by the time I climbed the steps to the condo. I stepped through the front door and stopped to pull in a deep breath.

Coffee.

Emma was up and had put a pot on for me.

"Is she a great sister or what?"

I freed Moss from his leash and followed him into the kitchen. He stood, loudly lapping up water as I poured a cup of coffee.

As I raised the mug to savor the first, rejuvenating sip, I saw the note I'd left for my sister on the counter. Below my writing, she'd drawn a smiley face followed by the words *Sorry, had to run. Talk later—E.*

"Really, Em?" I asked aloud.

Had she not read my note?

Aggravated at my sister's sparse reply, I tried calling her, but got her voice mail. I decided not to leave a message. I was going to have to head to my first appointment soon and wouldn't have much time to discuss the Ortega situation in detail. I pushed the issue to the back of my mind and headed to take a shower.

After our walk, I'd needed a caffeine boost to remain ambulatory, Moss, in contrast, seemed indefatigable. I was still toweling off when he started dancing around me asking to go for a ride.

Once upon a time, Moss had often joined me on errands and appointments with clients. He loved to ride in Bluebell and acted not only as a deterrent to theft but as backup on the rare occasions I'd ventured into areas where it was needed.

Things changed the night Emma had brought the kitten home. Voodoo had been worn-out, malnourished, and frightened. Moss had taken one sniff of the kitten and morphed into a helicopter parent. He'd been hovering less and less, as Voodoo had gained strength and it was obvious my dog wanted to get out of the house for a bit. Today, he was revving to go.

"Need a break, huh, big guy?"

Go. Ride!

I was hesitant to leave Voodoo alone for very long. Her claws were small but could shred a roll of toilet paper with no problem. I hated to imagine the damage she could do to the couch if deprived of her playmate for an extended period.

I decided to let Moss ride along to my first appointment, which happened to be with a woman and her cat who lived in Marsh Landing, which wasn't far.

Moss would get his ride and a break from kitty-sitting duty and I could swing back by the condo to drop him off and check on the kitten before I headed to R-n-R to talk to Boomer.

I grabbed Moss's leash and we headed out the door.

Marsh Landing is a luxe country club neighborhood which, like most, had a guard posted at the gate. In order to gain entrance, you had to be on the list and know where you were going. The homes were expensive. Many of them, especially those along the water, were mini-mansions. Mrs. Hurwitz's place was no exception.

Leaving the windows partway down to catch the cool marsh breezes, I left Moss in Bluebell with some water and a kiss on the head. My client opened the door and ushered me into the living room.

"The vet said he was fine, but I can tell. Something just isn't right with him."

I nodded and studied the "him" in question.

Her cat, Sir Thomas T. Lipton III, or just Thomas for short, was a handsome orange tabby with bright, golden eyes and a long, triangular face. He gave me a cursory glance then closed his eyes to nap. When she'd made her appointment, Mrs. Hurwitz had explained that Thomas had started "acting crazy" a few weeks before. He'd destroyed a set of curtains and was meowing to be let outside—something he had never been allowed to do.

"You said he's always been an inside cat. Has he escaped lately?" Sometimes a taste of the outside world inspired a rebellious streak.

"No. He hasn't gotten out in years."

"Can we bring him to the window where he damaged the curtains? I'd like to observe his behavior." And ask him what the problem was.

Luckily, I could say things like "observe" and "watch for his reaction" to cover the fact that I was having a mental conversation with an animal.

As soon as we made it to the window, Thomas became fixated on the thick, wooden plantation blinds, leaping up to claw at them with an obsessive intensity.

"See? He's gone crazy," Mrs. Hurwitz said.

I opened the blinds and peeked outside. A squirrel chided me from a tree less than ten feet away, its tail waving as it called out a warning to its kits.

Bingo.

I glanced down at Thomas.

Squirrel!

I had to grin. Squirrel, indeed. A whole family of them.

Hearing the chattering of the young squirrels as they raced around the tree had flipped the hunting switch in the typically lazy house cat. Interestingly enough, after speaking with him for a few minutes, he revealed what he really wanted was a way to watch the squirrels.

I explained my "theory" to Mrs. Hurwitz and suggested Thomas's cat tree be moved to the window and for the blinds in the upstairs bedroom to be kept open. I also invited her to call in a couple of days if he hadn't calmed down.

All in all, the session had taken only about thirty minutes, putting Moss and me back home in less than an hour.

With slight trepidation, I scanned the condo for Voodoo, searching for any sign of destruction as I headed to where she slept in my bedroom.

Apparently, the kitten hadn't moved.

She blinked squinty, sleepy eyes at me when I turned on the lights, spread her tiny mouth into a tiny yawn, and went back to sleep.

Emma arrived just as I was pouring coffee into a to-go mug.

"Where have you been?" I asked, snapping the lid onto the cup.

"Running a few errands. Why, what's wrong?"

"I have three hundred things I need to talk to you about."

"Really? Three hundred?"

"Okay, more like five, but that's not the point."

"Sorry," she said with good-natured sarcasm. "I had to pick up a new iPad to use while the cops have my stuff." She held up the slim, white box.

"You could've just used my laptop."

"Windows?" She made a face. "No, this Mac girl will stick with what she knows."

She opened the box, lifted the new tablet out, and plugged it in to charge.

"Listen, Tony left me a message. He said it was about you." I fished my phone out of my purse and played it for her.

"Well?" I asked when she didn't offer a comment.

"Well, what?"

"What the hell is he talking about, Em?"

"I have no idea. If I had to guess, I'd say he didn't like that you hadn't returned his calls." She lifted a shoulder. "He knew you'd respond if he mentioned me."

"Don't you think he sounded a little desperate?"

"Tony was good at manipulating people."

True enough. "What about the time stamp? He called me the morning he died. And the last thing on his computer was a newspaper article about me."

"How do you know that?"

I explained Jasmine's phone call and subsequent request for my help finding Heart. I went over everything that happened at Ortega's house, including my run-in with Boyle. I also told her Kai's story about Boyle's suspicions of my involvement with Sartori.

"Well," Emma mused, "you can't blame Boyle for drawing a connection between you and Sartori. She's right."

"Come on, Em. I've only met the guy once."

"After you saved his daughter. Even if you forget about Logan and his weird gift—or whatever you want to call it—look at it from her perspective. A month ago, Sartori's daughter, Brooke, runs away. You inexplicably decide the girl's in danger and start looking for her."

"But—"

"I know." Emma held up a defensive hand. "You had intel from a tiger who knew Brooke had been kidnapped. But I'm going to go out on a limb and guess you haven't told Boyle about your ability."

I made a face.

"Right. Bottom line here is this—you risked your own neck to find Brooke and, ultimately, saved her life."

"Yeah, well, I had help," I said, giving her a pointed glance.

Emma waved away the comment along with her involvement in the girl's rescue.

"I'm trying to point out that in Boyle's mind, what you did makes you and Sartori allies."

I wanted to scoff, but it actually made sense. Especially considering Boyle's history with Sartori and her partner's betrayal.

"And," I said, hesitating before jumping in with what I wanted to ask, "there was something about the way Kai defended her. He called her Tammy."

Emma turned to walk out of the kitchen, motioning for me to follow. "I need to dig out an old briefcase to use. Keep talking, I'm listening."

"What do you think?" I asked my sister, stopping at the door to her closet.

"About what?" She pulled a slim, nylon briefcase off one of the upper shelves.

"About Kai and Boyle. You're better at this stuff than me. Do you think they could, you know . . ." A quiver of anxiety did some interesting things in my stomach, but I took a sip of my coffee and pushed on. "Have a thing?"

My sister eyed the bag critically and said, "I'm going to assume by 'this stuff' you mean interacting with *Homo sapiens*, in which case—" Emma stopped when she lifted her gaze to me.

Whatever expression my face wore made her sigh and set the briefcase aside to focus on me. "If Kai has a *thing*— it's for you."

I made a face. "Doesn't mean he can't have a thing for someone else."

"True, but I don't think so."

I wasn't convinced, and my sister knew it.

"Does this sudden suspicion have anything to do with Dane Harrington?"

I started to reject the idea but thought better of it.

"I don't know, Em. Maybe it does, maybe it doesn't." I slumped against the door frame to mull it over.

Until recently, I would have denied a breakup from so long ago would still be affecting me. But I'd learned just how difficult the past could be to ignore.

"It's so stupid," I told her, studying the lid of the travel mug.

"No, it isn't. You were young. The blush of new love is a powerful thing, kiddo."

"We spent every day together for over six months. I thought I knew him." I looked at Emma, willing her to understand even as I struggled to do the same.

My sister's face had hardened like it always did when I talked about Dane. I hadn't told her about my relationship with Dane Harrington—yes, *those* Harringtons—until recently. Emma was still recovering from finding out I'd not only dated a member of one of the most wealthy, influential families in the Southeast, but that he'd dumped me when I told him about my ability.

"Come on," she said, taking my arm, "I need a cookie if we're going to talk about that jack-hole."

We headed back into the kitchen. My sister opened the freezer and took out the box of Thin Mints.

"Is that the last box?" I asked when she opened it and I saw it contained only one sleeve of cookies.

"We'll have to ration." She handed me a cookie and I bit into the crisp, cold, mint-chocolatey goodness.

Moss heard the crackle of the bag and came trotting in to beg for his share.

"You are sooo out of luck," I told him.

Treat?

I took a dog treat out of the pantry and gave it to him. Moss dropped it on the floor and looked at my Thin Mint with unsuppressed longing.

"Never going to happen," I said.

With an affected snort, he picked up his treat and moped off into the living room.

"I didn't think dogs liked chocolate."

"Oh, they like it. But it's toxic."

"Speaking of toxic, let's get back to Dane."

I finished off my cookie. "He didn't just break up with me, Em, he never talked to me again. One day we're making plans to meet his parents and possibly build a life together, and the next day—poof!"

Dane had left me with a "Dear Jane" letter during the middle of our romantic vacation—*in the Bahamas.*

"And really, so what?" I said, growing angry with myself. "So a guy dumped me, big deal. The man you married, who vowed to protect and honor and love you—he almost killed you. What right do I have to be all wounded?"

"It's not about rights. He hurt you. If you stubbed your toe, would it hurt any less just because someone else you knew broke their foot? You can think, 'Wow, I'm lucky I just stubbed my toe.' And it's good to put things into perspective but it's still going to hurt."

"How do you do it? Move past everything. Forget."

"I don't forget. I think about it every day. I've learned to channel my emotions into something productive." She wrapped up the Thin Mints and placed them back in the freezer. "As far as the Kai-Boyle thing goes, it seems to me Kai is just trying to be up-front. By telling you about Boyle's issues with Sartori, and, by extension, you." She held up her hand to ward off any protest. "Warranted or not, he's looking out for you. That's what you do for people you care about."

"Yeah, I know. I wish he wouldn't call her Tammy, though."

My sister rolled her eyes. "Oh! I almost forgot, you know how I tried to get someone from the news to come cover the auction at Happy Asses?"

I nodded. "They couldn't spare anyone that night for some reason."

"Right. Well, the reporter I talked to, Anita Margulies, has offered to come do a profile piece on Wednesday."

It was great news. "Did you tell Ozeal?"

Ozeal Mallory, owner of Happy Asses Donkey and Big Cat Rescue, lived in a humble, one-bedroom apartment above the facility's commissary and worked tirelessly to keep it operating.

"I let Hugh tell her. Ozeal has him to thank. Anita, the reporter, took one look at him, found out he volunteered at a rescue facility, and was hooked."

"Hugh has that effect on people."

"Not everyone," she said, giving me a pointed look. "Anyway, I was hoping you could come for the interview."

"Um . . ."

She must have heard the panic in my voice because she amended, "Don't worry, Anita doesn't want to talk to you. She wants to pet the pretty animals. And to answer your question, I'm including Hugh in that statement."

"And you want me to referee? Come on, Em."

"Why not?"

"Haven't you seen *When Animals Attack*?"

"Why do you think I want you to come? Hugh told Anita all about Boris and how they want to build a new enclosure for him. We have to get some shots with the tiger."

I shook my head. In truth, I didn't think Boris, the Siberian tiger to whom she was referring, would repeat his stress-induced paroxysm of rage, but it bugged me when my sister thought I could snap my fingers and make magic happen. I appreciated her confidence in my ability, but I wasn't all-powerful.

"Come on," she insisted. "Can't you just Zen-mojo him like you used to do with Coco?"

See what I mean?

"Zen-mojo?"

"You know what I'm saying."

"First of all, Coco was a poodle. There's a slight difference."

"There you go—they're practically the same."

I waited several seconds before responding, then said, "Weird."

"What?" Emma asked.

"Nothing. I thought you really liked Hugh. But I guess you'd be okay watching him lose a limb."

"Come on, Grace. It's not for me, it's for Ozeal."

Ozeal dedicated her life to the well-being of the animals in her care—many who'd been abandoned, abused, or neglected. I couldn't say no, and my sister knew it.

"Fine. When?"

Emma beamed. "Three. She says it shouldn't take more than an hour or so to get everything they need."

"Works for me."

"Great. Listen, I'm playing catch-up with clients most of today but Wes and I are going to grab a late lunch around one if you can join us."

I promised to try but know the chances I'd make it were slim. If Boomer had a lead on Heart, I'd have to follow it, if not, I'd need to find another lead. Either way, it was turning out to be a busy day.

I drove through the gates of R-n-R at a little past ten. The Jeep Cherokee was parked in the same place it had been the day before. Boomer's truck was parked next to the Jeep. At least I assumed the pickup belonged to Boomer, as it looked identical to the one I'd seen him driving away the day before.

Are my detective skills good or what?

Standing next to the truck's bed, digging through the open aluminum toolbox, was Hunter. He glanced up as I pulled in next to him and parked.

I hopped out of Bluebell and walked around the tail of the truck toward him.

"Morning," I said.

He looked up at me and nodded a greeting. "Mr. Parnell isn't back yet, but Boomer's here." Hunter motioned absently toward the adjacent field, where a tractor was parked at an oblique angle. The crunch of tires on the gravel-and-shell drive made Hunter glance over my shoulder and frown.

I turned to see what had inspired the reaction. A big camper-trailer was slowly trundling down the drive.

It looked a lot like my parents' Winnebago, except for the horses clearly visible through the last few side windows.

"Whoa," I said, impressed with the size of the vehicle.

Hunter muttered something under his breath, then said to me, "Can you do me a favor and take these to Boomer?" He handed me a heavy-duty plastic box which, judging from the label, was a set of socket wrenches.

"And tell him the new boarders are here early. I've gotta let these people know where to go."

The kid didn't sound happy about it.

I wasn't sure if it was because he didn't like his boss or just didn't like to be stuck dealing with people. I could sympathize, either way.

Leaving Hunter to his task, I headed toward the tractor but, as I approached, saw no sign of Boomer.

I walked around to the front and discovered a pair of jean-clad legs sticking out from under the front at an angle.

Hearing my footsteps over the tall grass, he said, "Boy, you are slower than molasses in January. We got to get this field mowed or the boss will have both our asses. Here."

His hand appeared suddenly, palm up, expectant. His fingers were thick and gnarled in the way that men who spent their lives using them tended to be.

I squatted down, handed him the tools, and was about to introduce myself when Boomer let out a deep sigh.

"Well, these would work if I was fixing a Kubota, which I'm not. Don't you know the difference between metric and standard? Damnation and hellfire—" He angled his head toward me and stopped, obviously expecting to see Hunter.

"Hi," I said.

"Pardon me, ma'am. I didn't mean to cuss in front of a lady." He touched the brim of his ball cap in a rueful, if somewhat awkward, recumbent salute.

"Hunter asked me to give you those and tell you the boarders are early."

"Shit."

I arched a brow as he wriggled out from under the tractor and sat up.

"Pardon me—that was uncouth." He had a boyish grin and a spark of humor in his bright blue eyes.

I guessed his age to be around sixty, but he seemed to be the type of man who remained attractive at any age.

"One of those days?" I asked.

He let out a truncated laugh. "Yeah, you could say that." He flicked his gaze over me. "Things are lookin' up though."

His easy charm reminded me of Hugh, making me want to return his smile with a bit of sass.

"Guess you don't think I'm much of a lady, after all."

Unfortunately, Boomer didn't know me or my sense of humor. His smile faltered and he pulled himself to his feet.

"No, ma'am, that's not what I meant at all," he said, the playfulness evaporating. "What can I help you with?"

Damn. Why did I have such a talent for turning people off? I let it go—nothing I could do about it now.

"I was hoping you could tell me about a Friesian horse you had here not long ago."

"What about him?

"I'm actually trying to locate him."

"Oh?"

"This was the last place he was seen." By a cat. But I left that part out.

"You saying he was stolen from here?"

I opened my mouth to protest, but for all I knew, it was the truth.

"'Cause that's a serious claim," Boomer said, his anger becoming more evident with each word.

Crap.

"That's not really what I meant."

"What did you mean?"

"It's just that his owner is really worried and—"

"We take care of our horses here, ma'am."

"I never assumed otherwise, but—"

A shrill whistle cut off my blundering explanation. We both looked toward the sound. Hunter stood at the entrance to the field. Seeing he'd gotten our attention, he beckoned with a sharp, sweeping wave.

"Excuse me," Boomer said and began walking to where the boy stood. A hitch in his step made his gate jerky, but his long legs covered the distance quickly.

Seeing his summons was being answered, Hunter turned back to the new guests.

I started after Boomer, then noticed the socket set lying in the grass. Not wanting to leave the tools on the ground, I picked them up and headed back to the main area of R-n-R.

The man I'd seen driving the . . . what would you call it? A recreational horse vehicle? RHV? Sounded like a new type of flu. Recreational *equine* vehicle? REV. Much better. The driver of the REV had parked and was busy unloading one of the horses. He seemed comfortable and assured, his horse relaxed. The mark of an experienced horseman. Off to the side, a woman holding a squirming toddler spoke to Hunter.

As I neared, I caught snippets of their conversation: Hunter explaining Mr. Parnell was on his way and assuring her it wouldn't be a problem to get them settled in the meantime. Boomer led the first horse into a small paddock next to the field where the campers were supposed to park while the man worked at unloading horse number two.

Lucy and Scout, the resident horses at R-n-R, approached the fence opposite, curious about the new visitors. Hoping the morning wouldn't be a total loss, I headed to talk to the horses.

Lucy and Scout, however, we're no more informative than Minerva had been. Yes, they'd seen a Friesian horse. No, they didn't know what had happened to it. I was able to discern there was some commotion ending with Cappy bleating late into the night. Looking for little Nelly, I was sure. I thanked them both with a pat and considered my next move.

I could wait for Mr. Parnell, but things seemed a little hectic. Probably better to come back later.

As I headed to Bluebell, I started to set the socket set on Boomer's toolbox, then, thinking they might slide off if he drove away without seeing them, put the tools in the truck's bed. I noticed a hand-lettered sign advertising fresh guinea fowl eggs and smiled. I liked guineas, boisterous as they were, and it took a certain kind of person to successfully keep a flock.

The truck's back window sported a number of decals and stickers, including one that featured a stick-figure drawing of a rider being thrown off their horse along with the caption I DO MY OWN STUNTS.

At least he had a sense of humor about some things.

I also saw a row of parking decals dating from '07 to '09 with the name of a polo club located in Wellington. In all honesty, I didn't know much about the sport. The extent of my polo knowledge had been gleaned from *Pretty Woman*, but I was sure there was a lot more to it than fancy hats, champagne, and divots. Polo, like anything involving riding and handling an animal as large and powerful as a horse, had to carry some risk. I wondered if a fall during a match had precipitated Boomer's limp.

A question I probably wouldn't get a chance to ask him as it seemed he'd decided not to like me.

One thing I had learned from him—I needed to change my tactics when I talked to Mr. Parnell.

In my defense, Boomer had admitted to having a bad day, but there was a good chance Mr. Parnell would be having one, too.

I decided to come back after lunch and make an assessment then. It would give me time to think of the best approach, something I clearly needed to work on.

How to Lose Friends and Irritate People, a practical guide by Grace Wilde.

My mind inadvertently jumped to what Kai had told me about Detective Boyle and I pushed the thought away.

I left R-n-R and, once again, looked for Nelly as I drove along. Finding Mr. Parnell's lost goat would be a good ice-breaker, right?

My phone rang just as I was getting good and lost.

The number on the screen had a New York City area code. Who did I know from New York?

"Hello?"

"Grace, it's Jasmine." The static was better than the day before, but her voice still sounded hollow and tinny.

"Hey, listen, I may lose you, I'm in a bad area."

"Sorry? Oh, you mean on your mobile." She pronounced the word with a long *i*—mow-bile. "No problem. I was just ringing to ask if you'd found anything."

I winced, realizing I probably should have already called her with an update.

"Nothing much, yet."

I told her what little I'd learned visiting the stables and my plans to go back and talk to the owner.

"But he was there?" Even with the bad connection, I could hear the hope bolstering her words.

"A *Friesian* was there," I corrected.

"But the note," she said, referencing the scrawl Tony had made about R-n-R. "It can't be a coincidence."

"It's unlikely. I'm working on the assumption the horse was Heart. I'll know more after I speak to the owner."

Fingers crossed, anyway.

"You don't happen to have come across any paperwork," I asked. "A bill of sale or something? Just so I can prove to the stable owner I am who I say I am."

"No, sorry. Mary is still looking through Tony's papers, and now that the police have his computer—well, I hope they would let me know if they found anything."

"I have a contact I can ask," I told her, thinking I'd get Kai to put a bug in Charlie's ear.

"Grace, can you ring back as soon as you know something?"

"I will. Um, sorry about not getting caught up with you before. I just didn't have much to tell you."

"No worries, really. I'd rather you spend time looking for Heart than mollycoddling me."

"I do have something I want to ask you," I said, stopping to idle at a dirt road leading into the state park.

I wasn't sure how to word my question so I just spit it out. "Tony left me a message the day he died. He said he needed to talk to me about my sister, Emma. Do you have any idea what he might have meant?"

There was a long pause. "No idea. Odd. I felt sure he was trying to reach you because of Heart."

Crap! Had I just put my foot in my mouth and implicated my sister in Ortega's murder?

"It probably had something to do with the auction," I said, wishing I'd kept my mouth shut. "Which reminds me— Tony was the winning bidder for my services, so technically, you don't have to pay me."

"Actually, I was thinking about that. In addition to paying your fee—which I will be doing, no arguments, please—I'd also like to offer a reward for Heart."

"That's a great idea."

"I should have thought of it before." She sounded tired and it occurred to me Jasmine was probably having to make funeral arrangements and was burdened with any number of other issues, but I had to ask the next question.

"How much?"

"I was thinking ten. Would that be enough?"

"Ten . . . ?"

"Ten thousand dollars."

"It's a good start," I said. "I'm going to find him, Jasmine."

"I know. Thank you."

After hanging up, I stared out the windshield, hoping I hadn't bitten off more than I could chew.

"Like that's ever happened," I scoffed aloud.

Step one was, well, figuring out where I was.

A chain stretched across the path in front of me. To one

side a sign banning motor vehicles was posted; it also gave the name of the trail.

I retrieved the map gifted to me by the hikers the day before and had begun searching for the name when it hit me.

I'd just spoken to Jasmine on my cell. Maybe my GPS app was online.

Sure enough, it opened without too much delay and I was able to orient myself and determine how many rights and lefts it would take to find civilization and, hopefully, I thought as my stomach grumbled, lunch.

By a quarter after noon, I was on my way back to R-n-R with a to-go bag and a plan.

Boomer's truck was gone when I arrived. Parked in its place was a newer, less careworn white pickup with an illustration of the R-n-R logo on its side along with the slogan YOUR STABLES AWAY FROM HOME.

Not the catchiest, but it got the message across.

Boomer's assumption that I was maligning the stables by insinuating something had happened to Heart on their watch had made me worry about talking to Parnell.

But that had been before my conversation with Jasmine.

Now, I had a plan.

Keeping it in mind, I moseyed up to the house's front door. The sign hanging in the window indicated they were open for business, so I turned the knob and stepped inside.

To the left, where I imagined the living room would normally be, sat a large oak desk fronted by a set of visitor chairs. Both they and the desk chair were done in an odd shade of steel blue leather. In front of the window, a macramé planter cradled one of those variegated spider plants. All of this, when viewed in concert with the abstract peach, mauve, and turquoise painting on the wall, reminded me of an '80s dentist's office.

A row of metal filing cabinets acted as a divider to what might have once been a dining area. The temptation to open the cabinet's drawers and flip through the files made my fingers itch. But I knew I'd never have time to get far. Instead, I edged over to the desk to see if it yielded anything of interest.

There was a brochure from a company called Farmstead Properties who claimed to be "the farm and ranch special-ists!", a card from a place that sold new and used tractor parts, and a file folder labeled "Receipts."

I started to open the file for a quick peek when footsteps clunked on the parquet floor. I snatched my hand back and stepped away from the desk. A few moments later, a man holding a half-eaten sandwich on a paper towel appeared from around the cabinets.

"Help you, ma'am?" he asked.

"Mr. Parnell?"

"Call me Rusty." He was tall, a little bowlegged, and paunchy enough to put a strain on the pearly snaps of his plaid shirt.

"I'm sorry to interrupt your lunch."

"No bother," he said and moved behind the desk to set the sandwich down next to an open can of Coke. "What can I do you for?"

He sat and I followed his lead, lowering myself onto one of the chairs opposite.

"My name is Grace Wilde. I'm hoping you might have some information on a horse that boarded here not long ago."

"You were here earlier, asking about the Friesian."

"That's right." Giving him my most professional smile, I laid the magazine, open to Heart's picture, on his desk.

Time to implement the plan.

Step one: establish credibility.

"I've been hired by the owner to find him. I'm an animal behaviorist. My skills and experience with animals make me uniquely qualified to locate an animal if it goes missing." I'd spent most of my lunch break coming up with that line. Mr. Parnell was not impressed.

"Hmm." He looked over the magazine and took a swig of Coke.

"What can you tell me about his time here?" I asked. When he hadn't answered after several seconds, I added, "Anything you might remember would be helpful."

I'd chosen my wording to make sure I wasn't insinuating any wrongdoing on his part.

He took his time to reply, seeming to guard his words as carefully as I was.

"I'm afraid I can't tell you much. He wasn't here long."

"Do you remember anything odd happening? Did anyone take an interest or ask questions about him?"

He pursed his bottom lip and shook his head. "Not that I know of." He tilted back in his chair, making the springs groan in protest. "Look, I'd like to help, but I've got some paperwork to do, so . . ."

It was clear he expected me to leave. Darn it! No time to artfully move to step two of the plan.

"Well . . ." I stood, took one of his cards from its little display stand and shoved it into my back pocket. "Thanks for your time," I said, picking up the magazine.

He gave me a dismissive nod.

Now or never, Grace.

A door banged opened somewhere beyond the row of filing cabinets and Hunter clomped into view a few moments later.

"I'm . . . Oh, sorry."

"She's just leaving. What is it?" Parnell asked Hunter, completely dismissing me.

Before turning to go, I held out one of my cards to Mr. Parnell. He took it grudgingly. "There is a reward offered for the horse, so if you think of anything, give me a call."

Just as I was shutting the door behind me on my way out, I caught a glimpse of something through the beveled glass. Parnell, tossing my card directly into the trash.

My knee-jerk reaction was to walk right back into his office and hand him another card, saying something snarky, like "here's an extra just in case you lose the first one," but maturity prevailed.

I left R-n-R wondering if Parnell simply didn't want to get involved or if his reticence signaled a more sinister motive.

If so, what would it be?

CHAPTER 8

I was almost to the beach when my phone erupted into a rousing version of the sea chantey "Randy Dandy Oh." Emma had assigned the ring tone to our uncle Wiley. An eccentric old man with a love of sailing, the sea, and pirates.

"Hey," I answered as quickly as I could. "Everything okay?"

The last time my uncle had called me I'd ended up in a disco-era gold lamé jumpsuit.

Don't ask.

"Well, yes and no," he answered. "Actually, I'm calling for a friend. She rescued a dog—well, not really a dog. She's like Moss."

"A wolf hybrid?"

"Yep. Though she's more." He paused. "Let's just say she needs your help."

I heard a woman's voice call out something in the background, followed by a loud crash.

"Wiley?"

"We're fine. That was just a ficus plant. I'm not sure whether or not she's trying to kill it or play with it—either way, it's a goner now."

"Give me the address. I'll be there as soon as I can."

I've met plenty of people claiming to own a wolf or wolf-dog hybrid when what they really had was a mixed breed dog or, in some cases, a purebred Siberian husky with agouti coat coloring, which to the untrained eye resembled a wolf.

I'd even heard horror stories of purebred huskies and other northern breeds being seized and either euthanized or "returned to the wild."

Wolf-dog or not, my uncle wouldn't have called me unless there was a serious problem.

I found the address easily and was soon knocking on the door to the tidy little brick home. I glanced around the neighborhood while I waited. It was a quiet street; I didn't hear any dogs barking or the squeal of preschool children. A lone, dark sedan rolled lazily by but no other traffic came or went.

Wiley answered the door—a relieved smile lifted the ends of his handlebar mustache when he saw me. As always, he wore a beret. Cottony tufts of white hair sprouted from under it.

"Thanks for coming, Gracie."

"Sure. What's going on?"

A slim woman with close-cropped salt-and-pepper hair appeared as he ushered me into the brightly lit foyer.

"This is my friend Janie," Wiley said.

I nodded a greeting and shook her hand. She was probably in her seventies but had the energy and quick, fluid movements of a much younger woman. Had her features not been pinched with lines of worry, I would have called her beautiful.

"Wiley says you have a special gift with animals," Janie said.

"You have a rescue you need some help with?"

"My late husband used to raise shepherds. He did Schutzhund training, so I've been around big dogs, but this . . ." She let out a troubled sigh.

"How long have you had—" I waited for someone to fill in the dog's name for me, and Janie quickly obliged.

"Pretty Girl. You'll understand why I call her that when you see her. I haven't had her long." She glanced at my uncle, suddenly uncertain.

"It's okay," Wiley told her. "You can trust Grace."

"Every morning, I go on my walk," Janie began. "The route I take goes through the neighborhood, then all the way around the park, about thirteen miles. Three times in the last month I saw a dog running loose in the street. I managed to catch her and found the owner, but he didn't seem to care that she was getting out. A couple of weeks ago, I walked by his house and noticed she was on a chain in the backyard. I guess she was climbing the chain-link fence and his solution was to tie her to a tree."

I exchanged a look with my uncle but let Janie continue uninterrupted.

"I walked by the next day and she was still tied up. The poor thing was panicking. Trying to get loose. I was afraid she'd hurt herself, so I knocked on the door to let her owner know what was going on."

She paused and pressed her lips into an angry, bloodless line.

"Let me guess," I said, trying to keep a hold of my own temper. "He didn't care."

"No. He did not." Her words were crisp and filled with contempt. "And when I told him I was going to report it as animal abuse, he—" Janie's voice wavered and she broke off. Her hands balled into fists at her sides.

Wiley stepped closer and patted her on the back. My uncle's face had turned grim as he took up the story. "He told Janie if she reported him, he'd just shoot the dog and be done with it."

The anger I felt toward this anonymous owner threatened to bubble over into rage.

I forced a calming breath. I'd be no use to anyone if I let myself get emotional.

"What happened?"

"I came home," Janie said. "Got my bolt cutters, walked back to his house, into the backyard, and cut that damn chain."

I felt my brows raise in surprise and more than a little admiration.

Janie squared her shoulders and set her jaw. Anticipating a rebuke perhaps.

Ha! Not from me, sister.

"I like her," I said to Wiley. He smiled, light returning to sparkle in his eyes.

I looked at Janie. "But . . . ?" There was always a "but" with these stories.

Janie's posture deflated slightly. "Things were okay for a couple of days. Then, she ate my couch."

I gave her a sympathetic nod.

"The next day, she tore a hole in the back door—which is made out of solid wood panels."

"Impressive," I said.

"She got into the refrigerator, too."

I winced, imagining what that cleanup would've been like.

"Have you been taking her with you on your walks?" I asked, trying not to sound accusatory.

"I brought her with me once, but I was afraid that awful man might see us even though I don't walk past his house anymore. I tried a different route, but her reactions to new things can be unpredictable. Sometimes she's skittish, and she's so big . . ."

"It's okay," I said, beginning to suspect my uncle was right about Pretty Girl being a wolf hybrid. Not that it mattered much. Sure, it was good to know what you were dealing with but, in the end, the most important thing to consider was temperament and whether she'd be amenable to training.

"Why don't I meet Pretty Girl and I'll see what I can do."

"That would be great."

As we walked through the house, the evidence of Pretty Girl's destruction was evident. Not only was the couch noticeably absent from the living room, I spotted torn curtains and a table lamp without a shade. The back door had been chewed and clawed, quite literally, to shreds.

"How is she around new people?" I asked Janie, though I had a feeling I knew the answer.

"Pretty shy, actually. She was very hard to catch that first time. In fact, I'd given up and was walking away when I noticed she'd started following me. I stopped and sat on the curb for a few minutes. Eventually she walked right up to give me a sniff. Now, she practically knocks me over if she hasn't seen me in a while."

"No vet visit, yet?"

"I wanted to take her but I was afraid she'd panic."

"Maybe you can give her a quick check-up." My uncle suggested.

"I can try."

After a couple of slow, centering breaths, I opened the back door.

Devastation reigned on the screened-in back porch. The ficus tree my uncle had mentioned during his phone call looked like it had been put through a mulcher. The large clay pot lay broken on its side, dark potting soil strewn all over the concrete floor.

In two places the screen was torn. The lower portion of the door was missing altogether.

I pushed through it into a backyard that had probably once been more . . . manicured. Now, holes were dug here and there, a couple of bushes had been vigorously gnawed on.

The canine standing in the middle of the yard studied me with eyes the color of sunlit amber. Had her coat been white instead of black, I'd have said she was the spitting image of a two-year-old Moss.

Pretty? Check.

Wolf-dog? Check.

Temperament and trainability?

"Let's find out," I said.

Turning slightly so I wasn't facing her, I knelt, and reached out to Pretty Girl with my mind. A quick, gentle assessment told me she was wary, but curious.

I widened the mental conduit, showed her I meant no harm. I was a friend.

While continuing to convey lots of positive stuff, I called her to me.

Come.

She stayed where she was.

Stubborn. Just like Moss.

Something strange happened as I thought of my dog. It

was almost as if the idea of Moss, the distilled, beautiful, wild, loyal, brave essence of my dog, reached out and connected with Pretty Girl.

So intrigued by the sudden Mossomeness I was projecting, Pretty Girl trotted to me with no further hesitation.

Kindred? She sniffed around me looking for Moss.

Uh . . . not exactly. But we'll set up a playdate.

We spent a few more minutes chatting. She relaxed more than I had expected, which was good.

After another couple of minutes, the wolf-dog allowed me to do a rudimentary checkup. All was well on that front.

With a farewell pat and promise to bring Moss for a visit, I stood and went inside to find Janie.

From what I'd seen, the woman didn't lack in the moxie department, but I still believed it would be best to be very clear about the amount of work required to keep Pretty Girl both mentally and physically fit.

Janie promised to do her best, and I offered to bring Moss over to help. With a little luck and a lot of determination, we'd make the home a happy one—for everyone.

My uncle walked me outside to Bluebell and thanked me again before saying, "I heard about Anthony Ortega."

"You did?" I asked surprised. My uncle didn't own a TV and hadn't had a newspaper delivered since the Reagan administration.

"Janie likes to watch the news."

"Ah. So it's like that, huh? You old fox, you."

"Old." He grinned. "Not dead."

We shared a laugh over that then he said, "How's Emma?"

"She's fine." I didn't want to worry him with details of her arrest or say anything about Boyle's one-sidedness.

He nodded but didn't seem convinced.

"What?" I asked.

"Death, even the death of a despicable bastard like Ortega, can have an affect on the people who knew him. Keep an eye on your sister, okay?"

"I will."

I let what my uncle had said ruminate as I drove toward

the beach and realized I hadn't actually asked my sister how she felt about Ortega's murder.

"Great sister-skills, Grace."

Just before I'd made it over the Intracoastal Waterway, traffic came to a complete halt. When I saw the flashing lights of a police car ahead, I eased Bluebell over toward the median to try and get a better look at what was causing the holdup.

And couldn't see squat.

After what seemed like an eternity with no forward movement, I decided I had time to check my messages.

I'd missed three texts while I'd been working with Pretty Girl. One was from a client asking to reschedule an upcoming appointment. The two others were from Wes and Kai, both asking me to call.

I took care of my client first with a quick text message, then started to call Kai. Before I could pull up his number, my phone rang.

"Miss Wilde? This is Hunter, um, from R-n-R. I heard you were offering a reward if anyone knows about that Friesian."

"The owner is, yes."

"There's one thing, I don't know if it'll help, but I just talked to the driver who delivered him. She told me something happened that day."

I waited but he didn't elaborate. "Hunter? What happened?"

"She was followed."

"Followed? By who?"

"Don't know. Lily Earl, that's the driver, she makes stops here pretty regular, so I asked if she'd hauled a Friesian lately. She told me she had and she remembered because she had been followed that day."

"Can I talk to Lily Earl? Is she there?"

"No, ma'am, she's left already. I would have called sooner but I had to . . . uh . . . get your card from Mr. Parnell."

"I'm sure he had put it somewhere special."

"Well, uh . . ." He drifted off, not sure what to say.

"Do you have a number for Lily Earl?"

"No, ma'am, but I know where she'll be tomorrow." He gave me directions to a place not far from R-n-R called The Oaks and predicted Lily Earl would be there by nine in the morning.

"Hey," I said before he hung up. "Any sign of Nelly?"

"Not yet. I'm starting to feel kind of bad for Cappy, though. I think he misses her."

"I think you're right."

After hanging up, I considered turning around and heading back to the woods near R-n-R to search for the little goat, but knew by the time I got there it would be nearing dark and any hope of finding her would be futile.

Oh—and I was still stuck in traffic.

The gridlock inspired me to call Jasmine to give her a quick update, minimal as it was.

She answered with an anxious "Grace?"

"Hey, Jasmine. I just called to let you know that I haven't gotten positive ID on Heart, yet, but I'm going to talk to the woman who delivered the Friesian to R-n-R tomorrow morning. I'm hoping she'll have some paperwork on him."

"Something to give the police?"

"Right. I'm sure they'll look more closely at his disappearance if I can prove Heart was the horse delivered to R-n-R." Even Boyle couldn't deny that. "I was wondering if you happen to have any other photos of Heart? Maybe something that shows more than just his head?"

"They took a massive number of photos at the shoot, so there must be. I know the photographer—I'll ask him."

"That would be great." I wasn't sure how much it would actually help, aside from giving me a better mental picture of what Heart looked like to compare with any information or images I might acquire.

I thanked Jasmine, hung up, and called Wes.

He answered by saying, "Amazing Grace, what are you doing?"

"Sitting in traffic on Beach Boulevard.

"Stimulating."

"Yep. I'm not going anywhere any time soon. What's up?"

"I wanted to let you know you missed a fabulous lunch," he said. "Any progress on your search?"

"Nope," I said on a long breath. "There's something I wanted to get your take on, though." I told him about the last message Ortega had left me claiming he needed to talk about Emma.

"Your sister mentioned it at lunch," he said.

"He was lying, right?" I asked Wes.

"I think he was trying to manipulate you."

"That's what Emma said."

"You think there's more to it?"

"It just seems weird, but I can't put my finger on exactly why."

"Maybe it's the irony. His last phone call ended up being to a woman who despised him." There was a pause as Wes let out a musing, "Hmmm. Actually, allow me to recant that last statement. I'm sure there were plenty of women who despised him, so statistically . . ."

I didn't hear the rest of his words because my attention had been snagged by what was happening several car lengths ahead.

"Wes, I've got to call you back." I hung up and put Bluebell in park.

A motorcycle cop had arrived on the scene and more than one motorist had gotten out of their vehicle to watch or use their cell phone to take photos and videos of what was going on.

Near the front of the line of cars, one man was waving his arms and clapping. Not at the police, but at something on the ground.

"Great." I pushed open Bluebell's door and hopped out onto the street.

As I got closer, I could hear the man shouting, "Ha! Go!" as he clapped.

The first officer said, "Sir, return to your vehicle. Now."

"I am late for important business." The man's accent was foreign and thick. If I had to guess, I'd say Russian—but

I'm only going with that because he sounded a lot like Chekov from *Star Trek*.

I looked down and spotted the source of the problem.

Stretched across the road was a very large, very agitated alligator.

Just great.

The motorcycle cop, a big dude who looked like he probably rode a Harley when not in uniform, turned his attention to me while his fellow deputy continued to order Chekov back into his car.

"Ma'am, you need to return to your vehicle."

How best to handle this? I thought about claiming the gator was mine but that seemed unwise. I was pretty sure losing track of your pet ten-foot-long alligator would be frowned upon by the lawmen.

I decided to go with my fallback strategy.

"My name is Dr. Wilde, I'm a veterinarian specializing in herpetology." I motioned to the gator and smiled. "Specifically, large reptiles."

The two deputies and Chekov stared at me.

When you can't dazzle them with brilliance . . .

"I thought I could lend a hand," I said. "Maybe get this guy out of the way?"

Moto-cop looked at me intently. "You're a herpetologist?"

Uh-oh.

"A vet," I corrected, but the fact that he knew what herpetology was didn't bode well for my little white lie.

The first deputy seemed to be deferring to Moto-cop. Chekov looked at all of us and said, "You, little lady, git rid of lizard. Yes?"

"It's not a lizard," Moto-cop said. "It's a crocodilian."

He'd intended the comment for me. A test, or to prove he knew his reptiles? Was this to be a power struggle?

I had no idea.

Okay, here's the truth. I don't know everything about animals or their behavior. In fact, I'm pretty fuzzy when it comes to details.

Do I know the difference between a tapir and a tarsier?
Yes.

Tapirs are large rainforest-dwelling mammals with prehensile noses and have striped babies that are pretty freaking cute.

Tarsiers are tiny, rainforest-dwelling primates with gigantic eyeballs and have tiny, furry babies that are also pretty freaking cute.

Could I expound on the behavior of either of these animals?

Not a chance.

There was one thing I was pretty sure of, though, and that's that an alligator in the middle of the road being harassed by humans was not going to be a friendly animal. And no matter how much Moto-cop knew about them, he wouldn't be able to defuse the situation as quickly and peacefully as I could.

When in doubt, pretend like you're already in charge.

"Okay, good." I gave Moto-cop a decisive head bob. "You have some knowledge of these animals. And you"—I looked at the other deputy—"you arrived on the scene first. Do you know if the animal has been injured?"

I wasn't sensing any pain radiating from the gator, but couldn't be sure. Plus, I wanted to take control of the situation.

"It came out to road in front of my truck," Chekov said. "No one hit it."

I nodded. I'd need to take a closer look both mentally and physically to be sure, but first things first. I said to Chekov, "Thank you for your help. For your safety, please get back in your truck."

The cops backed up my request with a couple of stern looks and Chekov complied.

"Now, Officer"—I looked at the first deputy's name tag—"Barrows, would you kindly back your cruiser up a bit, give the gator some space? While you"—I turned to address Moto-cop—"stop traffic on the other side of the median. Okay?"

"What are you going to do?"

"Get him to go that way." I pointed across the street to the wide, marshy reed bank leading to the Intracoastal Waterway.

He looked like he was going to ask me to elaborate on my plan, but I nipped that in the bud by saying, "We've got to get traffic stopped, though. You know how fast these guys can move. If he decides to make a break for it, he could get hit."

Moto-cop nodded and went across the median to stop oncoming traffic.

While everyone was busy, I took the time to focus on the gator. When I'd first walked up, his mouth had been open aggressively. Now he sat, still frightened and disoriented, but no longer in defense mode.

"That's right, buddy," I murmured. "Good gator."

Want to go home?

I tried to imagine the cool, soothing water of the marsh. The heavy scent of green, growing things, of salt and decay. I pictured the flash of silver fish scales in the sun.

Home.

The word was a low bellow in my mind. I knew my brain had translated the gator's thoughts to construct the word. But it was still neat to feel it form in my head. To know that such a primitive creature understood me.

I smiled.

Start walking, buddy. Home is closer than you think.

He started walking forward and I followed slowly, urging him on. When he'd crossed the road and was sliding down the embankment, I wanted to do a fist pump and happy dance but stuck to a whispered "Yes!"

I turned to Moto-cop as he came to stand next to me. To my surprise he was grinning like a kid.

"Nice job."

"Thanks."

He put up his hand to keep traffic at bay so we could cross to where I'd left Bluebell.

"Maybe you want to go herping some time," he said.

"Um . . ." Herping? What the hell was herping? "Well, I . . ."

"I'm sure you're probably married or something, but I thought I'd ask. You don't meet many girls who are into herps."

I felt heat crawling up my neck into my cheeks. Moto-cop was asking me on a herp with him. Sweet Lord, take me now.

Thankfully, we'd reached Bluebell. I opened the door and climbed in as fast as I could, smiled, and called, "Thanks for all your help!" Then shut the door, shifted into drive, and pulled away.

Wincing a little, I glanced in the rearview mirror. That was when I noticed the same sedan I'd seen earlier appear behind me.

Lily Earl wasn't the only one being followed.

CHAPTER 9

I watched the sedan for several minutes and, when I was certain it was the same car, called Kai.

"I have a hypothetical question for you," I said when he answered.

"Okay."

"If you thought you were being followed, what would you do?"

"You think you're being followed?"

"Hypothetically."

I could hear him sigh before he said, "I would make sure I was actually being followed."

"By doing . . . ?"

"Where are you?"

"Just passing the water park on Beach Boulevard."

"Take a left at the next street. Don't use your blinker."

I put my phone on speaker and set it on my lap so I could simultaneously drive, listen, and keep an eye on whether or not the car stayed behind me.

"Okay, done. Now what?"

"Did they turn, too?"

"Yes."

"Maintain a normal speed and take another left."

I did.

"Are they still behind you?"

"Hypothetically?"

"Grace . . ."

I glanced in my rearview mirror. "No, they kept going."

"Good. Take two more left turns. That will get you back to where you started."

"So . . . I went in a circle"

"Correct. The chances that someone will do a complete 360 the same time as you is pretty slim. If you see them again, you'll know."

"It was probably my imagination," I said and explained what I'd learned from Hunter about the delivery driver being followed.

"Now I have a question for you," he said. "What are you doing tonight?"

"I don't have anything planned."

"You want to get together for dinner?"

"Sure. Where do you want to go?"

"I have an idea. I'll pick you up at six."

"A surprise?"

"Yep."

"Sounds good."

"And if you see that car again, don't bother with trying to lose them. Call me—I'll take care of it."

Macho-man stuff usually brought my hackles up, but hearing the protectiveness in Kai's voice made my insides go all soft and gooey.

A few minutes later when I checked the rearview mirror for the tail, I noticed I was sporting a dopey smile to go with the warm fuzzies.

The happy-balloon I'd been floating on deflated as something important dawned.

I was going on a real date—with Kai.

Though we'd been seeing each other—or trying to when our crazy schedules allowed—for a few months, this would be the first time Kai had come to pick me up for a real, honest-to-goodness date.

Which meant I'd have to wear . . . something.

Clothing.

I'd have to wear, well, not the grimy jeans and dirty T-shirt I was currently sporting, for sure.

My gifts are many and varied—animal telepathy, unyielding tenacity, sarcasm . . . Wardrobe selection is nowhere on the list.

I needed Emma.

I tried her cell, muttering a curse when it went to voice mail.

I left a message and hoped I'd find her at home. Within five minutes, I pulled into the condo's lot and that hope evaporated. Not a sleek new Jaguar anywhere in sight.

Crap!

Moss jogged into the foyer to great me, Voodoo fast on his heels. He nudged me for a pet then asked to go out for a potty break. I obliged him and asked that he wrap things up as quickly as nature would allow.

Promising treats, I urged Moss up the stairs and through the front door, then called Emma again.

Voice mail.

"Seriously, Emma," I panted into the phone as I scooped a serving of dog food into Moss's bowl and started opening a can of kitten food for Voodoo. "Sister in need of assistance. I'm jumping in the shower. Get your ass home."

I was in and out of the shower pretty fast, but drying my long hair took forever. I'd hoped by the time I was finished, Emma would have at least called me back.

Nope.

With a sigh, I set the phone on the counter and knew I couldn't put it off any longer. It was time for war paint.

The last time I'd attempted to apply makeup to myself had been a bit of a disaster. I ended up looking like a clown having a bad day.

"Come on, Grace," I said to my reflection. "You can do this."

Shoulders squared, I marched to my sister's bathroom, where all manner of cosmetics were available. Not that I planned on using many. Maybe a little tinted lip gloss, some powder to take away the shine, and a little mascara.

Emma had a lighted, magnifying makeup mirror. I clicked it on, leaned in, then jerked back when I saw my reflection.

Good grief. Talk about exposing flaws. Had my pores always been that big?.

I saw some loose powder in a container and decided to try it. I dabbed the brush in the powder, tapped the side the way I'd seen Emma do, then, taking a deep breath, I turned back to the makeup mirror and began.

Things went smoothly until I applied the lip gloss. It took about a minute, but just as I started on the mascara, my nose started running, my lips began to tingle then burn as if I'd been sucking on a jalapeño pepper.

"What the . . . ?" I ran to grab some toilet tissue and rub the gloss off my lips. I hurried back to look in the makeup mirror and figure out what had gone wrong. My lips were pink and swollen but the tingling burn had started to fade.

An allergic reaction?

Sniffing, I studied the rest of my face carefully, looking for signs of hives. With relief I found none and went back to applying the mascara. With slow, careful movements, I swiped the wand over my lashes and was almost finished when, without any warning whatsoever, my body betrayed me.

I sneezed.

Sneezing mid–mascara swipe is *bad.*

I poked myself in the eye.

My vocal cords produced a sound that was equal parts pain, anger, and frustration followed by a string of some of the most inventive curses I'd ever heard, much less uttered. I squeezed my eyes shut and bounced up and down on the balls of my feet.

Moss, alarmed by my yowl, came sprinting into the room. *Grace!*

"I'm okay, buddy."

Okay? He came to my side to assess the situation and I gave his head a reassuring pat.

I'm fine.

The tears that pooled in my eyes began to fall. I tilted my head up to the ceiling and blinked rapidly, trying to stem the flow, but it was no use. Because, folks, when you poke yourself in the eye with a tiny, cylindrical brush covered in mascara, your eye thinks you've stabbed it with a miniature pinecone dipped in acid.

I paced back and forth, trying to convince my brain that I had not, in fact, blinded myself.

"Grace?"

My sister's voice preceded her into the bathroom by about half a second. Squinting and blinking against my blurred vision, I turned to face her.

"Whoa." The sight of me actually made her recoil, which I took as a bad sign.

"Mascara," I said by way of explanation.

"*American Horror Story*," she corrected.

I didn't want to look, but her words made me turn to the full-size mirror. I stared at myself in shock. Somehow, the powder I'd used was two shades lighter than my skin. Tears streaked down my cheeks in dark rivulets. A clump of toilet paper clung to my chin.

Oh. My. God.

"What inspired this assay into the world of cosmetics?" Emma asked.

"Kai." A slightly hysterical giggle gurgled out of me. "We're going on a date."

"Oh!" My sister's eyes flared wide. "Okay . . . Don't worry, I can fix this."

I started to laugh and pointed to my reflection. "With what?"

But Emma had already moved past me to open a drawer.

"How much time do we have?" she asked, handing me an elastic headband to push my hair out of my face.

"Maybe fifteen minutes."

With a grim nod, Emma got to work. She started the hot water running in the sink. Grabbed a jar from the counter and unscrewed the top. Plucking a washcloth from the basket on the counter, where she kept them rolled into neat spirals, she snapped it open with a flick of her wrist and smeared it with a glob of cream.

"Wash," she said, handing me the cloth.

I leaned over the sink and obeyed.

"What are you going to wear?" Emma asked, astutely noting I was standing there in my underwear.

"I have no idea," I sputtered, still scrubbing.

"Where is he taking you?" Some of the calm in her voice had slipped.

"He said it was a surprise," I said, defensively. Straightening to look at my sister's reflection I added, "How the hell am I supposed to know what to wear on a *surprise* date?"

"Calm down," she soothed, handing me a towel. "I have the perfect dress. When he gets here, I'll answer the door and scope it out. We can either dress you up or down as needed."

"Okay, yeah, that sounds good."

"Finger," Emma commanded, holding up a tube of what looked like liquid foundation.

I curled my lip at the stuff.

She sighed. "It's BB cream."

"Bee what?"

"It will blend with your skin tone, trust me."

Still making a face, I let her squirt a dab on my finger.

"Put it on like you would moisturizer. Then, use this"—she placed a round container of peachy-colored blush along with a fluffy brush on the counter—"followed by this"—she added a tube of lip gloss to the procession. "Remember, less is more."

When I emerged from the bathroom a couple of minutes later, my sister had laid a dress on her bed along with a myriad of accessories.

"Here, let's start with this," she said, handing me the dress.

It was a pretty, dark red and purple print number that wrapped around the front and tied in back. The style usually worked on my figure.

"Damn," my sister said, crossing her arms and regarding me with a small shake of her head as I finished tying the dress. "I'll have to give it to you now. You fill it out in places I never can."

"Yeah?"

"Va-va-voom." She took my shoulders and turned me to face the full-length mirror.

She was right, the V in front dipped down just enough to show a hint of cleavage and accentuate my waist.

"When he gets here all we have left to do is choose between the flats or heels, clutch or baguette, and decide whether to add earrings and bracelets and—"

The doorbell rang.

My sister grinned at me and actually clapped her hands in excitement.

I really needed to get out more.

Moss looked from me to Emma as she rushed out of the room to answer the door.

"It's Kai," I told him. "Go say hello."

Treat! My dog wasn't asking me, but hoping Kai would get suckered again. Head and tail high, he trotted through the door to try his luck.

Emma returned a minute later.

"Kai's looking deliciously casual." She glanced over the extra stuff strewn about the room. "Just the flats and you're good to go."

"Thank God."

"Have fu-un," she singsonged the words and I gave her a grateful smile before heading out to where Kai was waiting in the foyer.

"I'm not falling for it this time." He was shaking his head at Moss, who sat, head cocked, tail swishing slowly, looking up at Kai.

"Moss, go ask Emma for a treat."

My dog abandoned his efforts with Kai, immediately turning to jog back to my sister's room.

"Unfaithful mutt," Kai teased.

"When it comes to food," I agreed.

Kai focused his attention on me and though his jaw didn't exactly drop, he did let his gaze linger in all the right spots, finally, and most important, on my eyes.

"You look great."

"Thanks. So do you."

He wore jeans and a deep plum-colored T-shirt that complemented his skin tone and made his green eyes seem a shade brighter than usual.

They sparked with a hint of mischief.

"Where are we off to?" I asked.

He didn't answer, instead asking, "Do you mind if we take your car?"

"You want to go on a date in Bluebell?"

"If that's okay."

"Sure." I grabbed the keys and my purse off the foyer table and followed him out the door.

He stopped when we reached Bluebell and held out his hand.

"You want to drive, too?"

"If I may."

My curiosity kicked into overdrive and I searched his face for some clue to what he had planned. The only thing I discovered was that it was difficult to stay focused on ferreting out the truth when distractions like the firm, yet somehow sensual shape of his lips kept snagging my attention.

With a mental head-shake, I handed him the keys, and he walked around to the passenger side, opened the door, and helped me climb in.

Within a few minutes we'd made it onto Third Street and were headed north. I looked out at the familiar buildings, but quickly gave up trying to divine a destination.

"Give me a hint."

"Okay," he said. "I've got one coming up right now."

He flipped on the blinker and pulled Bluebell into a narrow parking lot. I'd passed the place a hundred times, and didn't need to check the business's sign to know where we were.

"A car wash!" I said, clasping my hands over my heart with a mawkish gasp of delight. "Won't the other girls be jealous!"

"You asked for a hint," he said, maneuvering toward the cavernous opening of the automated car wash. "Try out some of your investigation techniques on me."

"Um . . ." I thought about it as Kai cranked down the window and paid the machine. He put Bluebell in neutral and we started forward on the conveyer belt.

"Is this some sort of Hawaiian courting ritual?"

"Nope."

"You like playing antenna roulette?"

His forehead creased as he regarded me.

"You know," I said, "car washes and antennae don't always mix." I put my fists together and mimed breaking something in half.

"Shit." He started to open the door but I put my hand on his arm to stop him.

"Just kidding. Bluebell's antenna is built-in."

He relaxed back in the seat and gave me a look of mild reproach.

"What?" I asked. "Misdirection is an investigation technique, right?"

Kai didn't answer but his lips curved in amusement.

We lurched farther into the car wash. Rotating strips of fabric slapped soapy water over Bluebell and were followed by the rhythmic spray of synchronized jets of water.

"You feel comforted by the womblike sounds?"

He barked out a laugh and gave me an amused look. "Womblike?"

"I'm reaching," I told him. "The obvious answer is that you want Bluebell to be clean."

"Correct."

"But why?" We'd come to the end of the car wash and I had to raise my voice to be heard over the giant blow-dryers.

Still smiling, he shrugged without answering me and a minute later had pulled back onto the street.

Ten minutes after that, we turned off Third Street where it ended at Atlantic Boulevard.

The area had been spiffed up over the years, with planted palms, brick-paved walks, and quaint cafés. But as we drove away from the ocean, the palms became more sparse, and soon an overabundance of twenty-four-hour pharmacies and strip malls lined the street.

I'd never seen the large parking lot serving the strip malls more than half full, but tonight it was overflowing with every type of vintage and antique sport utility vehicle I could think of—and I could think of a lot.

"Is this a car show?"

"An impromptu one," Kai said.

"A cruise. You brought me on a date to a car cruise?"

"Buddy of mine from work has his ear to the ground. I asked him to let me know the next time one was going down with the truck and SUV crowd."

We rolled slowly past the vehicles. Chrome glinted, paint gleamed, the earth shook as one of the hot rods roared to life.

"Look! Do you know what that is?" I pointed at a blocky two-door. We parked and I hopped out of Bluebell to walk toward the smaller SUV.

"It's a Scout. My dad had one that looked just like this except ours was a weird avocado/army green color." I peeked through the open window. "He taught me how to drive in one of these," I said, grinning at the memories conjured by the sight of the spartan interior.

"This one's in great shape."

"She's only had one owner," a man said as he approached.

"I'm guessing that would be you," I said.

"Yes ma'am. Bought her in 1968."

"Straight-6 or V-8?"

He reached past me through the window and popped the hood. "Take a look."

I admired the beautifully restored engine and was soon chatting easily about torque and towing. Suddenly, I realized Kai was probably bored out of his gourd, but when I glanced over at him, he was standing off to the side, watching me with a satisfied smile.

Giving him a quick grin in return, I turned my attention back to answer a question the man with the Scout had asked about Bluebell.

We traded stats and stories for a few more minutes, then parted ways.

Someone had cranked their radio and oldies music

drifted on the breeze. Kai laced his fingers through mine as we moved on to admire other vehicles. The feel of his calloused hand sent a buzz of electricity up my arm, making my whole right side feel warm and fuzzy.

"Thanks for this," I said, glancing up at him. "And thanks for making sure Bluebell was presentable."

"I didn't want to embarrass her in front of her friends."

That was when it happened.

There are moments in life when a little part of yourself breaks away from the whole to float over and settle into someone else's care.

I felt it—subtle though it may have been. Like the shift of a pebble on a slope. It might seem insignificant, but in reality it's those pebbles that precede the avalanche.

The thought brought on a sudden wave of panic and made me freeze midstep.

"You okay?" Kai tightened his grip on my hand, probably thinking I'd stepped in a pothole. Nope, just freaking out over the realization I was falling for him.

Deep breaths.

"Yeah," I finally said. "I just haven't eaten much today—I'm starved."

"Want to go to Culhane's?"

"Sounds great."

The popular Irish pub was comfortably crowded inside. The music and conversations, though loud and lively, somehow managed to stop just shy of raucous.

Despite the crowd, we didn't have to wait long for a table or our food. Kai ordered a Guinness and the fish and chips and I went with a Smithwick's and Kaye's Pasta Mac, which promised to be baked to perfection.

"Are you sure you're okay? You seem distracted."

"I'm sorry, it's just . . ." That I'm having emotional palpitations over the idea of falling in love. "Worried about Heart."

"Haven't made much progress?"

"Not as much as I'd like," I said and attempted to shift my attention to my search for the missing horse. "I tried to talk to the owner of the boarding stable today. Well, I *did* talk to him but he didn't want to talk back. And one of his employees, Boomer, thought I was making accusations rather than just asking questions. It's like I have a talent for rubbing people the wrong way."

"You don't rub me the wrong way." The way he said it made my heart speed up. I wasn't sure how much of my reaction was due to pleasure and how much was panic. I envisioned a skier vainly trying to outrun the slope as it collapsed behind him.

I took a sip of beer in an attempt to mask my sudden, inner turmoil and I told myself not to draw parallels between my relationship with Kai and natural disasters.

"I certainly managed to ruffle Detective Boyle's feathers." As soon as I said the words I regretted them. What would possess me to bring Boyle into the conversation?

"Grace—"

I held up a hand and said, "Sorry, I forgot. It's Tammy, right?" The comment came out a bit more caustic than I'd intended.

Kai leaned back to regard me with narrowed eyes.

"Are you trying to prove that you *can* rub me the wrong way, or just using sarcasm as a smoke screen?"

I shrugged. "I'm also adept at jumping to the wrong conclusion and the silent treatment."

"Wow," he said in an unenthusiastic monotone. "The total package."

"Now look who's being sarcastic."

"You shouldn't dish out what you can't take."

I batted my eyelashes at him and, in a breathy drawl, said, "Why, Mr. Duncan, are you flirtin' with me?"

"Yes."

That shut me up.

"What's going on with you, Grace?"

What could I say? *I'm too immature to process grown-up feelings so I'm acting like a ten-year-old?*

"I'm sorry. Can we go back to when I was rubbing *other* people the wrong way?"

He held my gaze, letting the seconds creep past before

finally saying, "Lucky for you, I have a weakness for petite brunettes with ESP."

"Hey! I'm almost five foot three—that's solidly average."

"Five foot three, huh?"

I sat up a little straighter and said, "Let's get back to the folks at R-n-R." I could understand Boomer's reaction to my questions, but I'd worded them more carefully with Mr. Parnell.

When I told Kai this, he said, "Usually, if someone acts guilty it's because they are."

"You think Parnell could be involved in Heart's disappearance?"

"I didn't say that. He might have simply been too busy to talk or, as we've discussed, been rubbed the wrong way."

He smiled as he said it, so I wasn't really worried he'd hold my earlier lapse into snarky sarcasm—snarcasm?—against me.

"Still, it's worth looking into," he said. "I can check the place out, off the record."

Kai knew how I felt about him digging on my behalf. Before I could protest the idea, he asked, "What do the animals think of him?"

"I haven't asked." Knowing Kai would press me for clarification, I continued, "I don't always get a reliable answer."

"Why not?"

"Asking an animal's opinion on a human is tricky. Not only is the answer subjective, just as it is with other people, but it can be very skewed."

"Give me an example."

"Take Dusty," I said, talking about Kai's sweet, independent cat. "He loves you. He thinks you are the greatest guy in the world."

"You saying I'm not?"

"That was a bad example," I admitted. "But let's go with it for a minute and suppose you weren't really such a great guy. Not in an overt way. Animals tend to pick up on people who are totally psycho. But let's say you were a bank robber or had a gambling problem or something."

"As long as I keep giving him tuna," Kai said, "he'll tell everyone I'm awesome."

"Right. The opposite can be true, too. I've met animals who disliked people because of the way they spoke or laughed."

"Makes sense."

"I've gotten better at asking for specifics, but even then, I end up with less-than-useful information. Details about how a person sleeps, or how comfortable their lap is, that sort of thing."

"You're right, that's not very helpful. I'll see what I can find out about R-n-R and Parnell and let you know."

I nodded. If he didn't think it would be an issue with work, I wouldn't protest.

We finished up and headed outside into the balmy evening, then wandered toward Bluebell.

Many of the cruisers had closed their hoods and headed off. The vacant spots had been filled by the folding chairs of those who decided to stay awhile.

We reached Bluebell and I asked, "So, any more surprises tonight?"

"I don't know." He inserted the key into the passenger-door lock and paused to look down at me. "What did you have in mind?"

His pupils had dilated the way a cat's do when it's ready to pounce. Awareness flooded over me in a hot wave. Absurdly, a line from *Top Gun* popped into my head: *Take me to bed or lose me forever.* I didn't say it out loud, but that didn't seem to matter.

Kai leaned close to murmur something in my ear just as a nearby engine growled to life.

Startled, I glanced toward the sound. That was when I saw it. The sedan.

It drifted along Atlantic Boulevard like a shark coasting on a current searching for prey. Whatever Kai had started to say was lost. I straightened and stepped to the side.

"That's it." I pointed. "That's the car that was following me."

Kai's head snapped around and a heartbeat later, he was sprinting toward the street.

I rushed after him. The sedan didn't gun its engine and roar away with squealing tires; it just sailed past and melted into the flow of traffic. Before Kai reached the sidewalk, it was gone.

He was still starring after it when I reached his side. Suddenly, I felt foolish.

Maybe it hadn't been the same car after all.

Kai had already pressed his phone to his ear when I turned to tell him so. Even with the music and street noise I could hear him giving the license plate number to someone.

He finished the call and looked at me.

"What is it?"

"I don't know, maybe I was wrong." I didn't want him to get into trouble, especially if I was just being paranoid.

"What makes you say that?"

"If it'd been the same car, wouldn't whoever's driving have sped off when we spotted them?"

Frowning, Kai looked back to where the car had disappeared from view. "Not necessarily." He turned back to me and said, "Come on, we'll talk in your car."

Once we'd settled into Bluebell, he asked, "What was it about the car that made you think it was the one following you earlier? Don't think about it, just tell me the first thing that comes to mind."

"The dust, I guess. I mean, it's hard to be sure, but the sides looked dusty."

"Like Bluebell was."

"Well, yeah," I said, though I hadn't made that connection.

"Why would someone be following you?"

"I don't know. It has to be connected with Heart's disappearance, though."

"Because the delivery driver was followed?"

I nodded. "I don't know the details yet, but Hunter made it sound significant. Maybe the guys following me are looking for Heart, too."

"Why?"

"I'm guessing it has something to do with Tony's murder."

Kai seemed to consider that, then started Bluebell's engine and drove out of the parking lot back toward Third Street.

"There's no way anyone could have known where we were going tonight, which means they followed us from your place."

"But I lost them earlier, while we were on the phone," I reminded him. "I did the around-the-block-circle thing."

"Then you either have more than one tail or they know where you live."

A disturbing thought.

Rather than taking the direct route to the condo, Kai turned into a neighborhood with a lot of twisting roads.

I kept watching for headlights, but none appeared behind us.

We pulled into the condo's parking lot and Kai walked me inside.

"I didn't see your sister's car. Do you think she'll be back soon?"

"Doubtful."

He looked around, almost as if checking for an intruder.

"The coast is clear," I told him. "Moss would have let me know otherwise." My dog had heard us come in but was being lazy and was content to stay on the couch with his kitten.

"I'm going to take a drive and look around," Kai said. "See if I can figure out where they've been watching from. Keep the door locked, I'll be back soon."

Kai left and I turned the dead bolt with a sigh.

"Well, isn't this great." We'd gone from *Top Gun* to *Mission: Impossible* in twenty minutes.

The double entendre of that thought made me want to bang my head against the door.

I shouldn't have said anything about the stupid sedan. In an attempt to stave off depression, I took my laptop to the couch and decided to spend the time looking up dark, four-door cars for sale. I was hoping to pair the body style of the car I'd seen to a make and model, but after scanning a half a dozen images, they started to blur together.

I scrolled to another image, and decided to amuse myself by channeling Jake, saying in a possible impersonation of the detective's Buffalo accent, "Yo, the car look like this?"

"Yep."

"How 'bout this?" I asked, bringing up another photo.

"Yes."

"This?"

I carried on like that for a minute and came to the conclusion that eyewitness testimony couldn't be trusted. Which made me worry Kai was on a wild-goose chase.

What if I wasn't being followed? I tried to think of where else I'd seen the car. Not just behind me, but driving past . . . just before I went in to see Pretty Girl. The car had driven by, dark windows, dusty side panels—it hadn't registered at the time, but I was sure it was the same car.

A *ding* from my laptop told me I had new mail in my in-box. I closed out the sedan search and opened my e-mail.

I deleted the spam offering "Cheap Viagra or Cialis now!" But saw the latest two e-mails were from Jasmine.

The first supplied me with a link to a page on the LaPointe website.

I clicked it and was treated to a viewing of the commercial starring Jasmine, Heart, and a blond model driving an antique sports car.

Music dipped and swelled as the scenes cut back and forth from car to horse, highlighting the curve of the car's gleaming fender then the regal arch of Heart's neck. I got that they were drawing a parallel between the beauty and power of the horse and car, and the strength of the women commanding both, but wasn't sure what any of it had to do with selling jewelry.

I watched the video a few more times, with near equal admiration for the car and the horse, then moved on to the second e-mail from Jasmine.

In it was the message "Hope these help" from Jasmine along with an attached file that contained the photos I'd asked for.

"That was fast," I mused.

More out of curiosity than any real hope of finding something useful, I scrolled through the photographs. There were hundreds of them. All original and unretouched versions.

I came to the photo of Heart and Jasmine and fetched the magazine to compare original to the final image. Playing an impromptu "what's different?" game.

Hey, might as well keep killing time, right?

In the advertisement, I noticed that a small blemish on her cheek had been removed and her skin smoothed. A stray lock of hair blowing in an awkward position near her lip had been erased, and fullness had been added to her hair.

Suddenly, I understood why looking at Emma's fashion magazines made me feel self-conscious.

Kai called as I was frowning at the photo.

"I'm walking up your stairs."

"On my way." I set the laptop aside and I reached the front door just as he knocked.

"Any luck?" I asked, opening the door to let him in.

"No."

I looked up at him, wanting to say . . . something.

"What?" he asked.

But I wasn't sure I knew.

"Come on, Grace, talk to me. Tell me what you're thinking."

I was thinking I was sorry he'd spent his night off driving around looking for a phantom sedan. I was thinking how nice his shoulders and biceps looked with his armed crossed.

Most of all, I was thinking I wanted him to kiss me.

My phone rang. I'd forgotten I was still holding it, and the sudden noise made me jump. I glanced down at the screen, frowning when I saw the call was blocked.

"Hello?"

"You're being followed."

"Who is this?" I asked, though I thought I knew.

"Just watch your back, sweetness."

"Logan?"

But he'd hung up.

Kai was staring at me, clearly waiting for an explanation. Unfortunately, I didn't have one.

"Did I just hear the name *Logan*?" he asked with maybe a little too much control.

I nodded. My lingering surprise prevented me from doing much more.

"What did he say?" Kai asked.

"He told me to watch my back. That I was being followed."

"You're sure it was him?"

I nodded. "He calls me sweetness."

"I see."

Okay, that was obviously the wrong thing to say.

"Not that I like it—I don't," I rushed to explain. "But that's how I knew who it was."

"Right."

"Well," I said, desperate to find another angle to the topic, "at least we know Logan's not the one following me."

"Actually, it seems he is."

"Um . . ." I didn't know what to say to that. Kai seemed to expect me to say something, but only one thought kept circling through my head.

If I ever saw Logan again, I was going to turn him into a real ghost.

Needless to say, the date ended soon after that with Kai cautioning me to keep the door locked and bidding me a cool good night.

CHAPTER 10

I moped into the kitchen. The digital clock on the stove read a few minutes after nine thirty. Pathetic.

Emma had left a note in the usual spot. I scowled when I read it.

Looking forward to your walk of shame! xo E

My sister had nurtured high hopes for my date. But there would be no "walk of shame" for me after being out all night.

Frustration made me crumple the note and toss it in the trash. Instead of making it in the bin, the balled-up piece of paper bounced off the rim and rolled over the floor.

Voodoo streaked into the kitchen from out of nowhere and pounced on it.

Ha!

The kitten's mind was a tangle of excitement over the appearance of a new toy. She batted the paper around, then abruptly abandoned it when she rediscovered another toy she'd knocked under the refrigerator.

I bent to steal the note back just in time to see the little yellow toy spin out of sight.

Gone! She let out a pitiful meow.

"Hang on, lunatic, I'll get it for you." I started to look for a wooden spoon or something to use to fish it out for her, but before I had a chance to find something suitable, Voodoo had rolled onto her back and was having a great time reaching and swatting under the fridge. I left her to her kitty fun.

There were probably a legion of toys under there by now.

Too restless to sleep, but not ready to closely examine Logan's call and Kai's obvious and understandable reaction to it, I decided to get ready for bed then continue my perusal of the photos Jasmine had e-mailed.

I paused when I came to the studio shots. It was weird to see Jasmine standing in the same position as the photos taken outside, her hand raised to touch an imaginary horse.

Visible in the background was a lighting pole, some sort of gray fabric, and even a beefy dude standing to one side. I looked at the magazine again and could see how they'd layered one image over the other, superimposing the real jewels over the fake and adding lens flares and sparkles to create something more perfect and beautiful than could be possible in reality.

"I will never believe what I see in a magazine advertisement again," I told Moss, who was stretched out on the couch beside me.

Finally, I came across a series of photos of Heart and searched the images for any identifying features. Some Friesians had white stars on their foreheads, but as Jasmine had said, Heart was solid black. The high resolution made it so I could zoom in and out of each photo, but, even so, I couldn't find any unique scars or other markings. I decided to transfer a couple of images to my phone anyway.

At least I wouldn't have to keep showing people the magazine, which put much more emphasis on Jasmine and the LaPointe jewels than the horse. I also had a much clearer mental image of Heart to use with any animals I came across.

With a sigh I closed my laptop and called it a night.

• • •

I should have gotten out of bed when my eyes inexplicably sprung open at four a.m.; instead, I told myself it was too early and went back to sleep.

Never a good idea. Oversleeping makes me a groggy mess.

Morning brain fog has always been an issue for me but that day, it was worse than usual. My eyelids felt twice their normal size and I stumbled, almost clipping the door frame with my shoulder as I headed to the bathroom.

My mind was so lethargic, it took me a minute to lock on to Moss's and Voodoo's locations and even longer to discern whether they needed to be tended to. Both were napping on the couch.

I soaked a washcloth with cold water and scrubbed my face, hoping that would scour the sleep from my brain.

"Coffee?" Emma asked from the door to my bathroom. She held up a mug—my favorite oversized one with I LIKE BIG MUTTS AND I CANNOT LIE printed on it.

I grunted an affirmative and she set the mug on the counter.

"I already took the fluff-mutt out for a jog. You up for some training?" she asked.

I lifted the mug, took a swig of coffee, and nodded. "Sure."

She studied me with her astute Emma-eye, and I waited for her to ask me about my big date. Instead she said, "I'll meet you downstairs in ten minutes."

My sister had converted a section of her garage into a martial arts dojo. Mostly, she trained in aikido, occasionally branching out into other disciplines. She'd nagged me into participating when I first moved in with her. I was surprised to find I actually enjoyed it.

Among other things, the classes helped alleviate frustration, which was something I certainly needed that morning.

I finished my coffee, pulled on my white *gi* and tied my even more white belt around my waist.

Oh well, you had to start somewhere, right?

Slipping into a pair of flip-flops, I checked on Moss and Voodoo—both were still sleeping on the couch—and headed down to the dojo.

Emma wasn't wearing her *hakama*, the wide-legged pants worn by many traditional Japanese martial artists.

"Takeda Sensei's not coming today?" I asked.

Emma always dressed properly for the elderly instructor. So did I, for that matter.

"Next week," she said. "I thought we'd focus on footwork today, so I decided it would be better if you could see my feet."

Apparently, my sister was going to wait for me to bring up the topic of my obviously botched date with Kai. I didn't want to discuss it, knowing she'd tell me I was an idiot for pushing him away. And she'd be right.

Whatever. I had other things I wanted to talk about.

"What do you think?" I asked Emma as we sat on the tatami mat, going through a few stretches before our warm-up. "About Jasmine."

"If you're asking me if I think she killed Tony, my answer is no."

It hadn't been what I meant, but I went with it. "Maybe she had someone do it for her."

My sister shook her head. "I was there. I saw the look on Jasmine's face. She was beside herself." Emma sat with her legs outstretched then folded forward at the waist, touching her chest to her knees as she reached past her feet. She made the movement look easy.

"She could've been faking," I suggested, struggling to mimic my sister's flexibility—and failing.

"She wasn't," Emma answered, voice muffled by the fabric of her *gi* pants. Drawing in a deep breath she sat up and looked at me. "Trust me, I know people. It wasn't Jasmine."

I started to ask who else would have wanted Ortega dead when my sister swung her legs open and rolled her body forward into a split.

"You make me feel like a hippo flopping around next to a ballerina."

She chuckled. "Don't you remember *Fantasia*? The hippos *were* ballerinas."

"That's why it was called *Fan*tasia and not *Real*tasia." I pointed out. "What about Mary?" I asked, changing the subject back to potential murder suspects. "She probably hated Ortega. I would have if I'd have worked for him."

Emma, being my sister, followed my train of thought without a problem.

"It wasn't Mary."

"You never know," I insisted. "He could have been planning to fire her."

"Tony couldn't tie a necktie without her. He wasn't going to fire her."

"Maybe they were having an affair."

My sister stood, then gave me a flat look.

"Think about it," I said, warming to the idea. "Ortega gets engaged, brings Jasmine into Mary's territory, and she loses it. Takes him out."

"We're talking about people, not wolves," my sister said.

"A wolf would attack the invader, not its own pack member."

"Come on. Time to exercise something beside your mouth."

We trained for almost an hour. It felt good to let everything else go and get absorbed in the movement and technique until I took a breakfall a little too hard.

Breakfalls are a way of hitting the ground so as to *break* your *fall* when an opponent throws you.

I'd gotten the hang of it—mostly. But my arm was still healing from being wrenched to the side not long ago by someone who was trying to kill me.

"Shoulder?" Emma had noticed my wince.

"Yeah, it's okay. Still twinges sometimes."

The truth was, the repetitive, jarring falls were taking a toll.

Emma, ever perceptive, said, "Why don't we call it quits for today?"

As we walked together back to the condo I thought about

what Uncle Wiley had said and asked,. "How are you doing? I mean, none of us liked Tony, but . . ."

"That didn't mean I wanted to find his body." She finished the sentence for me.

"But you're okay. Nothing left unsaid or anything. No regrets?"

"No. I'm just glad he can't hurt anyone anymore."

"Don't let Detective Boyle hear you say that," I said as I followed her into the kitchen to grab a glass of water. "She'll show up with a pitchfork and mob of angry villagers."

"You think she's that bad?"

"Don't you?"

"Maybe."

"What happened last night?"

I shrugged then gave her the CliffsNotes version. "Everything was great until I saw that stupid car."

"And you're sure it was the same one?"

"The more I think about it, yeah. In fact"—I paused, remembering something else—"I think I saw it the first time I went to R-n-R. I was going really slow, trying to find the turnoff. All the other cars that came up behind me went around, except for a dark sedan."

"How did that ruin the date? You could have damsel-in-distressed him right into bed."

I gave her a look.

"What? It works. Trust me."

"It might have worked—until Logan called."

She blinked at me. "Come again."

"You heard me."

"Explain."

I did, though there wasn't much to say.

"Ookaaay."

"I didn't know what to do, Em. I mean, Kai is standing there looking at me like, 'Is that who I think it is?' so I told him it was. Then I totally messed up."

My sister waited.

"Kai asked me how I knew it was Logan, and I told him Logan calls me sweetness."

My sister has very expressive brown eyes. Right then, they were spread wide, clearly asking, *You did what?*

"I know. I tried to explain but I just made it worse. I didn't know what to say, so I shut up. After a couple of minutes, he left."

"Okay. Here's what you need to do—call him."

"And say what?"

"I'd start with 'I'm sorry.' Make it clear you're just as baffled by Logan's call as he is."

"Ugh." I propped my elbows on the counter and dropped my face into my hands. "I feel so incompetent. Why couldn't I think of the right thing to say?"

"Wouldn't hurt to throw that in, too. Tell him you didn't know what to say, and you're sorry." When I only grunted, my sister continued, "Here's how apologies work—the longer you take to say you're sorry to someone, the less likely they'll be to forgive you."

I straightened and faced my sister. "It's not that I don't want to apologize. I do. I'm just afraid I'll screw it up."

"Be sincere and it will be fine."

"There's always Moto-cop."

"Who?"

I told her about the gator-induced traffic jam and Moto-cop's offer to take me herping.

By the time I'd finished, Emma was laughing so hard she had to support herself with one arm on the counter.

"I figured out what he meant later," I said. "Herpetology—herp. If you go looking for amphibians and reptiles, you're herping."

"Please stop." Tears were running down her cheeks.

I shrugged. "I wouldn't mind going herping."

• • •

Knowing I'd be in an area with spotty cell coverage the rest of the morning, I tried to call Kai before I left to find Lily Earl. I'd spent a significant amount of time fretting over what I was going to say, so when I got his voice mail I stammered, "Um—hey, it's me. I . . . Call me back."

I hung up before I could start rambling and realized I'd completely forgotten to ask Kai to talk to Charlie about keeping an eye out while he was searching Ortega's computer for any info on Heart.

I looked back at my phone and grimaced. I couldn't call back and ask him for a favor. Not until we talked.

I called Jake instead.

He answered with his typical "Yo."

"Hey, Jake, how's it going?"

"What do you think?

"Okay, we'll skip the small talk. I suck at it anyway."

He snorted at that.

"I have a favor to ask."

"If it has anything to do with the Ortega case, the answer's no."

"It doesn't. Not really. I've been hired by his fiancée, Jasmine, to find his missing horse, Heart."

"Who?"

"Boyle hasn't told you about it?" I explained as quickly as I could.

"Okay, yeah, I remember hearing about that. I'll let Charlie know. Hope you find 'im."

I dropped my phone in my purse and headed out the door.

Before walking down the stairs, I took a moment to scan the parking lot and street for suspicious, dark sedans but saw none.

Nevertheless, I kept an eye out as I headed to find Lily Earl.

At a little past ten I pulled through the gates of The Oaks and saw immediately why Lily Earl would want to visit. The place was gorgeous.

At first, it was hard to tell the difference between the house and barn. Both structures were designed similarly in a nouveau Craftsman style with thick, angled columns supporting deep, open porches. Even the house's portico was mimicked by that on the stables. Ultimately, it was the vehicles and placement of fencing that gave it away.

I spotted a truck, not quite as big as a semi, but close, coupled to a massive horse trailer.

Parking, I walked over to it to determine if Lily Earl was nearby, but her cargo had either already been dropped off or was yet to be loaded because the stalls, all eight of them, were empty.

I scanned the vast property, wondering where the driver might be and decided the barn was my best bet.

I took two steps inside and froze.

"Whoa."

Without a doubt, I'd just entered one of the most luxurious stables I'd ever seen.

The lights lining the center aisle were housed in wrought-iron globes accented with real horseshoes.

R-n-R was a nice place. Clean and homey with that nice layer of dust you expect in a barn. There was no dust at The Oaks.

I glanced up in search of cobwebs and saw a cat dozing on a rafter. I smiled up at the cat. Maybe the two places weren't that different after all.

"Can I help you?"

A young woman, maybe a couple years my junior, stepped out of one of the stalls to my right. She wore riding breeches, boots, and a pale blue polo sweater. Her long auburn hair was secured in a braid that fell over one shoulder.

"I'm looking for Lily Earl," I said.

A smile lit her face, showcasing dimples.

"I imagine she's in the office flirting with my daddy. Come on, I'll take you."

We walked past several horses: a palomino, a lovely bay, and a chestnut.

No Friesians.

"Are these all walking horses?"

"That's all we have. My name's Bonnie, by the way."

"Grace."

"Nice to meet you. Here we go," she said, heading up a trio of steps leading to a door. "They're probably in the kitchen pretending to be more interested in coffee than one another."

She pushed the door open with a wink and called, "Daddy! Someone's here to see Lily Earl."

We walked into what looked more like a formal study in a manor house than an office attached to a barn.

Bonnie led me through to a kitchen bigger than many I'd seen on my recent house hunting adventures.

A man and woman stood on opposite sides of the kitchen island, each leaning on their elbows toward the other and cradling coffee cups in their hands.

The man straightened and turned toward us as we entered and I saw the second reason Lily Earl would be excited to visit The Oaks.

"Daddy, this is Grace. Grace, this is my father, Sean Breen."

"Mr. Breen," I offered my hand.

"Sean," he amended as we shook.

I turned my attention to Lily Earl, who looked at me with what seemed like equal parts curiosity and annoyance.

"Sorry to interrupt," I said. "I was hoping to ask Lily Earl a couple of questions about a horse she delivered to R-n-R stables about a week ago."

"The Friesian," she said and, seeing my surprise, added, "Hunter told me someone was asking. And it's the only horse I've delivered lately where something strange happened."

"Let's start with the something strange," I said.

"This sounds like a story that calls for coffee," Bonnie said and began making two more cups.

"Well," Lily Earl began, "right off, I noticed there was a car following behind me. Which isn't that unusual. People sometimes drive along with their horses. But when I stopped to gas up I noticed these two guys poking around the trailer. It was almost like they were trying to get inside. Of course, I asked them what they were up to and they claimed to be checking on a friend's horse. It's just . . . they weren't horse people."

"What do you mean?" I asked.

"You could just tell. When I walked up, one guy was making a comment about how filthy horses are. And he had a weird accent. Thick. I don't know—Greek, maybe."

"And the other guy?" I asked.

"He was just too"—she paused to summon the right word—"spiffy."

"Spiffy?" I repeated, trying to picture what she meant.

"Like he was wearing a suit?" Bonnie asked.

"Not a suit with a tie. A sports coat and slacks. But it was his shoes that I remember. They were shiny as a chrome bumper."

Shiny. I thought about what Minerva had said about the shiny bells. This could be a fit.

"Do you remember what kind of car they were driving?"

"It wasn't a truck or anything. Just a regular car. Dark. Black or dark blue, maybe."

The dark sedan?

"Was there anything else you remember about the men?"

"One of them had a couple tattoos, couldn't say what they were of, though. There was something else a little weird, not about the men."

I waited.

"Dr. Simon showed up just as Boomer was taking the horse into the stables. She seemed, I don't know, anxious to check him out."

Both Bonnie and Sean looked surprised at that.

"What?" I asked, glancing around the group.

"Dr. Simon, well, she sits a wee bit high on her horse."

"He means she's snooty," Bonnie translated.

"She doesn't do checkups," Lily Earl added. "Or get dirty."

"I thought you said she was a vet." Staying clean, especially in a rural area, would be a challenge.

"She doesn't act like one," Bonnie said.

"Struts around acting important, mostly," her father added.

I looked around at each of them in turn. Stop the presses. Could it be? Had I finally found a *clue*?

"Do you know where her office is? Does she have a practice?"

"As far as I know she works out of her home," Sean said.

"Do you have an address?"

"Just a phone number. She only just moved here a couple of months ago," Sean said, pulling a phone out of his breast pocket. He found the number and recited it to me. "Right now, the closest cell tower's down. I'm not sure you'll reach her."

"Boomer would know her address," Lily Earl said.

Boomer again.

Dang it, it was looking like I was going to make another attempt to talk to the man.

"Do you have Boomer's number?" I remembered seeing it on the sign advertising eggs, but hadn't written it down.

Sean found it and gave it to me, then said, "It's his home number. He's there most evenings."

"You could just go by," Bonnie suggested. "He lives right next to R-n-R."

"Hunter told me you work for the Friesian's owner?" Lily Earl asked.

"Yes, she's offering a reward for Heart's return."

"Heart?"

"The horse." I felt a flutter of apprehension. Was I tracking the wrong Friesian? "Didn't you see his name when you made the delivery?"

"The paperwork only lists their registered name."

I did a mental head-slap. "Right, and a lot of horses are called something else. Nicknames."

She nodded. "I can't exactly ask them to tell me, can I?"

"No, that would be crazy."

I relaxed and made a mental note to ask Jasmine for Heart's registered name, which was something I should have already thought to do. "Actually, do you still have that paperwork?" This could be what I needed to get Boyle to take the case seriously.

"I might still have my copy in the truck. What day did you say it was?"

"I'm not really sure. Probably around a week ago."

She looked thoughtful. "I turn in my paperwork at the end of each month, so I should have it."

Bonnie's interest in the mystery seemed to have swayed Lily Earl to help and we all walked out to her vehicle together.

"This is an impressive setup," I told her as she went through her paperwork.

"Thanks." Lily Earl smiled. "She's almost paid for."

Her smile faltered and she started flipping through the papers again. "This is weird. I don't have anything about a Friesian anywhere. The paperwork is missing."

Lily Earl promised to try to get a copy of the missing paperwork but didn't seem optimistic. Her contractor was old-school and didn't use computers, which meant there was only one paper copy floating around somewhere.

It was still early and I had time to go to R-n-R to try to catch Boomer and make nice. Before turning to leave I asked, "You haven't seen a brown and white goat wandering around loose by any chance, have you?"

"Actually, yes."

"Really? When?"

"Last week. On the road between here and R-n-R. Just walking right along the side of the road. I was going too fast to stop without injuring the horses but I did turn off and circle around. By the time I made it back, she was gone."

She? "You knew it was Nelly?"

Lily Earl nodded. "I stopped in at R-n-R and told Boomer. He lives pretty close by, so he said he'd look. I guess they still haven't found her?"

"Not yet."

"I'll keep an eye out, then. For the Friesian, too."

I thanked her, gave her a business card, and headed to Bluebell. I'd just opened the door when Bonnie came running from the barn.

"My dad found Dr. Simon's address." She held out piece of notepaper. "It's not far."

She gave me directions that seemed simple enough, not that I'd been having much luck lately in that department.

I handed Bonnie one of my cards. "If you think of something that might help."

"I'll call. I hope you find him."

I nodded a thank-you, climbed into Bluebell, and headed down the drive.

Was it terrible to admit I was relieved I wouldn't have to talk to Boomer to get the vet's address?

Oh well.

Actually, I kind of liked the guy. Thinking of the I DO MY OWN STUNTS bumper sticker made me smile. But I needed to save my limited people-pleasing skills for my talk with Kai and helping with the interview at Happy Asses.

I paused before turning onto the road and checked my phone, both to see if any calls had come through and to determine if I had a signal. No to both, which meant I would have to track Dr. Simon down in person if I wanted to ask her about Heart.

A quick check of the clock told me it I had a little over half an hour before having to head to Happy Asses, so I followed the directions Bonnie had given me. As I made the final turn into the neighborhood, I passed a parcel of land marked with a FOR SALE sign. I recognized the name on the sign. Farmstead Properties. Parnell had one of their brochures on his desk.

Was that the reason he'd brushed me off? If he was looking to sell, he'd want to avoid any scandals.

No one had mentioned R-n-R being on the market, but I hadn't asked.

The question would have to wait because, a moment later, I found myself in front of Dr. Simon's house. The driveway was empty, but I wasn't completely discouraged. Hoping her car was in the garage, I climbed out of Bluebell and started toward the house.

I hadn't made it more than a few steps before someone said, "If you're looking for the doc, she ain't home."

I turned to see a small, elderly woman standing on the opposite side of a hedge of rosebushes that lined the drive. She wore a vibrant orange University of Florida sweatshirt and matching pants. Her visor, too, displayed the school's logo—a fierce alligator, mouth open to display a profusion of teeth.

I wondered if the woman had ever been herping. The thought produced an involuntary chuckle.

The woman narrowed her eyes.

Apparently, laughing while looking at someone's clothing is not the best icebreaker.

For once, I knew what to say.

"Go, Gators."

Her wrinkled cheeks gathered up in a smile. "Go, Gators," she responded.

And just like that, we were comrades.

"You know Dr. Simon?" I asked.

"I do," said Gator Lady.

"Do you know if she keeps regular hours?" The woman seemed the type who kept her eye on things like that.

"She leaves in the morning, then sorta comes and goes, you know. The doc's real busy."

Which meant I'd have to rely on luck if I wanted to catch her either at home or on the phone.

I looked back at the house, wondering if I could leave her a note.

"I hate to see her go," the older woman said. "But, family's family."

"Go?" I glanced at Gator Lady. "What do you mean?"

"She's moving back home. Said her momma was having health problems."

"But didn't she just move in not long ago?"

"Rented the place first part of September. Paid six months in advance."

"Are you the landlady?"

"You think I'd let that *Loropetalum* get that leggy?" She pointed at a shrub with burgundy-purple leaves and several long, spindly shoots sprouting in all directions.

I wasn't much of a gardener, but shook my head in solidarity anyway. Gator Lady pointed out another problem planting—something even less pronounceable—and before she could get too carried away with the critique, I pointed to her roses.

"I just noticed all these are orange. And you have hydrangeas, too." They weren't blooming this late, but the large, serrated leaves made the bush easy to identify. "I'm guessing they're blue, to go with the orange roses?"

"What other color would they be?"

We shared a laugh, and I waved good-bye to my new friend, wishing everyone was so easy to connect with.

Football, go figure.

• • •

The breezy morning had settled into a beautiful, sunny afternoon. The only clouds in the sky were wispy confections of white fluff which, thankfully, carried no threat of rain. Humidity was low, the temperature mild. I was no expert on filming news spots but conditions seemed to be pretty optimal.

Someone had decorated by stacking bales of hay here and there. In the field between the gazebo and the donkey pen, a life-sized scarecrow, complete with overalls and a floppy, felt hat sprouted from the ground. At its base was a hand-painted sign welcoming visitors to the pumpkin patch. Two upright bundles of multicolored corn stood on either side and pumpkins dotted the grass.

"Grace!"

I turned toward the excited voice and smiled at the pretty teenage girl jogging toward me. Her high ponytail swung in tempo with her steps. She had dyed the ends of her dark hair a deep teal. The color flashed like a peacock feather in the bright sun.

"Hey, Brooke. A pumpkin patch, huh?"

"Isn't it cool?"

"Sure is."

"We give the cats pumpkins to play with every year around this time and Emma thought it would be cool to make it so people could come pick their own pumpkins and feed 'em them themselves."

"Feed who?"

"The cats. Well, not all of them. Samson, he's one of our caracals, doesn't like them. And they don't really eat the pumpkins."

"More like claw and shred?"

"Pretty much. They love it! We'll be doing a drawing for

each cat, then the winner gets to come behind the fence with us."

"Not in the enclosures," I said, alarmed at the thought.

"No, just behind the people fence. Emma thought it would be a good way to bring in new visitors. If you don't win the drawing you get to keep the pumpkin anyway. And there will be other stuff going on. Ozeal will have Jack-Jack out for the kids to pet and take pictures with."

Jack-Jack was an adorable mini-donkey. He was smart, friendly, and, aside from a few specific issues, well behaved.

Thinking of him made me wander to the fence.

The little donkey trotted over when he saw me, barking out a shrill, excited bray.

"What's he saying?" Brooke asked me.

In a moment of insanity, I'd decided to tell Brooke the truth about my ability. So far, I hadn't regretted it—much.

"You don't have to be telepathic to know," I told her.

"Come on, Grace."

I'd promised Brooke I would translate on occasion. In return, she'd promised not to tell anyone about my ability or talk about it in front of people.

"He wants his Skittles."

Skittles! Jack-Jack confirmed as I pulled the small packet of candies out of my back pocket. Soon, the rest of the herd had gathered at the fence, all asking for their share. When all the treats had been doled out, Jack-Jack made a soft sound.

Grace! My name was infused with snapshots and thoughts blending together. A request to play a game interwoven with gratitude and suffused with a handful of Skittles.

"Maybe in a little bit, buddy. I have to help with these shenanigans first," I said, giving his soft velvety nose a quick rub.

"What?" Brooke asked.

"He wants to play tag."

"Tag?"

"I'll show you later." I was far too conscious of the fact of a news crew's presence to keep discussing Jack-Jack's request.

"So," I said changing the subject, "how's Josiah?"

"Good. Mr. Reedy stays with him a lot."

"Oh?" I asked, thinking of Reedy's five pit bulls. "Who takes care of his dogs?"

"They stay with Josiah, too. In fact, one of them, Scarlett, even gets to sleep in the bed. She pretty much stays with him all the time."

I remembered the sweet, even-tempered dog.

"His doctor says it helps to have an animal to take care of. Keeps him occupied and, you know, more focused."

I did know. Josiah's head injury had affected his grip on reality. Having someone like Reedy, grumpy old coot that he was, keeping track of Josiah's meds was essential. A therapy dog was icing on the cake.

"How's your mom doing?" I asked Brooke.

"Better. She decided to go back to rehab, so I'm staying with my dad."

We rarely talked about her father. The less I knew about the crime boss's life, the better. But I couldn't help but ask, "And Logan?"

She gave me an elaborate shrug. "I haven't seen him."

"Really?"

Her eyes went wide with innocence. "What? I haven't."

I knew Brooke viewed Logan as her guardian angel and would never think otherwise. Guardian? Yes. Angel? Not in a million years.

"Even if I had seen Logan," she said, "it's not like the cops could catch him anyway."

I nodded, conceding the point. You don't earn a nickname like the Ghost without good reason.

"He called me last night."

"Shut up. Seriously?"

"Seriously."

"What did he want?"

I debated how much to tell her, then decided she might actually be able to shed some light on the situation. After all, Logan worked for Brooke's father—that had to give her some insight.

"He warned me to watch my back."

"For what?"

"He didn't say. Any idea why he would call and warn me?"

"No, I mean, except—"

I waited.

She looked away, chewing her lip as she thought.

"I think," she said, still not looking at me, "maybe he feels kind of bad about what happened. You know, because he didn't tell you everything when you were looking for me, it put all of us in danger."

"So he's making up for keeping me in the dark before by giving me vague warnings now?"

"I don't know. I guess."

"Well, you can tell him when you *don't* see him again, I said, thanks, but no thanks. He can take his mysterious phone calls and . . ."

I trailed off when I realized Brooke had stopped listening. Her attention had become focused on something over my left shoulder.

Turning to follow her gaze, I discovered the subject of her fixation. A boy, maybe a little older than Brooke, had emerged from the barn. He was a tall, broad-shouldered kid with a mop of dark curls. Even from this distance, I could guess he was related to Ozeal.

"Friend of yours?" I asked.

At my words, Brooke yanked her gaze away from the boy. A flush crept up her neck to flood her cheeks. She seemed self-conscious and almost shy—completely unlike the tough, streetwise kid I'd met not long ago.

The boy saw us and came over.

"You're Grace?" he asked, after flashing a broad smile at Brooke.

"I am."

"This is Cody. Ozeal's his aunt," Brooke said, still blushing prettily.

"Do you need help with the hay?" he asked me.

"Hay?" I had no idea what he was talking about.

"Oh my God," Brooke said. "I totally forgot. Emma

wanted to see if you had room in the back of your car for a few bales of hay."

"For . . . ?"

She shrugged. "Decoration, I guess."

I didn't ask what my sister planned to festoon with hay bales, just handed Brooke the keys to Bluebell. I'd let the kids deal with finding enough room in the catchall that was the cargo area for "a few" bales of hay.

Turning to the main part of the rescue facility, I saw Ozeal, Emma, and a woman I assumed to be the reporter Anita Margulies approach from the direction of the commissary. Trailing behind them was a rotund, bearded man walking next to Hugh. Emma gestured a couple of times, pointing out this and that. The group stopped near the cougar cages.

The reporter, dressed in a crisp, royal blue button-down shirt and navy slacks, conferred with her cameraman. They nodded and positioned Ozeal with her back to the cougar enclosure.

Emma saw me watching and waved me over.

The man hoisted the camera onto a shoulder and as I neared the group, I heard Anita Margulies say, "Three. Two. One. Ozeal, can you tell us more about your plans for the new tiger exhibit?"

"Well, as you can see behind me, the cougars are currently living in a much smaller enclosure."

I sent a mental greeting to the cougars who had spotted me and come to the front of their cage to say hello.

"We'd like to move the cougars over to where Boris, our tiger, is now," Ozeal continued. "But to do that, we'll have to make significant changes to the fencing."

An understatement, I thought. Cougars climbed. Tigers didn't. Not very well at least. In order to contain the smaller, more agile cats, the large area would need to be completely enclosed.

"There are a few varieties of steel netting available, but, as you can imagine, it's a bit expensive."

"And the tiger, Boris, where would he go?" the reporter asked.

"Into a brand-new enclosure." Ozeal smiled broadly and

I noticed her lips were tinted with a hint of color. Someone had talked the practical, no-frills woman into wearing makeup.

I cut a sidelong glance to my sister. Emma was beaming with the overzealous pride of a stage mom as she watched the interview.

"There's a spring-fed pond located on the property just north of us." Ozeal motioned to her right. "It would be a perfect place for a tiger."

Ozeal continued to lay out her plans for Boris's new home. It sounded like a total tigertopia. Suddenly, I understood why she needed the publicity. Procuring the land, building the enclosure . . . it would cost a small fortune.

Not that Boris didn't deserve it.

They finished up the interview and my sister turned to me. "Grace, this is Anita Margulies."

I nodded a hello to Ozeal then shook the reporter's hand before being introduced to her bearded cameraman, Phil.

"So you're Emma's sister. It's nice to meet you." The woman's smile was bright and wide but there was a glint to her eyes that made me wary. "We're ready to get some shots of just Hugh and the tiger in the enclosure interacting. Can you play-fight with him like you can with a puppy?"

I shook my head. "Not a good idea."

"No?" The reporter glanced at me then pouted at Hugh. I noticed her hand was still on his arm. "You're sure?"

I gave Hugh a pointed look. "Given your history with Boris."

"History? What history?"

Hugh flashed her a carefree smile. "Boris got a little frisky with me a few weeks ago. It wasn't a big deal."

I felt my brows creep up to my hairline. *Frisky* wouldn't have been the word I'd use to describe what had happened.

I didn't bother to contradict him, just shook my head and said very calmly, "Sorry. No play-fighting. Boris is very sweet and incredibly well socialized. But he's still a tiger, not a tomcat."

"Grace—" Emma tried to interject, but I kept talking.

"Boris has four-inch claws. One swipe, even an unintentional one, could cause real damage. It's not worth the risk."

Hugh raised his hands and spoke in a tone I'd heard him use once on an angry porcupine. "I agree with you, Grace. Wrestling around with Boris isn't safe."

I felt my shoulders relax a bit.

Truthfully, I didn't know if I could stop a tiger in full-on attack mode and I didn't want to find out. If something upset the big cat, it would come down to a battle of wills, which, when prepared, I usually won. Stubbornness has *some* perks.

With Boris, the link to the wild was latent, but it was there— shimmering just under the surface, something I'd learned first-hand. The good thing about my previous brush with Boris's inner beast: I wouldn't be surprised by its ferocity.

Still, I was going to have to bring my A game to keep us both safe.

"Okay," I said, looking around the group. "Let's get started."

"Wait!" Brooke, who had clearly finished loading hay bales into Bluebell, jogged to a stop next to me and reached into her back pocket. "I made it for Boris last night. Is it okay if he wears it?"

She looked from Ozeal to me. I blinked at the spangled strap of leather. Ozeal gave a "fine by me" half shrug.

"Wow," I said, taking the collar from Brooke "I didn't know they still made Bedazzlers."

"Isn't it pretty?" She smiled proudly at her creation. "I used one of my old belts. It already had the studs on it but I added the rhinestones."

"It's perfect," Emma assured her.

"You've worn this?" I asked.

"Grace—" Emma made my name into a gentle reprimand for what she probably assumed was going to be an insult to Brooke's fashion sense. Please. Like I was a qualified judge?

"It's a good thing." I waved off my sister's rebuke. "Boris loves Brooke. Putting something on him that smells like her will put him at ease."

I'd come to realize one of the reasons Boris liked me so

much was not so much for my ability to communicate with him, but that my dark hair and light eyes reminded him of his favorite human, Brooke.

The girl beamed. "So, you think he'll like it?"

"I do." I turned back to the rest of the group. "Just let me know when Hugh's ready. I'll take care of Boris. Brooke, you can help me." Hugh, Ozeal, and the news crew started to walk away, but I touched my sister's arm, holding her back.

I stepped away from Brooke and said quietly, "I'm not sure about this woman, Em. She's . . . shifty."

"She's a reporter, of course she's shifty."

"And did you see how touchy-feely she was with Hugh?"

My sister rolled her eyes. "He's the reason she wanted to do the piece, remember?"

I did. "Just make sure if anything weird happens, you take out the cameraman."

"Seriously? There's a chance of that?"

"Probably not. But the only thing worse than one of us getting mauled would be to have it immortalized on film to be played over and over on the news."

She stared at me, brows raised.

"I mean it, Emma."

"Okay. I'll take out the cameraman if anything happens."

I nodded and turned back to Brooke.

We headed through a small gate and around to the path that ran along the perimeter fence. "You think Boris will like his collar because it smells like me?"

"Yep," I told her as we walked toward the long cement-block building attached to the rear of the tiger's enclosure. "I just hope he doesn't like it too much."

"What do you mean?"

"You know how dogs chew up their owner's shoes and stuff?"

"Yeah."

"Well, usually they do that because shoes, socks, or whatever smell like a person they love and chewing on it envelops them in that person's scent, which makes them happy."

"So you think he'll eat his collar?"

"Only one way to find out, kid."

I pushed open the metal door to the tiger house. Bright afternoon sunlight streamed through the high, narrow windows and cast a rectangular spotlight on the superstar of that day's production.

The light made every exquisite detail of the cat's sinewy body stand out in high relief. He twisted his head around to look at us. The black around his golden green eyes gleamed, his pupils, despite the sun, enlarged slightly when he saw us, then contracted again.

With a happy, moaning growl, Boris rolled to his feet and stepped to the interior cage door.

He let out a few chuffs and pressed his forehead against the chain-link.

Pet.

I scratched him between the ears. As soon as we made contact, his thoughts streamed into my head.

More.

"Scoot back, buddy, I need some room," I told him as I pushed on the interior gate. At the same time, I mentally urged him to back up.

Boris obliged, and I slipped inside.

He bumped his head against my hip and slid his face along the crease of my jeans. The action both marked me as his and scratched a spot just past his whiskers.

As I went to fasten the collar around his neck, light caught the facets of the rhinestones and bounced off the walls in hundreds of tiny rainbows.

Boris watched the dancing lights for a moment with interest then nuzzled at my hand.

Pet.

I rubbed his ears and under his chin slowly, taking extra time to assess his mood and add a nice layer of good vibrations of my own.

"What's he saying?" Brooke asked.

"Not much, just happy to get scratched in all the right spots." I glanced over at her. "See if Hugh's ready, then come back and open the door."

She nodded and left. I took the opportunity to pull in a couple of deep breaths and push any negative feelings out of my head.

By the time Brooke returned, I was as calm and centered as I was going to get.

The guillotine door leading to the exterior enclosure operated on a pulley system. I signaled to Brooke that I was ready and she grabbed the rope and hoisted the door. The opening was about a three-by-three-foot square, plenty of space for a tiger, but a tiger and a person was a little tricky.

Boris and I both tried to go through at the same time and I got a little squished against the side in the process.

With a grunt, I stumbled through the opening like a wounded water buffalo, and tried not to think about the camera pointed in our direction.

Hugh, looking handsome and relaxed, sat on the thick log that lay across the center of the enclosure. Boris recognized him instantly.

Doc! He let out a chuff of happiness and greeted Hugh with a good-natured head-butt. Then, with a bit of encouragement from me, he turned and plopped down at Hugh's feet.

I gave Boris a pat and stepped back so I was out of the camera's frame.

In situations like this, I try to keep my mind set firmly in ready-for-anything mode.

Unfortunately, some things can't be planned for.

I'd been focusing on keeping the link open to Boris, and gently poured happy, friendly images and emotions into his mind, all the while halfway listening to the interview.

Hugh talked about how much tigers, and Boris in particular, liked water and how much the cat would love a pond large enough to swim in.

Boris, for his part, was acting like a ham. He rubbed his face on Hugh's knees and made happy-tiger sounds.

"What the hell?" Hugh's words prompted me to follow his gaze. I saw two sheriff's deputies approaching my sister. Taking point in front of the two men was Detective Boyle.

The camera swung around to capture the scene.

"Emma Olivia Wilde." Boyle's voice was loud and authoritative. "You're under arrest for the murder of Anthony Ortega."

Handcuffs snapped onto my sister's wrists and Boyle, still with her ridiculous escort, turned my sister and led her away.

Anita Margulies went into attack mode in the blink of an eye. She started asking questions about Ortega.

Understanding hit me when she jammed a microphone toward my sister and asked, "Was the murder retribution for the way he treated you? Or was it self-defense?"

This was a setup. A surge of outrage exploded through me and kept on going—right into Boris.

I wasn't physically touching the tiger but he reacted anyway. Before I could rein in my temper, the tiger belted out a snarl and shot to his feet. The target of his sudden, confusing rage was, of course, Hugh.

Without thinking, I grabbed the only part of the tiger I could—his tail.

I can promise you this: The warning you've heard about tigers and tails is completely, 100 percent legitimate.

Boris whirled on me, jerking his tail out of my hands as he spun.

Two things saved my life.

One—in the milliseconds that passed between realizing we'd been set up and facing vivisection via tiger, my emotions bounced all over the place. Fury, dread, disbelief, confusion . . .

Thanks to our mental connection, I'd brought Boris along for the ride and that left him disoriented.

But what really saved my bacon was this fact: I am a klutz.

The irony that I ended up being named Grace is a cosmic joke.

Half a second after losing my grip on Boris's tail, I stumble-stepped back, tripped, and landed with a splash in his little pool.

The shock of the cold water was enough to short-circuit all other emotions. Abruptly, I wasn't angry or frightened or anything. My mind was utterly blank.

Luckily, Boris's love of water filled the void with a single idea.

Play!

A moment later, he leapt into the water. Siberian tigers are the world's largest cat, weighing well over six hundred pounds. Even with the water as a buffer, I felt it when he landed on me.

I would have panicked, if the tiger suddenly standing on my chest hadn't been so delighted with our game.

His joy and excitement fluttered through me and, despite being trapped underwater, I felt my lips stretch into a smile.

All this happened in less than five seconds, but I was still running out of time.

Not just because I couldn't breathe—though that was a concern—but because the people who were no doubt watching didn't know Boris wanted to play, not kill.

To ward off any aggressive action from the humans, I raised my hand out of the water, waved and gave the thumbs-up signal.

Swim! Boris urged.

Sounds good, buddy. You've just got to let me up first.

Rather than pushing against his chest, which would have gotten me nowhere, I nudged the leg pinning me with my free hand. Boris understood my request and shifted his weight, sliding his paw off to the side.

Relieved, I moved to sit up, but couldn't.

What the . . . ?

It took every ounce of control I had not to start flailing around in terror.

Dimly, I realized my shirt must have been caught on one of the tiger's claws.

My oxygen-deprived brain struggled to cobble together a solution.

An idea came to me with the speed of a sedated manatee. I raised my hand out of the water a second time, opened my palm wide and focused every functioning brain cell I could to issue a single command.

Five!

Boris, gimme five!

The tiger lifted his paw and batted my hand, freeing my shirt from his claw. I popped to the surface, gulped in a breath, coughed, then managed to sputter, "Good boy."

"Grace?"

Hugh was on his feet, hand on the butt of his dart gun.

I wiped water from my eyes and maneuvered onto my knees.

"We're okay." I panted.

Ozeal had made it through the tiger house and was scrambling through the guillotine door.

"We're okay," I said more loudly.

I didn't dare look to where I'd seen Boyle leading my sister away. I couldn't even risk thinking about it.

To Hugh, I said softly, "Give me a minute with Boris, okay?"

He hesitated, then moved to where Ozeal was crouched. Both of them ducked through the opening, one after the other. After a few seconds, the door slid closed.

Boris watched Hugh leave and turned back to me, eyes hopeful.

As I begin to regain my senses, I understood what the tiger wanted. The reward for his trick.

Swim!

"Not much room in here," I told him, standing slowly and stepping out of the pool. Goose bumps rose on my skin almost instantly. "How about some catnip instead?"

Boris loved catnip and five minutes later he was happily rolling around with a bag of it and I was headed through the guillotine door into the tiger house.

Brooke, who had fetched the catnip and was now acting as gatekeeper, lowered the door behind me with a rasping *clang*.

"Thanks," I said as I moved through the next gate and secured the latch. "Did you and Cody happen to see a red backpack when you loaded that hay in Bluebell?"

She blinked at me, uncomprehending.

"I try to keep a change of clothes—" A more careful look at her face had me pulling up short. The girl looked almost as upset as she had the first time we'd met, when she'd believed I was trying to kill her, so her expression made me step back and ask, "What?"

After a second, I understood.

Through the closed door, to the tiger house, I could hear Anita Margulies peppering Ozeal with questions. Evidently, the reporter had followed my sister as far as possible, then doubled back to spring on Ozeal.

What had I expected? Of course the reporter would be asking questions. It was her job, but I didn't like what I was hearing. Not at all.

"Do you deny a connection to organized crime?"

"I don't know what you're talking about," Ozeal said.

"Do you know Charles Sartori?"

"Stay here," I ordered Brooke in a low tone.

Trying to ignore my dripping clothes and sodden appearance, I stepped out of the door and into the spotlight.

The reporter whirled toward me as soon as I opened the door. "Miss Wilde, what do you have to say about your sister's arrest?"

The camera swung to focus on me like the Eye of Sauron.

It took effort, but I ignored both the question and the camera and looked at Ozeal.

The usually unflappable woman seemed shell-shocked under the barrage of questions. It made me want to snatch the camera, throw it to the ground and stomp it into little bitty pieces.

"Is this facility a front for organized crime?"

"Four hundred," I said, keeping my voice as clear and steady as I could.

"Excuse me?" The reporter looked at me as if I'd spoken in pig latin.

"There are less than four hundred Siberian tigers left in the wild. Careless accusations put not only this tiger's home but his life at risk." I looked her in the eye. "It's appalling."

Her lips parted.

Yes. I just accused her of being a tiger killer.

Phil, the cameraman, started to angle his lens to point at the ground. The reporter noticed and shot him a look sharp enough to slice flesh. He straightened.

"People deserve to know the truth." Anita Margulies threw her shoulders back in defiance. "My source tells me there's a connection between this facility and Charles Sartori's criminal organization."

Apparently, Mrs. Margulies didn't know the big connection was Sartori's daughter, a sixteen-year-old girl who loved animals and volunteered to help them. I wasn't about to drag Brooke into it.

"Your source?" I scoffed. "You mean Detective Tammy Boyle, who herself has been investigated for probable ties to organized crime?"

Oh yeah. I went there.

Anita Margulies's eyes narrowed. I could tell she was weighing her options, but I didn't know what else to say to make her back off.

The tiger stats had been my trump card. I mean, really, what kind of a soulless degenerate would spit in the face of a critically endangered species?

My question was answered a moment later when she thrust the microphone into my face.

"What ties do you have to the Sartoris?"

"Anita." It was Hugh. He materialized to sidle up next to the reporter. Smiling, he gently pushed the microphone away then leaned down to murmur in her ear. An emotion I couldn't read slid over her face. Her brows knit and she turned to look up at Hugh with wide, questioning eyes.

He nodded.

The reporter's gaze lingered on his face a moment before it swept over me, Ozeal, and finally settled on her cameraman.

"Okay. Let's go, Phil." Phil looked as confused as I felt but he lowered the camera to do as he was bid.

"I'm not promising anything," the reporter said to Hugh.

"I understand," Hugh said, still smiling.

He did?

"Let me see you out," he offered with a sweep of his arm.

I wanted to be impressed and should have been grateful but, as I watched Hugh walk the news crew away, I felt bewildered and aggravated.

When he placed his hand on the small of her back, I couldn't take it anymore.

"I need to go check on my sister. Ozeal, do you mind if I use the office bathroom to change?"

Ozeal, who seemed just as confused as I was, simply nodded.

As luck and my own lack of preparedness would have it, I didn't have much to change into.

Before loading the hay into Bluebell's cargo area, Brooke and Cody had taken the time to relocate a few items to the backseat. I found my red backpack, which was supposed to be stocked with a change of clothes and a few other necessities.

I opened the pack and discovered it held two pairs of socks, a bra, and a light jacket.

Great. I could go to the sheriff's office soaking wet or dressed as a flasher. With a sigh, I tossed the pack onto the seat and slammed the door.

"Grace?" Brooke's voice was tentative as she approached.

I turned to her.

"I just wanted to say thanks. For not letting that lady talk to me."

"Sure."

"And"—she hesitated—"just . . . be careful, okay? You can't trust the cops."

I was beginning to think she was right.

CHAPTER 11

I tried to keep her advice in perspective as I drove downtown toward the sheriff's office.

Being the daughter of a Mafia boss, Brooke didn't have the highest regard for law enforcement officials. Still, something about her words struck home.

Obviously, I couldn't trust Boyle, but what about Jake, or even Kai?

My trust, once won, is not easily torn asunder. Which made me question if I really trusted Kai at all.

I pushed the troubling thought away and called Wes.

"I'm walking into the JSO now," Wes told me. "Where are you?"

"About fifteen minutes out."

"Text me when you get here. I'll call you as soon as I can."

He hung up and a moment later, my phone chimed, signaling I had a text. It was from Kai.

Just heard about Emma. Meet me at entrance.

I knew he was referring to the security checkpoint near the set of glass doors that led to the investigations division.

By the time I'd parked, the aftershocks of my

tiger-induced adrenaline rush were in full effect. My legs ached. My hands shook uncontrollably. I barely managed to climb out of Bluebell without my knees buckling.

It would pass, but I still hated trembling like a terrified terrier.

Striving for control, I walked as fast as I could up the stairs to the entrance of the Police Memorial Building and pushed my way through the glass front doors. I had to fight the urge to pace as I waited for Kai and busied myself by reading the names on the wall of fallen heroes.

So engrossed with my thoughts, I didn't hear anyone approach.

"Grace."

I glanced around—it was Hugh.

"What are you doing here, Romeo?"

"I wanted to see what was happening with Emma."

"Have you talked to anyone?" I asked.

"I went over to the jail but she must not be in their system yet. They sent me over here."

The jail was a mere covered walk away from the sheriff's office. Convenient.

"Kai is on his way," I said. "He should know more."

We stood there staring at each other for a couple of minutes in impotent silence.

"Can I ask you something?"

"Sure," I said, expecting he had a question about Emma or maybe even Ortega.

"What happened today?"

Where to begin? "The detective who arrested Emma is off her rocker, for starters," I said.

"I'm talking about what happened with you and Boris."

"Oh. That."

I'd planned to tell Hugh about my ability. Partly because he was dating my sister but more because it didn't seem fair that Brooke should know when Hugh, a friend and colleague, didn't. Still, I didn't really want to talk about it in the foyer of the sheriff's office.

"I'll tell you about it later, okay?"

"Yeah, okay."

"What did you say? To the reporter," I asked.

He gave me a half grin. "Only what she needed to hear."

His gaze drifted away from my face to settle somewhere behind me. The cocky expression shuttered slightly and I knew he wasn't looking at Kai before I heard the words "Miss Wilde."

Still, the voice set my teeth on edge.

Boyle.

I tried to school my features into a placid mask before I turned to face her.

"Detective," I said with a calmness I didn't feel.

"I'm glad you're here. Would you come with me, please?" Something about the way she said it brooked no argument. I thought about digging in my heels just to be ornery, but was curious what new trap she might try to spring.

I glanced back at Hugh.

"I'll let him know," he said.

I gave him a nod and went with Detective Tammy Boyle.

We walked down the long, vaulted hallway leading toward the homicide unit. The hall was deserted, all the doors closed. The sun had set and the skylights over our heads had become a dull, gray line.

Boyle didn't lead me into the homicide unit, as I'd expected. Instead, she opened the door to a claustrophobically small interview room and motioned me inside. She asked me to sit. As I did, I noticed a file folder lying on the compact table.

The detective sat across from me and critically eyed my clothes and still-damp hair.

"J Beverly Hills," I said.

She blinked at me.

"It's the conditioner I use. Great stuff. Kind of pricey, but it smells amazing."

I started to call her out on the trap she'd set for Emma by tipping off Anita Margulies, but Boyle opened the folder and slid a piece of paper over to me.

"We've recovered a series of text messages from your sister's phone."

The printout was an exchange between Emma and

myself. The time stamp before each message showed the texts to have taken place from 4:57 to 4:59 p.m. the day before Ortega was murdered.

The first was from me. I read silently.

Me: *Tony called again . . .*

Emma: *Ugh! Idiot*

Me: *What do you want me to do?*

Emma: *Nothing. I'll take care of it*

I made a show of turning the paper over as if checking for more texts, then looked up at Boyle.

"And?"

"This." She tapped the paper lightly. "It shows intent."

"Intent to do what?"

"I think it's pretty clear."

And I thought she was pretty crazy. I barely managed to catch the words before they flew out of my mouth.

There was more to this talk—I could feel it. Boyle was trying to maneuver me, into what position I wasn't sure, but if I wanted to avoid it, I was going to have to keep my trap shut.

Boyle gave me her cool cop-stare.

I met it, wondering when she would figure out it didn't work on me.

"The medical examiner has finished the autopsy on Anthony Ortega. Would you like to know the cause of death?"

I didn't answer.

She didn't elaborate.

We looked at each other for a full minute. I took the time to make a few observations.

Boyle's eyes were an appealing dark brown—large and liquid like a horse's, but there was no warmth in them.

She had freckles, just a few, sprinkled over her nose. They were cute. People probably took in the big, brown eyes, freckles, and petite frame and underestimated her. I wouldn't make that mistake.

"Do you know what a spiral fracture is?" Boyle finally asked.

Of course I knew; I had a medical degree, after all. I still didn't say anything.

She kept her brows raised, waiting for me to answer.

I didn't oblige.

"No? Huh, I would have thought you would have learned that in veterinarian school."

Veterinarian school? I had to hand it to her, Boyle knew how to push buttons.

"Spiral fractures are caused by rotational force on a bone. A twisting." She mimicked the motion with her hands like she was wringing out a wet towel.

I said nothing.

"Your sister has bruises and scrapes on her knuckles." Boyle flipped over what I'd thought was a blank piece of paper. It was a photo of the back of Emma's hands. "We documented them the first time we brought her into custody. Do you know how they happened?"

I wanted to spring to my sister's defense, tell Boyle the scraped knuckles were from hitting the heavy bag in the dojo, but I pressed my lips together.

"We've recovered a note from your sister's computer. In it, she mentions never letting Anthony Ortega hurt anyone again."

She sat back and regarded me.

"You understand what all this means, don't you? Your sister is going to be charged with *first-degree* murder. Do you know what that is? Life in prison or the death penalty."

A cold knot began forming in my stomach. Not of dread or fear but of anger.

"Bullshit." I think the fact that I'd spoken surprised her more than the word.

"I see."

I shook my head, disgusted. "No you don't. You, *Tammy*, are one of the least perceptive human beings I've ever had the misfortune to meet. You only see what you want to see. It doesn't matter what I tell you. You've made up your mind." The truth of my words pressed down on my shoulders like a lead blanket. Fighting against the feeling, I stood and took the few steps required to reach the door.

It was locked.

I turned back to see Boyle regarding me with a smugness

that told me she wasn't going to let me walk out of an interview a second time.

"Am I under arrest?"

"If you want to help your sister, you'll sit back down and talk to me."

"No." My voice was surprisingly mild given how badly I wanted to leap across the room and throttle her.

"Look, I'm trying to help her, Grace. Tell me about the abuse. I know Tony had it coming—"

The door swung open and Kai leaned into the room.

"Grace," he said, with an expressionless glance at Boyle, "your attorney is looking for you."

I followed him into the corridor and away from the interview room. My shoes let out sodden squeaks as we walked and I was reminded that my hair was a tangled mess. I went to comb my fingers through it and saw they were still trembling.

A combo of no food, worry, anger, and the lingering epinephrine in my body.

Kai noticed the tremors. "Are you okay?"

"Yeah, I just need to eat something. Thanks for rescuing me."

He wasn't appeased. "What happened? You're soaked."

"Boris almost drowned me." I dismissed his look of shock with a wave and a shrug. "My fault."

The knots in my shoulders relaxed a little when I caught sight of Wes. Like always, he looked as polished and put together as a *GQ* model.

Hearing us approach, he looked up from his phone and gave me a gentle smile.

A hundred questions leapt to the front of my mind but leading them all was "Where's Emma? Is she okay?"

"She's fine. She's being booked."

"Can I see her?"

"They won't be finished until after visiting hours are over. We'll come back in the morning."

I searched my friend's face; he looked confident, as always, but his expression cooled when he looked at Kai.

The two had met a couple of times, but to prime his memory I said, "Wes, you remember Kai."

He inclined his head. "Of course. Though right now I'm going to advise you not to speak with Sergeant Duncan unless I'm with you."

"Why? He's not on the case."

"It doesn't matter. Until we have a chance to go over a few things, it's better if you don't speak to the police at all."

"But—"

"It's okay," Kai said. "He's right. Go get something to eat." He glanced at Wes. "She shouldn't be driving."

"I'll be fine."

"Yes," Wes said, "because you're coming with me."

He started to lead me away but I turned back. "Kai, I'm sorry. Last night . . ."

"Was my fault," he said. "I'll call you tomorrow."

· · ·

Wes had insisted I ride in the town car while he took Bluebell to pick up Chinese.

I showered and, much to Moss's disappointment, no longer smelled like tiger water.

It sounds a lot more alluring and exotic than it is, trust me.

I'd just donned my most comfortable sweatpants and a T-shirt Wes had given me with the words I KISSED A DOG AND I LIKED IT on it when I heard the front door open.

A moment later Wes called out, "Honey, I'm home!"

Moss let out a truncated howl of excitement and charged out of my bedroom to assault Wes and scarf down as many fried wontons as possible before I arrived to spoil the fun.

"Those are hot, big guy," I heard Wes warn as I started down the hall.

Moss didn't care. He was bolting the last wonton with nary a crunch when I walked into the dining area.

"People food isn't good for you," I told him.

Moss licked his chops and begged to differ. *Good.*

Wes had already set plates on the dining table and was pulling cartons out of the paper bags.

I fetched napkins and a couple of glasses of iced tea.

"You'll be glad to know I wasn't followed," he told me after taking a few bites of fried rice. "At least not that I could see."

"Ha!" I said around a mouthful of Vegetarian Delight. "I knew that's why you wanted to take my car."

"I have to keep one of my girls out of trouble." His tone had become very un-Wes-like.

The food seemed to solidify in my throat and I had to swallow hard to get it down.

"You're worried."

"I don't like the vehemence with which the police are pursuing Emma."

"Boyle." I said the name with enough asperity to elicit a barely audible growl from Moss.

Wes gave me a questioning look and I told him what had happened at Happy Asses. It was a testament to our friendship that rather than asking about Boris, Wes focused on Boyle and Margulies.

"Are you sure Margulies was tipped off?"

"You should have seen how fast she pounced on Emma."

"Reporters can be pretty quick on the rebound."

I thought about it. It had all happened in a blur. One second, I was tuned in to tiger-TV, the next, Boyle and her deputies were leading Emma away in handcuffs.

"Even if someone did leak the story," Wes added. "It might not have been Boyle."

"Who else could it have been?"

"Actually, there are quite a few people involved in processing an arrest warrant. Any of them could've tipped off Anita Margulies."

"It was Boyle, Wes, I'm telling you. The woman has a screw loose."

"Let's move on to the JSO. What did you tell her?"

"Nothing," I said, defensively. "I exercised my right to remain silent."

Wes gave me a look.

"Mostly," I amended.

He waited.

"I didn't say anything about Emma. I just told Boyle she was a biased twit."

"Tell me everything."

I did.

Wes listened then took a few minutes to mull over what I'd said. "I think Boyle might want Emma to confess by saying she acted in self-defense."

"Because of her and Tony's history?"

Wes nodded.

"How would she even know about Emma's past with Tony?"

"Mary knows. She could have told Boyle."

"Mary?" I hadn't realized Tony's housekeeper had been privy to what had happened to Emma. I'd been away at school and had never gotten the full story.

"She agreed not to talk about it," Wes said. "But that was before Tony died. She'd have no reason to protect his reputation now."

"Or she's trying to lay the blame on Emma to cover her own guilt."

"What makes you think Mary had anything to do with Tony's death?"

"I don't know. It's just a feeling." I couldn't put my finger on why, but I was suspicious of Mary.

"I'm not sure Mary could have done it," Wes said. "When Boyle asked you about spiral fractures did she tell you Tony's arm was broken?"

"No."

"Did she mention a cause of death?"

I shook my head.

"Commotio cordis."

It took a minute for me to remember where I'd heard the term. "Like the little boy who got hit in the chest with a baseball a couple of years ago?"

"I'm still waiting on a copy of the report from the medical examiner, but from what I understand, cause of death is listed as heart failure due to a blow from an unknown object."

"How can that be ruled a homicide?"

"Boyle is basing her case against Emma on her history with Tony and her experience as a martial artist."

"She thinks Emma twisted Tony's arm with enough torque to break it, then what?"

"She hit him in the chest with something that stopped his heart."

"This isn't *Kill Bill*. No jury would buy that Emma killed him with some mystical death-punch."

"That depends."

"On what?"

"On whether or not Emma knows how to do it."

CHAPTER 12

The warmth and stillness of the air made it feel more like the start of a muggy June day rather than an autumn morning. Little droplets of moisture had gathered on Moss's coat, making his fur look like it was covered in dozens of tiny, dull crystal balls.

A crystal ball would have been nice to have or, better yet, a magic wand.

Where the heck was Dumbledore when you needed him? Oh yeah—he was dead.

"Man, I need some coffee and a shot of Prozac."

Moss was feeling sluggish, too. I couldn't tell if he was mirroring my gloominess or paying the price for eating one too many wontons. Either way, he was happy to cut our run short.

Voodoo trotted down the hall toward us as soon as we walked inside. She squeaked out little complaints at our absence as she approached. When she reached him, she head-butted Moss's legs then moved on to me.

Hold! She asked me to pick her up. I was happy to oblige.

I made coffee, cuddled the kitten, and felt better.

The pocket of my shorts started singing "I'm Too Sexy."
Right Said Fred? That was a new one.

How did my sister manage to mess with my ring tones?
She was the ring tone ninja. A rinja.

I fished the phone out of my pocket and smiled when I
saw the caller ID.

Hugh.

Of course.

"Hey."

"You up?"

"Mostly."

"Want a bagel?"

I hadn't until he said the word. "Yes."

"I'll be there in twenty."

Luckily, I'm low maintenance. I hurried into my bedroom, set Voodoo on the bed, then darted into the bath to
take a quick shower.

My hair was still wet, but it was combed and I was
dressed when Hugh arrived.

We headed into the kitchen and I poured Hugh a cup of
coffee while he took the deli paper–wrapped bagels out of
the bag.

By some unspoken signal, we agreed to eat standing at
the counter.

Moss came into the kitchen to beg for a bite of bagel
before I'd had a chance to unwrap it.

Anticipating this, I'd already secured my mental shield
and was able to ignore my dog. Mostly.

He whined.

I turned my back to him and said to Hugh, "If he gives
you the sad face, just ignore him."

"You're the boss." He grinned and took a bite of his bagel.

"Sorry about last night. I should have called." I'd thought
about it when I didn't see him on the way out of the JSO,
but let myself zone out in the town car and had completely
forgotten about it by the time I went to bed.

"It's okay," Hugh said after a sip of coffee. "I ran into
Wes. He brought me up to speed."

"Then you didn't come by to ask about Emma."

"I talked to Ozeal last night. She's worried about Boris. These outbursts aren't like him. She's afraid he has some sort of neurological disorder. I wanted to get your opinion."

"Boris is fine." I hesitated, not sure what to say. I needed to tell Hugh the truth about my ability.

I remembered what Sonja had told me a few months ago when we'd talked about Hugh. The man wasn't blind and he wasn't a fool. If I told him the truth he would believe me.

Still, the words wouldn't come. Hugh had started talking again about Boris, outlining a couple of theories explaining the tiger's abnormal behavior. But I was too busy psyching myself up to listen.

"It wasn't Boris," I spoke over Hugh's hypothesizing. "Yesterday was my fault."

"Okay." He waited for me to explain.

"Boris got upset because of me."

"I didn't see you do anything."

"It's not what I did. It's what I thought." *Spit it out, Grace.* "I have that ability."

"To do what?"

"Communicate with them, you know . . ."

"You mean—" He made a vague indication toward his temple.

I caught myself before I could wince.

"Yeah, like that."

"Well," he said philosophically. "That explains a lot."

I waited.

"You don't think it's crazy?"

He let out a quick laugh. "No. I've seen what you can do. You think I'm stupid?"

"Sometimes."

"I still don't get what happened with Boris."

I sighed. "Basically, when I saw what was happening with my sister, I whammied him with a big dose of anger."

"You can do that?"

"It wasn't on purpose."

"Whatever, Beast Master."

I rolled my eyes. "See? This is why I never told you. I knew you'd come up with something ridiculous like Beast Master."

"Beast Mistress?"

"I swear to God if you start calling me Beast Mistress, I'll make Boris eat you."

"You wouldn't do that. I'm too pretty."

I wrinkled my nose in distaste.

The insult rolled off him like water off a beaver's butt. "Emma thinks so."

I thought about the ring tone she'd programmed for Hugh and laughed. "You're right about that."

Suddenly, the levity and banter felt wrong.

"I'm worried about her, Hugh."

He sobered and studied me for a long moment before saying, "The first time I saw your sister, I remember thinking it must have driven your daddy crazy, having two beautiful daughters to worry about. I mean, I knew how you were."

"What does that mean?"

"You're"—he hitched a shoulder—"you know."

"No." I crossed my arms. "How am I?"

"Well, not very approachable. Not that it's a bad thing," he added hastily. "That's my point. You're guarded."

"So?"

Funny how I had managed to tell him my biggest secret and was suddenly feeling defensive about my lack of social prowess.

"I thought Emma would be, too."

"Emma? Guarded?" I scoffed.

"What I'm trying to say is she's tough. Not in the same way you're tough and maybe not for the same reasons, but you shouldn't worry about her."

"Did she tell you? About Tony, I mean."

"Only a little, but it was enough." Hugh's expression changed as he spoke. A flash of flint-hard ferocity lit his hazel eyes.

His magnetism was not diminished. If anything, the intensity made him more appealing.

The thought sparked an idea.

"Do you have any contacts at the port?"

The change of subject threw him for a moment. "Where, here?"

"Miami." Jacksonville's port, though busy, didn't allow the import of animals.

"I've dealt with a few people, why?"

"Tony Ortega was having a horse brought into the country. A Friesian named Heart."

"Emma mentioned it. He was stolen, right?"

I nodded. "I think it has something to do with Tony's murder. The cops have blown it off because there's not really a paper trail on the horse."

"There has to be, if he was shipped here."

"Tony was supposedly keeping everything under wraps to surprise his fiancée, but now, I'm thinking there's more to it."

"What's Heart's registered name?"

Crap!

"I forgot to call and ask. Hang on." I grabbed my phone and found Jasmine's number. The call went straight to voice mail. I left a message about Heart's registered name and asked that she leave a message or send a text when she could.

"Boyle said she'd had one of her investigators check it out," I said to Hugh. "But I'm thinking someone with substantial veterinary experience might find out more, or think of alternative questions to ask."

Hugh's excessive charm didn't hurt, either. Someone who might not be candid with the cops would talk to Hugh.

"I'll see what I can find out about Heart. I've got to go talk to Ozeal before I head into work."

"Um, Hugh, what I told you about my ability. I don't tell many people."

"I shouldn't mention it to Ozeal?"

"If you don't mind." It seemed silly, especially considering how many people now knew. Sometimes I felt like my life was one of those giant, intricate domino patterns. Every swirl and line precisely built and perfectly aligned. It felt like someone had knocked over the first domino. It was only a matter of time before the chain reaction got going to topple what had taken so long to build.

"I'd rather tell her myself, I guess."

"Sure."

"When are you going to talk to Emma?"

I glanced at the clock on the stove. "Soon. Wes is sending a car for me."

"A car? Like with a driver?"

"It's how he does things." I was so accustomed to Wes's penchant for being chauffeured around, I never gave it much thought.

"Must be a decent lawyer," Hugh said as I walked him to the front door.

"Wes is a spectacular lawyer."

CHAPTER 13

After Hugh left, I went to finish getting ready—a task consisting of brushing my teeth and putting on shoes. Back in the kitchen, I noticed Moss's water bowl was almost empty and had gone to the sink to rinse and fill it when there was a knock at the door.

The quick rapping of "Shave and a Haircut" was followed by the sound of the door opening and Wes calling out, "Grace?"

"Kitchen," I answered.

He appeared a moment later.

Moss, knowing either from the knock or some doggy sixth sense that Wes had arrived, came trotting in to say hello and see if his friend had brought more wontons.

"You're a glutton for punishment," I said to Moss.

Wes bent to give Moss a good pet and asked, "Are you hoping for a handout, huh?"

"Always." I set the water bowl on the floor.

"Tell her, big guy. Say, 'Mom, I'm sooooo hungry!' Tell her."

Moss hungry.

Nice try.

"I wasn't expecting to see you until I got to the jail," I said to Wes.

He straightened, all playfulness gone. "I need to talk to you—" He was cut off by the sound of a fist pounding on the front door.

Moss echoed the enthusiastic knock with a trio of belly-barks.

Wes and I exchanged a look. "You expecting anyone?"

"You mean like the police? No."

"Police?" he asked.

"Who else knocks like that?"

I followed Wes to the door, not surprised to see Boyle and two deputies when he opened it. Boyle, on the other hand, seemed caught off guard to see Wes.

She quickly covered her reaction and held up a piece of paper. "This is a warrant for all hardware, software, and digital storage media belonging to your sister," Detective Boyle said.

"A warrant for what?" I looked up at Wes, hoping he would translate.

"They'll be taking Emma's computer stuff."

"But they already have everything, except the iPad she just bought."

"Not everything." Boyle looked at me like I should know what she meant. I didn't.

Wes took the warrant and began reading over it. Everyone stood there looking at Wes. Just as things were getting awkward, he handed the warrant back to Boyle and said, "If you, or your deputies, take so much as a Kleenex from my client's home, I will move to have the search and seizure declared illegal and therefore inadmissible. Are we clear?"

"Crystal." Boyle seemed unruffled by his warning.

I stepped back, expecting them to enter, but Wes moved to block the door. He turned to me and the look on his face told me it would be bad if they found what they were looking for.

"Grace, can you make sure Moss is out of the way?"

I nodded. Moss was standing next to me, and I grabbed his collar and walked him into the kitchen. A few moments later, Wes and the deputies passed. One of the cops started rifling through the living room. Wes followed the second officer as he turned down the hall leading to the bedrooms and home office.

Boyle, of course, came into the kitchen, where Moss and I were trying to stay out of the way, and started systematically going through each drawer.

Voodoo, startled by the strangers and noise of the search, came running into the kitchen to hide under Moss.

I told the kitten it was okay and after a few minutes, she crept out of the kitchen to watch the humans from a safe spot under the dining table.

As Boyle made it to where we stood near the island, Moss and I moved to the other side of the kitchen.

She searched each cabinet, the pantry, even opened the stove and microwave. From where I was in the kitchen, I could see the deputy had opened the entertainment center and was looking through the DVDs.

Boyle opened the fridge and started going through its drawers and when she moved on to the freezer I couldn't take it anymore.

"Help yourself to a Thin Mint while you're in there. We keep them next to the severed heads."

The detective ignored me and finally let the door close with a *whomp*.

"We've catalogued all the items taken from your sister's office, car, and briefcase Sunday. We're missing something."

"Oh?"

"It's something your sister mentioned to you."

"When?"

"Sunday. She asked you to handle a party for her, didn't she?"

"Yes."

Boyle looked at me expectantly.

"You're going to have to give me a better hint," I told her.

"She told you about a file on her computer. She asked you to download it to a thumb drive and give it to her colleague."

"Right."

"Where is it?"

"I gave it to Kendall."

"No, you didn't. We asked her."

"Well, she's mistaken. I remember printing the file."

"I'm not talking about the file, I'm talking about the thumb drive."

She held up the warrant, as if that would help me understand what a thumb drive was.

Wes and the deputy he'd been shadowing approached from the hall. The officer shook his head, then held up a plastic evidence bag with a small black rectangle inside. "I found a USB stick, but it's not yellow."

Yellow USB stick?

Oh hell.

A memory leapt into my head.

Sunday night. Jake and Boyle waiting outside as I rushed to find the file for the party and copy it to a USB stick. Moss nudging under my hand as I tried to plug the USB stick into my sister's computer. In a blur of yellow it had sailed into the kitchen and landed . . . somewhere.

It took all my willpower not to start scanning the kitchen floor to make sure it wasn't sitting out in plain sight. Thankfully, Voodoo chose that moment to come careening into the room, chasing her favorite toy, a ball with a little jingle bell inside.

With the kitten as an excuse to look down, I glanced at Voodoo then let my eyes slide furtively over the floor and along the base of the cabinets.

No sign of the USB stick.

Looking back at Detective Boyle, I said, "Listen, I admit to e-mailing a file from my sister's computer before you took it. I'm sure you saw that in her out-box. I left the original copy of the file on her desktop. It was a bunch of stuff pertaining to the party that night. Nothing nefarious."

"And the USB drive she mentioned?"

"I couldn't find it. That's why I e-mailed the file."

The second deputy stopped at the entrance to the kitchen, looked at Boyle, and shook his head. By some unspoken directive, both men turned and walked through the foyer and out the front door.

Voodoo bumped into my foot as she chased the ball and it rolled away to bounce off the bottom of the fridge.

In a flash of sudden, terrible clarity I knew where the USB stick was. I'd seen it, or rather part of it, a few nights before.

With deliberate effort, I pulled my gaze away from the base of the refrigerator.

Detective Boyle scrutinized me.

Don't look guilty, I ordered myself. *And don't look at the fridge.*

"You're sure you haven't seen it."

"Yep."

I tried to think about something else, but kept seeing the yellow USB stick in my mind's eye—spinning under the fridge. I focused on Boyle's face and had started counting freckles on her nose when I heard something slide across the floor. I glanced down at Voodoo and saw, with horror, that my kitten had abandoned her jingle ball and was focused on something under the fridge.

I realized too late that my thoughts had probably inspired the kitten to investigate the area.

Damn cats and their infernal curiosity.

Before I could think of a way to distract the kitten, Voodoo nudged the yellow USB stick out from under the fridge. In a heartbeat, it was batted across the marble tiles, clattering over the floor to bounce off the cabinet.

There was nothing I could do—the kitten was headed straight for us, pouncing and slap-shoving at the yellow rectangle in crazy kitten abandon.

The stick clattered between Moss's legs and I did the only thing I could think of.

Moss, sit!

I let him feel my urgency and, for once, he didn't try to bargain for a treat, but planted his furry rump on the floor.

Good boy!

Voodoo, whose attention span was only a little longer than a gnat's, lost interest and scampered off to get a drink of water from the freshly filled bowl.

"So." I looked from Boyle to Wes. "Are we done?" I didn't wait for an answer. "Great. Wes will show you out."

Boyle hesitated, her eyes narrowing in suspicion. She

swept her gaze around the room then reluctantly followed Wes to the front door.

As soon as I heard the door close, I peeked into the foyer and motioned to Wes to return to the kitchen.

"You're not going to believe this," I said in an unnecessary whisper. Urging Moss to stand, I retrieved the USB stick from the floor. Wes had stopped at the entrance to the kitchen with his face angled away, eyes shut.

He held up both hands palms out and said, "Wait. Don't tell me."

I curled my fingers around the USB stick and stuffed it into the back pocket of my jeans.

"Okay."

Wes lowered his hands and looked at me.

"I don't want to know."

"But—"

He held up a peremptory hand. "It would be unethical for me to tell you not to hand over something like that to the police. Point of fact, it would be unethical for me to know you have it in your possession. Do you understand?"

I nodded, then said, "One thing's bugging me. Hypothetically."

Wes gave me an exasperated look, but didn't tell me to shut up, so I continued.

"Why does Boyle want the yellow USB stick? What does she think is on it?"

"In my humble opinion, she's interested in it because Emma asked you to get rid of it. It was the only thing Emma wanted out of the house before the police came to take her computer."

"She didn't ask me to get rid of it, she asked me to give it to Kendall."

"Which amounts to the same thing."

"But, if I'd given it to Kendall, the cops would have just found her and gotten it anyway."

"True. Unless Kendall would have known what to do with it."

"What are you talking about, Wes?"

"I'm only suggesting Emma's intent may have been to keep it away from the police." He glanced at his phone. "We are now very late. Come on, we'll talk in the car."

"Uh, wait . . ." What was I supposed to do with the USB stick? I didn't want to take the very thing the police were looking for to a building crawling with cops. "Give me two seconds."

With a perceptive nod, Wes headed outside.

I gave Moss a treat for his assistance, thought about dropping the USB stick in the box of doggy biscuits, and then decided to bury it in the junk drawer Boyle had taken extra time searching.

Grabbing my purse and phone, I hurried out the door.

"Now, tell me everything you know about this Kendall person."

"She's a party planner, she works for the Ritz. Here"—I grabbed my phone from my purse—"I have her number."

Wes entered it into his phone, then looked up, waiting for more information.

I shrugged. There wasn't much to say. Kendall knew and respected Emma and seemed happy to do her a favor. The young woman dealt with the pre-party chaos without batting an eye.

"Did she ask you about the phantom USB stick?"

"No. In fact, she hardly looked at the printout I gave her on the party."

Wes considered that and I felt obligated to add, "Though that might have been because it came out magenta. The printer's out of the other colors."

"Anything else?"

I shook my head, then remembered a tidbit. "She told me Emma helped her get a job in the business."

"When was that?"

"I don't know. If skill is an indicator, I'd say a while ago. She was good. Reminded me a lot of Em."

"Did she say how they knew one another?"

"No, I assumed it was from work, but that wouldn't make sense, if Emma got Kendall a job. Did you ask Emma about Kendall?" I asked as the driver glided onto A1A.

"No, but I will." Wes opened the little cooler built into the town car's side panel and pulled out a small bottle of Perrier.

I shook my head when he offered me one.

All the talk about Kendall and parties made me realize something with a start.

"Holy crappoly! Today's Thursday." Emma worked events Friday, Saturday, and Sunday. "The weekend's almost here."

Wes saw the panic in my eyes and patted my knee. "It's okay. I'm having Emma's calls forwarded to Claudio. He's delegating."

"Oh, thank God." I sank back into the plush leather seat. Wes's assistant, Claudio, was superhuman. I was pretty sure he could juggle the scariest things on the planet. Swords, chainsaws, flaming batons, weddings . . .

"Which reminds me, have you heard of the Sanctuary of Saint Giles?"

"No, why?"

"They called asking to speak with Emma."

"What is it, a church or something?"

"I thought so, too. Maybe related to a wedding, but when Claudio asked for details, they refused to give any."

"Did you ask Emma?"

"She said it was a charity she'd given to, but . . ."

"What?"

"I don't know." Wes looked out the window for a moment then back to me. "Something about the way she brushed it off seemed strange."

"Like she didn't want to talk about it?"

He shook his head. "It's probably nothing. There's something more important I wanted to tell you before your visit with Emma."

"Okay, what's up?"

"When I saw her earlier, she was"—he appeared to be searching for the right word—"down."

"She's in jail."

"It seems to be more than that."

"Did you tell her Claudio is handling the events for her?"

"Yes, and she was grateful but"—he sighed and rubbed his eyes—"I don't know how to explain it. She wasn't herself. I wanted to tell you for two reasons. One, I don't want you to be taken aback when you talk to her."

"What's the other reason?"

"I want you to make sure she knows I'm on her side."

• • •

Wes had been right about Emma—she wasn't herself.

I asked her if there was anything she needed or something I could do to help but she just shook her head.

I tried to come up with a way to at least let her know I still had the USB stick but knew Boyle would be watching and listening to everything we said.

"Wes is working on getting you out of here."

She nodded.

"I know you didn't kill Tony. You wouldn't have been there if he hadn't been trying to contact me."

"Grace." She reached over to clasp my hand, and the handcuffs scraped over the tabletop as she moved. I stared down at the shining metal and felt a lump clog my throat.

"Look at me."

I did.

"This is not your fault."

"It's crazy," I said with more despair than I'd intended. "That's what it is. Crazy and stupid. And the cops are crazy and stupid to think you did it."

"Not really."

My mouth dropped open in shock.

She smiled and I got a glimpse of my sister peeking through the stoic veneer.

"They're looking at the easiest, most logical target. It's what they do. And with good reason."

"Occam's razor," I muttered.

"Exactly."

I arched my brows.

Her smile widened; she loved surprising people. "I hoped

once the police started peeling layers away from Tony's life they would find a more viable suspect, but it seems that's not the case."

"You don't seem very upset."

"Oh, I'm upset. But it won't do me much good. I figure you and Wes will be doing enough stewing for all of us."

"He's doing all he can, you know."

"Of course. He needs to get some rest. So do you."

"Your boyfriend called me at the crack of dawn." I told her, knowing she'd know I was talking about Hugh. "He wanted to come over and talk about how great you are."

"Did he?"

"We talked about Boris, too."

Emma's eyes widened as she got my meaning. "Well, I'm glad you talked about it. It's been a long time coming."

"He said he's going to visit you later."

"That will be nice." Her face softened and I was struck again by the realization of how much she liked him.

Anger bloomed through me in an unexpected wave.

My sister had dated plenty of guys. Men fell all over themselves to talk to her. But Hugh was different. They'd connected.

The thought of her missing out on a second of that connection pissed me off.

"Grace?"

"Sorry, what?"

"How's the hunt for Heart going?"

My anger fizzled out at the mention of Heart.

"Slowly." I told her everything I'd learned, then said, "I feel like I'm letting him down, Em. All I know for sure is he's not with Jasmine, which means he's not where he should be. I don't even understand why anyone would steal him in the first place."

"Why don't you ask Sonja? The ASPCA keeps information on stuff like that, don't they?"

They did. "Emma, you're a genius."

"I have my moments." Her smile was almost as brilliant as usual.

I detected the sound of muffled voices in the outer corridor. A glance at the clock confirmed our visit was almost over.

"Gracie." My sister squeezed my hand so I'd meet her gaze. "I think it's time to call Mom and Dad."

I nodded. "Yeah."

• • •

The visit was over more quickly than I'd have liked. But rules were rules. Wes needed to stay and go over some things with my sister so I headed out to find the town car and catch a ride home.

I was enveloped by the scent of roasting coffee as soon as I stepped outside.

A half a block away, the Maxwell House plant must have been making a giant batch of hazelnut. It smelled amazing. I paused, drew in a breath, and, despite the growing warmth of the day, immediately wished I had a steaming cup in my hand.

Maybe I needed to cut back.

I rejected the idea before it had fully formed and turned to walk toward the parking area.

Jasmine called while I was standing at the curb waiting for my ride.

"I'm sorry for the delay getting back," she said. "I'm at the airport on my way to Texas to help Tony's family make arrangements."

"Of course." I knew the Ortegas were from somewhere in Texas, so it stood to reason his funeral would be there. "Thanks for getting back to me."

"Heart's registered name is Heart of Midnight. Though I believe his paperwork lists the name in French. Which would be *Coeur de Minuit*."

I asked her to text it to me so I'd be sure to get the spelling right.

"Have you found anything?" she asked.

"No, but I have a friend who's going to make some calls."

"I'll be on a flight soon and have some obligations later but if you find anything . . . I could really use some good news."

"If I get any, I promise to call."

A few seconds after hanging up, the text with Heart's French name appeared. I forwarded it to Hugh and hoped he'd make headway with the info.

Just as the town car pulled to a stop at the curb, I heard, "Grace, you got a sec?"

It was Jake.

Wes's driver had gotten out of the car to open the door for me, but I motioned for him to wait and turned to the detective.

I started to ask "What's up?" but remembered what Wes had said about how many people would have been privy to Emma's imminent arrest. The question I ended up asking was: "Did you know? When I talked to you yesterday morning, did you know about Emma?"

"You mean did I know your sister was going to be arrested? Yes."

I don't know why, but I was surprised he admitted it. Jake, being a detective, noticed.

"You expect me to lie?"

"I expected you to feel bad about it."

"How I feel ain't gonna change things, Grace. But if it makes a difference, I'm sorry."

"There was a news team there. They recorded the whole thing."

"I heard." He paused, jowls drooping in a frown. "That's not how I would have done it, but it wasn't my call."

I just looked at him.

"Listen, you asked me to look into the missing horse. I did."

"And?"

"Boyle *did* have one of our guys check to see if any horses like the one you're trying to find came through the Port of Miami. I double-checked with him, and he's gonna get me a copy of the paperwork. I'll let you know as soon as I get it."

"Thank you." I turned to go.

"Grace." I waited. "I heard about the tiger getting a little out of control."

I shot him a frigid look. If he was insinuating Boris was vicious, I was going to hurt him, friend or not.

He raised his hands in a nonthreatening gesture. "I just wanted to tell you, I'm glad you're okay."

I inclined my head and walked to the idling town car.

During the ride home, I sent Sonja a text message asking her if she had plans for lunch. She still hadn't responded when the car dropped me at the condo, but it was well before noon.

Moss didn't bother to get off the couch when I walked inside. He offered a sleepy greeting and went back to sleep.

Lazy dog, I chided. But he'd already dozed off.

I couldn't blame him. Voodoo had reached the stage of kittendom where the wee hours of the morning seemed like the ideal time to play. Moss hadn't had a good night's sleep in a week; I'd let him be.

With I sigh, I took my phone from my purse and looked at the screen. It was almost eleven. My parents were early risers, no matter what the time zone. Unless the Winnebago had sprouted wings and flown over the Pacific, they'd be up. If they were close to a cell tower, they'd answer.

I pulled in a fortifying breath and called.

It was a difficult conversation. For one thing, my parents were on the fringe of an area with no cell service so I had to repeat everything twice before they made it over a mountain and suddenly had good reception. I told them not to worry. They told me they would be home in three days. At first, they played with the idea of Mom catching a flight out of the nearest airport but finally decided it would be safer to have two drivers working in shifts.

I love my parents. Sure, they fought and squabbled from time to time like any couple, but in the end, when it mattered, they stuck together.

I found myself wondering if I'd find someone who'd be willing to be stuck with me, no matter what, then shook off the thought.

Sonja had texted me back while I'd been on the phone with my parents. It was her day off and she suggested we meet for Mexican.

Just after twelve I slid into the booth across from her.

She grinned, "I ordered you a margarita."

A waiter brought the obligatory chips and salsa and a moment later two margaritas the size of aquariums were placed in front of us.

I blinked at the colossal drink. "I guess you heard about Emma."

"No, what?"

I took a giant sip of my margarita and I gave her the shortest version I could.

Sonja's brow furrowed even as her eyes widened in alarm. "I can't believe it. What did Kai say?"

"He's not on the case. The woman running the investigation is a real piece of work, though."

"What can I do?"

"Actually, I need help finding a horse." I explained and brought up one of the photos of Heart I had on my phone.

"And you said this was Tony's horse? Is that what the thing at the auction was all about?"

She had been standing next to me at the auction when Tony's winning bid had been announced.

"I can't think of another reason he'd want to hire me."

Sonja looked back at the photo of Heart before handing the phone back to me. "He's handsome," she said.

"Do you think someone would take him because of that?"

"People take horses for all sorts of reasons. Just like people will steal a dog or a bike or anything else. Thieves are thieves. They want what you got—they figure, why not?"

"Yeah, but a horse?"

"You'd be surprised."

The waiter came to take our order. I hadn't even looked at the menu so went with the standby cheese quesadilla.

"Have you shown his picture around the equestrian center?"

"No, but I will. It's weird," I said after another tangy sip of my margarita. "The people after him aren't horse people." At least according to Lily Earl, and I trusted her judgment.

Sonja's face went grim. "You don't have to be a horse person to work for a slaughterhouse."

I would not go there. "That doesn't add up, either. The

delivery driver, Lily Earl, said two men followed her all the way from Miami. I think they're the same men who were arguing at R-n-R the night Heart was taken."

"Why do you think that?"

"Minerva saw them."

"Minerva?" she asked.

"R-n-R's resident barn cat. She heard men arguing the same night Heart went missing."

"How do you know it's the same men who followed the driver?"

"Shiny bells."

"What?"

"That's what Minerva said—'shiny bells.' She was associating that with the men arguing. At first, I thought she'd been talking about bells that were shiny, but maybe they're two separate things. Lily Earl said one of the men who followed Heart wore noticeably polished shoes."

Much faster than seemed possible, two scalding-hot plates were set in front of us.

"Okay," Sonja said, "the shoes cover the shiny but what about the bells?"

"I don't know. It could have been anything. I heard it, though. It was a jingling sound."

"You heard it? When?"

"When I was talking to Minerva."

She canted her head and arched her brows. "You hear things when you're communicating with animals?"

The way she said "hear things" made me sound like a crazy person. The thought brought my hackles up until I remembered I was talking to Sonja, who, unbeknownst to me, had become aware of my ability years ago, and never judged or questioned it.

I nodded. "I hear, see, feel, smell . . ."

"Smell?" She made a face.

"Yeah. Not always, thank God."

"Then you're plugged in completely."

"Yes and no. I can't jump into an animal's head and sift through their memories. I can only perceive what they're thinking in that moment." I took a gooey bite of quesadilla. "Sometimes, what I hear is part of the memory and other times it's like an association." I tried to think of the best way to explain. "You might think of your favorite movie and the theme music starts playing in your head. Like *Jaws*."

She shuddered.

"You're afraid of sharks?" I was genuinely surprised. I knew a lot of people were afraid of sharks but that was usually due to lack of understanding, wasn't it? Sonja had a degree in biology.

She squeezed her eyes shut. "Don't tell me how amazing they are, I know. In theory, they're beautiful animals. I have a better chance of getting struck by lightning, blah-blah."

"Twice," I amended. "This is Florida, remember?" If the Sunshine State didn't average more lightning strikes than any other state, I'd be surprised.

She glared at me. "But I am still scared of them. And I do not want to meet one—ever. Sharks are like torpedoes with teeth. And I'm black," she said, as if I'd never noticed. "I probably look like a seal or something."

The gurgle of laughter that bubbled out of my throat caught me off guard and made me laugh harder. It felt like I hadn't had a good laugh in a year. It felt great.

For a while after that, we took our time eating and chatted about unimportant things.

Somehow, we segued to Detective Boyle—who Sonja agreed sounded like a piece of work.

I thought of the Saint Francis medallion Sonja had given me not long ago and asked, "Have you heard of a Saint Giles?"

"Sure. He's one of the Fourteen Holy Helpers." Knowing I'd have no idea what she was talking about, Sonja continued, "They're a group of saints who protect against disease and other health problems."

"So a Sanctuary of Saint Giles would be a hospital?"

"Or a long-term care facility for people with severe disabilities. Why?"

"My sister donated to a place called the Sanctuary of Saint Giles."

"Nice of her."

Yes, but it was still odd.

Letting Saint Giles go for the time being, I told Sonja about another, more worrisome mystery—the USB drive.

"Why are you assuming it's something bad?" Sonja asked.

"I don't know. It's just a feeling."

"Maybe you're just overthinking."

"Me? Never."

"My suggestion? Find out what's on the drive, and go from there. You can worry about it when you know for sure."

• • •

With a bracing breath, I plugged the USB stick into my laptop and clicked the drive's icon. It opened, revealing a single file folder. When I tried to open the folder, a box appeared. I couldn't open the file without the password.

Why would the information on the file be password protected?

One way to find out.

I started typing in passwords I knew Emma used, making it through four or five before running out of steam.

I looked around the room for inspiration, then got up and rummaged around my sister's office, looking for her social security number. I tried it, then her birthday, and after thirty minutes entering as many variations of everything I could think of, including "Graceisawesome" and "Graceisnumber1"—you know, just in case the password had to contain a number—was no closer to gaining entrance to the information on the file.

"Okay, how about, p-a-s-s-w-o-r-d."

Nope.

"Any guesses?" I asked Moss.

Pizza?

I grinned. "I don't think she loves it quite as much as you do, big guy."

If Moss ever had to come up with a password for something it would either be "treat," "pizza," or quite possibly "Moss-Handsome."

With a sigh, I ejected the USB drive and disconnected it from my laptop.

Maybe the password would come to me later. Or, better yet, Emma would be released and I could ask for an explanation.

I stood and was scanning the living room for the best place to hide the little yellow stick when my phone rang. I leaned over the coffee table to see the caller ID and froze.

Jake.

In a fit of paranoia worthy of a schizophrenic tripping on 'shrooms, I backed away from the phone, whispered a curse, then stuffed the USB stick under a couch cushion before answering.

"Jake, what's up?"

"I got some info on the horse."

"Heart? What is it?"

"Only one horse matches his description, but it can't be him."

"Why not?"

"Your horse is fixed, isn't he?"

For a half second I wasn't sure what he meant. "Oh, yes. He's a gelding. Wait, you're saying the only Friesian they have on record entering the Miami port was a stallion? You're sure?"

"In the last month, yeah."

I didn't want to believe it.

"But that would mean—"

"It ain't him. Sorry, Grace."

I hung up, flopped down onto the couch, and stared at a spot on the wall. I thought about Jasmine, who was in Texas hoping I'd deliver good news. I thought about Heart, wherever he was, and wondered who I was kidding to think I could play detective and bring the two back together.

After several minutes of staring, the silence started getting to me and I flipped on the television and channel surfed for a little while, brooding.

Sensing my mood, Moss came to nuzzle under my hand. *Okay?*

"Yeah, I'm fine. Just worried and unbelievably discouraged."

Moss trotted away only to return a moment later with Voodoo dangling from his mouth. He plopped the slobbery kitten on my lap, gave her face a quick lick, and looked at me.

"What?"

Your kitty.

For a moment I didn't understand—then his intent settled over me like a warm hug. Moss was offering me one of the things he loved most, hoping it would make me feel better.

"Thanks, big guy." Emotion made my voice waver. What would I do without this big pain-in-the-butt dog?

I love you, too. Grabbing his ruff, I pulled him in for a hug and kissed his muzzle.

He swished his tail a few times then climbed back onto the couch, turned in a circle, and huffed down with a groaning sigh.

Tears blurred my vision. I scratched the kitten under her chin and she tilted her head back, eyes drifting closed in kitty bliss.

Her purr, an almost hyperactive rumble, was loud and constant. Her thoughts were an oscillating thrum of satisfaction and sleepiness.

Leaning my head back, I let the kitten's serenity seep into my head. I was dozing lightly when I heard the newscaster say, "The latest on the Ortega murder—"

I opened my eyes and tried to focus on the TV. It was like trying to pull my brain out of quicksand. Groggily, I remembered how to shield my mind and slowly managed to wrest my thoughts free of Voodoo's.

Blinking at the television, I sat up and grabbed the remote off the coffee table. Turning up the volume in time to hear the desk anchor say, "Yesterday, our crew was on site when the arrest was made." They showed a clip of Emma being led to the deputy's car. Any lingering serenity I'd borrowed from Voodoo evaporated.

"Her attorney had this to say."

A recording of Wes followed. He looked calm, confident, and serious as he addressed a cluster of reporters outside the Police Memorial Building.

"My client is saddened by Mr. Ortega's tragic death. She

is, of course, innocent and we feel confident she'll be exonerated of any involvement soon."

"A source close to the investigation says that Ortega's fiancée, model Jasmine El-Amin, and her driver, Clarence MacEntire, are possible witnesses to the murder," the newscaster continued.

A blurry photo of a man holding a car door open for Jasmine flashed on the screen as the report continued.

"Originally from England, Miss El-Amin is said to have recently moved to the couple's beach home, where the murder took place.

"Joining us now is Anita Margulies, who is on location. Anita?"

The reporter appeared, standing in front of Ortega's house. The gate was closed, but the exterior lighting made the home's façade clearly visible in the background.

"As many of you know, Anthony Ortega's body was found Sunday," Anita Margulies said, looking well coiffed and serious. "Details are still coming in, but I *can* confirm his fiancée and her driver are being listed as witnesses. We can't be sure, as details are still emerging in the case, but it seems obvious, with the arrest of his ex-wife, Emma Wilde, that the police have substantial evidence implicating her in his death. Again, we can't speculate on the details but their relationship raises a number of questions. Was jealousy a factor? Perhaps some financial ties between the victim and his ex-wife were being threatened due to the upcoming marriage. Again, we can't speculate, but it's clear there's more to the story, Chris."

My heart rate and blood pressure had been steadily rising with every sentence.

They couldn't speculate?

I wasn't going to sit idly by while Emma was being slandered.

Before I'd really thought about it, I was up and headed for the door.

Not even sure where I was going or what I was going to do, the decision was made for me when I opened the door and nearly collided with Kai.

"What are you doing?" My anger at Margulies and her *speculations* made my surprise seem more like an accusation.

"I was on my way to a scene off Bay Meadows and thought I'd stop by to check on you."

I gave him a dubious look. Ponte Vedra was not on the way to Bay Meadows.

"Can I come in?"

I nodded and opened the door.

"First, I wanted to apologize for bailing on you the other night. I'm sorry I let Logan's phone call bother me so much. I think I've made it clear that logic goes out the window when it comes to you."

"Ditto," I said, which made him smile.

Kai has a terrific smile.

"I know we shouldn't talk about Emma, but I do want to help you if I can."

"Can you arrest Anita Margulies for being a lying bitch?" I told him about the news report and the poorly hidden insinuations. "She made it sound like Emma had already been convicted. I should have let her go into the enclosure with Boris when he snapped—he would've taken her out."

Kai arched an eyebrow at my vehemence. My rant had attracted Moss's attention and he came trotting into the foyer to give Kai the cool wolf-stare.

Kai glanced at my dog. "I guess we're not really friends."

"He knows I'm upset, so he's upset. And what am I doing? I'm not even supposed to talk to you about any of this."

"That's not true. We can talk about Heart. I found out something interesting about Rusty Parnell."

"The guy who owns R-n-R."

"Nope. Rusty Parnell doesn't own it, his sister, May, does."

"Then where is she?"

"Undergoing cancer treatment."

"And he's taking care of the place while she's in the hospital?"

"That's one guess. Though it doesn't seem he's ever been

involved with the place. She inherited R-n-R from their parents over fifteen years ago."

I wondered if medical bills had driven him to want to sell his family's property, then reminded myself that wondering about Parnell and R-n-R was pointless.

I blew out a breath and sank back against the wall. "I appreciate you looking into it, Kai, but it doesn't matter. Heart isn't even here. I got the info from Jake. The only Friesian who entered the port was a stallion. Heart is a gelding."

"Could be a clerical error," he suggested. "We're talking about importing from overseas. There's a language barrier to consider."

"Well, I can't check Lily Earl's paperwork—it's missing."

"You said the vet was there when Heart was delivered to R-n-R, right?"

"Right."

"Well, would she have noticed if he . . ." Kai trailed off, a pained look on his face.

"If he had been cut?" I asked, just to see if Kai would wince. He did.

Men. So sensitive about their nether regions.

"Would you prefer the term *neutered*?" I asked. "How about *castrated*?"

He flinched. "I'd prefer we didn't talk about it."

I tried to hide my smile but failed.

"You think this is funny?"

"Maybe a little."

"Back to the vet," Kai said.

"I haven't been able to reach her. I talked to her neighbor, who told me the good doctor was in and out and doesn't have a set schedule. How do I catch her at home?"

"You could always try doing what the telemarketers do—catch her at dinnertime."

CHAPTER 14

It was after dark by the time I reached Dr. Simon's little blue house.

Gator Lady was nowhere in sight, though I noticed a TV's flickering glow seeping around the curtains of one of her windows.

Whatever she was watching, it was loud. Probably a recording of a favorite Gator game.

An excited canine mind zoomed into my range before I'd rung the bell.

I could barely make out the dog's muted barks but I knew that something was amiss.

The dog was more than excited, he was . . . distraught.

Dr. Simon's front door was solid except for a series of small, rectangular windows ascending across the upper part of the wood. Standing on tiptoe, I squinted through the glass and was just able to make out an open living area and past it, a dining room set.

The dog let out a barely audible whine, and I realized the poor thing had barked himself hoarse.

He was desperately hungry and judging from the dark

lumps and small puddles decorating the hardwood floor, I guessed he hadn't been taken out for quite some time.

I tried to get a look at the dog but couldn't get high enough to see down at such an acute angle. I could, however, see through all the way to the rear of the house. The interior was dim, but I could make out a set of windows flanking the solid back door. Almost solid, I realized, squinting against the murky light. There, in the lower part of the dark rectangle, was the faint outline of what looked like a doggy door.

Light flooded the porch in a blinding flash.

I took a step away from the door, expecting it to swing open. Nothing.

The lights must have been on a timer.

The desperate barks continued and I focused a little bit more intently on the dog's mind, aligning my thoughts to his.

Roscoe hungry.

Okay, Roscoe. As soon as the dog felt my connection, he began pleading in earnest.

Please, Roscoe hungry! Thirsty. Please!

This wasn't the poor-me-I'm-starving kind of begging Moss would do to con someone into giving him a treat. Roscoe had not been given food or water.

Gator Lady had said Dr. Simon was moving. Could she have abandoned the dog?

I knew the answer.

"Hang on, little guy," I muttered.

I turned and hurried back down the path leading to the driveway. With single-minded purpose, I marched between Bluebell and the garage doors and had rounded the side of the house and taken several steps when reason caught up with me. The security lights were blazing everywhere.

With a sighed curse, I slowed. And tried to walk in the least suspicious manner possible.

Only to find the gate in the six-foot privacy fence locked. *Crap!*

There were no crossbeams to use as footholds on my side and nothing in the area I could use as a leg up.

I studied the gate, hyperaware of the fact I was acting

surreptitious while literally standing in a spotlight. Whatever I was going to do, I needed to do it fast.

There was a cluster of palms between Gator Lady's house and the gate. But I had a clear view of a pair of windows. She might glance out and see someone climbing the fence and call the cops.

I was pretty sure I hadn't left Duval County, which meant if I got caught, the Jacksonville Sheriff's Office would be responding. I might be able to spin a story of breaking into the house out of concern for the dog's safety to a Saint Johns County cop and get off with a warning, but I didn't want to risk Boyle catching wind of my little rescue mission. I had no doubt she would toss me in jail in a hot second if she got the chance.

Adding a breaking and entering charge wouldn't do me—or, more important, my sister—any favors.

But I couldn't just leave the poor dog.

I tried calling Sonja for help but, as I knew it would be, the cell signal was nonexistent.

I got back into Bluebell and started driving, keeping my eyes on the road while intermittently checking my phone for a signal.

I slammed on the breaks when I saw something I recognized. The little faux water well with the overflowing petunias. I'd passed through this part of the neighborhood a few days ago.

Dr. Simon lived on one of the streets bordering Jennings State Forest.

I dug through the detritus on the passenger seat and finally found the rudimentary map I'd gotten from the hikers. After a quick scan I found what I was looking for. The cross street I'd come to was listed on the very edge of the map.

I made two left turns, and soon rolled to a stop at the same trailhead I'd found a couple of days before.

The chain swooped from pole to pole barring access to the wide, dirt path. To the side of each pole, a berm had been built to discourage motor vehicles. Easy enough to bypass with Bluebell.

Wincing as branches scraped along the passenger side, I angled around the pole and heaved over the small hill. The undercarriage rasped over the sand, but a moment later we were clear and bouncing along the trail.

I gave Bluebell's dash an affectionate pat.

Though it was much darker in the woods than it had been on the street, I eschewed turning on the headlights, opting for fog lights instead. I was hoping the beacon of Dr. Simon's array of exterior lights would be visible through the trees and didn't want to dull my night vision.

"Disco," I said aloud as I caught a glimmer through the branches.

I parked and remembered the hay bales in Bluebell's cargo area. I was not going to be able to get to my toolbox, which meant no flashlight or screwdriver. A quick search of the glove box yielded a two-inch Swiss Army knife and a fancy wooden chopstick I used to secure my hair into a bun on occasion.

Better than nothing. I carefully traipsed through the woods toward the house.

Like some homes that backed up to woodland, Dr. Simon's yard had been privacy fenced only on the sides. Along the back was the shorter, wire fencing erected by the Forest Service.

I paused in the shadow of a large pine tree to scan the area. The place was lit up like the Fortress of Solitude on Christmas. The coast seemed clear, so I hurried to the fence and quickly climbed over into the brightly lit yard.

Keeping my stride casual, I headed to the back porch.

I'd come to a decision during my trek through the woods.

My plan was to climb through the doggy door, make sure Roscoe had food and water, poke around a little, and assess the situation.

What I found would determine whether I took him with me or not. Either way, the first step was getting through the dog door. Fortunately, I was familiar with this model.

The exterior had a thick rubber flap, magnetized at the bottom to help it stay closed. I peeled it up and out of the way so I could get to the hard, plastic "security" door, then placed the chopstick where the latch of that door locked it in place.

A little shake, a little twist, and voilà, it slid up and out of the way.

I tucked the chopstick into my back pocket, stuck my head through the opening, and was greeted with more ebullience and fanfare than a superhero.

Roscoe, who turned out to be a papillon, licked my face and danced in happy circles.

Hello! Hungry!

Kisses!

"Okay, buddy, hang on."

It took a minute to wriggle through the opening. I had to stretch and contort to avoid the piles of poo around the back door.

Twister: the Excrement Edition.

Finally securing a safe place to put my hands, then my knees and eventually my feet, I stood and began my search for dog food.

"Where's your food, Roscoe?"

Food!

The little dog dashed around the corner and reappeared a few seconds later dragging a plastic dog bowl with him.

He set it in front of me, spun in a tight circle, then pranced to one of the lower cabinets and bumped the door with his nose.

Sure enough, I opened it to find a bag of dog food.

I poured some in Roscoe's dish then got a cereal bowl from one the cabinets, filled it with water and set it next to the food. The little dog took two bites of food then went straight for the water. He drank with an eagerness that made me think he'd been without for a while.

Where the hell was Dr. Simon?

As if answering my own question my gaze landed on a purse resting on the counter next to a pile of mail.

I opened the bag and peeked inside, then, for no other reason than I'd seen people do it in movies, I lifted out the wallet and looked over its contents. Driver's license, credit cards, cash—whoa. Make that *lots* of cash.

I didn't get an exact count, but it was at least two grand.

With a wary look around, I stuffed it all back in her purse. Her purse, wallet, and cash were here. But where was she?

Could something have happened to the vet? People fell and injured themselves at home all the time. And with the cell service out . . .

"Hello?" I called out. Waited. Aside from Roscoe's happy munching—nothing. The rest of the house felt empty. Still, it would be better to take a look around. I didn't make it a habit of breaking into people's houses and felt a little jumpy and nervous as I started down the hall to what I assumed were the bedrooms. The first door opened to a bathroom. I flipped on the light, but other than some truly unfortunate wallpaper, saw nothing remarkable. Next came a bedroom, empty except for a floor lamp. Across the hall was another bedroom—also empty. The master was at the end of the hall.

I clicked the switch and heard the hum of the ceiling fan as it began to spin overhead. The room remained dark, and I felt for a second switch. Finding none, I glanced up at the fan. It was capped with a globe that should have contained a light.

The fixture hummed and began to sway slightly. A gentle ticking sound punctuated each oscillation.

It probably would have been soothing, had I not been skulking around in the dark. Squinting up, I searched for a pull chain on the fan, but didn't see one.

"Should have dug through hay for the flashlight."

By the ambient glow from the window, I was able to make out a walk-in closet to my right. Turning on that light revealed there was no one in the room.

There was an open moving box to the side of the closet. I did a double take when I saw the diploma.

Auburn—my alma mater.

Except, something wasn't right. I pulled the framed certificate out of the box for a closer look and saw the diploma had slipped a little in the matting to reveal another document underneath.

Flipping the frame over, I opened the back and found a

second diploma for someone named Simone Grant who'd earned a degree in business from Ohio State.

A third claimed Caroline Smith, Esq., had attended Loyola.

Could they all be fakes?

I found the answer in a second box nestled inside the first. The stack of identification badges and driver's licenses were from all over the country. Though her hair color and style changed, sometimes dramatically, between IDs, and different glasses and even eye colors were listed, I knew I was looking at the same woman.

There were also two U.S. passports issued in different names and a dozen business cards.

At least I'd figured out why Dr. Simon didn't act like a vet. She wasn't one.

Who was she?

Where was she?

Abandoning the box and its contents, I continued my search.

Next to the bed, I found an iPhone. It was newer than mine but I was still able to navigate to Dr. Simon's messages and her call list. Three out of the four most recent calls were local numbers; one was listed as "blocked."

The rapid *click-clack* of the dog's toenails on the hardwood floor sounded and a moment later, Roscoe pranced through the doorway toward me.

I glanced at him and asked, "You need to go out? Give me just a sec."

But he didn't want to go out, he wanted me to pick him up and hold him.

Cuddle!

He balanced back on his hindquarters and scooped down at the air in front of him with his front paws.

All the time his big, liquid brown eyes were a picture of longing.

Please cuddle?

"Has anyone said no to this?" I asked and scooped him up. He wriggled ecstatically for a moment, gifted me with a half a dozen doggy kisses, then settled into the crook of my arm.

I turned my attention back to the phone. I went to the voice messages; there were only two and I listened to each in turn.

The first was from Boomer. He sounded annoyed. "Lucy's colic is better, but I'd still appreciate a call back."

A slow chill oozed over my skin when I heard Tony's voice.

"I got your call. I may have a solution to our problem."

I started to replay the message but the phone buzzed in my hand and a warning flashed on the screen.

Low battery.

I looked around the room for a charger. I'd taken a step toward the dresser across the room when tension rippled through the little dog.

Though I'd paused to listen, I couldn't hear anything over the humming, *tick-tick-tick* of the ceiling fan.

Roscoe had gone rigid. Something about his reaction told me it wasn't Dr. Simon returning. A moment later, the sound of muffled voices confirmed this theory.

Men's voices.

I crept toward the hall, thinking I might overhear what was being said, when two things happened in quick succession.

First, I heard the front door's lock click.

Second, as the door opened, one of the men said in a distinctive accent, "It smells like shit in here."

The instant he spoke, Roscoe began to tremble and whimper. Instinctively, I reached out mentally to calm him—the moment I'd connected to his mind a series of images flashed through my head.

It was like crash-landing into someone's nightmare.

The sound of crying.

Fear.

That accented voice speaking harsh, cold words filled with menace. A woman's muted, agonized sobs.

I choked back bile and clasped my hand over my mouth.

As I wrestled my mental shield into place I realized I was still standing in the doorway to the bedroom.

In moments, I'd be in plain view of the two men—no, the two *murderers* who'd just entered the house.

I spun in a futile circle, struggling to keep my wits about me as the echo of the dog's memory bounced around my head.

The need to flee made my legs burn.

But there was nowhere to go.

Hide!

I scurried into the walk-in closet, clicked the light off, and slid behind the open door. A few seconds later I heard the same voice growing louder as the man moved down the hall.

"Where's the dog?"

"I don't know, but there's crap everywhere."

"Grab her stuff. I'll get her purse."

The bedroom light clicked on, spearing our hiding place with a thin beam of light.

I absurdly wondered how the hell the man had managed to turn on the light then realized it didn't matter.

In order to get as flat as possible, I'd lifted Roscoe high onto the side of my shoulder, which made his muzzle level with my ear. He was panting—not hard, but in the confined space he sounded like a revved-up, mini–Darth Vader.

I was going to have to quiet him down or we were both done for. I would be, anyway.

I closed my eyes and focused on making myself completely calm. The sound of movement drifted in from the bedroom but I didn't allow my mind to register it, instead I worked at clearing my head until it was filled with layers and layers of white, hazy nothingness, like the snow on an old black-and-white TV.

When I was sure I could snuff out whatever terror flared in his mind, I turned my attention to Roscoe. Keeping my eyes closed and my thoughts focused, I cautiously opened my mind to his.

The need to run away made him squirm in my arms.

Easy. It's okay.

His thoughts were an unintelligible tangle of fear. I tried to soothe buzzing panic with blanketing calm.

I don't know how long it took, but eventually the little dog's breathing became even.

I allowed myself to become aware of the creaking

floorboards as the man moved around the bedroom, then I heard something else—a jingling sound.

Almost like . . . bells.

I tilted my head to peer through the space between the door and the jamb.

A leanly muscled man with spiky dark hair stood at the dresser. His back was to me, so I couldn't see his face, but as he moved I could see he was wearing latex gloves.

He pulled an armload of garments out of the dresser and stuffed them into an oversized, black trash bag before proceeding to the next drawer. He paused in his efforts and with one hand began patting the thigh of his loose slacks. The movement made whatever was in his pocket jingle.

This had to be one of the men Minerva had seen in the barn. The same guy Lily Earl described.

Mr. Jingles grabbed the jewelry box off the dresser and tossed it into the bag.

He turned to scan the room and I eased away from the opening. As much as I wanted to get a look at him, I knew if I could see him, he could see me.

A moment later, his footsteps clomped toward the closet. Squeezing my eyes shut, I held my breath and said a silent prayer.

Light flooded the closet.

If he started pulling clothes off the hangers near the door, he'd see us.

I had no weapon. No room to move.

Mr. Jingles stopped just on the other side of the door. I could feel his presence.

The pocket jingling started up again.

My heart pounded so hard against my breastbone I was sure he could hear it.

Footsteps echoed closer, then the second man spoke.

"What the hell are you doing?"

"She had too much crap. Look."

"Christ." The second man moved past Mr. Jingles, ramming the door against me as he entered the closet.

Roscoe trembled.

Stay calm, I urged him.

Calm and still.

I heard the scrape of hangers sliding over the rod. "Here." There was a muted rustling of fabric. "Go put those in the back with her. It doesn't have to be perfect."

"I don't think I want to take orders from you anymore."

"No?"

"No."

"Tough shit."

"We wouldn't have had to come back if you had listened to me."

"It was too risky to move the body before. The lady next door was out in her yard—you think she wouldn't have noticed someone else drivin' Simone's car?"

"You could have let her go."

"So she can talk to the first cop who comes asking questions? I don't know what they call it in your country, but here, that's bad business. And I don't do bad business."

"We lost the girl because of you. If we don't find the horse—"

"Don't threaten me." The second man growled the words. There was a tense silence.

"I'll kill you before you can pull the trigger, cowboy."

Trigger?

When had a gun come into play?

A part of me—an obviously insane part—longed to peek around the door just to see what was happening. The rest of me wanted to melt into the wall and disappear, get away from the Bad Guy Smackdown happening two feet from my face.

"You try any of your moo-shoo crap, I'll blow a hole in you the size of Dallas," Cowboy said.

Mr. Jingles muttered what was probably a scathing insult in a language I didn't recognize.

"Talk English, punk."

"We need to get out of here. There isn't room for everything."

"So leave it. It just has to look like she left if anyone comes looking. We ain't U-Haul."

The tension eased but I didn't take a full breath until both men were out of the closet.

After several minutes of nothing more than footsteps coming and going, I started to think they would be leaving soon.

Sure enough, a few minutes later the closet light was turned off, followed by the one in the bedroom.

Darkness enveloped us. I started to relax until I heard Mr. Jingles say, "Where is her phone?"

Crap!

I glanced down at the cellphone in my hand.

What was I going to do with it?

I listened as one of the men rummaged around the room for a minute before moving down the hall.

They were going to come back. Eventually, they would look more thoroughly and I would be dead.

Think.

The lights were out. If I was quick, I could scoot from behind the door and toss the phone onto the bed. I eased around the door and peeked around its frame.

The room and hall were empty. Rather than risking the phone bouncing off the bed and clattering to the floor, I took three steps into the room, shoved the phone partway under a pillow and tip-toe sprinted back into the closet.

"I already looked in there," Cowboy said as Mr. Jingles walked into the room.

I heard the *jingle-jingle* as he tapped his pocket, then a low, derisive curse. A moment later he walked out of the room.

One of the worst things about being trapped in a closet for almost an hour while murderers discuss the best way to dispose of a body and gather their victim's possessions, is the total lack of an opportunity to pee.

Fear had kept my bodily functions in check until the house grew quiet and I became fairly certain the coast was clear.

I waited another few minutes, barely daring to breathe, before easing around the closet door. I strained my ears but was able to hear little more than my own thrumming pulse. What was I doing? I had a set of much more keen ears to ask.

Roscoe, bad guys? Where? I highlighted the question with rough images of the two men.

Roscoe's plumed ears pricked. *Out.*

At least they weren't in the house or garage. I crept to the bedroom door then made a run for it. The problem with running in situations like this is that once you start, it's hard to stop. I tucked Roscoe in my arms and sprinted across the backyard like a running back headed for the end zone.

The wire fence slowed me down, but not by much. With Roscoe snug in one arm, I scrambled over the obstacle. It may not have been nimble but it was quick.

I'd taken several, loud crashing steps into the woods before I managed to stop and slide into a shadow cast by one of the pine trees.

I had to think. Crashing blindly through the woods would announce my location to anyone who might be lurking—not helpful. I also didn't relish the thought of tumbling ass-over-elbow into a thicket of saw palmettos—a plant that got its name from the sharp teeth that lined its stems.

Forcing a steadying breath I closed my eyes and listened. Crickets sang and a light breeze rustled through the pines.

I checked with Roscoe—he didn't hear anything menacing either, so I took my time and picked my way through the brush until I saw light glinting off Bluebell's chrome grille. The sight brought on a wave of relief.

I even considered squatting next to her back tire to use the bathroom but decided I could hold it. Better to haul my cookies out of there—my bladder would have to wait.

I climbed in behind the wheel, shaking like a nervous Chihuahua. I tried to get a grip on my adrenaline so I could one: put the key in the ignition; and two: drive.

Focusing on a couple of deep, calming breaths, I tried to get control of my racing heart.

Roscoe turned his attention to the backseat so suddenly and fully, I knew without having to read the dog's thoughts—there was someone behind me.

CHAPTER 15

Easing Roscoe off my lap onto the floor so I'd have room to move, I cranked Bluebell's engine while slowly reaching under the seat, where I kept my homemade stun gun. It was more of a stun stick, actually. About the same length and girth of an empty paper towel roll, I'd confiscated it from some teenagers who'd been using it on a dog, and it had come in handy in the past. I'd had to use it only once, but I'd have no problem using it again.

My fingers brushed over the rubber cylinder when a voice behind me said, "Don't."

Knowing someone was lurking behind me didn't stop me from flinching with a yelp. It didn't stop me from grabbing the stun gun, either. I spun over the bench seat, ready for an attack, and froze when I saw the man lounging in my backseat.

Though he sat casually with one arm draped over the seat back, a coiled readiness radiated from him.

"Logan?"

My first instinct on seeing him wasn't so much fear as the desire to zap him for scaring the crap out of me.

He must have read my mind because the corner of his mouth quirked in amusement.

"I took the batteries out," he said.

Scowling, I lowered my arm, then reached up to click on the domed ceiling light so I could see his face. Not that I'd ever found Logan's expressions very readable, but light always keeps the monsters at bay, right? I lowered the stun stick, then narrowed my eyes. "My Glock?"

I kept my gun secured in the cargo area.

"Still in its locked box."

As if a lock would have stopped him.

He lifted a sprig of hay to his lips, just like a good ol' boy.

Roscoe decided he needed to be introduced to our visitor and hopped into the seat to prop his front paws on top of the seat back.

"Is that a dog or a big furry bat?" Logan asked.

"He's a papillon. The ears are a prerequisite."

"I like the wolf better."

Roscoe wagged his tail—low and submissive. The little dog leaned forward, stretching his head as close to Logan as possible, trying for all the world to get a good sniff and maybe a lick or two.

"I think he wants to be my friend," Logan said.

"So much for papillons being smart." Not that I could throw stones. Roscoe wasn't afraid of Logan and deep down, for a reason I couldn't fathom, I wasn't either. Which made both of us stupid.

I blew out a ragged breath and slid to sit sideways, folding one leg under me. Roscoe promptly hopped into the cradle of my lap and settled there with a sigh.

"What are you doing here, Logan? And what was with the cryptic phone call?"

"Just trying to give you a heads-up."

"You might want to try to be a little more specific."

"I'll take that under advisement."

"Why are you following me?" I asked.

"I'm not, but I have been keeping an eye on some . . . let's call them bad guys, who *are* following you."

Which confirmed I was the "girl" Mr. Jingles and Cowboy had talked about. I suppressed a shudder.

"How is Sartori mixed up in all this?" I asked.

"He isn't."

"Come on, Logan."

"Mr. Sartori keeps on top of any new players who come into the area. It was impolite for them to show up without contacting us first. I've already had a chat with them about that. They assured me they'd be leaving very soon. I've been keeping tabs on them to make sure they do."

I thought about that.

"During your tab keeping, have you seen a big, black horse around?"

"No, and if that's what you're after, I'll give you some advice. Forget the horse."

"It's not just about the horse, Logan. My sister has been arrested for Tony Ortega's murder. If these guys did it, I need to find something linking them to the crime. Who are they? What do they want with Ortega's horse?"

"I don't know why they would be interested in a horse."

"They didn't say anything to you about why they were in town? Do you know their names?"

"No."

"No what? No, you don't know their names or—"

"No, I'm not telling you anything else."

"Why?"

"Because it will get you killed."

"Come on, Logan, please. Just give me something. Anything I can tell the police to help them realize my sister is innocent."

"Are you sure about that?"

"What?"

"That your sister is innocent."

"Of course."

"You don't think she could kill someone if she had to?"

Logan had seen how skilled my sister was.

I met his eyes. "She didn't."

He lifted a shoulder, chewed the bit of hay. "If you say so."

I didn't want to listen to anyone else suggest Emma might be guilty.

"Why do you care if my life is in danger, anyway?" I asked, both to change the subject and because I really wanted to know.

"I pay my debts."

"You don't owe me anything."

"Most people would be grateful for my help."

"You're not helping me."

"I'm not helping your *sister*," he corrected. "There's an old Polish proverb I've always liked: Not my circus, not my monkeys."

"Nice."

"If your sister knew the risk you were taking, she'd agree with me."

He was right. But that didn't mean I could just give up.

With a frustrated growl, I dropped my head into my hands and scrubbed my tired eyes.

Kai would believe me when I told him what Roscoe had witnessed, but Boyle?

I wasn't even sure Jake was ready for that much info—I knew I wasn't.

"Do you know Dr. Simon's real name?" I asked, I lifting my head to look at Logan. The backseat was empty.

"No way." I hauled myself up and peered over the seat. Gone.

I wasted little time wondering how Logan had managed to disappear.

"Freaking Ghost." I buckled up, Roscoe tucked against my side, and headed out of Jennings.

There'd been nowhere to turn Bluebell around so I drove straight on the dirt road. According to the map, it would take me much farther south than I needed to go, but I was happy to put some distance between the bad guys and myself.

Something flashed in my headlights and I slammed on the brakes. Stunned to see what was spotlighted in the road.

A goat.

"You've got to be kidding me." I started to chuckle at my own pun then winced as I almost lost control of my already stressed bladder.

I got out of Bluebell and started toward the goat.

"Nelly?"

She let out a gentle *mbaaaaaa*.

I'd found her—now what? The answer seemed obvious.

"Come on, Nelly. You're coming with me." Scooping the goat into my arms, I hauled her back to Bluebell and set her in the backseat. She was tired and didn't protest as I urged her to stay still and calm as we drove.

When the dirt road emptied out onto pavement, I stopped.

I couldn't go back to R-n-R. Mr. Jingles and Cowboy might be watching. On the other hand, they could just as easily be waiting for me at the condo.

Crap.

Crap-crap-crappity-crap.

I wasn't thinking clearly. I was hungry, freaked out, and really needed to find a bathroom.

"First things first," I gave Roscoe a reassuring pat and aimed Bluebell toward civilization. I stopped at the first gas station we came to, and when I made it back to Bluebell after my potty break I discovered Nelly, being a goat and capable of climbing just about anything, had relocated to the front seat, where she was curled up next to the papillon.

"You guys are buddies, huh?"

Friend, Roscoe assured me.

"Good. One less thing to worry about."

Now, I just had to figure out my next step. I had to get home to take care of Moss and Voodoo, but it would be stupid to go alone and risk running into Mr. Jingles and Cowboy.

As soon as my phone showed I had a signal, I called Kai.

"Grace, I've been trying to get ahold of you. Are you okay?"

"Those guys following me—the ones who followed Heart, too. They're bad people, Kai."

"Where are you?"

"East of Jennings State Forest. I'm fine. But I need your help."

•   •   •

I'd touched on only the basic points but Kai didn't want me going home, or anywhere else, alone. He promised to be waiting for me at the condo.

I didn't see his truck when I pulled into the lot. Instead, he'd driven an SUV with the sheriff's office logo visible on the sides and rear. He stood, casually leaning on the back bumper, waiting.

Also visible, I noticed, was his police-issue Glock strapped into a gun belt.

I parked next to the SUV and got out.

"Making a statement?" I asked when he'd come around the vehicle.

"Might as well."

I nodded, and with a frown, he looked over my shoulder into Bluebell.

"Is that a goat?"

"Nelly. I told you about her, at least I think I did, she was lost—" I stopped myself. "Never mind, I'll explain later. Here, take Roscoe." I opened the door, scooped up the little papillon, and handed him to Kai. Using one of the slip leads I kept in the glove box, I urged Nelly to disembark, which she did with more grace than I'd have thought possible.

"What are you going to do with the goat?"

"Nelly," I corrected. She had a name, after all. "I'm going to take her inside and do a quick exam to make sure she's okay. After that . . . I don't have a plan after that."

I was keyed up with that weird, exhausted jitteriness that comes with being stressed to the point of insanity.

Moss was thrilled with his new houseguests. Voodoo, not so much. One bleat from the goat and the kitten took off to hide under my bed.

I got my backup medical kit and knelt on the living room

rug to give Nelly a cursory checkup. She seemed no worse for her adventure.

"Not even a scratch," I told Kai as I zipped the kit closed.

He had taken the initiative to pour me a glass of wine. I stood and took it gratefully.

"Do we need to put her somewhere?" he asked, looking at the goat. She'd already settled onto Moss's doggy bed with Roscoe curled at her side.

"They're okay for now," I said after tasting the wine. "I just want to take a minute to catch my breath."

I set the glass of wine on the side table and with a long sigh dropped onto the couch.

Suddenly, I'd lost the desire to do anything but sit.

Kai joined me a moment later and let me space out for a few minutes.

Moss went to check on his kitten. Voodoo was still under the bed. Not because she was afraid, but because she'd discovered how well her claws penetrated the filmy fabric underside of the box spring.

And was tearing into it like a baby velociraptor.

At least it was my mattress. She could rip it to shreds. I didn't care.

After not nearly enough downtime, I heard Kai say, "Grace?"

With a nod, I straightened, retrieved my glass of wine, and angled to face him. "I should start at the beginning, right?"

He nodded. "From when you got there."

I made it through most of the story before he started asking questions.

"So you broke into Dr. Simon's house to rescue Roscoe?"

"Technically, as a consultant for animal control, I'm approved to employ certain tactics in the rescue of an at-risk animal."

"You didn't just rescue the dog. You snooped."

"That wasn't the plan, I swear." I lifted my right hand to emphasize my solemnness.

"Why did you go through her purse?"

"I don't know. It was there. What was I supposed to do?"

"Call the police."

"I couldn't. No phones, remember? When I realized her wallet and cash and all that was in her purse, I decided to look around and make sure something hadn't happened to her. Which of course it had."

"Explain again what Roscoe told you."

"It was more show than tell, unfortunately."

"Take your time."

I didn't want to remember what the papillon had shown me, but after taking a fortifying sip of wine, I did as Kai asked.

"I don't know how it started. Roscoe's memory was triggered by the sound of Mr. Jingles and Cowboy talking."

"Those are the bad guys?"

After explaining how I'd come up with the nicknames, I continued, "I heard them arguing with Dr. Simon, or Simone, or whoever she was. They were angry, especially Cowboy. Dr. Simon was"—I squeezed my eyes shut—"she was crying. Begging for her life. It didn't matter."

"It's okay. Come here." Kai set my wine aside and pulled me into a hug. I sank into the warmth of his embrace and drew in a shaky breath. He smelled wonderful. I indulged for a minute, then eased away.

I still hadn't made it to Logan's appearance. I knew that part of the story wasn't going to make Kai happy, but there wasn't anything I could do about that.

"There's more," I said, looking him in the eye. "Logan was there. Not with Cowboy or Mr. Jingles," I hastened to clarify, as if that would mitigate things. "He was in Bluebell, waiting for me."

"Logan."

I nodded. "He scared the crap out of me."

Kai didn't say anything for several seconds. "And?"

"He told me the men were dangerous. Like I couldn't have figured that out." I went over what Logan had told me.

"Another warning?"

I nodded. "I think he was more interested in why they'd been following me. I told him I didn't know. The only connection is Heart."

"Does Logan know who these men are?"

"I got that impression, but he wouldn't tell me. He said it would get me killed and then friggin' Houdinied on me."

Kai shook his head then leaned back to gaze up at the ceiling—which meant he was either deep in thought or trying to get his temper under control.

I was going to guess the latter.

When he still hadn't responded after a full minute, I said, "What?" I was too tired and upset to hold my tongue—not that I'd ever needed an excuse.

Kai looked at me. "I don't like that Logan has developed this *interest* in you."

"I don't think he'd hurt me, if it makes you feel any better."

"It doesn't."

Kai searched my face, eyes fierce and filled with an emotion I couldn't name but could certainly feel. He reached out and tucked a lock of hair behind my ear. The gesture was so tender and at odds with the intensity of his expression, I was still trying to wrap my head around whether or not he was mad when he slid his fingers through my hair, clasped the back of my neck, and kissed me.

Heat sparked between us and before I was able to form a more coherent thought than *Yes!* we were horizontal, tearing at each other's clothes.

Kai tugged his shirt over his head, tossing it aside to expose the smooth, rippling muscles of his torso.

I'd pulled him down into another kiss when I heard Roscoe let out a long, pitiful whimper. Without thinking, I mentally reached out to quiet the little dog.

Bad idea.

Ever have a disturbing image pop into your head at the worst possible moment?

The instant my thoughts connected with Roscoe's, I was hit with a playback of Dr. Simon's murder.

I sucked in a shocked breath and shoved at Kai's chest.

He jerked back.

"What? What's wrong?" he asked as I scrambled away.

I yanked my mental shield up to try to cut off the memory, but it was too late. Images bounced through my head. Screams echoed. I clapped my hand over my mouth and tried not to throw up.

"Grace, are you having a panic attack?" He sounded almost as horrified as I felt.

I pressed my eyes shut, shook my head, and fought off a wave of nausea. I couldn't let Kai think he'd done this to me. I held my hand out to him.

He took it, eased closer, and then touched my cheek with whisper-soft fingers.

"It's okay. You can talk to me, baby."

My heart trembled a little at his words. He'd called me baby, and—Lord help me—I *liked* it.

I offered him as much of a smile as I could. "Nothing spoils the mood like the flashback of a murder."

"Come here." He pulled me into his arms and froze.

A low growl vibrated only inches away.

Moss.

He must have gotten a dose of my terror and decided Kai was to blame before I'd shielded my mind.

I tried to reassure Moss. *It's okay.*

Guard.

I eased away and slightly in front of Kai. My dog's lips were folded back in a very serious display of fangs and intent.

Kai's not hurting me, see?

The growl subsided. Moss leaned in to sniff my face.

Okay?

I'll be fine, I promised with a pat.

He gave Kai a warning look before turning to walk away.

"Well, that was . . . different," Kai said once Moss had disappeared down the hall.

"I'm sorry." I buried my face in my hands, beyond embarrassed. "By the time I realized Roscoe was having a nightmare, it was too late."

I looked at Kai but he wasn't paying attention.

"Should she be doing that?" He pointed over my shoulder.

I shifted around to see Nelly standing on her hind legs,

both forehooves planted on the wall as she nibbled at the tasseled curtain tieback.

"No—" I stood and made a move to take it away, but the goat managed to yank the tassel free before I made it. "Give me that!" I wrested the maimed tangle of threads out of her mouth.

"Emma's going to kill me."

"Can we put Nelly somewhere else?" Kai asked. "Somewhere less edible."

I nodded. "On the deck."

He stood and pulled on his shirt. "Why don't you let me help, then we can talk a little more."

It didn't take long. Goats loved to climb but the outdoor furniture was sturdy enough to handle it. After bringing anything nibbleable inside and moving the potted plants into the hall bath, I lugged Moss's dog bed outside, got Nelly a bucket of fresh water, and then added a bowl for Roscoe when it became evident he wanted to bunk with his new buddy.

Wes returned my call just as I was closing the sliding glass door.

I told him what had happened, assured him I was safe, and he promised he'd be there in fifteen minutes.

It took him ten.

Being the only one of us who'd skipped dinner, I ate leftover Chinese and tried to remember every detail.

"Do you have any idea when the murder took place?" Wes asked.

"I don't know. A couple days, maybe. Gator Lady—the neighbor—she might have a better idea. I'm only going by how hungry Roscoe was and how many accidents he had."

"Hopefully, someone has reported her missing. Then we can go over there and take a look," Kai said.

"I don't know if she's the kind of woman who'd be reported missing," I said and told them about the IDs and diplomas.

"Can you remember any of the names she used?" Wes asked, sliding the notepad he'd been using toward me.

I tried, but could remember only Caroline and Simone.

"It's okay," Kai said. "Con artists tend to use names that are easy to forget."

"So who are these people?"

"Most criminals aren't masterminds," Kai said, "hatching plots from poorly lit basement lairs. They're just thugs."

"So I'm giving them more credit than I should?"

"In the brains department? Probably. People like this are devious and that can seem like cunning, but really, a thug is just a thug."

"How do we find these thugs?" Wes asked.

"I ran the plate on the car they were driving," Kai said. "It came back registered to a man from Boca Raton. But I'm still running it down."

"What about Dr. Simon?" I asked. "I'm telling you what I saw and heard. Even if you leave Roscoe out of it, doesn't it count for something that these men were talking about getting rid of her and her stuff?"

"It does with us," Wes said.

But that didn't make me feel any better.

Neither did listening to Kai and Wes discuss theories. I was exhausted.

I didn't want to think about murderers and con artists. I didn't want to talk anymore.

"I'm going to grab a shower," I announced to no one in particular. Both men paused to look at me but neither protested, so I headed into my bathroom, stripped, and stood under the hot water until my fingers began to prune.

I wrapped myself in the superfluffy robe Emma had given me for my birthday and was twisting my hair into a towel when there was a knock at the door.

Steam from the bath rolled out as I open the door.

"You don't look much better," Wes said.

"Thanks," I grumbled, but knew he was right. "I don't think I can talk anymore tonight," I told him as I sank onto my bed.

From the other side of the bedroom door, Moss let out a soft *woof.*

Without me having to ask, Wes turned and opened the door. Moss trotted in, Voodoo on his heels.

I picked up the kitten and curled onto my side.

Happy kitty vibes began thrumming into me at once.

"Kai says he's staying on the couch. Are you okay with that?"

I nodded.

"Do you need anything before I go?"

"Kai needs a blanket." I started to get up but Wes stopped me by leaning over to kiss my forehead. "I'll take care of it. Rest."

I did a quick mental check on Nelly and Roscoe—both were sound asleep.

Moments later, so was I.

• • •

The next morning I pulled myself out of bed and, still half asleep, shuffled toward the kitchen. I stopped when I saw Kai foraging through the cabinets. Suddenly, I was wide awake.

Shirtless, barefoot, hair mussed with sleep—he looked *good*.

Roscoe chose that moment to prance up to me. I glared down at the little dog.

"You're lucky you're cute."

Cuddle!

I scooped the papillon into my arms—it wasn't like he wanted to have a murderous nightmare and booty-block me.

"Were you talking to me or the dog?" Kai asked.

"Both." I stepped all the way into the kitchen. "Are you making me breakfast?"

"Looking for coffee."

"Even better." I got the bag out of the freezer. And enjoyed watching him go through the steps.

"Moss didn't want to go outside with me," Kai said as he worked on the coffee. "But I put food in his bowl and gave Roscoe some, too. I opened a can of cat food for Voodoo. I wasn't sure about Nelly."

"I have some hay in Bluebell, but she'd probably like to go out and browse a bit. I need to take the dogs out, too."

"Let me change into my running gear and I'll come with you."

"Running gear?"

"I always have a bag with gym shorts and a change of clothes."

"Smart," I said, thinking of my unprovisioned backpack.

Kai retrieved his bag from the SUV while I hunted up a couple of spare leashes.

Twenty minutes later, I was coxing Nelly off the grass while Kai waited with Moss and Roscoe when disaster struck.

"What in the name of—Is . . . is that a *goat*?"

Mr. Cavanaugh, our less-than-magnanimous, somewhat cantankerous, complete ass of a neighbor.

As far as I could tell, he disliked just about everything. Especially yours truly and any animals within twenty miles of his person.

I kept my back to the man as he stammered down the stairs.

Kai saw my pained expression, but seemed to be waiting for me to say something. Probably because Cavanaugh was talking to me.

"I'm speaking to you!"

I turned to face him. "Oh—Mr. Cavanagh, hi! Isn't this great?" I motioned to Nelly.

"Great? It's . . . It's . . . ." He seemed to be quivering with too much rage to force more words out.

"This is Nelly, she—"

"It's a *goat*!"

"Yes!" I said with so much forced enthusiasm I thought my face would break. "She is part of our new lawn maintenance program."

"What?"

"Didn't you get the ballot from the condo association? It was voted in last month."

"Ballot? What ballot?" His liver-spotted face started turning purple.

"Nelly is much more economical and better for the environment than traditional lawn equipment."

"You can't keep a goat here. I won't stand for it!"

"Oh, she's just here to trim the grass."

He narrowed his rummy eyes. "I'll be looking into this."

"Sure."

"And if I see that animal going in or out of your unit, the board will hear about it."

He gave me the stink eye all the way to his car.

"Have a great day, sir," I called out and waved as he drove out of the lot.

"The lawn maintenance program?" Kai asked as we walked up the stairs.

"By the time he finds out the truth, Nelly will be back at R-n-R. Assuming I can get an escort."

"I'll go with you tomorrow."

Kai's phone was ringing when we walked in the door. I left him to take the call while I put Nelly out on the back deck with some hay and fresh water.

Roscoe and Voodoo had become fast friends and were chasing each other around the living room when I came inside.

I headed for the coffeepot.

"We found the sedan," Kai said a minute later when he was off the phone. "The plates are a match."

"That's good, right?"

"It was dumped and set on fire. Charlie's on his way to take a look, but Jake thinks it's a total loss. They did a good job torching it."

"So, no evidence?"

"Probably not. And worse, we don't know what they're driving."

"Yes, we do," I said, straightening away from the counter. "Dr. Simon. They took her car. I remember them saying they needed to drive it when the neighbor wouldn't be watching."

"I'll let Jake know. I've got to run home and get ready for work but I'll call as soon as I hear something." Kai picked up his bag and I walked him through the foyer to the front door. He stopped before opening it. "Grace, promise you'll stay inside unless someone is with you. And by someone I don't mean Moss."

"Okay, but isn't there something I can do? Give a statement or anything."

He regarded me with an odd expression. As if a thought was just dawning on him.

"Kai?"

His attention snapped back into focus. "What about talking to Nelly? She's been wandering all over the area, maybe she saw what happed to Heart."

My lips parted in a surprised smile. "That's a great idea. You're a genius." I stood on tiptoe and kissed him. I'd meant it as a quick, appreciative peck but once my lips touched his, it was like an electromagnet had been charged.

My arms came up to snake around his neck while his locked around my torso. We eased away from each other a few seconds later, a little breathless.

"This has got to stop, Grace."

I tried to blink away the brain fog. Not sure of his meaning, I said, "Um . . . it does?"

"Yeah, it does." His voice was a rough-hewn whisper. "If we don't finish this soon I'm going to lose my mind."

"Oh, right." My knees had gone suspiciously weak as his intentions became clear.

"Um . . . maybe we can wait until my sister is cleared of murder?" I asked only half sarcastically.

"I'm not making any promises." He gave me one last scorching look and added, "Use the dead bolt." Then shut the door.

I engaged the lock, then turned to rest my back against the door. Nelly stood watching me from a few feet away.

"Don't look at me like that, missy. I got some questions for you."

I'd wanted a distraction from my impending—what? Appointment? Liaison? But asking Nelly to describe where she'd been and what she'd seen was more than I'd bargained for.

Nelly, like most goats, explored her surroundings with her *mouth*.

Which meant I sat in the living room listening while she categorized every weed, stick, and who-knew-what she'd sampled.

Most of the time, the visual feedback was limited to shades of dull green. I had no idea what she was talking about and no clue how to use the information.

I was offered a reprieve when my phone started playing salsa music.

"Wes."

"Got a minute?"

"Is that supposed to be funny?"

"No, why?"

"Sorry. Kai has me on house arrest."

"I'm glad."

"Any news on Emma?"

"My sources say the state attorney is rethinking the murder charge."

"That's great."

"Not exactly. There's more of a precedent for manslaughter in regards to COD being *commotio cordis*."

"What about Mr. Jingles and Cowboy?"

"Until there's more to go on than the testimony of Emma's sister, the state attorney isn't willing to hold off. She'll be formally charged today."

CHAPTER 16

"Have you caught the bad guys yet?" I asked Kai when he called a few hours later.

"No, but Jake put out a BOLO for Dr. Simon's car. It will take time, but if they're in the area, we'll find them."

"I know one way you could find them—"

"Forget it."

"But—"

"We are not using you as bait, Grace."

"But it would work, wouldn't it?"

"You're not risking your life to try to catch these men."

"I wouldn't be risking my life, not if you guys were there, like a setup or a sting or something."

"This isn't a cop show, Grace, we don't put civilians in danger to catch suspects."

"Right, I know that. I think being cooped up all day is getting to me."

"That's one reason I called. I wanted to bring you lunch."

"Lunch sounds wonderful."

"What are you in the mood for?"

Honestly, I was in the mood to get the hell out of the house, but would settle for having a hot guy bring me food.

"They're charging Emma today," I told him after we'd settled on sandwiches.

"I'm sorry."

"I just feel so useless. I keep thinking, if I can figure out who took Heart and why, I'll be one step closer to understanding why Mr. Jingles and Cowboy are after him. That's the key, isn't it? If I figure out what they want, then maybe you guys will know who to look for."

"And you think figuring out who they are will clear Emma?"

"It can't hurt."

"No, it can't. But I think there's something else you can do."

"What?"

"I talked to Tammy—she's really hung up on your involvement with Sartori."

"What can I do about that?"

"She knows you asked me to help find Brooke, but she assumes it was at Sartori's request."

I narrowed my eyes. "You want me to tell Boyle about my ability."

"I can back you up, Grace. We can show her there's an explanation for every suspicion she has about you."

"You really think she'll believe me?"

"Yes."

He had a lot more faith in her than I did. "Did you call and offer to bring me lunch just to butter me up?"

"I'm offering to bring you lunch because I want to see you."

"Then I accept your offer. And I'll think about it."

"You might want to talk to Wes. See if he wants to do his honey badger impression."

"Honey badger?" Wes was going to love that.

"Just check with him and see if he has a problem with you talking to her. I know how he is about that kind of thing."

I talked to Wes. He didn't have a problem with it if I didn't.

The thought of opening up to someone like Boyle made my lip curl. But I would do anything to help my sister.

To make use of the time, I reexamined how I'd approached Nelly earlier. I was going to have to narrow the concept if I wanted any hope of success.

Maybe the problem wasn't so much how broadly I'd phrased the question, but the perspective.

Instead of asking her to recall what she'd seen recently and weighing the question with an image of Heart as I thought of him, maybe I needed to have a goat's-eye view.

I went back to my laptop and watched the commercial featuring Jasmine and Heart, focusing on the segments that showed his legs. Then I combined the movement with the other full-length photographs I'd seen of him. Trying to memorize every detail of his lower half, as if seeing from a goat's perspective.

Holding those images in my mind, I sat on the couch in front of where the goat stood, balanced on the corner of the coffee table.

Nelly.

I reached out both mentally and with my hand, then offered the composition to her.

Have you seen this horse?

It happened in a flash. The image of Heart I'd given Nelly fluttered back and forth from desert sands to green pasture. It lasted only for a second, but I knew.

It was Heart.

She'd seen Heart. He stood in a pasture ringed with tall pine trees. I saw a barn, chicken coops, and even got a glimpse of the house.

"Ha! Good girl." I stood up, grabbed her by the horns and kissed the little star on her forehead.

I was so excited when Kai knocked on the door a few minutes later I overwhelmed him with a flood of information before he made it into the kitchen.

"Hold on, start over. You said Nelly knows where Heart is?"

"Yes! She saw him." I tried to explain the goat-vision,

then noticed he was still holding bags of food. "Let's sit out back. I'll grab the drinks."

The day was bright and beautiful, the view of the Atlantic—breathtaking.

"You sure you want to move?" Kai asked as he unwrapped his sandwich.

"No—I love the beach. But I can't live with my sister forever. Look at the company I keep." I pointed at the animals lounging about.

"A motley crew," he agreed.

"Tell me about what Nelly saw."

"It was him, Kai, I know it. Heart was standing in a *pasture*. With *pine trees*. That wasn't coming from me."

He smiled.

"Any landmarks? A place you recognized?"

My excitement faded. "No."

"Well, you know Heart's close to where you found Nelly—a goat can only go so far."

"Maybe if I could drive around the area . . ."

Kai didn't bother to respond; he just gave me a look.

"How else am I going to find him?"

"Why don't you try Google Earth or one of the other online maps? You can go to the street view and see if you recognize any of the houses."

Having never done so before, Kai showed me how to take the little virtual man and drop him on a particular road.

"If you start at R-n-R, which is . . . here." He clicked back to the satellite image and pointed at an area that, when I canted my head, lined up with my idea of where the stables were.

"Okay."

"Then work your way out in either a spiral or a grid pattern."

"Sounds very *CSI*-ish."

"It's how I walk crime scenes all the time."

His phone chirped. After glancing at the screen, he said, "Speaking of which—I've got to go."

"You're not going to ask about Boyle?"

"I figured you'd let me know."

"Set up the big reveal. She already thinks my sister and I are criminals, so what's the worst that could happen?"

• • •

I began virtually combing the places around R-n-R but made little progress.

"I'm getting nowhere," I said to Nelly, who had curled up on one of the outside chairs to chew her cud and watch me mutter to myself as I stared at the computer screen.

A lot of the houses were set too far back from the road to see. I was probably getting a good look at only half of the area's homes, if that.

I sat back and looked at the goat.

The later it got, the less open the goat had been to chat. As it neared sunset, no amount of coaxing would convince her to focus on Heart.

Her instincts were telling her to take advantage of the nice, raised bed the chair provided, and snooze. Roscoe, freshly finished with a rousing game of tag with Voodoo, hopped onto the adjacent seat and flopped down to rest.

I saw how low my battery was and went inside to plug in the laptop. Then, in an attempt to distract myself from thinking about Boyle's imminent visit, decided to clean the condo.

Emma kept things neat and organized so it didn't take long to straighten both the living and dining rooms. I'd already put things to rights after Boyle's deputies ransacked the place . . .

I froze, then rushed into the living room, lifted the couch cushions, and snatched up the yellow USB stick.

Crap!

With everything that had happened, I'd forgotten about it. And now Boyle was coming back.

"Calm down," I told myself. She couldn't search the house again, could she?

I still had to hide the stupid thing.

Kai would be knocking on the door any minute.

With a growl of uncertainty and frustration, I ran into my bedroom and stuffed the USB stick in one of my boots.

Just as I walked back into the living area to make sure the couch cushions were straight, there was a knock at the door.

Kai had arrived with dinner.

"Before we eat, can we take everyone out for a potty break?"

"Sure."

I asked him to act as lookout as I smuggled Nelly out of the condo.

Having had dinner, the goat wasn't very interested in taking more than a little nibble here and there. About five minutes later, we hurried back inside, careful to avoid making any noise that might attract Mr. Cavanaugh.

"Thanks," I said after getting the crew settled. "And thank you for bringing me food again."

"I brought you this, too."

Kai held up a long rolled-up tube of paper.

I unfurled it and laid it on the dining room table. It was a copy of a huge aerial photograph. I recognized the property in the center.

"It's R-n-R."

"I calculated the probable distance a goat could travel in two weeks, given where she started and where you found her. Which makes this"—he traced his finger over a red circle—"the most likely area of travel."

"This is amazing."

"I thought it might be easier to work on both the computer and this map."

Kai handed me my pita wrap and a pen.

"Let's start eliminating properties where we know Heart isn't."

We ate and marked the map. I crossed out the places I'd virtually visited, then recognized The Oaks and marked it off, too.

Even though a good chunk of the search area was in Jennings, there were at least thirty homes on the map.

"Well, it's a start, at least," Kai said.

It was.

"Tammy will be here soon. How do you want to do this?" Kai asked. "Should I tell her, or—"

"No. I'll do it. But if you can think of anything to say that might make her a little more open-minded, that probably can't hurt."

"You really don't think she'll listen, do you."

There was a loud knock at the door.

"Let's find out."

I took Moss and Voodoo and put them in my bedroom. Roscoe and Nelly were on the back deck.

Kai let Detective Boyle in and we all took a seat in the living room.

"Thanks for coming, Tammy," Kai said diplomatically. "I know you think I'm not very objective when it comes to Grace, and you're right. But when it comes to what she's about to tell you, just hear her out. Grace."

This was my cue. I looked from him to Detective Boyle. I'd never seen a more closed-off, unyielding face.

"Okay." I blew out the word on a long breath. For Emma. I would do anything I could, if there was a chance it would help my sister. I looked Detective Boyle in the eye and told her the truth.

Boyle smirked. "You're psychic."

"Yes."

She crossed or arms. "Okay. Prove it."

I shook my head. I knew it was pointless.

She looked at Kai as if to say, *See?*

"Grace, please."

"Fine. My dog, Moss, is in the other room, I can have him howl or—"

"I don't think so." She cut me off before I could finish the sentence and looked at me like I was something that needed to be scraped off the bottom of her shoe.

"You think I'm stupid?"

By some miracle, I managed not to answer that.

"First, I want you out of the room," she said to Kai.

"Come on, Tammy—" But his exasperated protest was useless.

"You want me to believe this dog and pony show? We do it my way."

I shrugged, waved him off, and said, "The closest room is the hall bath. If that's okay with you, Sergeant."

Kai didn't wait for her to respond, just turned and disappeared down the hall. Boyle kept her unfriendly gaze on me, so I slumped back into the couch with as much nonchalance as possible and propped my feet on the block of driftwood that served as the coffee table.

It sounds hackneyed, right? Using driftwood as *anything* in a beach house. But my sister made it work. Emma—talented, beautiful, brave Emma. I still wanted to be her when I grew up.

The thought brought on a flush of tears and a wave of anger so cold it burned through my belly like a shot of cheap bourbon. I looked at Boyle, not bothering to disguise how I felt.

"You look upset," she said with a smirk I would have paid good money to see wiped off her face. Preferably with a porcupine.

"Wow," I said in a monotone. "It's almost like you're a detective."

"Sarcasm is the implement of a weak mind. A defense mechanism. You feel frightened or angry and you use sarcasm as a shield."

"And a psychoanalyst, too. Nifty."

Her smirk grew into a smile and I winced inwardly.

Okay, so she had a point. So what?

It was clear I wasn't going to be able to stem the flow of sarcasm. "Clearly, you don't understand my humor. So let's get on with your test."

"The goat. Get it to come inside through the dog door. You have thirty seconds. If you speak or make any movements, you fail."

I started to open my mouth to tell her she was nuts but I'd be damned if I was going to give her the satisfaction.

The problem was, the dog door, which was easily big enough for Nelly to fit through, had a proximity lock. It would disengage only if the sensor came within a foot of the door, and the sensor was on Moss's collar.

I thought about the one hanging outside just in case I

locked myself out. It was dangling from one of the light fixtures hanging over the table.

Nelly was a goat. Goats were climbers—she could reach it.

I let my eyes drift closed, pulled in a calming breath, and reached out with my mind.

Nelly.

The goat was happily snuggled up next to Roscoe on the chaise longue.

Nelly!

I felt it when she focused on me. I pictured where the sensor was hanging and encouraged her to go to it.

It took several precious seconds but I finally heard a *clunk* as she jumped off the chaise, followed by the clop of dainty hooves on the deck.

Come on, Nelly girl, don't let me down.

I focused more intently on the goat. For a moment, I could actually see what she was seeing. Looking at the world from her perspective in real time. It wasn't something I did often or for long—mostly because it gave me a splitting headache—but it had its perks.

I was sure Nelly had seen the sensor, because she was looking right at it.

Yes! That.

She climbed onto the chair and then the table.

Seeing the movement while stationary brought on a wave of vertigo. I grimaced and pulled my thoughts away from the goat's.

There was another *thunk* as Nelly jumped off the table followed by a clatter when she scrambled through the doggy door.

I opened my eyes and Nelly dropped the hard plastic disk to the floor and let out a loud *"Mbaaaaaa!"* Basically saying, *There. Happy?*

Yes! Thank you, Nelly, you are the smartest goat ever.

Kai came bursting into the room just as what was left of the outdoor light came crashing to the ground. Roscoe let out a flurry of alarmed barks.

Nelly hopped back a step and toppled over.

Kai muttered a curse followed by an apology. "I forgot about the fainting thing. Is she all right?"

Nelly?

Whoops.

"She's fine."

Boyle was looking from me to the door to the goat then back at me, her eyes widening the longer her gaze darted along that path.

Moss, never one to miss out on the action, let out a short yip-howl, wanting to know what was going on.

"It's okay, Moss."

Okay?

Everything is fine, big guy. Take care of your kitty.

I got up to open the back door for Roscoe. The little dog darted inside, tail waving like a flag, ears pricked into twin plumes of dark, feathery hair as he sniffed at Nelly, gave her muzzle a friendly lick of encouragement, then pranced over to me and did his "pick me up" dance.

I obliged, then turned to face Kai. We both looked at Boyle.

"What happened?" he asked.

"She asked me to get Nelly to come inside."

"But the sensor for the door is on Moss's collar. How did Nelly unlock the dog door?"

I explained about keeping the second sensor outside.

"So she did it." Kai looked from me to Boyle. I wasn't sure if he was talking about me or Nelly. Either way, he was right. Not that it would matter.

"No," Boyle said, standing. "It's a trick."

"Tammy, how can it be a trick? Grace has had the goat less than twenty-four hours. It's never been here." He looked at me for confirmation but Boyle was already shaking her head.

She'd collected herself somewhat but still seemed to be breathing hard.

Kai noticed. "It's okay. Believe me, I had the same reaction."

"It's a trick."

"Tammy—"

"It has to be a trick."

"It's not." Though Kai's voice wasn't angry, it had gained a slight edge of impatience.

Boyle searched his face. She didn't like what she found.

Her brows bunched in anger. "What is this? Is this is some kind of joke? Screw with Boyle, the easy target?"

"Come on, I wouldn't do that."

"You are a scientist, Kai."

"Yes, which is why you should listen to me. Okay? You think I didn't look at this from every angle I could? You think I didn't question my own sanity?"

"No," she said. "I think you are either so deep in Sartori's pocket to want out or too wrapped up in her to give a damn. I don't know which, and I don't really care, but I am done listening to you."

Boyle stalked through the house and slammed the door on her way out.

"I don't understand," Kai said. "She can't possibly think you somehow rigged this."

"She doesn't," I said, feeling oddly calm. "She knows I was telling the truth. It just freaked her out."

Nelly had recovered and wanted to go back outside. I asked Kai to accommodate her while I went to open my bedroom door for Moss and Voodoo. Roscoe followed Nelly and they settled back on the chaise longue. Moss trotted out of the hall in front of me and started sniffing around, reconstructing who had gone where. He paused for a moment where Boyle had been sitting.

Strong emotions leave a mark. I wasn't sure if it was the scent or something more nebulous but animals were sensitive to it. Whatever Boyle had been feeling made Moss let out a low growl.

"Now that that's over, I could use a glass of wine."

We went into the kitchen and I poured a glass of whatever Kai had opened the night before. He went for a beer.

"I'm really sorry, Grace."

"It's okay," I said and for the first time in a long time I meant it.

"I just don't get it," Kai said.

"I do. Come on, let's sit. I want to tell you about an idiot I dated."

Kai gave me a curious look but followed me back into the living room.

We sat on the couch. I took a sip of wine and said, tongue firmly in cheek, "It's a sad story of love and loss. His name was Dane Harrington and I thought he was perfect."

I told Kai everything. More than I'd even shared with Emma. Dane and I had been vacationing in a private bungalow in the Bahamas. It had been the most romantic place you could imagine. Right on the beach. Filled with candles and moonlight.

Paradise.

Until I'd saved a pod of dolphins and told Dane the truth about my ability.

"So . . ." Kai said. "He just left you there?"

"With a plane ticket," I said lightly. "You see, we'd taken his family's private jet to the island so it was the least he could do."

"Jet?" I watched as he made the connection. "Wait. *Those* Harringtons?"

I lifted my wineglass with a nod.

"Damn."

"Hey," I said in mock offense. "You're not supposed to be impressed—the guy dumped me."

"I didn't say he wasn't an idiot."

"You're forgiven. Anyway, I'm telling you this because you need to understand. Boyle is like Dane. She will never accept that I'm telling the truth about my ability. She can't. I saw the way she looked at me, Kai. She knows I'm not lying. But it still freaked her out."

"Did it freak him out? The Harrington asshole."

"Oh yes."

"His loss."

"One man's trash is another man's treasure?"

Kai touched my chin and gently guided my face toward his. "Any man who would think you were trash is a fool."

He kissed me, and I forgot all about Dane Harrington and Detective Boyle.

CHAPTER 17

Wes was coming up the stairs as Kai was leaving for work the next morning.

"Wes, hey," I said, my cheeks heating slightly. "What are you doing here?"

"I thought I'd swing by and check on you, but I can see you're in good hands."

Kill me now.

"I hope you took good care of her, Sergeant."

The double entendre was pretty clear. Somehow Kai managed to say with absolute sincerity, "It was my pleasure." Then, turning to me with a wicked grin, he said, "I'll call you later." And kissed me good-bye.

Wes managed to keep a straight face until we were inside with the door closed.

He raised his brows, made a show of looking me up and down, and said, "Well, look who's glowing this morning."

"New moisturizer," I said lightly and turned to head into the kitchen.

"I'm not touching that one," he said, following me into the room. Then—"Well?"

"A lady never kisses and tells. You taught me that."

"*Pfft!*" He waved a hand. "What do I know?"

"Coffee?" I held up the carafe.

"Fine," he said, shoulders drooping in defeat.

I poured him a cup and we shared a silent toast before turning serious.

"How'd it go with Boyle last night?" he asked.

"It was a disaster."

He grimaced. "That good, huh?"

"On the bright side, Kai is going to talk to her boss and explain his concerns regarding her conduct."

"You go, girl," Wes said.

"I told him not to, but he insisted. I think he finally realizes she's not acting very balanced."

"I've already spoken to her supervisor. Maybe another cop will help. If it gets enough traction, the state attorney will get involved. There will be a review of the cases she's been involved in, including Emma's. But it won't be enough to get the charges dropped."

I nodded. Kai had told me the same thing. "You know what's weird? I thought I'd feel all smug, proving I was right about her. But I don't."

"You feel bad."

"Not for her. For Kai. Boyle's going to hate him for going over her head. He knows it, but he's going to do it anyway because he's worried about her."

"Sometimes you have to choose between what is right and what is easy."

I canted my head. "Did you just quote Dumbledore?"

"I did," Wes said, taking a final sip of coffee before setting his empty cup in the sink. "Now, I'll quote another great wizard and remind you that there's no place like home."

"That was the good witch, Glinda."

He gave me a pointed look.

I rolled my eyes. "I'm not going anywhere. Don't worry."

• • •

Ever notice how spending all day at home isn't a big deal until it becomes mandatory?

The restlessness set in about twenty seconds after Wes left.

I tried to kill time by focusing on chores, with minimal success. It had taken only twenty minutes to straighten my room, start a load of clothes, and empty the dishwasher.

Drumming my fingers on the counter, I worked on the map for a while, managed to eliminate two more properties, then tried to get more detail out of Nelly regarding Heart's location.

I sat out on the deck, brain growing more numb by the second as Nelly enthusiastically enumerated the various herbage sampled on her adventure.

If I'd had I the slightest idea what plants she was talking about, I might have been able to use the information to locate Heart. Like breadcrumbs but with chlorophyll.

Sometimes the lines of communication become garbled.

Nelly didn't say, *I ate clover* or *the wild dill was amazing.* She didn't know what I called the plants. Her names were all about flavor and smells. Having never munched on most weeds, I couldn't hope to translate.

So I went back inside to the aerial map.

I knew Kai would be out of pocket most of the day. I had leftovers and would survive not getting a lunch delivery.

He called just after ten, sounding a little rushed.

"I'm going to give a deposition this afternoon, so I don't know how late it will be before we can take Nelly home."

"That's okay. I called R-n-R and left a message on their voicemail, so at least they know I have her. She's fine here for a little while. I'm actually more worried about Cappy."

"I'll let you know how things are panning out. The deposition is for a major case so it might take a while. I'll be able to check my messages periodically. But if you need something or see anything odd, call Jake. A buddy of mine from Saint

Johns is going to park his cruiser at the entrance to your place for a little while—he should be there any minute."

"You're setting me up with a bodyguard?"

"I want to let these guys know you're protected. If they understand there'll be a backlash if they mess with you, they'll be less likely to try something."

"I'm touched," I said, and though it came out a little silly, I meant it.

"I'll see you tonight. Call if you need me."

I smiled for a while after he hung up, until I remembered my sister was in jail facing a murder charge.

Emma would be ecstatic to know I was happy. But that didn't assuage my guilt.

I had to think of a way to help my sister.

Kai had once explained that in an investigation, connecting the dots would be possible only after I had *collected* all of them. My gut was telling me there were some dots on the USB stick.

I retrieved the drive from where I'd hidden it, grabbed my laptop, and headed out onto the back deck.

Sitting at the table with the ocean breeze to clear my head, I plugged the drive into the USB port and clicked the icon. The box requesting the password popped onto the screen. I drew in a slow breath before starting to type.

In theory, the file had something to do with Ortega.

What did I know about him?

I typed his name, then deleted it.

"Don't focus on theory," I muttered to myself. "What do you know?"

Emma had wanted me to give the USB stick to Kendall.

With a shrug, I typed the girl's name.

The file opened.

I stared at the screen for a minute, too shocked to read over the contents. Once I started, I wished I hadn't.

There were separate folders, all about Anthony Ortega. One was labeled "Photos Hospital." I didn't open that one. I'd seen what he'd done to my sister firsthand, I didn't need to see it again.

If that had been the only thing on the drive I would have understood why she didn't want anyone to see it. But the other folders contained bank account information, addresses and phone numbers of people Ortega knew, and dates and location of travel.

Often, the data was annotated with Emma's shorthand.

I slumped back in the chair.

"What the hell, Em?" I wanted to haul my sister into one of those interrogation rooms at the JSO myself and demand to know what was going on.

Why did she have an encrypted file outlining every detail of her ex-husband's life? And why hadn't she ever told me about it?

Anger made me want to snach the USB stick out of my laptop and toss it into the Atlantic.

I didn't, because suddenly I realized what was keeping me on edge.

Fear.

I was afraid.

Not just because murderers had been following me. This was a different type of fear. One that had been growing since the moment I'd heard Ortega's last message. I hadn't recognized it before because it was the bone-deep, pervasive, nagging type of fear that cloaks itself in other emotions. Annoyance and anger. Frustration and doubt.

I was afraid, not only because Emma was in trouble, but because she had been lying to me. For years.

There was an explanation. There had to be.

Logan's words oozed into my mind.

What if she was guilty?

"No."

It was one thing for Emma to have secrets. Everyone did. But to believe she was capable of murder? I couldn't accept that.

Whatever reason Emma had for keeping this file didn't matter. It was in my hands now. I had to figure out what to do with it.

I started going through the subfiles, starting with the most recent, dated September 1. There were pages of bank statements with certain transactions underlined and notations in my sister's shorthand. I could read most of what she'd written, though little made sense. Several transactions were marked with *CA*, which was my sister's shorthand for cash.

So far, most of the transactions listed were marked *CA*.

Just when I thought I would start going blind and I'd never come across anything that made sense, I saw a name I recognized. Simone Grant. Dr. Simon had an ID in that name.

Next to a payment of $15,000 to Simone was the word *Services*.

Barf.

I redoubled my efforts, looking more closely at the other names on the list and saw a second name I recognized: Yosef Khalil, Heart's trainer. Who'd apparently received $1,000 from Ortega.

I frowned when I realized he could have been paying him for something legitimate. Equipment, medication—it didn't do me any good to make that connection.

Everyone knew Ortega had been in Morocco.

I scanned over the page looking for payment or a record of Ortega's purchase of Heart from LaPointe. But I didn't see any reference to the eccentric billionaire. Could it have been listed as his estate? I delved into the search anew and after almost an hour learned Ortega had, in fact, paid the Pearl of the Sand, a company owned by LaPointe, $20,000 in cash. No notation of what was purchased.

I sat back and glared at the file.

My gut told me there was information in it I could use. But I just didn't know what I was looking at.

I got a pen and a legal pad and wrote down every name listed, from the payment to the Pearl of the Sand to the last entry in the file.

Thirty-six people.

Mostly men.

I started searching the Internet for each name but quickly came to the conclusion that doing so was pointless.

Even starting with the less common names, there were dozens of people with the same name living all over the world.

I tried to narrow the results by adding Tony's name to the search but didn't come up with anything that seemed relevant.

After two hours, my head was pounding and I was ready to give up.

It would take days to research each name and I didn't even know what I was looking for.

Sartori had given Cowboy and Mr. Jingles a deadline to wrap up whatever business they had and get out of town.

Logan would make sure they honored the decree. Soon, the men responsible for two murders would skip town. Even if Kai was successful in his attempt to convince the higher-ups in the sheriff's office to reassign Boyle, it would be too late.

Emma had already been charged with murder. Unless the state attorney was provided with significant evidence to clear her, she would be tried.

As hard as it was to believe, as impossible as the idea seemed, my sister could go to prison.

The truth was, I didn't know how to use the information in front of me, and I couldn't very well ask Kai about what was on the USB drive and couldn't talk to Wes about it either. As much as Hugh would want to help, I was pretty sure he wouldn't know any more about Ortega's criminal activity than I did.

"Think like a criminal," I told myself. Like a criminal . . . Or I could go with option B and *ask* a criminal. Someone who wouldn't be compromised ethically or feel obligated to turn it over to the police. Someone who knew the identity of the players involved.

Logan.

He had refused to give me information but, in theory, I now had their names. How could he claim telling me more would put me in danger if I already had the information?

It was worth a shot.

I didn't have any more of his infamous cards featuring nothing but a phone number—I had given them to the cops.

Not that the cards would do much good; Kai told me the lines had been disconnected.

"I need the bat signal." I said, looking out over the horizon.

"Ghost signal. Whatever."

Suddenly, I had an idea.

I grabbed my phone and called Brooke.

"You know how to get in touch with Batman?" I asked as soon as she picked up.

There was a long pause, then: "Officially?"

"Unofficially," I promised. "I just need to get his input on something."

I could have asked to speak to her father but the thought made me balk. Odd that I felt more comfortable talking to Logan than Charles Sartori. Hey, the devil you know.

"I can get him a message," Brooke said.

"Perfect. Have him call me."

"Grace, is everything okay? Like, with Emma?"

"I hope so, kid."

About four seconds after hanging up, I started having doubts about my decision to contact Logan.

What was I thinking? I was just proving Boyle right, wasn't I?

Screw it. Boyle already believed I was a criminal, probably a mutant criminal.

Still, did I really want to get Logan and by extension, Sartori, involved?

If it meant I'd find a way to help Emma, yes.

What was I going to say to Kai?

CHAPTER 18

There had to be something I could do to take my mind off worrying while I waited for Logan to call.

I looked out at the Atlantic, longing to go for a mind-clearing walk. Not an option, what with murderers lurking about.

My leg jiggled up and down as my body tried to burn off restless energy.

I glanced around at all the dozing animals. Moss had woven himself around the table's legs and was sprawled at my feet, and Nelly, eyes half closed, contentedly chewed her cud in the shade of one of the large potted palms while Roscoe snoozed on the cushion of the chaise longue.

Voodoo was dead to the world in my lap.

I could always hitch a mental ride with one of them. Zone out for a while.

The thought had some appeal, though considering my state of mind, could just as easily backfire and have the opposite effect. I didn't want to foist my agitation on anyone else nor did I want to witness the havoc the animals could wreak if they got restless. Best I kept my brain to myself.

Maybe I could go to the dojo and hit the heavy bag? The complex's garages were detached, forming a solid wall between the condo's lot and A1A.

Surely I could make it across the parking lot safely. Especially with a Saint Johns deputy parked near the entrance. I could even go let him know I was headed to the garage for a little while.

I lifted Voodoo from my lap, intending to set her next to Moss to continue napping but before I could do so she stirred, tangled one paw in my hair, and started biting and batting it with sleepy, kitty glee.

Okay, let's go see if the deputy is still on watch.

I closed out the file then removed the USB stick and shut my laptop.

Tucking the USB stick in my back pocket, I carried the notepad and laptop in one arm and Voodoo in the other.

I'd left the door open to let the condo air out after my cleaning spree. But too much sea air was hard on everything from electronics to cabinetry.

With my elbow, I slid the door closed with a rasping *thunk.*

Moss hardly registered our departure, which said something for his level of sleepiness.

I set my laptop and notebook on the corner of the island and began to unwind Voodoo from my hair.

The peephole in the front door wouldn't give me a view of the parking lot. In fact, I wasn't sure I'd be able to see past the stairs even if I broke the rules and stuck my head out the door.

The only windows facing that way were in the laundry room and small, adjacent bath. Knowing I'd have to climb onto the washer and dryer to see out the laundry room window, I headed for the bath.

The potted plants Kai and I had relocated turned the space into a mini-jungle, much to Voodoo's delight. I set the kitten on the floor to explore while I headed to the window. Its opaque glass was patterned like some shower enclosures, but it opened a few inches. Not much of a view, but I could see the parking lot. The Saint Johns County police car was gone.

Dang it!

Kai had sent me a text with the deputy's name and warned me that the man would have to leave if he got a call.

No dojo. No beach walk. Did Emma still have her yoga DVDs?

I snapped the window closed and nudged Voodoo away from a large fern.

Scoot, kid.

"We're going to do some downward dog."

She scampered off in front of me but just as I was stepping into the hall the kitten came running back.

Alarm rippled from her like heat from a mirage.

Here's a little food for thought about cats: If they were inclined to take on the task, cats would make better watchdogs than most dogs. They hear and, in most cases, see better than dogs and are generally more sensitive to unusual sounds.

The problem is, even if they cared enough to bother—and let's be honest, we're talking about cats here—felines can't bark, which makes it difficult to warn of an intruder.

Unless you happen to be telepathic.

Man! Voodoo shot past me in a blur of frightened fur.

What? I asked, confused.

Man! She repeated the word along with the image of a pair of dark boots and pant legs. I let out a squeak, scooped the kitten into my arms, slammed and locked the bathroom door.

All in all, not the smartest move. I was now stuck in the small room with no way out and nothing but a toilet brush and some attractive foliage to use as a weapon.

If I opened the window I could yell for the cop or better yet, send out a mental distress call to Moss.

I was readying to do so when someone on the other side of the door said, "Grace?"

Even over my pounding heart I recognized the voice.

"Logan?"

Still clutching Voodoo to my chest, I opened the door.

"You rang?" It was a passable impersonation of Lurch, but I wasn't amused.

"Are you trying to give me a heart attack?"

And why hadn't Moss warned me of Logan's presence?

A quick mental check told me my dog was completely conked out. I relaxed slightly.

Logan must have come through the front door. Had I left it unlocked?

"How did you get in here?"

"I'm more interested in how you knew I was here. You knew I was in your truck, too. How?"

"I'm psychic," I said drily.

His gaze flicked over me in a way that made me want to squirm and I suddenly became aware of how much bigger than me he was. Being someone who didn't like to show weakness and still embarrassed by the pathetic squeak I'd made when I realized someone was in the house, I made myself step forward. The move left Logan with two options—he could either move to let me pass or stay and make me bump into him.

Logan stepped back a fraction. Far enough to let me into the hall, but just barely.

The dim light of the hall seemed to accentuate his size.

Maybe I was a foot shorter and holding nothing more than a kitten but I wouldn't be intimidated in my own hall-way, dammit.

I glared up at him. "Are you finished?"

"Finished?"

"Looming."

He quirked a brow and let several seconds tick by before taking a step back. I brushed past him and started down the hall. I'd have to get a handle on my nerves before Moss woke up. I wouldn't want my dog to take a bite out of Logan.

Then again, maybe I did. It would be nothing less than he deserved.

I put Voodoo on the love seat where she liked to sleep and looked out the sliding glass doors. Moss was still fast asleep on the back deck.

"Some guard dog," I muttered to myself.

"Nice goat," Logan said, coming up behind me.

"Thanks." I turned to face him. "I'm sure you know that's not why I contacted you. I wanted to show you this." I handed him the notepad with a list of names. "The men who've been following me are on there somewhere. I want to know who they are."

"Where did you get these names?"

"It doesn't matter. Just tell me what I need to know."

"You're not going to stop, are you?"

"No."

"Tell me where you got the names."

I shook my head.

He tossed the pad onto the counter.

"No source, no intel."

"They're from a file on Tony Ortega."

"May I see it?"

"Just tell me what you know. Please."

Logan crossed his arms. Waited.

Finally, he said, "One of the first rules of negotiation: Know what's at stake and he with the least at stake, wins."

We both knew I was the one with the most to lose.

"I'll show you the file. After you tell me everything you know about Mr. Jingles. He's the one with the Greek-sounding accent."

"His name is Erjon Hoxha, and he's not Greek, he's Albanian."

"That's it?"

"That's all I know."

I didn't buy it, but it was clear he wasn't going to tell me more until I showed him my source, so I turned on my laptop, plugged in the USB stick and opened the encrypted file.

"This list has some interesting contacts. Your brother-in-law was mixed up with some bad people."

"Does that mean I should give this to the police, to prove Tony had contacts with whoever?"

"I wouldn't."

"Why?"

"No one on this list was caught standing over his body."

"What about Mr. Jingles, Hoxha," I corrected. "Or Cowboy?"

"What about them?"

"You promised to tell me what you know, Logan."

"I tell you what, give me this USB drive, and I'll see what I can do to put Hoxha and Cowboy in the right hands."

"Not mine to give."

"Then I can't help you."

"Okay. Deal. But only after Emma's cleared."

"I'll see what I can do."

He laid a key on the counter. "You shouldn't hide a spare key outside. It's too easy for the wrong person to find it."

He turned and walked out the door.

Damn.

Not only had I contacted Logan, I'd just made a deal with him.

What else could I do?

Time was running out. I didn't exactly trust Logan, but I didn't think he was lying.

• • •

After Logan left, I spent time pacing around, chewing on my lip, and worrying.

Pointless.

There was no laundry to do, so I decided to clean out the fridge. It didn't take nearly long enough.

I sat on the couch next to where Voodoo was tottering over the cushions and tried to find some inner calm.

The kitten attempted to leap from the couch to the coffee table and didn't quite make it. She did, however, manage to snag the magazine with her claws and pull it down on top of herself.

Bubba! Panicked, she sped off toward Moss, seeking protection from the scary paper thing that had attacked her.

He gave her a reassuring lick and, courage restored, she bounded out of sight.

Kittens are such adorable, manic little things.

I bent to retrieve the magazine. It had fallen open to the often-studied photo of Jasmine and Heart.

Sighing, I looked at the ad and wondered what would happen if I failed.

Would whoever took Heart hurt him? Had they already?

My phone rang and I snatched it up, desperate to derail that train of thought.

"We found the vet's car," Jake's gruff voice rumbled over the line.

"Yeah?"

"We're bringing the two guys in right now."

"That's great, Jake." Logan had kept his word. I wasn't surprised, per se, just shocked that he'd done it so quickly. Which made me wonder what was on the USB drive that he wanted.

"Grace?" Jake said. "You listening?"

"Sorry. What?"

"I know you're thinking this means Emma's in the clear."

"It doesn't?"

"Thugs like this, sometimes they want to talk, sometimes they don't. Just sayin', don't count your chickens."

"Chickens?"

A flash of insight hit me.

"You know," Jake said, "before they hatch."

"Right. Thanks, Jake," I said in a rush and hung up.

"Chickens," I muttered then closed my eyes and tried to remember the details of what Nelly had shown me.

Heart, in a pasture. Pine trees. A barn. And what I'd thought were chicken coops.

Not chickens. *Guineas.*

On impulse, I started to call Kai then remembered he wouldn't be able to answer so sent him a text instead.

I know who has Heart! I went on to explain briefly and asked him to call when he had a few minutes to talk.

I was sure I knew where Heart was, and therefore, who'd taken him, but I still didn't know why.

I tried calling Jasmine, and when she didn't pick up, left her a message to call me back.

Walking out onto the deck, I took a deep, cleansing breath of tangy salt air and let my eyelids drift closed. A half a second later they sprung open and went wide.

To the south, a wall of bruised clouds darkened the horizon.

Crap!

I rushed inside and opened my laptop. A quick look at the weather website I'd been checking over the last few days confirmed my fears.

The line of storms was headed onshore. I snatched up my phone. It took a minute to find the number I was looking for.

It rang at least ten times before a good old-fashioned answering machine picked up.

"This is Grace Wilde. If you're there, please pick up—it's an emergency." I waited a couple of seconds. "Okay, I'm going to say this as quickly as I can. Heart, the horse I've been looking for and am fairly certain you have, is terrified of storms. It's a long story, the why isn't important. You need to know—" The machine cut me off.

"Dammit." I redialed.

Busy.

I walked outside, counted to ten while I watched the bloom of angry clouds roil closer, then tried the number again. It started ringing. I knew I couldn't just leave a message and hope for the best. I glanced at Nelly. I couldn't leave her in the condo, either.

The answering machine picked up again.

"Heart—the horse. He has to be blindfolded during storms. It's the only thing that will keep him calm. Otherwise, he'll panic and hurt himself. Let me know you got this message. You don't have to admit to anything, I just want to know he's safe. My number—" The machine cut me off again.

"Really?"

A spear of lightning flashed in the distant clouds.

No time.

"Roscoe, you're on kitty-patrol. Nelly, Moss, let's go." I grabbed a slip lead and Moss's leash. "We've got a horse to save."

CHAPTER 19

I loaded Nelly into Bluebell first, then hurried to the other
side to open the door for Moss, who hopped in to join her.
I started to close the door and noticed Nelly was chewing
on something besides her cud.

A stiff piece of white paper jutted from the side of her mouth.

"Give me that." I reached past Moss and plucked the
paper from her lips, frowning when I realized what it was.

A card. Plain but for a phone number printed on one side.

Logan.

He must have left it in the seat the other night.

Shaking my head, I shoved the mangled card into my
back pocket, shut the door, and climbed in behind the wheel.

As I pulled onto A1A, I redialed the number. Again, I
got the answering machine.

"Blindfold the horse before the storm if you want to keep
him safe," I said in a rush. "Listen to the other messages if
you need the details. I'm on my way to you now."

The storm chased us all the way there. Pressing closer in
the rearview mirror with every mile.

Finally, I turned off the paved road toward R-n-R, then

turned again and followed a narrow, bumpy lane to where it ended.

I climbed out of Bluebell but paused before opening the back door to allow Moss to join me.

Heart might be afraid of dogs. The horse was sure to be agitated; I didn't want to add any more stress.

I turned toward the barn, then did an about-face and went back to Bluebell. Walking around to the other side, I opened the door to see Nelly had stretched her neck over the back-seat into the cargo space and was nibbling on something she shouldn't. The goat wouldn't frighten Heart, and I couldn't leave her to damage herself or Bluebell's seats, carpet, seat belts, or whatever else she could get her lips on.

"Come on, Nelly." I slipped a lead around her neck. "You're coming with me. Moss, stay." I laced the last command with the weight of my will. Letting him know it was important he do as I asked.

He yielded, unhappily, and gave me the letdown-yet-still-eager face through the window as I closed the door.

"Sorry, big guy. If I can, I'll come get you in a bit."

Nelly in tow, I hurried to the barn's massive set of doors, started to reach for the handle, and stopped.

A new padlock gleamed in the dusky light, mocking me.

I grabbed the lock and yanked. It remained steadfastly closed.

There was a crack where the two doors met and I peered through it, trying to get a glimpse of the equine I knew was inside. But the crack was too narrow and the interior too dark.

"Mind telling me what you're doing here?"

I turned and saw Boomer, who was standing near the corner of the barn and holding a very serious-looking double-bladed ax in one hand. He wasn't swinging it at me, and I didn't want him to, so I raised my hands as far as Nelly's lead would allow.

"Guess you didn't get my messages?" I asked.

He didn't respond, just studied me with a narrow-eyed gaze.

"Listen, there isn't time to explain," I said. "I know it's

asking a lot, but you need to trust me. We have to get a blindfold on Heart. Now."

A distant, muted rumble of thunder punctuated my words. A nervous whinny sounded from inside the barn, along with hooves shuffling over hard earth.

"Why do you have Nelly?" Boomer asked.

"I found her in Jennings. I'm planning to take her back to R-n-R, but I have to make sure Heart's okay first."

The wind picked up, making the treetops sway. Another strained whinny echoed from the other side of the door.

The world had become tinted with the odd yellow-green light that sometimes precedes a storm.

We didn't have much time.

"Boomer, please. We have to blindfold the horse. If we don't, he'll panic and hurt himself."

"Blindfold, with what?"

"I was going to use this." I motioned to the windbreaker I'd tied around my waist.

Heart snorted and uttered a louder, more agitated squeal.

The fear started radiating from him in cold, shivering waves. I pressed back with soothing thoughts, and he calmed, but I knew it was tenuous.

"Please," I said to Boomer.

The man reached into his pocket and tossed me his keys. I handed him the end of Nelly's lead, unlocked the doors, and pulled one side open. In the eerie light, Heart looked like a phantom emerging from the shadows. A Ringwraith's fell steed.

Boomer limped inside, turned on the lights, and the horse was transformed into the beautiful animal I'd been looking for.

"Heart." I was so relieved, I wanted to rush forward and fling my arms around his neck.

Heart's ears pricked at the sound of his name. I felt his flutter of hope and anticipation—then his eyes adjusted to the light and the feeling faded.

He'd seen my dark hair and for a moment thought I was Jasmine.

"Sorry, handsome." *I'll get you together soon*, I

promised, then untied the windbreaker. "First, let's take care of this, okay?"

Heart shied as the first drops of rain began to fall. I reached out with soothing thoughts to calm him. As quickly as possible, I folded the lightweight fabric and, with Boomer's steadying hand on Heart's halter, tied the jacket over his eyes.

The horse calmed almost instantly. I let out a pent-up breath and gave his neck a gentle pat. Then gave him a quick, mental once-over to check for any physical issues. He was fine and dandy.

"How did you know?" Boomer asked.

"I told you, his owner was worried about him." I'd turned to look at Boomer and give him the full story when I noticed something unusual.

We were surrounded on three sides with hay bales. They'd been stacked like giant bricks to form a wall.

The brick-laying pattern started by one door, stair-stepped up and went all the way around to the other door. With both doors closed, the structure became a temporary horse stall in the middle of the barn.

A more thorough look around told me why the makeshift corral was necessary.

To the left, the stalls had been converted to chicken, or in this case, Guinea coops. The wall to the right was covered with various gardening tools. Several polo mallets were mounted above, and a few dangled from a hook.

A workbench and shelving lined the back wall, packed with an array of tools, paint cans, extension cords, and various other items sure to get a curious horse into trouble if given the chance.

The gap above the base where the hay wall started was large enough for a person to step up and over, providing access to the rest of the barn.

"I like the hay idea," I told Boomer, turning to face him.

"You know horses," Boomer said, still eyeing me a little warily. "If they can get into something, they will."

I nodded. "Not as bad as goats, though." As if to prove

my point, Nelly bounced up the pass-through opening to stand on the wall of hay.

Goats.

The rain and wind picked up and Boomer went to close the doors against the strengthening storm. I noticed he'd set the ax in the corner, which I took as a good sign.

Without any prompting, he turned to me and said, "I wasn't planning on keeping him."

"What happened? Why take him in the first place?"

"Our mare, Lucy, was getting over a mild colic. I'd been checking on her every few hours. I knew Parnell wouldn't bother."

"Because he wants to sell R-n-R?"

"I didn't know that at the time, but he'd made it clear he didn't care much about the animals. When Nelly got out, he just shrugged. Asked me how long it would take to fix the fence."

"It was up to you to check on Lucy."

He nodded. "It's quicker to cut across the back field than it is to get in the truck and drive all the way around. Mess with the gate, you know."

I remembered seeing how close his house was to R-n-R's barn on the aerial map. I also remembered a fence.

"How do you get onto the property?"

"There's a gate to access the riding trails."

I hadn't remembered seeing a gate, but I hadn't been looking.

"It was after midnight," Boomer continued. "That time of night, things are usually real still and quiet, but when I headed across the field I saw a car parked by the office. As I got closer, I could see there were a couple of people in the front. At first, I thought it was Hunter with one of his friends sneaking a beer or something. You know kids."

"But it wasn't Hunter." I had a good guess who it was.

Boomer shook his head. "One of them lit a cigarette and I saw his face. There was something about him. I can't say what, but it didn't feel right. We didn't have anyone scheduled to stay—and the gate should have been locked, so they weren't turned around or lost."

"Why not call the cops?"

"Couldn't. They'd have seen me if I tried to get to the office. I went as far as the shed so I could hear what they were saying. One of them had an accent—he said, 'We need to cut him open. We can't just shoot him.' The other said, 'Why not? Ortega can take care of the fallout. What does he care about a dead horse as long as he gets his money?' And I knew I didn't have time to make it home to call the police, either."

"How did you know the 'him' they were talking about was Heart?"

"Scout is the only other horse it could've been, and he's been at R-n-R for years. Why would anyone want to cut him open all of a sudden?"

"So you took Heart before they could hurt him."

"I've lost horses before. Working with them as long as I have it's bound to happen. But the last time—" He shook his head and looked away. "The last time, I swore: never again."

Thunder boomed loud enough to rattle the walls. We all jumped. Boomer and I both looked at Nelly, who had thankfully decided to lie down atop the hay and was in no danger of falling over. Heart shied but no more than any other horse might and as soon as the thunder rumbled past, he was still.

I cast my mental feelers out to Moss. He wasn't afraid of storms the way some dogs are, but I wanted to check in, anyway.

You okay, big guy?

Okay. Dinner?

Yep, he was fine.

Soon. I apologized for the late dinner and promised to make it up to him. He settled in to enjoy the white noise of the pounding rain and dream of the clucky, fluttery things he'd smelled when we had first driven up.

I looked past Heart toward the coops, where I could see the dark, speckled forms of the guineas as they roosted. Even over the pounding rain, their squeaking honks and soft whistles were audible. Guineas were renowned for raising the alarm if they spotted a threat. Real or imagined.

"What did the guineas think of their new barn mate?" I asked Boomer.

"Fussed a little when I brought him home that first night."

"Why didn't you call the police once you got back?"

"I was going to," he said. "It took some time to get him settled. Once everyone was quiet, I went back to see if they were still around, but the car was gone. I figured it could wait. The next morning I went to talk to Mr. Parnell, you know, tell him what happened. When I got to R-n-R, there was a man already asking questions. Said he was a cop named Ortega."

Tony had pretended to be a cop? It was almost laughable.

"I remembered hearing the men the night before saying someone named Ortega would take care of things."

"You thought they knew a dirty cop who would cover for them."

He nodded. "Parnell didn't want anything to do with it. Too worried about selling the place, I guess. So I tried to figure out what the hell was going on. Why anybody'd want to cut up a horse? I figured Lily Earl might know something but by then, I was neck-deep in this mess, didn't want to drag her into it."

"You're the one who stole her paperwork."

"And a fat lot of good it did me. Everything on it was fake. I called the contact number—no answer. I tried looking up his registered name. Nothing. I didn't know what to think, except someone wanted to hurt him, and I wasn't going to let that happen."

I looked at the dust-covered polo mallets and thought of the decals on Boomer's truck from Wellington. One had been from 2009.

Suddenly, I understood.

"You were in Wellington when . . ." I didn't have to explain; Boomer knew I was talking about the day over twenty polo ponies had suddenly, mysteriously died. It had turned out to have been an accident, a mistake with a vitamin dosage that ended in tragedy.

"That was one of the worst days of my life," Boomer said, voice rough. "They died. One after the other, and none of us could do anything."

My nose stung. My vision made hazy by the sudden tears. I couldn't imagine.

"I'm sorry." My voice was low and so thick with emotion, I was surprised he could understand me.

He nodded, blinking hard as he looked away.

"Nothing to be done about it, now," he said. "And trying to change that fact only leads to trouble. Believe me. Here I was, with a stolen horse and no idea what to do. I went over what I'd heard that night a hundred times but all I can figure is—these guys must have been smuggling something, so I looked him over."

"And?"

"Couldn't find anything. Until you came poking around. I talked to Lily Earl. She said you were looking for a gelding, but I had a stallion."

I felt my eyes widen. "Wait, you're saying . . ."

Boomer smiled. "Yep."

It made a crazy sort of sense. I knew there were companies that made testicular implants.

"So he's . . . augmented?" I asked.

"Not anymore."

"You took them out?" I asked, stunned. "How?"

"I've been working with horses longer than you've been alive and then some."

I had nothing against giving credit where credit was due but, really? No way.

"And he didn't mind?"

"Nah. Scar tissue made it painless."

I started to check with Heart to verify the story but remembered I'd already given him the psychic once-over and had detected no aches or pains. Besides, there was something I really wanted to know.

"What did you find?"

"I'll show you." Boomer got up and motioned for me to follow as he slipped through the person-sized gap in the hay wall and walked along the path he'd left to serve as both a walkway and a buffer zone to keep Heart clear of the wall of garden implements.

Boomer stopped before we reached the workbench and pointed up. Like you find in many barns, there was a loft and now that I was looking, I could see that what I'd thought was just the side support for shelving was really a ladder.

Before I could protest, Boomer started to climb.

"Hey," I said, "be careful." The ladder was a structural part of the barn's shelves but that didn't keep me from grabbing the sides in a pointless attempt to hold it steady.

Boomer reached the top, pulled himself onto the loft, and disappeared from view. A few minutes and some scraping sounds later, he returned, holding up a pair of what looked like plastic Easter eggs.

I squinted at them. Felt my brows arch.

They were *blue*.

"Oh, come on."

Boomer grinned and dropped one egg down to me. I twisted it open. Inside, a diamond necklace glinted, catching the light as only diamonds can. I lifted the necklace partly out of the egg. I was no expert but I was sure even one of the large stones would be worth a small fortune.

Mouth agape, I raised my eyes to Boomer. He shook the second egg, making it rattle like a maraca. Eyes twinkling, Boomer tossed it down, too. I'd started to open the second egg when I heard Moss let out a warning howl-bark.

Reaching out to connect with his mind, I became aware that someone had pulled in to park behind Bluebell.

I froze. The rain and distance may have masked the sound of the pickup truck, but it was obvious that the men who climbed out of the vehicle were trying to conceal their approach to Boomer's house.

Shhh, Moss. I urged him to stay quiet and alert.

He did, and I edged a little more closely into his thoughts to listen and watch through my dog's eyes.

The night was brighter. Shadows less dense.

One of the men paused to look in at Moss. Thanks to Moss's wolf-eyes, the man's features were clear. I'd seen him before—in one of the photos from Morocco.

It was the security guard. The one standing off to the

side in the photo of Jasmine wearing the real LaPointe jewels.

A faint, clinking ring came to me through Moss's ears.

Mr. Jingles.

There was a split second of disbelief, followed by a rapid-fire ping-ponging of thoughts.

Mr. Jingles and Cowboy were here. They must have followed me—but how?

I'd talked to Jake no more than an hour ago. They couldn't have gotten out of jail.

No time to worry about specifics. I wasn't sure how it was possible, or how everything fit together but I knew I didn't have time to worry about it now.

Thanks to Moss, I could track the men's movements. Mr. Jingles headed to the house; Cowboy was walking straight toward the barn.

I blinked the world around me back into focus. Boomer had turned and was moving to start down the ladder.

"Boomer, wait!" The fear in my hushed voice made him stop and glance over his shoulder at me.

There was no way to explain how I knew what I knew. There would barely be enough time for me to tell him to hide.

I touched my finger to my lips and sprinted down the pathway to the barn door. Opening it a crack, I peered out into the light rain.

Cowboy's figure was backlit by the wan light from the back porch. He was about fifty feet away.

No time to run—Boomer wouldn't even make it down the ladder.

I pulled the door closed and rushed back to the loft, gesturing frantically.

"Hide!" I hissed.

"What?"

I met Boomer's gaze and mouthed, *Hide*, with an urgent wave. For a moment, it looked like he would protest but Boomer was smart and wary enough to take my advice.

He eased back into the shadows and disappeared.

Cowboy had to be getting close to the barn. I thought

about Boomer's heavy, double-sided ax but knew I could never hope to use it, or any of the other tools for that matter. How much good would a weed-whacker be against a gun?.

I needed to think.

Easier said than done in situations like this.

One thing was certain, I didn't want to draw attention to the loft's ladder, obscure as it was.

I grabbed a bucket of grooming tools from a shelf and rushed back to where Heart stood.

As I set the bucket beside him, I realized I was clutching the eggs to my chest. If I handed the gems over, I was a goner.

I scrambled to where the water bucket sat on the hay bale, opened each egg, and dumped the sparkling contents into the water.

A rustle of footsteps sounded from just outside the door. I tossed the empty plastic shells to the far end of the makeshift stall and grabbed a brush out of the bucket.

The footsteps paused. Cowboy was probably peering through one of the cracks.

As calmly as possible, I began brushing out Heart's glossy, black coat.

A cool head would win over blind panic. These men were murderers. I was no match for them in the skill or ruthlessness department, I had to *think*.

What did I know about these men? They'd killed Dr. Simon. That fact didn't help in the anti-panic department, so I shoved it away.

Think. Think. Think.

What else did I know?

I remembered something I'd overheard while hiding in the closet with Roscoe.

I don't do bad business—that was what Cowboy had said. To him, murder was just business. Could I play on that? Find a way to appeal to that sensibility? Convince him I was just as ruthless and jaded?

If you'd asked me a couple of months ago to rate my lying prowess I would've put myself just north of the two-year-old-caught-with-a-forbidden-cookie level.

However, for better or worse, my skills at deception had improved. Not greatly, but I'd learned one important key to telling tall tales and getting away with it: commitment.

You had to *become* the lie.

A whisper of an idea formed in my mind. When the barn door creaked open, I was ready.

I kept up the brushing for a few strokes then glanced over my shoulder. Feigning mild surprise, I smiled and turned to face him.

"I thought you boys had already left town."

Cowboy didn't respond; he just glared at me with cold, dark eyes.

I didn't flinch or look away. One of the benefits of coming eye-to-eye with some of the scariest creatures known to man was that I was not easily cowed with a glare.

The gun Cowboy held was another matter, but I managed to keep my expression cool.

Any show of weakness would be a mistake.

I held the brush tightly in one hand and rested the other on Heart's muscular flank. More to conceal my shaking fingers than anything else.

I didn't want to open my thoughts to the horse—sharing my terror with him wouldn't do me any good.

The poor thing might rear or try to bolt. I was just as likely to get trampled in the confined space as Cowboy, so I kept my mind carefully shielded as I held his gaze.

Time seemed to move at the speed of a herd of turtles marching through molasses. Mr. Jingles finally broke the stalemate when he appeared in the doorway. Cowboy looked at his partner, who shook his head, which I took to mean he'd searched the house and found it empty.

They turned their attention back to me.

"Howdy," I said.

"Tony was right." I wasn't sure if Cowboy was talking to me or Mr. Jingles.

"There's a first time for everything," I said, letting my distaste show.

"You found the horse." Mr. Jingles was eyeing me the way someone might look at an unusual bug.

"I did. But not for Tony. I found him for Jasmine and to get the reward she offered."

"You won't be collecting," Cowboy said.

"Come on." I put my hands on my hips. "It's only ten grand. You got what you want, you can't be that greedy."

The men stayed silent. I looked back and forth between them and let my smirk fade. "You *did* get what you wanted, right?"

"What might that be?" Cowboy asked.

"Uh . . ." I tried to look surprised and innocent as I pointed to the empty plastic eggs on the hay-sprinkled ground.

Predictably, Cowboy raised his gun to point at me and snarled, "Where are they?"

"Your guess is as good as mine. I . . ." I trailed off then shook my head and muttered, "Damn."

"What?"

"Can't you guess?" I asked.

"I'm not in the mood to play games."

"I'm not the one playing."

He leveled the gun at my leg. "If I don't like the next three words out of your mouth, I'll blow your knee apart."

Don't faint, I told myself. *Don't throw up and don't crumple to the ground to beg for your life.*

I had to have some moxie.

He wanted to hear three words. I only needed one.

"Logan."

Cowboy's eyes narrowed.

I waited. Sometimes it was best to shut up and let people draw their own conclusions. I was hoping these two were going to come up with the same conclusion Boyle had, that I was in with Sartori's gang.

Ironic, given how much energy I'd spent trying to prove I wasn't connected to Sartori's criminal organization. Now my life depended on two very bad men believing the opposite.

"How do you know Logan?" Mr. Jingles asked.

"He works for my uncle."

"Uncle?" Cowboy scoffed. "You're saying Sartori is your uncle."

"Yep."

"You're lying. You're dating a cop."

"You mean Kai Duncan?" I tried to smile flirtatiously as I looked at each man in turn. "The sergeant's not my type. But don't tell him that."

Mr. Jingles let his gaze flick over me, though whether it was in admiration or doubt, I couldn't be sure.

"Tell you what," I said, "you can call Logan and—" I started to reach into my back pocket and almost lost my kneecap.

"Don't," Cowboy growled.

"Whoa. It's just his number." I held up Logan's card.

Cowboy plucked it out of my hand and frowned. "Did you drop it in a garbage disposal?"

"No, that's goat spit."

He almost dropped the card, but I pretended not to notice. "Unlike Mrs. Simon, or whatever her name was, I'm an actual vet who works with real animals."

Cowboy curled his lip in distaste.

"Hey." I shrugged. "Spit happens."

Neither man seemed to appreciate the joke.

"Call Logan. Tell him you have me and you want to trade. He'll do it."

Cowboy held out the card to Mr. Jingles. He declined and pulled a phone out of his back pocket. "I have his number," he said, and dialed.

I waited for him to curse and say there wasn't a signal. My plan was to then suggest we use the house phone and once we'd left the barn I'd make a run for the woods.

But Mr. Jingles didn't curse. In fact, it looked like he was waiting for someone to answer.

He must have a satellite phone.

Crap!

I heard him say, "We have Sartori's niece." His eyes shifted to me and I barely had time to consider panicking before he handed the phone to me.

I took it. "Logan?"

"Grace." He sounded resigned. "Where are you?"

I couldn't tell him. Doing so would let Mr. Jingles and Cowboy know Logan had never been here and therefore couldn't have taken the gems.

"Don't give me a hard time, Logan, you knew I was looking for the horse."

"I'm going to need more to go on, sweetness," Logan said.

I knew that, but aside from Boomer, only one person knew where I was—Kai.

I made a show of rolling my eyes as I tried to think of a way to discreetly pass this information to Logan. "You can be pissed later," I said. "I'm supposed to be meeting Kai and he'll get suspicious if I don't show. You know how long I've been working on him?"

"Kai knows where you are." It wasn't a question.

"That's ri-ight," I singsonged. "For*ever*."

I could tell my comments had made Cowboy suspicious. But I didn't want to give back the phone. Breaking the connection with Logan suddenly felt like cutting the cords of a parachute.

Cowboy stepped toward me and snatched the phone out of my hands.

"Rude," I said, crossing my arms in a huff.

Cowboy kept his gaze on me as he spoke into the phone, "You have thirty minutes to bring us what we want." I couldn't hear Logan's response and couldn't read Cowboy's expression.

Cowboy hung up and handed the phone back to Mr. Jingles.

For a couple of seconds, I let myself think, *Yay, Logan is coming!* Then reality started seeping in and I thought, *Oh crap, Logan is coming.*

He had nothing to trade for me, which meant he would have to resort to other tactics.

If he did something drastic to Cowboy and Mr. Jingles, where did that leave Emma?

Maybe I was jumping too far ahead. They'd given him a

mere thirty minutes. Which didn't allow Logan much time to get in touch with Kai and ask where I was.

I didn't want to imagine how that conversation would go. Would Kai even talk to Logan?

There were so many things to worry about, I wasn't sure which to pick first. But one thing was clear, I was going to need to come up with a plan B and be ready to exploit any opportunity that presented itself.

I heard Mr. Jingles say, "He'll try to sneak up on us."

Cowboy shrugged. "Keep an eye on her. I'm going to look around."

I watched him slip outside into the light rain, which left me one less bad guy to deal with. Though I didn't know if the remaining bad guy was armed. I thought not, but couldn't be certain.

"It's funny," my captor said. "Tony told us he wasn't working with Sartori."

"Tony said a lot of things." I turned and started brushing Heart again, hoping to sneak a glance at the loft where Boomer was hiding and avoid any questions I didn't know the answer to.

I could feel Mr. Jingles's eyes on me and the nape of my neck shivered and tried to crawl away to hide.

"I'm wondering, why did he hire Simone? I mean, she's good as far as cons go, but it seems foolish to have her set up shop and pretend to be a vet if he's got you."

"Good question. Too bad you can't ask him."

"You're right. It is too bad."

I glanced over my shoulder when I heard the jingling again. He was looking out the partly open door into the drizzling rain. I watched as he fished a pack of cigarettes from the inside of his jacket, reached into the jingle pocket of his pants, and produced a metal lighter. Flicking the flame to life with one smooth, practiced movement, he pulled in a lungful of smoke and turned his attention back to me.

"Tony and me went way back," he said more quietly, then glanced away, flicked ash from his cigarette, and exhaled a cloud of smoke. "I didn't mean to kill him."

"Right," I said, wondering if Boomer had heard the confession. If everything went south, maybe he could vouch for Emma.

"You didn't mean to kill Simone either?" I said more loudly than was necessary.

"Simone—that wasn't me. I pushed her to talk, sure." He lifted a shoulder as if to say, *Sometimes you just have to torture people, you know how it is.* "But I would have let her go. Killing women—" He made a face.

"Your partner doesn't have a problem with it."

"He's not my partner," Mr. Jingles spat. "He has the honor of a dog."

I snorted. He looked at me and I said, "I've found dogs to be far more honorable than men."

Time to steer the conversation in a new direction. "Why use a horse?" I asked, looking over at him. "It's not like jewelry can't be hidden in a hundred other places. Why go to all the trouble?"

"LaPointe is a paranoid bastard. No one and nothing was allowed off the estate without being checked."

"Everyone? Even guests?"

"Guests, family, it didn't matter. Even the cars were parked outside the security gate."

"That's why he had to have the replicas made. How did you manage to swap them out?"

"Once you were inside the estate, LaPointe didn't care. He'd let his dog walk around in diamonds."

There was enough bitterness in his voice to make a lemon seem sweet.

"Must have driven you crazy," I said, "Seeing all that wealth wasted on islands and cars."

"My mother died because I couldn't afford better doctors."

I almost felt sorry for him. But just because life wasn't fair didn't give you the right to take someone else's stuff and murder people.

Thankfully, Cowboy returned before I opened my mouth to express my views.

The two men started talking quietly. I strained to hear what they were saying, but they were smart enough to keep their voices too low for me to understand.

Out of the corner of my eye, I saw movement in the loft. Boomer was trying to get my attention. To better see him, I moved to stand in front of Heart. It was time to take the blindfold off, anyway. The rain had stopped and I hadn't heard any thunder in a while.

"You made it through the storm, didn't you, boy?" I spoke softly to the horse as I removed the makeshift blindfold and set it aside. Then, keeping my face angled as if I was looking up at Heart, I focused past him to Boomer.

He pointed to himself, then at the fluorescent light fixture mounted on the ceiling, and sliced a finger across his throat in a cutting motion. He then pointed at me and finally, the barn door behind me. He repeated the gesture a couple of times and I thought I understood what he was trying to say.

I'm going to cut the lights. You run away.

I risked a glance at Cowboy and Mr. Jingles. They were still talking without paying attention to me. I widened my eyes at Boomer, hooked my thumb at the men, and shook my head.

A couple of seconds later, Mr. Jingles left, presumably to be on the lookout for Logan.

How was I supposed to get past the guy with the gun?

Sure, cutting the lights might confuse things for a couple of seconds, but he'd hear me if I tried to slip by or open the second door.

Boomer nodded then repeated the message. This time, he pointed at me twice.

Not getting it, I frowned and, seeing Cowboy was watching me, fiddled with Heart's halter.

"Let's get this fixed," I said softly and pretended to straighten a strap as I tucked his mane out of the way, which gave me an excuse to be standing where I was with my face angled up.

Boomer waited until I'd focused back on him to start the charades again.

He pointed at me then pantomimed . . . what? He fisted

both hands, held them up, and bounced up and down. Ride? He meant for me to ride out of the barn?

"Oh no," I said, shaking my head as I fussed with the front of Hearts mane. "Look at these tangles."

I went back to the bucket to find a comb, hoping Boomer heard me well enough to know I was not keen on that idea, either. If I, a smallish-sized human, couldn't squeeze by Cowboy, how was Heart supposed to?

Comb in hand, I moved to stand in front of Heart again and started brushing out the lock of mane that hung over one eye.

Boomer, of course, was pointing and miming again.

It was starting to make me nervous. He was obviously out of Cowboy's line of sight, but I was afraid Boomer might knock something over with all that moving around. I thought about turning my back and just ignoring him but that didn't seem like a good idea, either. I was getting short on time to come up with an alternate plan.

After making sure Cowboy wasn't looking at me, I covertly gave Boomer my attention.

He motioned to the door, touched the tips of both hands together, and swung them open. Then, he mimed riding and repeated the door-opening gesture, only faster.

Boomer didn't want me to try and sneak around Cowboy, he wanted me to charge through the doors past him.

Would that be possible?

It wouldn't take much of a push to open the door but, still . . . I thought about the old westerns where the gun-slinger shoves open the saloon doors.

Not a big deal if you had hands.

But I'd be asking Heart to hit the door at a run and keep going.

I glanced at Boomer. He must have known I was thinking about it, because he nodded encouragement vigorously.

I'd seen the video of Heart; Jasmine had said he loved running.

I looked at Cowboy. He was alternating between checking outside and glancing at me. I swept my gaze over the door. No nails or splintered wood. If we hit it at an angle, it would bounce harmlessly off Heart's shoulder.

But then what?

The sudden darkness would give us a few seconds, but Cowboy still had a gun.

I tried to recall the details of the property I'd seen in the aerial photo. There was a large oak between the house and barn. The coops were on the same side as the old horse pasture, which meant fences, so we couldn't go right. Dense woods were just beyond the house to the left. Didn't want to go that way on horseback.

Once around the oak, it was a straight shot down the drive. On average, horses can gallop at around thirty miles an hour, which is at least three times faster than yours truly.

If I was lucky, I might be able to flag Logan down as he approached.

And if I stood there weighing the pros and cons much longer, I'd miss my window.

I looked up into Boomer's eyes and dipped my head. He gave me the thumbs-up, pointed to his wrist, and held up two fingers.

Two minutes to go-time.

I stepped over to the bucket, picked it up, and started rummaging through it. There was a currycomb, a regular comb, and two brushes. Good, because I was going to need to get rid of everything and flip the bucket over to use as a step stool.

"Can't believe there aren't any braid bands in here," I muttered.

I turned to Cowboy as if seeking commiseration—he scowled and looked outside.

Perfect.

Still holding the bucket, I took Heart's halter and moved him so he was facing the door at more of an angle and positioned myself on his far side, where I set the bucket on the ground. I pulled out both combs and set them out of the way then grabbed a brush in each hand and started grooming Heart.

Cowboy did little more than cut me a glance, he was so focused on watching for Logan, so I tossed the brushes noiselessly onto the hay, flipped the bucket over, grabbed a handful of mane, and was ready to go.

I'd started mentally preparing Heart for the sprint when I saw Nelly stand and start strolling around the top of the wall toward Cowboy.

Crap.

If Boomer cut the lights now, she would probably be startled, tumble off the wall headfirst, and hurt herself.

"Nelly, come down off of there."

I glanced up to where Boomer had been but he was gone—headed to wherever he needed to go to cut the lights. Which meant he wouldn't know to wait for Nelly to be safely on the ground.

Down? Nelly asked.

Yes. Come here, Nelly girl.

I started to let go of Heart's mane and scoot around the horse to grab the little goat, but she made it to where Cowboy was standing and hopped down onto the lower hay bale that formed the starting point of the wall's base.

I let out a sigh of relief, and everything went black.

Even though I was expecting the sudden darkness, it took me a fraction of a second to react.

Fingers locked in Heart's mane, I stepped on the bucket, vaulted onto the horse's back, and spurred him forward with my heels and mind.

Ya!

Heart surged forward like a Thoroughbred out of the gate. The door flew open with a hollow crash. I kept my head down, but managed to catch a glimpse of Cowboy stumbling.

"Ha!"

I felt a maniacal grin stretch across my face as I twisted to get a better look at what happened.

Bad idea.

I may have mentioned that, despite my name, I am not a very *grace*ful person.

Adrenaline can be helpful, boosting strength and dulling pain in times of great duress, but it did me no good in the coordination department.

I started to slip sideways and, spastic as I was, overcorrected and pitched myself off the other side of the horse. I hit the wet ground in a not-so-perfect breakfall and tumbled onto my hands and knees.

Curses sounded—not mine and way too close for comfort. I wasn't the only one rolling around in the mud. Less than thirty feel away, Cowboy lay sprawled in a heap with . . .

Nelly?

Oops.

You okay?

Okay.

"Filthy," Cowboy sputtered, crab-crawling away from Nelly. I didn't see a gun in either hand. He must have dropped it when he fell. He'd already been off-balance when we bolted; the little goat had finished the job.

Bowling for bad guys—caprine style.

Still spouting curses, Cowboy put one loafer-clad foot on Nelly's side to shove her away and I was on my feet.

"Hey!"

An arm snaked round my waist and hauled me backward. I twisted, aiming an elbow to the gut. Missed. But the hold loosened, which gave me the chance to duck and spin. I almost slipped away but a hand clamped onto my biceps and pulled me hard to the side.

The gunshot sounded in the same instant I heard an impatient voice say, "Dammit, Grace, get down."

We ducked around the oak's massive trunk and I looked up to see—

"Kai?"

He shoved me behind him and drew a gun out of his shoulder holster.

"Hoxha," Cowboy shouted. "You got her?"

He must have seen us struggling and assumed Kai was his partner.

"Yeah," Kai called back.

I grabbed his arm to stop him from saying more and whispered, "Hoxha's from Albania, he has an accent."

Kai nodded and moved to the center of the tree where its

trunk split into two huge branches. I wouldn't have been tall enough to see anything, but Kai could.

While Kai looked through the crook of the tree, I scanned the area around us. Aside from Heart, munching on a thick patch of grass near the corner of the house, nothing stirred.

I checked on Moss. My dog was sleeping through the whole thing. I shook my head, not as surprised as I should have been.

"He knows I'm not his partner," Kai murmured. "He's going back into the barn. Closing the doors." He turned to me and took my arm. "Come on, I've got to get you out of here."

"Wait. Boomer's in the barn." I kept my voice a whisper. "He's hiding but we can't just leave him."

"Didn't you just do that?" Kai asked with a pointed glance at Heart.

"Yes. But I thought Cowboy would come after me. I hadn't expected him to say in the barn. Nelly's in there, too."

I'd taken a second to focus on her and knew she'd already recovered from her spell and had rolled to her feet.

"Maybe we should—" I stopped when I felt Nelly's interest fixate on something.

A light. Not very bright, but goats see better than humans in the dark.

"I think Cowboy's using the light from his phone to look around the barn."

"How do you know that?"

"Nelly."

There was a long pause. Leaving one mental thread connected to Nelly, I turned and blinked up at Kai. It was too dark to see his expression, but I knew the wheels were turning as new questions about my ability cranked through his brain.

They would have to wait.

"What if he finds Boomer?" I asked.

"Where is he pointing the light?"

I reached out through the tendril to once again push into Nelly's mind. "The wall," I said, my voice sounding strange, "and the floor."

"He's probably looking for another way out."

I hated to tell him, but there wasn't one.

Then I saw something on the edge of where the glowing light penetrated the darkness. Standing with his back against the same wall Cowboy was searching was Boomer. He was feeling along, touching each garden tool one after the other as if looking for one in particular.

Nelly's vision allowed me to see better than Cowboy, but in a few seconds, the light would catch Boomer and the jig would be up.

"Boomer," I whispered, then took a deep breath and yelled, "Hey, jerkface!"

Cowboy's attention snapped back to the barn door.

"Yeah, you!"

"Grace." Kai's voice was a harsh whisper. "What are you doing?"

I squeezed my eyes shut and held up a hand. I didn't have time to explain and was stretching the limits of my ability by using Nelly to keep track of Cowboy and keep an eye on Boomer. Not to mention think of something to say to get him to turn the light away from where Boomer was standing.

My head had already started to pound. It was going to be splitting later.

Assuming we all lived that long.

Cowboy edged back toward the door, tripped over something, and cursed. Boomer used the opportunity—not to run or hide, but to move closer.

Dammit, Boomer, don't be a hero. The thought made Nelly *baaaa* in concern.

Cowboy spun to shine the light on her. Then he cursed and muttered something that sounded like "Freaking stupid goat" before turning back to the barn door.

Again, Boomer used the opportunity to slide closer. He'd found his weapon of choice: a polo mallet.

If you can't beat 'em, help 'em.

"Your partner's dead. But we can still make a deal," I called.

"Why's that?" Cowboy shouted, creeping up to the gap in the door to peek out.

"Logan and I need a buyer. That's what you do, right? Broker deals?"

Boomer eased closer as I spoke.

"Do we even know what he's looking for?" The voice wasn't Kai's.

Straining, I opened my eyes, turned, and saw Logan had appeared from somewhere to join the party. I nodded and muttered, "LaPointe, water bucket." Knowing it made no sense, I couldn't bring myself to care. Being in two places at once was taking its toll. My right eye wouldn't open all the way, so I closed it.

"Hoxha said you have someone lined up," I yelled to Cowboy. "Do you?"

"If I do?"

"Then we want to do business. Come out, we can talk about it."

"Does this bitch think I'm stupid?" he muttered to himself.

"*Psst*," Boomer said.

Cowboy started to turn but Boomer had whipped the polo mallet around and whacked him solidly across the face.

The light dropped out of sight; Cowboy crumpled.

I gasped and released my connection to Nelly. Blinking back the swirls of light that danced in my vision.

I hadn't realized Kai had been holding both my upper arms to support me.

"He got him. Cowboy's down."

We hurried around the oak tree and ran toward the barn. Every step sent a jolt of pain slicing into my skull.

The light in the barn came on and Boomer opened one of the doors, smiling when he saw me. I tried to smile back but the world tilted suddenly. Everything went red in a weird flash—then nothing.

CHAPTER 20

I awoke the next day in a freaking hospital bed.

My mouth felt dry enough to be populated by Jawas. I blinked and looked around for one of those miniature insulated water pitchers that seem to exist solely in hospitals. I spotted it across the room.

Tossing back the covers, I started to get up, but noticed a black cardigan folded on the arm of the visitor's chair. In the seat was a well-worn book. And a pair of cat-eyed reading glasses.

I froze.

Mom.

On the other side of the privacy curtain, I heard the door open.

I shoved my legs back under the blanket as I heard Wes say, in a quiet voice, "I'll be here if she wakes up."

"Thank you, sweetheart, we won't be long," my mother said.

The door closed and a second later, Wes appeared.

"Hey, you're awake."

"Water." I pointed. He poured me a cup.

"My parents?"

"Got in late last night."

"The doctors?" It should tell you something about the force of nature that is my mother that I asked after the well-being of the hospital staff before anything else.

Wes, having known my mother since we were in grade school, understood my question.

He smothered a grin. "Everyone is taking good care of you."

I sighed. The giant round clock on the wall read half past seven. "They went to get a bite to eat."

"Breakfast?" As soon as I said the word, I was starving.

Wes read my mind and stepped out to ask one of the orderlies for something to eat.

Without success, I tried to remember what had happened, so I asked Wes. "The doctors are saying you had a blood sugar issue. Kai seemed to think you had overtaxed yourself. There was some concern when you didn't wake up, but the brain scan was clean."

"I had a brain scan?"

"And it was *normal*. I know, who would have thought . . ."

I threw my straw at him.

Wes looked at the door and lowered his voice. "We need to go over a few things before your parents get back. The police are going to want your statement."

"Okay."

"And it's going to have to match Kai's."

I learned the official version was that Kai had gone with me to return Nelly to R-n-R. We'd stopped by Boomer's on the way. Kai had been walking back to Bluebell when the bad guys showed up. I had told them a tall tale, which gave Kai a chance to get the jump on Mr. Jingles, at which point I'd run, distracting Cowboy long enough to let Boomer whack him with a polo mallet.

Logan's involvement had been left out, which simplified things and kept Kai out of trouble.

"What happened after I passed out?"

"Kai came with you to the hospital, as soon as the police got there."

"Wait." I felt a flutter of panic. "Where's Moss?"

"I took care of Moss. He's at the condo with his kitty cat and a very cute little papillon."

"Nelly?"

"Happily reunited with her true love, according to Boomer."

I relaxed. "Thanks, Wes."

He nodded and went on to tell me both Cowboy, whose real name was Ricardo Sandoval, and Mr. Jingles, AKA Erjon Hoxha, had been arrested.

The men had turned on each other faster than you can say "honor among thieves."

Hoxha admitted to hitting Tony Ortega, though he maintained he hadn't meant to kill him. Both men blamed the other for Dr. Simon's—or Simone's—death. The police were still going over the crime scene, and no charges had been filed yet.

The men the cops picked up driving the car were talking, too. Saying Cowboy had paid them to drive the car north and dump it into the Okefenokee Swamp. The two geniuses, having no idea there was a body in the trunk, decided it would be fine to cruise around town for a couple of days before heading to Georgia.

"Is Emma being released?" I asked.

"The state attorney is dropping all charges. She'll be out later today."

I smiled up at Wes and we shared a celebratory hug.

"What about me? I'm getting out of here soon?"

"Last I heard. But I'll check."

• • •

My sister ended up making it home before I did, though not by long.

Not surprisingly, we both wanted the same thing—a shower. So after hugs and a very quick chat, we went to get clean.

The first visitor arrived before I'd finished drying my hair. By the time I'd dressed, there were five extra people in the house. Wes, my mom and dad, Hugh, and Uncle Wiley.

Before long, the number of well-wishers swelled and we were in the middle of an impromptu party.

My mom, who is one of those people who can whip together a dozen hors d'oeuvres with little more than mustard, crackers, and sheer determination, set about feeding the throng.

Champagne was poured, a toast was made, and I took my glass and slipped out back for a bit of fresh air.

"Taking a break?" I looked over my shoulder to see Kendall stepping outside.

"Yeah," I said, turning back to look at the gray-blue of the ocean as it blended into the darkening sky. "Parties tend to wear me out."

She came to stand next to me at the rail. "I remember. Grace, I want to apologize."

"For ignoring my phone calls or lying to the cops?"

"For not realizing why you really needed my help that first night. Has Emma told you about our little pact?"

"We haven't had much time to talk."

"Maybe I should let her explain her side, then. I want you to know this—she and Mary saved my life. You've looked at the USB?"

"Password: Kendall," I said, tipping my glass to her.

"That's because the hospital photos in it are mine."

I turned to her. "You mean you and Tony . . ."

"No. I never dated him. My sister did."

Well, that sounded bad.

"It was after Emma divorced him," Kendall said. "Carly's actually my half sister. We had different dads. But we were as close as sisters can be."

Kendall was using a lot of past tense.

"What happened?" I asked.

"She met Tony. He did his thing. Played the handsome millionaire, swept her off her feet. Carly finally realized what kind of person he was and called me."

"What did she say?"

"She was terrified. I could hear it in her voice. But every time I asked her what was wrong she just kept saying she missed me and she was sorry. Finally, she admitted being scared but didn't know how to leave."

Kendall stared out over the water. A tear hung on her lashes for a long moment then tumbled down her cheek.

"I told her to get somewhere safe and that I was on my way. Big sister, coming to the rescue. It takes five hours to drive here from Atlanta. I was too late."

"I'm sorry."

She pulled in a deep sigh and nodded. "Tony told the police he'd noticed she'd been showing signs of depression, so he'd taken her to her favorite restaurant to try to cheer her up. When they got home they argued, and he went for a walk on the beach. He claimed when he got back, he found her, along with several empty pill bottles, on the floor of their bathroom. He called 911, but there was extensive damage. She would live, but she would never be the Carly I knew."

"Saint Giles." I remembered what Sonja had said about the saint and the chance that the sanctuary would be a long-term care facility.

Kendall nodded. "She has to have round-the-clock care. Carly's dad works in Alaska. Our mom passed away a few years ago.

"I quit my job and moved to Jacksonville, vowing to find evidence proving Tony Ortega had poisoned my sister and made it look like a suicide attempt. But there wasn't any. She'd survived, so the police came to the hospital, asked the doctor a couple questions, and that was it."

"They couldn't treat it as a crime, because she didn't die?"

"I told the cops about our phone call, but they seemed to see it as more evidence that Carly was distraught. I pressed, but never got much traction."

I understood all too well.

"I was trapped in a nightmare, until Emma contacted me. I was renting this fleabag apartment—every penny I'd saved went to Carly's medical bills."

"Emma got you a job."

"She did that and more." Kendall turned to me. "Your sister showed me there were other ways to make sure Tony paid for what he'd done to Carly."

"So you were blackmailing him."

"No. We knew we couldn't be so overt."

"Then what?"

"The greatest and most prolonged booty-block the world has ever known," my sister said from the doorway.

"Language," Mary scolded as she followed Emma outside. I looked at the three women. "Meaning?"

"We used our combined resources to make sure Tony never kept a girlfriend for long."

I stared at my sister, speechless. She lifted the champagne bottle, and I reflexively offered my empty glass to be filled.

"Mary was our inside woman," Emma said as she poured. "She knew every bank account number, all his travel plans, even the names and contact info of his favorite call girls."

My jaw dropped open.

"Kendall"—Emma turned to top off the young woman's glass—"did most of the recon and I worked in the button factory."

"Button factory?" Was I hallucinating?

"Yep. Once Mary clued us in on a new target," Emma said, "we would find out everything we could about the poor woman. Everyone has their buttons—I figured out the best way to push them."

"In a way that facilitated a breakup," Kendall clarified.

"You . . ." I looked from Emma to Mary to Kendall then back to Emma. "You formed a secret society whose sole purpose was sabotaging Ortega's love life? That's—" I wasn't sure my personal lexicon had the right word.

"Crazy?" Kendall asked.

I shook my head.

"Felonious?" Emma supplied.

"It's the most brilliant, bad idea I've ever heard," I said. "I can't believe I wasn't allowed to participate."

"That was my doing," Mary said. "When I suggested the idea to Emma, I made her promise not to tell anyone. Kendall was involved for obvious reasons."

"This was your idea?" That surprised me.

"After what happened to Emma, I started gathering as much information on Tony as possible. I didn't know what to do with it, but it seemed to be a good idea to have some ammunition ready. He met Carly in Atlanta. I'd only seen her a few times before he took her to Europe. There wasn't time to—"

Kendall reached over and took the older woman's hand. "You did everything you could, Mary."

"When Carly"—Mary swallowed back tears and lifted her chin—"I wasn't going to stand by and let it happen again."

"That's why you gave Jasmine such a cool reception when she moved here," I said to Mary. "It was part of the plan. Make her feel homesick and unwelcome?"

"That," Emma said. "And Kendall heard through her contacts in London that Jasmine's dad had an affair with their housekeeper, so we had Mary push that button, too."

"I'd drop hints about how well I knew Tony," Mary said. "Let her see me give him longing looks. Nothing over the top."

"Still," I said. "Yuck." Which got a laugh.

I looked around the group and blew out a breath. "There's something I need to tell all of you. About the USB stick." I glanced at my sister. "I kind of promised to give it to Logan if he helped catch the bad guys."

"Who's Logan?" Mary asked.

"It's a long story," Emma said. "Do y'all mind if I make the call on this one?"

Both women shook their heads, their trust in my sister evident.

"We'll see you inside," Kendall said and went with Mary to rejoin the party.

Emma turned to me. "Spill."

I explained that I'd accidentally kept the USB, hidden it from the police, and though I'd finally figured out the password, I was having problems understanding how I could use the information.

"So you asked Logan for help?"

"How many other criminals do I know?"

"The number is growing, if you count us."

I realized Emma didn't know what really happened the night before. Assuming she'd heard only the official version, I told her the real story.

"Logan was at Boomer's. He and Kai came to save me."

"Together?"

"Apparently." I told her about pulling the Logan card, literally, and, that Kai was the only one who knew how to find me.

"I don't know what Logan said to Kai, or how it all played out. He was gone when I woke up."

"What is it with this Logan guy?" Emma asked.

"I think he feels like he owes me for helping Brooke. I'm guessing after this, we'll be even. As long as I give him the USB stick."

"He can have it, after I erase the photos. We don't need it anymore."

"Hey, girls." My mom slid the door open to stick her head out, and said, "We're ready to cut the cake."

I looked at Emma as we walked inside. "Cake?"

My sister shrugged. "Mom."

It was explanation enough.

As I moved through the living room, I did a mental scan to check on the animals. Voodoo was sleeping in the crook of Sonja's arm. Moss was in the kitchen panhandling and Roscoe was snuggled in my dad's lap.

The little papillon had fallen in love with my father. Before my parents left, I planned to ask if they wanted a traveling buddy. Judging from the way my mother had cooed at Roscoe when he did his little pick-me-up dance, I was pretty sure the Winnebago would be getting a mascot.

My phone chimed as I finished off my second piece of cake.

I fumbled it out of my back pocket, hoping it was Kai. The text was from a blocked number. It read: *Beach. Five minutes.*

Though I had I feeling I knew, I responded with: *Who is this?*

No answer.

Call me paranoid, but I wasn't about to walk out onto the dark beach without knowing the text was from Logan. Hell, I wasn't sure I should if I knew it *was* Logan.

Who is this? I typed again.

My phone rang.

"Hello?"

"Boo."

"Logan?"

"Four minutes. Shake a leg, sweetness," he said and hung up.

Yep, it was Logan.

I caught my sister's eye and she raised her brows in silent question, then followed me out of the noisy kitchen.

"Time to pay the piper," I told her as we turned down the hallway.

Emma and I ducked into my room long enough for her to plug the USB drive into my laptop and remove the photos from the file.

"Take the mutt," she said as she handed me the USB stick.

"Yes, ma'am."

"Hey," she said. I paused in the doorway and looked back. "Tell him I said thanks."

I nodded, and with the excuse of taking Moss on a potty break, went to meet a ghost.

•   •   •

Logan stood just off the path, facing the water. The light of the moon made the tips of the waves glow white as they rolled to shore.

I let Moss off the leash. He trotted to Logan, gave him a quick once-over sniff, and moved off to explore the nearby tide pool.

"I guess we need to come up with a code word so I can tell the difference between you and the other crazies inviting me to clandestine meetings," I said, stopping beside him.

"'Boo' wasn't a big enough hint?" he asked without turning to me.

"Point taken."

I followed his gaze to look out at the water for a few heartbeats, then held up the USB stick.

"Are you going to tell me why you want it?" I asked when he took it.

"No."

Didn't think so. "My sister wanted me to tell you thanks."

"For helping her or saving you?"

I hadn't thought about the saving-me part. I glanced up at his profile. "Both, I guess."

He nodded. "He's a good guy, your cop."

"I know."

"I asked him if he wanted me to back off."

"What did he say?"

Finally, Logan turned to look at me. "He told me he wanted you safe. And if I was a factor in that, he'd learn to live with it."

The night was turning out to be full of surprises.

Logan lifted a shoulder and turned back to the sea. "He could have just said that because you were being held hostage at the time, but I think he meant it."

I wasn't sure what to make of that.

Moss splashed through the pool.

"Isn't there a leash law?" Logan asked.

I turned to look at my dog as he jogged away, stopped, and shook. At least he didn't wait until he was standing next to me to throw off the water, which was what he normally did.

"You going to call the cops on me for not having a leash?" I asked, looking back at Logan. He was gone.

"Oh, no you don't," I muttered. "Moss! Come. Where's Logan?"

My dog responded to my call much more quickly than he would have if I had said, "Let's go inside." He trotted to where I stood. I clipped on his leash and said, "Where'd he go, huh? Where's Logan?"

Moss sniffed the ground then looked past me, with a swish of his tail.

Kai.

"No, not Kai, Logan." As soon as I said it, I understood what my dog had been trying to tell me.

I turned to see Kai emerge from the path between the dunes.

"Kai, hey."

"Hey." He smiled, and I knew he hadn't heard me asking Moss about Logan.

And oh, that smile. Even in the moonlight, it was toe curling.

"Your mom told me where I could find you." He stepped close, brushed a wind-whipped strand of hair out of my face, and studied me. "You look better."

"Yeah, well I—" I stopped as something occurred to me. "Oh."

"What?"

"You met my parents."

"Is that a problem?"

"No, it's just, weird. You met them in the hospital while I was passed out drooling on myself. Not quite how I pictured the introduction."

Moss chose that moment to ask to be acknowledged, and nudged Kai's hand with his muzzle.

Only having to bend a little, Kai ruffled Moss's furry neck and gave him a pat.

"It was good timing, actually," Kai said, still talking about the hospital. "They got to there just as I was being asked to go in and give a statement. You'll need to do that, too."

"Wes already talked to me about it. I know you had to . . . omit some details."

He nodded. "Adding Logan into the story would only muddy things up."

"I'm sorry." I didn't want him to have to lie.

"Don't be. It was probably good that he was there."

"Really?"

"Logan called me as Charlie and I were going over some of the photos from Dr. Simon's car. I saw what they did to her. They're lucky Logan was with me—I would've killed one of them to get to you. That would have been harder to explain."

CHAPTER 21

"Okay, that's enough fun for now." I led Moss and his new biggest fan back to Bluebell. "Ebony and Ivory. In you go." I opened the rear passenger door so Moss could jump into the backseat. Pretty Girl was close on his heels, leaping up to sit next to him. It had been only a couple of weeks since I'd first seen her, but Janie's black wolf-dog looked like she'd grown an inch.

Part of that was confidence, I knew. Not only did she have a stable, loving home, but once a week she had Moss.

Today, I'd picked Pretty Girl up from Janie's and brought her and Moss to R-n-R to meet some horses and goats. She'd behaved like a perfect lady and as a reward, I'd turned the two dogs loose in an unoccupied, fenced pasture. They'd run and sniffed and played until both of their sides heaved and their mouths stretched in panting wolf-smiles.

I'd already given them water, but put a bowl in the seat anyway. It would get stepped in, kicked, or knocked over, but Bluebell had seen worse.

I gave both canines a pat. Pretty Girl aimed a couple of

licks at my mouth, but I managed to press my lips shut and move out of range. She turned her attention to Moss, showering him with half a dozen kisses as her tail swished over the seat.

"She's got it bad," I told Moss.

Moss, handsome.

"Yes, you are." Smiling, I closed the door and turned toward the barn.

The crisp wind sent a flurry of fallen sweet gum leaves dancing across my path.

I hunched into my jacket as I walked.

It was warmer inside the stables but not by much. Hunter was busy mucking out one of the stalls. I nodded to him as I passed.

Heart was tethered in the center aisle near the washstand. The horse had been brushed and groomed until his coat gleamed like satin.

"Minerva, dammit," Boomer said, appearing from around the corner. "How's it going to look if Heart walks out of here covered in cat hair?"

Minerva was happily settled on Heart's back, doing the kitty impersonation of a loaf of bread. All four feet tucked under her body, she looked like a patchwork muffin sitting in the place where Heart's saddle would usually go.

"Is this your spot?" I asked the cat, remembering what she'd told me about meeting Heart and doing a "spot check."

Good spot, she confirmed.

Boomer had continued to grouse at the barn cat; she ignored him.

"Jasmine hasn't seen Heart in months—she won't care about a little cat hair," I said.

Jasmine had been cleared of any involvement in the LaPointe heist, and was finally on her way to see her horse. Discovering she'd been engaged to a monster had taken a toll on the model, but Mary seemed to think she would rally.

I had a feeling today would help.

I'd missed the goats' reunion, but they looked happy.

I offered Heart a Jordan almond, a favorite treat, according to Jasmine.

Heart took it with a whisper of velvety lips on my palm and crunched away.

"Today's the big day, boy. You ready to see Jasmine?"

Yasmin?

I grinned. A horse with an accent—why not?

A silver sedan pulled slowly through the gates of R-n-R.

"Boomer, you're up."

He grunted, untied Heart's lead rope, and started walking out the barn's open gate.

Minerva nimbly leapt onto the wall of one of the other horse stalls as they passed.

I followed Heart and Boomer, then stopped just outside the barn.

"You came for the reunion?" Hunter asked, as he moved out of the stall and came to stand next to me.

"Yep."

I watched the sedan park and the rear door open. Jasmine stepped out. Her face turned to the barn eyes locked on her horse. One hand was pressed to her chest the other came up to cover her mouth. For several seconds she didn't move. She just stared at Heart as Boomer led him forward.

Heart hadn't seen Jasmine yet but he sensed something had changed. The horse shifted his focus from Boomer.

Ears twitching, he cast his senses around in an attempt to discern the cause of the sudden shift he'd perceived. And then, he saw her.

The connection was instant. And though my link to Heart was minimal, the joy that rushed though my chest made me suck in a surprised breath.

Heart quickened his step. Jasmine rushed forward and threw her arms around his neck.

"I heard you're giving the reward to Boomer," Hunter said. "Even though you found him."

I nodded. It only seemed right, given that Boomer had saved Heart to begin with.

"So you're not getting anything?"

"I get to see this," I said as I watched Heart nuzzle Jasmine.

"That's it?"

"Kid, that's everything."

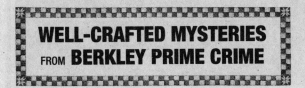

WELL-CRAFTED MYSTERIES
FROM BERKLEY PRIME CRIME

- **Earlene Fowler** Don't miss these Agatha Award–winning quilting mysteries featuring Benni Harper.

- **Monica Ferris** These *USA Today* bestselling Needlecraft Mysteries include free knitting patterns.

- **Laura Childs** Her Scrapbooking Mysteries offer tips to satisfy the most die-hard crafters.

- **Maggie Sefton** These popular Knitting Mysteries come with knitting patterns and recipes.

- **Lucy Lawrence** These brilliant Decoupage Mysteries involve cutouts, glue, and varnish.

- **Elizabeth Lynn Casey** The Southern Sewing Circle Mysteries are filled with friends, southern charm—and murder.

M5G0610